A TONGUE SO SWEET AND DEADLY

MORE BY SOPHIA ST. GERMAIN

COMPELLING FATES SAGA

A Tongue So Sweet and Deadly

A Promise So Bold and Broken

A Bond So Fierce and Fragile

A Fate So Dark and Delicate

ECHO SERIES

Echo of Wings

Echo of Deceit

A TONGUE SO SWEET AND DEADLY

COMPELLING FATES SAGA
BOOK ONE

SOPHIA ST. GERMAIN

kensingtonbooks.com

Content Notice: Violence, Torture, PTSD, Death, Gore, Spice, Some Swearing, Imprisonment, Orphans

KENSINGTON BOOKS are published by:

Kensington Publishing Corp.
900 Third Avenue
New York, NY 10022

kensingtonbooks.com

This book is a work of fiction. Names, characters, businesses, organizations, places, events, and incidents either are the product of the author's imagination or are used fictitiously. Any resemblance to actual persons, living or dead, events, or locales is entirely coincidental.

To the extent that the image or images on the cover of this book depict a person or persons, such person or persons are merely models, and are not intended to portray any character or characters featured in the book.

All Kensington titles, imprints, and distributed lines are available at special quantity discounts for bulk purchases for sales promotions, premiums, fundraising, educational, or institutional use.

Special book excerpts or customized printings can also be created to fit specific needs. For details, write or phone the office of the Kensington sales manager: Kensington Publishing Corp., 900 Third Avenue, New York, NY 10022, attn: Sales Department; phone 1-800-221-2647.

The K with book logo Reg US Pat. & TM Off.

ISBN 978-1-4967-6472-0 (paperback)

First Kensington Trade Paperback printing: June 2026

10 9 8 7 6 5 4 3 2 1

Printed in the United States of America

Chapter illustrations by Antonia Ansgariusson

Electronic Edition ISBN 978-1-4967-6486-7 (ebook)

The authorized representative in the EU for product safety and compliance
is eucomply OU, Parnu mnt 139b-14, Apt 123
Tallinn, Berlin 11317, hello@eucompliancepartner.com

To Tahoe.

Thank you for joining me on hundreds of walks when I needed inspiration.

HAVLANDS

Ellow

Asker

Korina

Eiatis
Sea

Vastala

CHAPTER ONE

The noise in the packed tavern was unbearable.

A relentless hum of chatter and clattering of glasses pounded against her temples, and Lessia cast a longing glance at the door behind her.

It had been a long day already, and the only thing she wanted was to climb into bed—to be anywhere other than this teeming, blistering room.

Even the snow swirling outside the dusty windows behind her looked more welcoming.

But she needed to show her face tonight.

She'd spent the past few nights holed up in her study, and Lessia knew word would get back to her king. If she stayed in tonight as well, his henchman would come looking for her.

She'd tested his patience before—two days seemed to be the longest time she could escape his watch.

Sighing, Lessia flicked her hair and forced her lips to curl into a sly smile as she waved to try to get Bren the barkeep's attention. A few patrons glanced her way, and she winked at two of the regulars when they raised their cups in her direction.

Bren was tied up, scrambling to take orders from thirsty soldiers who'd spent too many months at sea, so she rested her chin in one hand and traced the jagged outline of the wooden countertop with the other.

As she picked at the sticky surface, a drunken soldier barreled into her, jarring her arm off the counter and nearly tripping her.

Shaking her head, Lessia leaned back over the bar, but when the rough material of his uniform kept scraping against her arm, his hip painfully jutting into hers, she turned her head over her shoulder and glared at him.

"Could you move, please?" She pointedly glanced at the space beside him. "There's plenty of room for both of us to order."

The soldier swept his auburn hair out of his face and flashed her a drunken grin. "No need to frown, beautiful. I'm only trying to get a drink."

His eyes roamed over her black cloak and the long-sleeved black tunic she wore beneath, and he arched a brow. "I'd buy you one. But you're clearly not here to socialize."

With that, he turned back to the bar, leaning over the dark wood to give a wobbly wave to Bren.

Lessia rolled her eyes.

She knew her attire didn't do her any favors, not like the beautiful dresses other women in the tavern wore, their laced corsets accentuating their waists and the capped sleeves showing off their slender arms.

But it wasn't like she had a choice.

The soldier kept trying to get Bren's attention, and she couldn't help the smirk that pulled at her lips at his feeble attempts. The tavern was too busy tonight; there was little chance Bren would prioritize him over the many patrons he knew.

Especially when Lessia stood next to him.

A hand squeezed her shoulder, and she spun around, finding her best friend in one of those beautiful dresses she'd admired.

Gray, with white detailing trailing up the long skirts, the dress was simple but beautiful against Amalise's blonde tresses and huge blue eyes. And it had short sleeves, so she probably didn't have sweat dripping down her neck like Lessia did.

She dragged a hand through her wavy hair. "Is this one giving you trouble, Lia?"

Lessia shook her head. "I'm good."

When Amalise narrowed her eyes and a familiar wicked sheen glinted in them, Lessia stepped into her path.

Too often, a situation like this escalated into a brawl, and with tension already heavy in the air from restless soldiers, Lessia wouldn't be surprised if the whole tavern got involved after one punch.

That she was too tired for.

She let some of her own wickedness fill her eyes and offered Amalise an edged smile. "I told you I've got this, Amalise. You go back to whatever poor man you plan on dragging home tonight."

Lessia waved toward the table where the rest of their friends sat and where a group of soldiers and merchants hovered nearby to try their luck with the beautiful women.

Amalise scowled, but when Lessia kept her feet firmly planted, she shrugged and drew a breath to calm herself. Amalise could be a bit protective, and her temper rivaled Lessia's—which was one of the reasons they became instant friends when Lessia arrived in Ellow five years ago.

Finally, a smile overtook her face, and Amalise wiggled her brows, whispering theatrically, "I'm thinking the one over there."

She not-so-subtly pointed to a tall soldier whose eyes were fixed on them and who was clad in the same navy uniform as the man next to Lessia but with wavy black hair spilling far down his back.

Amalise pursed her lips when her eyes snapped back to Lessia's. "He's got better hair than me! I need to know his secret."

Lessia snorted. Amalise didn't need any beauty tips. She was already the most gorgeous woman Lessia had ever seen. And Amalise knew it.

Lessia's eyes trailed her friend as she approached the soldier. Her full hips swayed seductively as she stepped up one step too close, invading his space to whisper something in his ear.

Snickering to herself, Lessia turned back to the bar.

The soldier who'd bumped into her had managed to order a few cups of ale and slipped Bren some silvers.

Bren's eyes widened when they locked with hers, an apology ready at the tip of his tongue, but Lessia winked at him, gesturing toward the rest of the bar, where dozens of people leaned across the surface, desperate for his attention.

When he still hesitated, she waved her hand again, offering him a wide smile.

Although from the look on his face, she wasn't sure if it reassured him, as his posture remained tense when he finally approached another patron.

Shifting her eyes back to the soldier, Lessia tapped his shoulder. "I know you're new here, so I'll give you a pass this time. But me and my friends over there"—Lessia jerked her head toward the table where Amalise and a few others eyed them closely—"are thirsty. And we order first around here."

He seemed to prepare to respond with something snarky, but his gaze swept over her again, and his muddy brown eyes widened. "You're—"

"Half-Fae. Was it the ears? Or perhaps the teeth?" She couldn't help but let her lip curl, showing off her sharp canines, her grin creeping wider when the soldier inched backward.

"Or was it maybe the height?" Lessia straightened to her full five-nine stature, leveling her amber eyes with his frightened ones.

The soldier stared at her with the bar pressed into his back, the air around him crackling with nervous energy and fear seeping into his scent.

Lessia softened her gaze. "Is this your first time on Asker?"

His quivering chin dipped.

Gods, he must hail from one of the remote isles in Ellow if he hadn't encountered Fae or even half-Fae before. Not that there were that many half-Fae on the human isles—or in Havlands at all—but here on Asker, the capital island of Ellow, it wasn't unheard of to run into one from time to time.

The air shifted as the soldier's eyes narrowed. From the stale scent lacing his breath, it must have been ale bolstering his confidence, and his features twisted into a drunken sneer as he spat, "I don't know who you think you are, *halfling*, and I truly don't care. My friends and I just spent weeks at sea. We are thirsty."

Her guilt instantly melted away, and Lessia clenched her jaw not to snarl at him.

Shifting her golden-brown hair out of her face and balling her hands into tight fists to keep her unpredictable Fae emotions in check, she hissed quietly, "I am going to give you one more chance, soldier. My friends and I own this part of town—including this tavern. You may apologize for the vile thing you just called me by heading over to them and distributing the drinks you bought." She nodded toward the mugs of ale lining the bar behind him.

When the soldier scoffed and turned around to gather the cups and return to the rowdy group of soldiers he'd come with, a buzz filled her ears, and Lessia ground her teeth.

She shouldn't.

Using magic on humans was not only illegal, as she'd break the most sacred stipulation of the treaty between humans and Fae; she'd also despise herself for it later.

But her patience was truly running thin today.

And she had a reputation to uphold.

Casting a quick glance around the room, making sure no one looked their way, she blew out a deep breath and closed her eyes. The corners of her mouth lifted as her magic purred at the chance to be unleashed.

It had been months since she last used her so-called gift.

When her eyes flew open, she stared at herself in the dusty mirror behind the counter, and a shiver snaked down her spine at how her eyes glowed like molten gold in the dim light.

Apart from the pointed ears, she could be mistaken for human, albeit a quite tall female, but when she let her magic reign like this, there was no mistaking her Fae heritage.

Once again, she tapped the soldier's shoulder, and when his smug face snapped her way, his body stilled, his muscles locking.

"What the..."

The soldier backed into the counter once more, the ale in the two cups he held spilling onto his black boots.

Lessia closed the distance between them, gripping the

lapel of his uniform jacket and bringing her face to his. She let her hair fall forward again, two bronze curtains concealing her face from the other patrons.

"What—what happened to your eyes?" The soldier's voice shook as his gaze flitted between her hand and eyes.

Ignoring his question, she let magic seep into her voice, transforming it into a deep, seductive murmur as her eyes locked with his. "You will give those cups to my friends. And you'll continue to buy us drinks all night—courtesy of your big, big heart," she purred.

The soldier's eyes glazed over, his posture relaxing as he nodded.

Smiling, Lessia continued. "As a matter of fact, you'll be happy to do it. After tonight, you'll remember that the harbor and the east side of Asker belong to me and my friends. And you want to please us. Please be sure to inform your friends as well."

Lessia blinked, forcing the lingering magic back inside her until the unnatural glow left her eyes and her natural honey color returned.

Rolling her neck, she offered the soldier a sweet smile, tilting her head when he still hovered by the bar. "What are you waiting for?"

The soldier scrambled to gather all the cups in his hands, and Lessia laughed softly when he walked over and, with a smile on his face, distributed them amongst her friends, leaving a cup behind for her.

Grinning to herself, she lifted the mug to take a sip of ale. Even if she often felt like she cheated when she used her magic, since no soul in Havlands could withstand her commands, it was helpful in situations like this.

But Lessia's smile fell when cold, oily magic rippled over her skin, and her hand froze midair. With the hair on the back of her neck rising and her Fae senses blaring, she whipped around so quickly the ale sloshed over her hands.

Her heart hammered against her ribs as she beheld the silver-haired Fae slipping onto one of the high chairs beside her. The snow clinging to his gray cloak glittered in the dim light, and his tanned skin and the cascading waves of his shoulder-length hair shimmered—even in the depths of winter.

"That's what you waste your magic on? Some free ale and a simple human?" His deep voice rumbled through her, her heart beating in rhythm with his fingers tapping the bar.

Even with his glamour in place, the soldiers around them retreated, keeping a respectful distance—their dull human senses picking up on the danger radiating from the Fae.

Not that it surprised her. Full Fae could cast a glamour over themselves—could trick anyone into believing they were mere humans. But Merrick was one of the Fae king's most vicious soldiers, and not even a glamour could mask the cloud of hostility that clung to him.

She'd heard the stories about him growing up, how the Fae called him the Death Whisperer—how alone, he'd taken out entire companies of soldiers that dared stand against him.

Lessia shakily set down the cup and wiped her hands on her breeches. "Merrick."

Clasping her hands behind her back to prevent him from seeing them tremble, she swallowed. "To what do I owe this pleasure?"

She winced as her voice wavered, and cast a quick glance toward her friends.

Thankfully, they were occupied, toasting with the soldier she'd sent over and laughing as more of his friends joined them, each with drinks in his hands.

Silently cursing herself for staying in the past two nights, she waited, stiffening as his magic continued to dance over her skin.

The layers of clothes she wore did nothing to keep the oily vibrations off her. On the contrary, she could almost hear the magic whispering through the wool.

She'd have to take a bath and scrub every inch of her body to feel clean again.

Merrick angled his head, always careful to keep his eyes averted from hers, his long fingers impatiently running over the surface of the bar. Bren eyed her as he swiftly placed a goblet of golden liquor before him. When she inclined her head, Bren slipped away, hurrying to the other side of the bar.

"Where were you the past few days?" Merrick lifted the cup, swirling the liquid a few times before he took a long sip.

Lessia followed his movements closely as he elegantly set it down, his tongue darting out to lick a stray drop off his full lips.

He moved like a snake: everything about him cold and calculated, as if he could lunge any second and deliver a fatal bite.

Clearing her throat, she inched backward but stilled when the magic coating her skin tightened its grip, warning her not to take another step.

She shouldn't have sent the other guards home.

Merrick was the fourth Fae guard King Rioner had sent to watch over her. The others had lasted less than a week before they accidentally met her eyes and she sweetly asked them to leave and forget all about her. But Merrick had been a constant the past four years, not once meeting her gaze, not even allowing her a glimpse of the color of his eyes.

Although she was certain they were pure night—two dark windows peering into his lethal soul.

His magic nudged her again, like sharp daggers leaving stinging kisses on her back.

Lessia drew a deep breath. She only needed to assure him she hadn't forgotten about the king's orders; then she could leave, go home, and forget all about him until the next time he sought her out.

"I've been working. With so many taverns and gambling rooms to manage, I do have to spend time on paperwork as well. I can't be out every night."

Merrick remained quiet, but the air around him thickened with tension.

Lessia shuddered as she quickly continued. "I am planning on bringing some of the soldiers and captains home tonight, and my friends will ensure the soiree we'll host will be the talk of the town for days. I've already let them know who I am. The king will be pleased to hear that most people in Asker are familiar with my name by now."

His thick silver eyebrows twitched in irritation, the only emotion he ever allowed to cross the hard lines of his face.

At least when she was around.

But she doubted that face ever softened. There was a reason for his nickname, one she didn't care to find out.

"You know as well as I do that *our* king is not pleased. He ordered you to make a name for yourself here, Lessia. He did not order you to become a harlot, a human plaything."

Lessia stiffened, her nails digging into her palms until the smell of iron filled the air. But she wouldn't allow herself to correct him. It was better he thought that of her than knew what she actually did when she was out of his sight.

"Well, I do own most of the taverns in this part of town now. And I'm respected amongst the merchants and barterers who pass through, so we get the best goods at decent prices. Even with the prices rising, I can keep costs down." She swept out an arm toward the packed room. "That's why everyone comes here, why we're busy every night. I'd say I did pretty well. And I should expect our king would think so too."

When Merrick's nostrils flared, she clamped her lips shut.

Shifting, she studied his profile, the angry lines of his mouth as he sipped yet again from the goblet.

What she wouldn't do for him to turn his face to hers, to meet those evil eyes and tell him to leave. Perhaps ask him to forget who he was entirely, tell him to move to the abandoned shifter island and never return.

All Havlands would be better for it.

But no such luck. Merrick tapped the bar again, and Bren immediately slipped up to refill his cup.

"I guess you'll see for yourself soon enough," he said quietly as Bren shuffled off.

Lessia didn't think her heart could beat any harder, but when the tattoo on her arm burned in response to his words, burned for the first time in five years, she couldn't stop the gasp that escaped her. Her hand flew to cover her left arm, pulling at the tunic she wore to ensure it was covered.

Merrick downed the liquor and rose, towering over her as he turned to leave. She swore his lips curled slightly as his whisper brushed her ear. "King Rioner is coming to see you soon. He's calling in the debt you owe him. I'd say be ready, but..." His face dipped toward her arm, knowing exactly what was hidden beneath the layers of clothes she always wore. "It's not like you can escape it."

CHAPTER
TWO

She couldn't breathe.

Even when Merrick's magic finally released its death grip and his broad back disappeared as the tavern door slammed shut behind him, she had to lean against the bar to remain standing.

The Fae king was coming to Ellow.

He was finally coming for her.

Five years, she'd been out of his claws. Five years during which she'd almost forgotten the blood oath he'd forced her to swear to escape his dungeons.

But now her time was up.

Moving her hand to clasp at her chest, Lessia tried to draw deep breaths as flashes of darkness filled her vision, water dripping onto hard stone ringing in her ears, drowning out the sounds of the tavern. Her vision blurred as a crushing weight settled on her chest, and she desperately tried to force air down her lungs.

She couldn't do this here.

A warm hand settled on her back, and a strangled noise

left her when strong arms pulled her into a broad chest, shielding her from the room. Burrowing her face into the leather tunic, she let his arms envelop her—hide the tremors racking her body.

"You're not there anymore. You're never going back there. You're safe, Lia," Ardow whispered into her hair, his hands running up and down her back.

A dry sob shook her as his warm embrace reminded her of how she'd landed in the cellars in the first place, images of kind amber eyes and melodic laughs filling her mind, and overwhelming guilt constricted her throat.

"You're safe, Lessia," Ardow repeated.

He continued softly hushing her until her locked muscles relaxed, until air finally made its way into her lungs and her vision returned, the deafening sounds of the tavern following.

When the pressure on her chest lifted, Lessia finally pulled back and met her friend's worried eyes.

"I'm sorry," she whispered, her stomach twisting at the moisture lining his eyes as they trailed across her face.

Ardow gently cupped her chin. "Don't apologize. What happened?"

"It's—" Her voice vanished, the blood oath she'd sworn taking her air once more, forbidding her to speak of the king—to speak of anything involving him.

Ardow's eyes hardened, the warm brown deepening as his jaw clenched. "It's him, isn't it?"

She couldn't even nod, could only keep her eyes on his until Ardow bowed his head in understanding, his teeth grinding so hard she could hear it over the bustling tavern.

Ardow was the first friend she'd made when she'd come to Ellow. Being part-Fae, he hadn't shied away from her pointed ears. Instead, he'd stalked right up to her in a tavern not unlike this one and declared he was buying her a drink.

When he'd realized she'd only arrived in Ellow that morning, that she'd never set foot in human lands before that, he'd taken her in and offered her a spare room in his run-down apartment without another thought.

That's also how Ardow had gotten around the blood oath.

Lessia hadn't been able to explain why or how she ended up in Ellow, but he'd glimpsed the silver snake tattoo slithering up her arm one night when she made her way back from the washroom. With his Fae heritage, his grandfather being half-Fae, he knew immediately what it meant.

While she'd been prepared for him to throw her out headfirst when he saw the brand on her arm marking her a criminal, a Fae traitor, he'd only pulled her into his arms and whispered how sorry he was.

Soon after that, Ardow learned why she had nightmares, why the soft smatter of rain on a window made her flinch, and why she refused to sleep without a burning fire even during the warm summer months—getting to know the parts of her that she could never share or speak of.

Still, he didn't know the whole story.

There was only so much he could guess.

"I'm okay, Ard. I promise." Lessia glanced around the room, finding Amalise's eyes glued on her, a question in them.

She tried to roll her eyes to wipe the serious expression off Amalise's face, but when her friend's ones narrowed, she sighed.

Ardow had filled Amalise in when Lessia decided to trust her, and she'd become even more protective after that. Not that it was a bad trait, especially in a best friend, but Lessia wouldn't put either of them at risk, and now that her king was coming here...

Lessia steeled her spine.

She needed to find a way to keep them far away from him.

Dragging Ardow with her, she plastered a smile on her face and headed for her friends, swiping her half-full mug off the bar and downing the now-warm liquid.

She'd do what she did best.

Pretend, for a little while longer, that all was well.

CHAPTER THREE

Lessia shivered when the wind tore through her coat as they walked the winding path back to their home. Her friends giggled and gossiped beside her, and the drunken soldiers joined them, laughing and boasting about their adventures at sea.

Slinging an arm around her shoulders, Ardow tugged her close to his massive body to shield her from the icy gusts of snow that swirled around them.

The cliffs that Asker was built upon did little to shelter the town from the ocean breeze, which in summer was well needed but in the deepest winter caused ice to slither up the stone buildings lining the road, making the stone town seem as if it were made of crystal.

Ahead towered the white castle that once housed the monarchs of Ellow. Warm light flickered out of the many windows lining the tall walls, and soft music reached her ears over the wind.

The regent must be hosting some type of festivities.

She'd never been inside the castle, had never been invited when other merchants met to mingle there.

It wasn't too surprising. After all, she owned only a few rowdy taverns and the odd gambling room and had a bit of a reputation for being senseless and flighty.

Ardow squeezed her shoulders when they neared the metal double doors to the old warehouse they lived in. It was abandoned when Lessia found it, and she'd acquired it for a bargain from a desperate merchant who was shutting down his business. With Amalise's and Ardow's help, she'd turned it into a home over the years.

"I'm heading to the office quickly." Lessia slipped out of his embrace. "Keep them busy, will you?"

She flicked her eyes to Amalise and the two other women they typically spent their evenings with—Soria and Pellie—and the seven soldiers they'd dragged home, including the dark-haired one Amalise had spoken to all night.

Ardow nodded, but when he guided the rest left, up a spiraling staircase—toward the only room they allowed outsiders—Amalise doubled back, patting Ardow on the shoulder as she passed him.

Lessia arched a brow. "Have you tired of the soldier already?"

It wouldn't be the first time. Amalise loved to flirt, but no man stayed around for long. And even though Lessia teased her about it, her heart tugged when her friend grinned at her.

Amalise had lost her first and only love when she was eighteen. Six years ago, he'd gone out with a boat, working as a fisherman, as most men in Ellow who weren't nobles did, and after they'd been caught in a surprise storm, the only thing that returned was shards of wood crashing onto the beach.

Amalise had told her one night when they'd both drunk too much wine.

It was the only time Lessia had ever seen her cry.

Her eyes burned at the memory. Seeing Amalise so vulnerable had made Lessia share her own worst memory, one that hurt more than all the years she'd spent imprisoned. One that forever would taint any good memory she carried from her childhood.

One that still haunted her dreams.

"Where did you go just there?" Amalise's grin faltered, her eyes filling with worry as she placed a hand on Lessia's shoulder.

Lessia shook her head, pushing the laughing girl's face out of her mind. "Nowhere good." She tried to smile, but it ended up more of a grimace. "I'm heading to the office. You coming?"

Amalise nodded, and they shifted a large shelf blocking the hidden door to the right side of the warehouse.

As they opened the door and slipped in, muffled sounds filled the air around them: hushed voices and soft footsteps echoing through the large room before them, bouncing off the shiny, arched ceiling.

Lessia glanced at Amalise, and they both rolled their eyes at the same time.

"I guess it is too much to ask that they follow curfew." Lessia grinned.

When a head popped through one of the ajar doors lining the wall to the left, dark eyes widening and quickly disappearing, and a soft knock sounded on one of the walls separating the twelve bedrooms, everything fell silent.

Lessia couldn't stop a small giggle from escaping, and after one look at Amalise, they both erupted in laughter.

"We know you're awake. Come out," Lessia managed to get out in between fits of giggles.

Door after door opened and faces peered into the softly lit hallway, the firelight from the lanterns placed every few feet along the walls reflecting in their wide eyes.

Warmth spread in her chest when hesitant smiles lit some of the younger ones' features, and when Fiona, one of the youngest additions, squealed and ran for them, Lessia let the warmth fill her entirely, shrugging off the last remnants of haunting memories.

She opened her arms and lifted Fiona up, hugging her tight. "You been up to no good, little one?" she whispered before setting her down.

Fiona looked up at her, eyes rounded and feet planted firmly as she mock-glared back. "Always."

Lessia grinned at her while tucking a strand of dark hair behind Fiona's delicately pointed ear, careful not to touch the wide scar weaving up her neck. "Good, I'd hate for it to get boring around here."

Turning to the rest of the children, she searched for a new face, as another one should have arrived this morning. When she came up blank, she frowned and turned to Kalia, the oldest and the first child she'd ever offered a room here.

Now twenty-one, Kalia ran this place, and Lessia couldn't be more grateful for her help. Kalia was a kind soul, and most of the children trusted her immediately, making their transition and Lessia's life easier.

She'd met Kalia when they both were living on the streets of Vastala, and Lessia hadn't forgotten how the girl risked her life when King Rioner's men came for her. Even if her efforts were in vain, as soon as Lessia got out and was settled here, she'd sent one of the men now in her employ back to Vastala to find her.

Kalia had been living here ever since.

"He's not doing too well," Kalia said softly, ripping Lessia from her thoughts.

She gestured for Lessia to follow as she started walking toward the farthest bedroom.

Glancing at Amalise, who nodded and began shuffling the rest of them to bed, Lessia followed. Unease roiled in her gut as Kalia pushed the door open, and a small body lay curled up on the bed, facing the wall.

The boy was skin and bones, the clothes Kalia must have offered him hanging off his skinny shoulders. He didn't react when they entered, his eyes vacantly staring into the white wall beside his bed.

Even if he looked and smelled clean, his raven hair was matted, falling far past his shoulders, indicating how long he'd roamed the streets of Vastala.

Too long.

Lessia sat down on the creaking mattress and lit the lantern beside the bed, nodding for Kalia to leave them, her eyes sweeping the bedroom as Kalia quietly left.

The room wasn't much, but it was clean.

There were two beds, one still empty—the boy he would share this room with hovering outside to offer them privacy—and two small desks, each with its own chair. A worn rug covered the floor, and by the ends of the beds stood two small cabinets to store any belongings they might have. Not that this boy would have had much to bring with him, based on the state they'd found him in.

Her nostrils flared as she thought of the reason he'd been living on the streets. While the humans had learned something after the devastating war a century ago and finally treated most members of their society decently, the Fae hadn't evolved at all.

King Rioner's family still ruled the kingdom with an iron fist—as it had for millennia. The nobles and wealthy merchants were the only ones living comfortably, and the rest were left to fend for themselves as best they could.

And half-Fae...

Well, Lessia definitely preferred it here in Ellow. Even if humans didn't particularly care for them and often looked down upon them, they at least didn't leave half-dead children in the streets.

When the boy shifted, Lessia realized she was gripping the blanket beneath him so tightly she'd nearly pulled it—and him—off the bed. Drawing a breath to calm herself, she released her hold and placed a hand on the boy's shoulder.

He didn't react—didn't shy away from her touch—but didn't lean into it either.

It was as if she weren't even here.

"I know what you're going through," she said softly. "I lived on the streets of Vastala before I came here as well."

A chill raced down her spine as memories from her time on the streets flashed before her eyes. She'd been so consumed by guilt when she'd fled her family home that she hadn't dared use her magic for years. Instead, she'd done what the older half-Fae did—looked for scraps outside taverns, begged on corners, and tried to stay far away from King Rioner's sentries.

The sentries liked to terrorize them, and while they weren't allowed to kill without reason, when they grew bored as they marched through the usually quiet streets, they had no qualms about pitting half-Fae children against each other for food, clothing, or even blankets.

The boy's eyelids creased ever so slightly, so Lessia forced herself to continue. "I know the horrors you went through, but I promise you, you're safe now. It will be overwhelming, and humans can be strange sometimes, but you're safe here. We'll protect you, keep you warm and fed, and when the time comes, if you want to leave, we will help you find work, help you build a life."

She held her breath as the boy moved to lie on his back, his light gray eyes shifting between hers. When he remained quiet, she gently squeezed his shoulder. "Will you tell me your name?"

Silver filled his cloudy eyes, and he put a thin arm over his face. "I don't remember."

Biting her cheek to stop the choked sound traveling up her throat, Lessia nodded. "That's all right. You're starting a new life. It seems only fitting you should choose a new name as well. Many of the others have. Is there a name you like?"

He peeked at her, his arm still covering part of his face. "Ledger."

Lessia smiled at him. "Ledger. That's a pretty name. I think it fits you perfectly."

It truly did.

Like all half-Fae, he was beautiful. Even with the matted hair and the hollowness of his face, it was clear he'd grow into a handsome man. Perhaps not with the lethal beauty of the full Fae, but a more human beauty—a softer one.

"It was my friend's name." A sob racked Ledger's small body, and Lessia clutched the blanket again.

"He must have been a good friend," she got out, trying to draw a breath as a red haze filled her vision.

"He died. They killed him for stealing food for us. Why did they do that?" Ledger covered his face with his hands as more violent sobs shook his frame.

Her magic thrummed under her skin as she placed a hand on his back, and for a moment Lessia thought about removing his pain.

Within seconds she could make him forget about the friend—forget all about the life he'd been forced to lead.

Shaking her head, she forced the urge down.

She'd removed memories once...

After that day she'd promised herself never to do it again.

She couldn't undo what she'd done—would never return to the home where she'd lived the first twelve years of her life. But taking something so big away, the love he clearly harbored for the friend, was selfish—a quick solution that still wouldn't erase the traumatic events that colored the first years of his life.

Stroking the boy's arm, she responded quietly, "They don't know any better. They've been taught we're tainted, that we're diluting the Fae blood. But do you know what I think?"

Hands still pressed to his face, he shook his head, the bed shifting with the movement.

"I think they're also scared of us."

Ledger hiccuped, but a sliver of gray peeked through his fingers. "W-why would they be scared of us?"

She sighed. "Because we're different. The human in us makes us more open, more understanding of how the world is changing. Ellow might have a ways to go, but it's better here. And it will continue to get better. Vastala hasn't changed their ways in millennia, and perhaps they never will. Not unless there is a shift. I think the king is worried that if we grow to large enough numbers, that's exactly what might happen."

Ledger hiccuped again, and while he didn't respond, the tremors running through him came further and further apart. Lessia continued stroking his arm until his coiled muscles loosened, the sobs quieting.

As she was about to ask if he needed anything, the boy

cleared his throat. “Do you think my father will realize I’m gone?”

Ledger peered at her, and the hope that filled his eyes broke her heart.

Most half-Fae who ended up here were the result of a one-night affair or a Fae going against the king’s orders and falling in love with a human. Since it was forbidden to wed humans, it was rare for the relationships to last.

And even if they did...

Few humans survived them, survived the harassment and the nobles who took it upon themselves to right what they felt had been wronged.

Most of the children here had a dead parent and a parent who’d left them in the streets or the wilderness, pressured by their families or neighbors.

They were considered the lucky ones.

As if living in squalor, begging for scraps, and being spat on was luck.

Offering Ledger a small smile, she brushed a stray hair out of his face. “I could lie to you and tell you he will. But I don’t know, Ledger. If he comes for you, we won’t force you to stay if you don’t want to. You are not a prisoner here.”

In the four years she’d done this—brought these children here for a better life—not a single parent had come for any of them.

He nodded, satisfied with her answer, and when a small yawn escaped him, Lessia smiled again. “Time for bed. Kalia will make sure you have everything you need, but you can always send for me if you need me. Just ask for Lessia.”

As she made her way to the door, Ledger whispered, “Did your family come for you?”

Swallowing, Lessia responded, “I don’t have a family.”

But she couldn’t stop the memory of gentle hands in her

hair, the smell of fresh grass, and the sense of happiness flickering to life. A girl with a face the mirror to her own, giggling as she chased her. But when that face twisted with pain, emptiness replacing the happiness in the golden eyes, Lessia bit back a whimper.

She hadn't been able to save her.

But she'd made a vow that no more souls would lie heavy on her conscience.

With a final glance at Ledger, whose eyes had now shut, the hardness in his face softened, she forced a small smile, then walked out of the room.

CHAPTER FOUR

After helping her move the shelf back into place, Amalise waited at the bottom of the spiral staircase, one hand resting on the metal railing. As she approached her friend, Lessia cast a mournful glance over her shoulder.

She wished there was something more she could do for them.

Keeping them locked up like this drove even the calmest crazy some days.

But she'd brought them over illegally—hadn't dared to risk that they'd be turned away at Ellow's borders. So they had to wait until they turned sixteen, when most folks in Ellow started to work, before they could be introduced into society, each with an individual backstory of how they'd ended up here.

"Don't."

Her eyes found Amalise's, and Lessia frowned. "Don't what?"

"Don't feel guilty." Amalise's blue eyes held hers captive.

"You've done so much for them. This is more than they could ever ask for."

Lessia shook her head. "Living like prisoners? Just because they have a bed and food doesn't mean they're free."

"But they're alive." Amalise took a step toward her. "They get to live, Lessia."

A shard of ice pierced her chest, and Lessia tore her eyes away, slamming a hand against the wall as she thought of the young girl who didn't.

"You can't blame yourself forever, Lessia."

Amalise tried to put an arm around her shoulders, but Lessia shifted away.

She couldn't stand the compassion when she was the one at fault.

She needed to do better by these children.

Give them the life another had been robbed of.

"You were a child, Lessia. It wasn't your fault. You couldn't have known," Amalise pleaded.

"Please stop," Lessia whispered. "I can't think about this."

"But you need to. At some point, you need to let it go. She'd want you to. We all know why you bring them over, and of course we support you. Gods, I've come to love those little bastards despite all the chaos they cause. But you need to see the good you're doing!"

Lessia shook her head, her eyes following the swirling snow outside the rounded window beneath the stairs.

This burden was one she'd carry for however long she would live.

She could rescue every child in Havlands, and it wouldn't be enough.

It would never be enough.

"Lessia." Amalise reached out for her again, and this time, Lessia let her take her hand and pull her closer. "Please, you need to at least try. The darkness will consume the light you've created here if you don't. That I can't bear."

She shifted her eyes to Amalise's worried blues, trying to keep the hollowness that filled her out of her honey ones.

"I'll try," she said, although the emptiness of the promise echoed in her ears.

She could try all she liked.

But she'd never forgive herself for what she'd done.

Amalise raised a brow, and she forced a weak smile.

Her friend didn't smile back. Instead, Amalise's eyes bore into hers, her hand impatiently brushing a lock of hair out of Lessia's face.

When Amalise's mouth opened and closed a few times, Lessia braced herself. "Just ask."

Her friend sucked in a breath. "What happened back at the tavern, Lia?"

Lessia opened her mouth to respond, groaning when the words she wanted to say stuck in her throat.

Gods, she hated that she couldn't just tell her. It was exhausting trying to find ways around her king's orders—devastating to see the look of disappointment in Amalise's eyes, even as she knew Lessia couldn't help it.

Throwing her head back, she stared at the metal beams lining the tall ceiling. The white paint around them was chipping—they'd need to get that fixed soon.

And given what Merrick had told her tonight...

Moving her gaze back to Amalise's sharp eyes, she let out a soft breath. "You know how I told you there might be a time when I must leave for a while?"

Amalise's brows pinched, but she nodded.

"I'm afraid that time might come sooner than I'd like." She couldn't help her face from scrunching up, the words coming out choppy as her throat thickened.

"Oh, Lia." Amalise dragged her into her arms, and each held on tight to the other.

Pulling back, Lessia gave her a crooked smile. "We have tonight. I can't say how much longer, but let's not waste it." She gently nudged her shoulder when Amalise's gaze dropped to the floor. "You're supposed to be the carefree one."

Amalise shoved her back. "Not all of us can go around being all serious all the time. Honestly, I can never understand how the rest of Ellow doesn't see through the disguise, see what a boring bastard you truly are."

With a snort, Lessia dragged her up the stairs, where soft murmurs and the smell of liquor and arousal filled the air.

As they took the final step, Lessia tried to put the guilt and apprehension out of her mind. If this was truly her final night with her friends, she didn't want to waste it giving them more reasons to worry.

Squeezing Amalise's small hand, she lifted her gaze to the dimly lit sitting room.

Pellie straddled a soldier in one of the plush leather chairs before her, while another slowly stroked her back. One of his hands wrapped in her copper hair, tilting her head so the soldier beneath her could kiss her neck. Soria was nowhere to be seen, and Lessia realized two of the other soldiers must be with her.

With a wink, Amalise sidled up to the man she'd spent the evening with, taking the goblet he offered her and throwing it back. Flashing him a seductive smile, she slipped her hand into his and pulled him toward her room. But Lessia didn't miss the glance she cast her way, the slight frown between her brows.

Swallowing, she walked up to Ardow and sat down on the arm of his chair.

"All good?" He raised a dark brow when she leaned back and a sigh escaped her.

"Yes, the papers were all in order." Lessia kept her eyes on the room so as not to let him see the worry she was certain burned in them.

Two soldiers leaned against the wooden countertop before them. They took sips from cups of liquor in between spells of laughter, and when their smiles turned her way, the carefree expressions tugged at her heart.

She'd had that here.

Not often.

But there had been nights she'd forgotten all about the king, about what she'd left behind in Vastala, and had just been in the moment with her friends.

But now her time was up. She didn't know what the king wanted, but it couldn't be good. And she couldn't risk bringing her friends into it.

Especially with the secret they harbored in the rooms beneath them.

Pellie waved goodbye as she dragged the soldiers down the stairs, no doubt bringing them to her apartment, and Lessia nodded at her before she disappeared.

Soria and Pellie were key to keeping up the appearance that all she and her friends did was drink and bring home different men—and sometimes women—to warm their beds. While neither knew of the children or what truly went on in the warehouse, they were aware they were a distraction, and they made the most of it, both enjoying the freedom they'd been offered.

A few years ago, Lessia and Ardow had helped the sisters get away from their abusive mother and now paid for their apartments and living expenses. The sisters were clever enough not to ask any questions that might risk their newfound freedom, knowing there wouldn't be any answers anyway.

Lessia remained quiet while Ardow and the soldiers talked, the men telling them of their lives in the navy. They'd been at sea the past three years, traveling between the human isles to ensure peace, but had been called back with the elections in Ellow coming up.

Lessia nodded. She hadn't been here the past election, had only arrived right as it wrapped up. But she'd heard it could get intense.

When her eyelids fluttered, Ardow followed the soldiers to the door while she cleaned the dirty cups and wiped the spots on the counter where they'd spilled some of the liquor.

Leaning against the bar, she smiled at the scruffy leather chairs and the scarred wooden table before them—the first furniture they'd brought in here. She, Ardow, and Amalise had slept in those chairs, poor as ever, while they searched for the first place to open a tavern.

"You daydreaming over there, or did you fall asleep standing?" Ardow grinned at her from across the room, his arms folded over his chest as he leaned against the doorframe.

She smiled back at him.

He was devastatingly handsome, even with a slightly rumpled leather tunic and his dark hair tousled from him dragging his hands through it all night. With his muscled build, six-foot-two stature, and broad shoulders, he rarely had to fight for a man's or woman's attention when he wanted it.

Ardow wiggled his brows. "Admiring me?"

Rolling her eyes, she blew out the candle beside her and hurried to the door, where light trickled into the dark room. Ardow stepped aside to let her out, and she let out a breath when she left the darkness behind.

She winked. "Always."

When she made to walk to her room, Ardow caught her hand, and she turned her head over her shoulder to look at him.

"You want company tonight?"

Lessia bit her lip. It had been a while since Ardow warmed her bed, but she was exhausted and confident she'd have nightmares after the meeting with Merrick.

Shaking her head, she said softly, "I think I just need to sleep."

Ardow's smile didn't falter. He only nodded and kissed her cheek. "Good night, Lessia."

Waving at him, she slipped into her room, making sure the fireplace was lit and lifting a lantern off the wall to bring inside before she closed the door behind her.

CHAPTER FIVE

When she woke, the stars still winked at her through the floor-to-ceiling windows behind her bed.

Amalise had laughed when she'd picked this room—they'd moved in during summer, after all, and the window faced south, so her room was bathed in sunlight most hours of the day. But she'd stopped laughing, understanding instead filling her eyes, when Lessia had refused curtains, unwilling ever to block the sun again.

In winter, though, the sun barely peeked over the horizon in Asker, the island too far north. She'd hated it at first, had only ever known Vastala, where it was warm year-round, the Fae island several weeks south by ship.

But she'd gotten used to it. Even if she still hated the dark, the snow made up for it, and the coastal town was still bright and perhaps even more beautiful in winter, with ice coating every building, making the town sparkle.

After a quick stretch, she pulled on soft trousers and a long-sleeved black tunic before throwing her cloak over her shoulders. She sighed as she straightened the clothes she'd haphazardly thrown over the chair in the corner of her room last night.

In winter, she got fewer stares, fewer people wondering why she bundled up, why she wore long-sleeved tunics even in the blistering sun.

Following a brief stop in the kitchen, where she gobbled down a few pieces of dried meat and an apple, she went to the actual office. They'd built it in the back of the building, far from where the children slept.

Pulling apart the curtains, she let what little light there was in, setting down the lantern she'd brought from her room on the side table by the door.

The fireplace already burned bright, its orange flames dancing across the large wooden desk and the many papers strewn across it. Ardow must be up—there were more papers for her to sign, a new shipment of liquor coming in that they had first right to.

Lessia picked at the paper, but instead of picking up the quill to begin signing and checking what appointments she had today, she rose again, heading toward the small bookshelf. She pulled out an old book containing maps of Havlands and shifted a few other books to the side, then stole a quick glance at the door before she took out a key hidden in the book and opened the safe.

With her heart pounding in her ears, she pulled out the papers she'd hoped she'd never have to see again.

After closing the safe and putting the books back in their place, she sat back down at the desk and stared at them for a long while, her throat dry and eyes burning.

A firm knock interrupted her thoughts, and as Lessia snapped her head to the door, her eyes widened. Pulling at some of the other papers, she covered the thin pile.

Waving for the man to come in, she forced her lips to curl. “I’d almost forgotten it was the end of the month. Good to see you, Zaddock.”

Zaddock smiled back at her, his neatly combed brown hair not showing any signs of the walk here and his black uniform perfectly pressed. “Good to see you too, Lessia. I hear business is booming.”

Outside the door, several of his men stood posted, all bearing black masks to cover their faces and their hands resting on the swords by their hips.

Lessia held back a shudder.

She’d been intimidated by Regent Loche’s men since the first day she got here, by those terrifying masks they never took off.

But she guessed it was the point.

Tearing her eyes away from them, she nodded and opened a drawer to pull out the thick envelope he sought. “It’s been good. Prices are going up, though, so it’s getting more expensive to keep everything running.”

Accepting the envelope, not bothering to open it, Zaddock gestured to the chair opposite her. “Can I sit for a moment?”

Her stomach churned, but she forced her smile to remain. “Of course. What’s on your mind, Zaddock?”

Racking her brain, Lessia tried to think of what he could want.

She had not once been late with tax payments, and while the taverns and gambling rooms she, Ardow, and Amalise owned were not upscale, they made sure they followed all Ellow’s rules. None of them would ever risk having the regent and his men look into their businesses.

Zaddock tapped his fingers against his knee as he studied her, his face tilted and dark blue eyes soft.

She understood why the regent chose him as his collector. From the outside he looked gentle—kind, even.

But she knew better.

She'd heard what Zaddock and the rest were capable of if someone went against their leader.

"Regent Loche doesn't want to do this, but as you mentioned, prices are increasing. And with this harsh winter, the farmers and fishermen are struggling."

Her shoulders lowered an inch. "So he's raising taxes?"

While it wasn't optimal, since they barely made more than what they needed to cover for the children living here, everyone living in the warehouse had a roof over their heads and warm beds to get into at night, and she'd just have to be more careful with the food she purchased. Lessia knew too well what it was like to be cold and starving, and if she could keep someone else from experiencing it, she would.

Nodding, Zaddock picked up a small dagger lying on her desk, observing it for a moment. "He is. But as I'm sure you've noticed, we have had several ships come in the past weeks, and we're expecting more. With the elections beginning soon, the soldiers are needed here to ensure everything goes smoothly."

Her eyes trailed the dagger, how the shiny blade reflected the firelight, before she responded. "I have. It's been good for business. Although some of these men have been kept at sea for too long. There has been more trouble than usual."

Zaddock put the dagger down and met her eyes again. "Yes. Loche is willing to make you an offer. If you hire more men to keep the soldiers from beating each other—and anyone else, for that matter—to a pulp, he'll hold off on raising your taxes for now. While you might not have the most decadent of venues, the soldiers seem to prefer them."

He quieted for a moment, but she heard the underlying message.

He could not understand whyever someone would prefer their taverns over the upscale ones close to the castle or in the western part of Asker.

Sucking her teeth, she mulled it over.

More men meant more salaries. However, a few of the older boys in the house were getting anxious about getting out, and perhaps it would be a good way to introduce them into society. Ardow, Bren, and the rest of her men could keep an eye on them while they worked, and since they were half- or at least part-Fae, they were strong enough to take on a drunken human.

Lessia reached out a hand. "Tell Loche we have a deal."

CHAPTER
SIX

Her fingers ached from signing hundreds of forms, and irritation still pricked her skin from an earlier conversation with one of her suppliers.

He'd never liked her, didn't trust her Fae heritage, but he'd never been so blatantly rude and dismissive as when she'd tried to argue with him over the ridiculously high price he was asking for plain meat.

Making a mental note to let Ardow know they needed a new supplier to replace him, even if it would cost them more, she threw herself on the unmade bed in her room.

Staring up at the white ceiling, she waited for the door to open.

Amalise had been out all day. She'd brought some of the children to the forest to have them let off some steam, but they should be back any moment now, and Amalise always came straight to her room to give her updates on how they were faring.

Shadows from the moon rippled across the beams in the ceiling, and a yearning for summer came over her. This winter had been harsh, longer than the four others she'd spent here, and there didn't seem to be an end in sight. There'd been dark clouds rolling in, a hint of snow filling the air when she let the last merchant out of her office.

A sharp pain slicing through her arm made her involuntarily curl into herself, her hand flying to cover the tattoo and dread crawling up her spine as she hesitantly pulled back the sleeve.

No.

Her body buzzed when the silver serpent slithered up her forearm, its eyes blinking and its tongue viciously lapping her skin.

A pull twisted deep in her gut, and before she realized what she was doing, she walked out of her bedroom, unable to stop even to pick up her cloak.

In a trance Lessia walked down the spiraling staircase, out the double doors, and onto the cold, dark streets. Pressure built in her chest at the little light outside, but her limbs wouldn't bring her closer to the path where the metal lampposts lined the road. Instead, they led her out toward the cliffs, toward the wild sea roaring below.

She sucked in a breath.

Was she about to walk off?

Disappear into the dark waves?

But as she closed her eyes, her feet an inch from the steep drop, her body turned, leading her north, away from the town, following the slippery, dark cliffs.

Soon, the city was far behind her, with only black cliffs to her left and the dark forest to her right. Shivering, she tried to manage her breathing and squash the panic clawing at her lungs.

She didn't jerk when Merrick's oily magic lathered over her skin; she was almost grateful for the sticky warmth shielding her from the harsh wind. And she was more than a little grateful for the lantern he held as he fell into step with her.

A hood covered Merrick's face, the silvery cloak billowing behind him as she followed him left, where a lone figure in a dark cape stood upon a tall cliff.

They approached in silence, each dropping to one knee before him.

Lessia winced as the wet stone cut into her skin, immediately soaking her trousers.

"It's been a long time, Elessia Gyldenberg."

When Merrick didn't rise, she didn't dare either. "It has, my king."

It was quiet for so long Lessia almost wondered if he'd left, when the king ordered, "Get up."

Shakily rising to her feet, she stared at him.

The hood of his dark cloak covered his face, but she glimpsed the gilded doublet he wore underneath, coupled with a bejeweled belt and several glittering rapiers hanging from it.

If she hadn't been so afraid, she might have snorted.

He probably wore that overly decorated crown beneath the hood as well.

"Is something amusing you, Elessia?"

Even if she couldn't see his eyes, she knew they were narrowed, and she could smell the wisps of anger in the wind.

"No, Your Majesty." She didn't bow her head—he couldn't look directly at her, so he'd never know.

But magic tightened around her neck, forcing her eyes down, bending her head forward until it was all she could do to keep a whimper from escaping.

"That's enough, Merrick." The king waved his hand lazily. "At least for now."

When his magic released her, she snapped her head to the side and couldn't stop herself from snarling at Merrick, her hand reaching out to pull off his stupid hood to teach *him* a lesson.

A low laugh rumbled from him, so chilling she stopped herself, clasping her hands behind her back.

She wasn't a fighter, had never learned combat—hadn't required it when all she needed was to lock eyes with someone to control them.

Even if she was able to get one of them to look at her, King Rioner himself had commanded armies long before she was born—had fought every type of creature in Havlands.

The king laughed darkly. "So there is some fight left in you. Last I saw, you were so broken I wasn't sure you'd survive the travels here."

The musty smell of wet stone immediately filled her nostrils, and the fear she'd felt when his guards finally dragged her out of the cell wrapped like an icy hand around her heart.

She'd been blinded by the light they'd robbed her of for years when they threw her down before the king. With splitting pain tearing through her skull, she'd barely been able to hear the king offer her the blood oath.

Lessia bit her cheek, forcing the memories from their last meeting deep down.

She wasn't that desperate little girl anymore; she was stronger now, and she had people who depended on her.

Even if she'd make sure they didn't have to much longer.

"I'm glad. What I need you for will require some strength. From what I've heard, it can get quite grisly." The king tilted his head, but still, she couldn't make out a single one of his features; only the hood shifting betrayed his movements.

When he didn't continue, she gritted her teeth. "What may I do for you, Your Majesty?"

Intertwining his long fingers, the king chuckled. "I thought you'd never ask."

He paused for a moment, and her pulse quickened, echoing in the quiet night.

The king snickered again, before he continued. "I need you to run for regent of Ellow."

Lessia's heart stopped.

CHAPTER SEVEN

King Rioner elegantly jumped off the cliff, closing the distance between them.

A few feet away he stilled, the gemstones adorning his weapons glinting in the moonlight.

Lessia stared at him, her mouth falling open. "What do you mean, run for regent?"

She'd expected he'd use her for something dangerous, perhaps even something evil, but this?

What would the king have to gain in the human elections?

"*Your Majesty*," Merrick snarled at her.

She was tempted to tell him to speak like that to her face but drew a shaky breath to calm her temper. "I apologize, Your Majesty. Could you repeat what you said?"

King Rioner stood unnaturally still before her. "I should think I was quite clear. I need you to partake in the human elections, run for regent."

Lessia threw out her arms. "I won't win, Majesty. My magic doesn't work that way. I— I can only control one person at a time. I thought you were happy with Loche. He opened the trade with the Fae, he allowed us half-Fae to live here and be part of the society. He even allows Fae to come to Ellow should they like. So, why?"

The air crackled with tension, and Merrick's magic tightened its deadly fingers around her shoulders and neck, but she forced herself to keep her gaze on the king. Flexing her hands to conceal their shaking, she waited, the sharp breaths she let out seeming too loud in the deafening silence.

"Are you questioning me, Elessia?" King Rioner's voice was soft, but there was a lethal edge to it that had goose bumps pepper her neck.

She was certain he was about to end her when he took another step forward, but then the king halted again. "I don't need you to win. I need you to partake. You will run, participate in whatever they make their running regents do, and get close to Loche and his men."

King Rioner shot a look at Merrick before he continued. "I guess you need some information for what I need you to do." He picked at his cloak. "We've found spies in our castles, boats have disappeared off our coast, and Fae have gone missing—important Fae. I *was* happy with Loche. For a human, he doesn't disgust me as much as the rest of them do, but if he has anything to do with this, I need to know so that we can retaliate. If he's broken our treaty, war will come upon Ellow."

Her pulse thrummed in her ears.

Retaliate?

There was a reason there hadn't been a war for a hundred years. The last one had been so devastating that the Fae and humans finally bonded together to stop the bloodshed. And now her king was contemplating it again?

As if he sensed her thoughts, King Rioner snarled, "I don't want war, I lived through the last one. But strange things are happening in Vastala, and I need to know why. I need to protect my people."

A scoff made its way through her throat before she could squash it, and the next moment she was on the ground, stars dancing before her eyes from the blow Merrick delivered. Shaking her head to get her vision back, she didn't anticipate the second blow, either, and her face crashed into hard stone before she could throw her hands out.

Warm blood rushed down her face, but she whipped around, pushing to her feet to face the two cloaked males.

When Merrick made to approach her again, the king held up a hand, and the Fae froze.

"Yes, be a good male and listen to your master," she spat, blood streaming into her mouth when she smiled at the growl that left Merrick.

She'd not fought back last time she'd been in the king's claws.

When they'd beaten her, she'd accepted it.

Welcomed it.

The pain and grief inside her had been so raw when she was caught, she hadn't cared if she survived. The king's dungeons were where she belonged for what she'd done.

But now...

There were others to fight for.

And if she died tonight, she wouldn't have time to set everything up so they would be safe.

"You bore me. Elessia, you will join the elections to get close to Loche and the rest of the participants to see if he, or anyone else in Ellow, is the one behind this. I don't care how, but you will be beside him every step of the way. You will be standing there as the vote is cast. And as you're well aware, you may not breathe a word about me or anything related to my involvement, or our involvement together. You will tell everyone you want the disgusting *halflings* better represented, and that you're willingly participating. Make it believable, would you?"

She flinched when the tattoo on her arm burned in response to the command, the oath she'd sworn to serve him reminding her that she didn't have a choice. Blood chilling, she stared at the king as she memorized every word of his command.

What he'd told her to do.

And most importantly—what he'd not told her to do.

King Rioner began to make his way to the cliff again, to the water he controlled, which would transport him back to Vastala in minutes instead of weeks.

Turning back, he continued. "If you succeed in finding me the information I need, I promise to release you from your blood oath, and you can stay here with your pets should you like. As a free female."

When the bond between them flickered with the truth of his words, her heart began hammering against her rib cage.

The one advantage with the blood oath was that it went both ways: a vow from King Rioner couldn't be broken, as any vow he forced from her couldn't be escaped.

She could be free.

She could stay here, stay with Amalise and Ardow and the rest of the people she loved.

"One more thing."

The smile that overtook her face fell when the king gestured to Merrick.

"Show her what happens if she fails."

Lessia didn't have time to react before a fist connected with her stomach and she doubled over.

CHAPTER EIGHT

Whispers, and something wet and warm lying across her forehead, woke her. She furrowed her brows, then groaned when the motion made knives slice through her head.

"Take it easy, Lia. You've been out for a while," Amalise whispered.

Forcing her eyes open, Lessia stared back at her friend, at her wide blue eyes, at the angrily set jaw.

Ardow hovered behind her, his fists clenched so tightly his knuckles were white.

"Who do I need to kill?" Amalise cast a glare around the room, as if whoever had done this would appear out of thin air.

Lessia followed her eyes, realizing she was back in her own bed, the moon hanging high in the cloud-filled sky mocking her through the window.

She cleared her throat. "How did I get here?"

The last thing she remembered was hard stone, and bone-chilling wind brushing her cheeks.

Amalise shifted her glare to her, hissing quietly, "Who, Lia?"

Lessia's mouth opened and closed, but invisible fingers tightened around her throat, and she drew a wheezing breath as they restricted the air flowing into her lungs.

Ardow placed a hand on Amalise's shoulder, jerking his head at Lessia. "You know as well as I do that she can't tell us. But I have a pretty good idea of who did this to her."

Amalise sliced her eyes to Ardow. "Is it her king? This has something to do with what happened at the tavern, doesn't it?"

"I think so." Ardow sat down on the bed, the mattress shifting with both him and Amalise on it, making Lessia cringe as the movement sent sharp pain through her joints.

"Sorry!" He piled a few pillows between them, keeping her steady until they all got comfortable. "I think your king is coming for you, or has already, perhaps, based on the state of you."

Lessia fidgeted with the blanket they'd placed over her, her eyes darting between her friends.

Ardow nodded to himself. "Yes, he's having you do something for him. Are you leaving?"

Grateful that she could at least offer them that, she shook her head and tried for a weak smile. "I'm running for regent."

Her friends' stunned silence almost had her giggle.

Gods, she'd be made a fool.

Never had a half-Fae been in a leadership position, and with her reputation...

Jerking up, ignoring the sharp pain in her head, she stared at her friends with wide eyes.

This must be why the king had been so adamant she come to Ellow, that she make a name for herself until he called upon her.

But that was five years ago, and he'd mentioned recent events as the reason he needed her in the election...

Not that she thought it was beneath him to lie—but to risk this? Risk her being exposed as a spy, risk war? Something must have been going on for a while, something he was more afraid of than the bloodbath there'd be if humans and Fae once again became enemies.

Shuddering, she fell back against the pillows.

If he was having her do this, she'd need to find out what he really was looking for. If only so she could protect the people in this house, protect the land that had become her home.

She'd follow his orders.

She had to.

But he'd not explicitly forbidden her to do other things while she did.

"Regent?" Amalise stared at her. "I don't know why I never saw it before, but I think you'd actually be a great regent. I mean, if you weren't blood-sworn to the evil Fae king and all."

She couldn't stop the giggle this time, and soon Ardow and Amalise followed. All of them were gasping for air by the time they settled down.

Shaking his head, Ardow shifted so he could lie down next to her. "Lessia, regent of Ellow." He nudged Amalise. "You're right, it doesn't sound so bad. But you know the nomination is tomorrow already?"

Lessia nodded, ignoring the unease churning in her gut.

It was better it was coming up quickly.

If King Rioner was concerned enough to risk war, she needed to figure out why fast.

And she'd need to be smart about it. Everything she was

told by the regent she'd have to relay to her king. And if it was something that would put Ellow at risk...

She'd have to be careful with what and how she found out.

The sooner it was over, the sooner she would also be free. Would never again have to put her friends at risk because of the actions and choices that led her here. Would never again have to look over her shoulder for Merrick, or anyone else the king might think to send.

But they weren't there yet.

Lessia cleared her throat. "I don't think I can move. Ardow, can you please go get the leather folder that's in the top drawer of my desk? I need to speak to you about something."

His brows crashed, but Ardow got up and slipped out of the room.

Amalise immediately took his place, sticking her cold feet under the blanket.

Lessia wrinkled her nose. "Get those away from me."

"Or what, you'll pounce on me with that bruised body of yours?" Amalise smiled at her, moving her feet closer. "Nothing's broken, by the way, and even though your face was all bloodied when you were brought here, it seems they spared it for the most part. But you'll definitely be walking funny for a while."

Lessia smacked her. "Who brought me here? I was—"

Apparently she could not even tell her where they'd been, and she nearly choked as the oath thickened her throat.

Amalise smacked her back, oblivious to Lessia once again being silenced, but then propped up on an elbow to look at her. "Some soldiers found you. They were kind enough to wrap you up in a blanket, but you were still blue when Ardow carried you up here. You nearly scared me to death, Lia."

Cautiously shifting her arm, Lessia bit her lip not to grimace as she wrapped it around her friend's shoulders.

"What is this?" Ardow barged into the room, the folder open and the papers in his hands as he stuck them under her nose. "What *is this*, Lessia?"

Lessia swallowed as she stared at the yellowed papers she'd had drawn up a few years ago. "I'm signing everything over to you two."

"No!" Amalise flew up, joining Ardow to glower down at her. "You're joining the election. So what? You can still come back here from time to time while it's running, and even if you're elected, you can still help, perhaps even more!"

"Amalise, if something happens to me, I need to know they're okay—that you are okay. If everything goes how I hope it will, I'll be back, and you can sign my portion back to me. Please tell me you understand?"

It broke her heart to see them stare at her like this, anger and fear dancing across their features, but finally Ardow dipped his chin.

"I don't like it. It feels like you're preparing for something to go wrong." He smacked the papers down on her bedside table so hard the lantern on it shook. "And we can't even help you, because you can't tell us how!" His voice broke, and Lessia reached up to pull him to her.

Ardow let her drag him onto the bed, and she reached out to Amalise, who slowly lowered herself down, even as she pulled at her hair in frustration, making knots in her blonde waves.

"You *are* helping me," Lessia said quietly. "You've been helping me for years. And I can never thank you enough for it. But I need to ask this one thing of you, even if I can't tell you why."

When they bowed their heads, she squeezed their hands.

It was true.

She wouldn't have survived without them.

She'd been so broken when she arrived in Ellow. Not just from the years in the king's cellar, from the abuse and torture they'd put her through. But from the heartache of what she'd done to her family, from the memories of the streets, from the friends she hadn't had time to seek out before she was put on a ship away from Vastala.

Ardow and Amalise had sat with her during the long nights the memories wouldn't leave her mind, had listened and cried when she told them her darkest secret, and most importantly, had immediately helped her when she told them her plan of rescuing those who suffered like she had on the streets.

She breathed through her nose as apprehension, guilt, and warmth tangled inside her.

It felt as if the emotions would burst out of her body—too many, too intense, too conflicting, hurting more than her sore limbs and pounding head.

With a shakier voice than she liked, she said, "I need to sleep. I feel like I've fallen down a cliff."

Ardow and Amalise mumbled to each other as they walked out, but she couldn't make out the words as she tried to keep herself together.

Involuntary shudders convulsed her body as she stared up into the ceiling, praying she'd find a way to make it through while keeping Ellow, and everyone in it, safe.

Sleep came late that night, and when it did, Lessia wished it hadn't.

Memories of the cell and her family fought for dominance in her dreams, and no matter how much she tried, she couldn't change the outcome of death and destruction that followed as she tried to right the wrongs she'd caused.

CHAPTER NINE

The smell of food woke her, and with a groan, she pushed herself out of bed, every single limb and muscle aching. Dropping the blanket wrapped around her body, Lessia peeked down, holding her breath.

Black-and-blue bruising covered parts of her stomach, legs, and arms, but it was better than she'd thought.

Amalise was right—no broken bones.

Casting a glance at herself in the mirror beside the bed, she found her face free from bruising, even if her nose was a little red still from when it smacked into the stone.

Her amber eyes were red lined as well, her skin paler than usual, but that could also be attributed to her not eating last night. Picking at her bloodied and matted hair, she sighed and made her way out of the room, into the bathing chamber.

After a freezing bath, the delicious scents from the kitchen making her forgo warming the water first, she stepped out with dripping hair, her usual black trousers and tunic on.

Ardow stood with his back to her, freshly made bread on the counter beside him and steaming plates of meat and grains already standing upon the wooden table in the middle of the room. Gray wintry sunlight seeped through the window, left cracked open to avoid the room filling with steam from whatever was brewing in the large pot Ardow stirred.

"Morning," he chanted as he spun around.

When she raised her brows and gestured to the many plates, he offered her a sheepish grin and shrugged. "Couldn't sleep, so I stayed occupied."

Lessia smiled as the love she held for him won over the unease from last night. "I'm not complaining. This looks delicious."

Rubbing her stomach, she lowered onto a chair, holding back a grimace when her legs protested.

As Lessia popped a piece of meat into her mouth, she groaned.

She and Amalise were lucky Ardow could cook. Neither of them had ever learned, and they might have starved those early days when they couldn't afford to go to a tavern, or even buy much at the market, if it hadn't been for Ardow's skills.

"That good?" Ardow slipped onto the chair beside her.

She only nodded, stuffing her belly with the bread he offered. They ate silently for a while, until she could barely take a sip of water without nausea roiling in her gut.

Leaning back in her chair, she patted her stomach. "I definitely overdid that. I will miss this, Ard."

When his eyes lowered, she silently scolded herself. "I mean, I guess it'll just be a few days, right? Then I'll be back here for you to fatten me up."

He snapped his eyes to hers. "You know the election process takes months, don't you? And you'll need to stay with the other nominees for its full course."

"No?" Her stomach flipped when he eyed her again, his brown eyes narrowing.

"Gods, Lessia. It's a whole bunch of events and tests. How do you think people would know who to vote for if not?"

She shrugged. She'd never thought of the election—she'd known it was coming up, but everyone assumed Loche would be elected again, and she didn't particularly care either way.

As long as whoever ruled left them alone, let her run her public businesses and continue her secret occupation, they could go back to a monarchy for all she cared.

Fidgeting with her tunic, she reminded herself she didn't need to win.

She only needed to get through—find out what the king sought, and find out why he was having her do this.

The apprehension shifted into resolve.

She would do this.

She'd made too many mistakes in her life.

This time it would be different.

It was an election. How hard could it be?

Ardow tapped the table impatiently. "Lessia, it's not a game. They take this very seriously. And I fear this one will be worse, given how things turned out when Loche took power."

Unease rippled across her skin, but she shook her head, pushing it away again. She didn't have a choice, and the prize at the end—her freedom—was too great for her to let fear take root.

Lessia rested her elbows on the table, putting her chin in her hands. "What happened when Loche was elected? I thought he was the most well-regarded regent in the last century?"

Ardow rose and picked up some of the plates, casting her a warning glare when she made to help.

Sighing, she leaned back.

Her body would probably thank her for it.

"He is. By the commoners, at least, by the fishermen and farmers. But not the nobles, Lessia. Even if we got rid of the greedy royal family after the war, there was always—and I mean always—a noble as regent. You know they still own most of the land, control the ships, and keep most of the wealth to themselves. Even if it got somewhat better, it wasn't until Loche that things started to truly change. What you've seen the past years isn't how it always was."

Ardow glanced out the window, drawing it shut.

"Loche was a bastard-born nobody, Lessia. He came out of nowhere but had built a network of allies across Ellow, across every human inhabited isle in Havlands. No one knows how he did it. He just showed up on nomination day with that gang of terrifying men of his and won the election."

Lessia picked at a burn mark on the table. "All right, but he has done good things for Ellow. Everyone must see that, so I don't understand why this election would be worse?"

"Not everyone, Lessia. He raised the taxes significantly for the nobles and has been distributing some of the families' lands to allow farmers opportunities to grow their businesses. They are angry, and they are still powerful. They're going to try to overthrow him, and might very well do it with the help of other candidates who nominate themselves for regent."

Ardow walked up to her chair, forcing her to bend her sore neck to look up at him. "It's going to be dangerous, Lessia. These men... they won't hesitate to get rid of someone who gets in their way."

She reached out to grip his hand. "I don't plan on getting in anyone's way, Ard. I am going to participate, but that's it. I'll keep my head down, stay out of trouble. Regardless, they don't have anything against me except me being half-Fae. Most will probably not even look at me twice."

Despite her words, cold sweat kissed her forehead.

The people of Ellow tolerated her presence in the taverns, mostly because they usually were intoxicated enough not to care about anything other than their next cup, or whoever they flirted with for the night. But someone with Fae heritage taking part in the elections?

It was unheard of.

Ardow's jaw clenched, and he brushed his fingers over her arm, right over her tattoo. "If you don't think whatever you're expected to do will get you into trouble, you're not as clever as I thought you were. And I know you don't believe it, but I have a feeling you're going to do better than you think, Lessia. You're a natural leader, and I'm worried it won't just be the nobles coming after you. Loche and his men won't take nicely to someone challenging him. He expects it from the nobles, but you... He's dangerous, Lia. Shit, I am *this* close to stopping you. I have a bad feeling about this."

Lessia shifted his hand away, covering the tattoo with her own. "You can't stop me, Ard. I have to do this. And you cannot get in my way."

He dragged a hand through his hair, his eyes half-crazed. "What if I try? You'll use that mind control of yours on me?"

She couldn't stop a snarl from escaping. "I can't believe you said that! You know I never have, and I never would."

Rising to her feet so quickly the chair fell over, she made to sprint out of the room, but Ardow wrapped his hand around hers, spinning her.

"I'm sorry." He dragged his other hand down his face. "Fuck. I'm so sorry, Lia. I shouldn't have said that. I know you never would. After what happened with your—"

She snarled at him again. "Don't."

Thickness clogged her throat when bloodied golden-brown hair flashed before her eyes. Squeezing them shut, she forced the memory away, drawing deep breaths to clear her mind.

"I'm sorry," he whispered. "I'm just worried for you."

She looked up at him, her heart aching, and lifted a shaky hand to cup his cheek. "I know. I'm sorry too. For everything I cannot say, and for whatever I'll keep from you in the future. But I promise, I will be careful, and after—" She couldn't say it, but she let hope shine through in her eyes.

His eyes softened. "There could be an after?"

She only stared at him, but the corners of his mouth curled and he pulled her into a hug, lifting her off her feet. A huffed breath rushed through her teeth when his embrace pressed on the bruises, and he quickly set her down, his grip loosening.

"You go kick some ass in that election, and *after*, we're going to celebrate for a month." Ardow pulled back and winked at her. "Maybe more."

Heading toward the door, he motioned for her. "Come on, I'll help you get packed."

CHAPTER TEN

Lessia's chest felt as if it were splitting wide open as she walked through the icy roads of Asker, her feet dragging, not because her body ached but because she had to force herself to put one foot in front of the other to leave her home behind and head toward the square where the nomination would take place.

She hadn't been able to say goodbye to the children, hadn't been able to look into their eyes and pretend everything would be fine. And Amalise had refused to meet her gaze as they said a quick goodbye at home.

She'd almost broken down then.

Couldn't bear forcing her friend through another goodbye, even if she prayed this one wouldn't be permanent.

It had taken Amalise a long time to open up, and now...

She rubbed her burning eyes, swallowing against the dryness in her throat.

She didn't have a choice.

Even if the king had offered her one, she might have chosen to do this for the chance at freedom, might have agreed to anything to escape the danger she put them all in daily.

And if there was truly a risk of war, she needed to do everything in her power to stop it.

An arm slipped over her shoulders, pulling her closer, and she shot Ardow a grateful look when he didn't acknowledge her frustrated stomps but kept his gaze on the glittering path, his eyes darting between the homes lining each side of it.

Amalise had arrived in Asker about the same time as Lessia, hailing from Gostkan, a small isle in the north of Ellow, but Ardow was born here. According to him, all nominees were allowed one person to accompany them for protection or support—or perhaps both—during the election. And while she'd hated herself when she told Amalise, Ardow was the obvious choice.

His parents weren't nobles, couldn't be, with the Fae blood running through his father's veins, but they had influence over the farmers in the south. And he knew more about the election, and the participants, than her and Amalise combined.

She needed him.

Amalise knew it as well, but it would take a long time for her to forgive being left behind.

Amalise's protectiveness made her take on the riskiest missions, always being the one to travel on the ships to Vastala—even though she was human. But this time, Lessia couldn't allow her to do so. There was too much at stake, too much to gain, so even if she knew Amalise would feel like she'd stabbed her in the back, she'd had to ask Ardow.

She only prayed her best friend would forgive her.

"She will," Ardow said softly. "She hates that she doesn't have control, Lia. But she'll forgive us. She probably already has."

Lessia frowned at him. "How do you always read my mind?"

Rolling his eyes at her, he squeezed her shoulders again. "You wear every emotion on your sleeve. It's not that difficult. But you should probably work on it. We're nearly there."

Lessia snapped her eyes forward.

The narrow path before them opened into a wide square, the houses surrounding it taller than the ones in the rest of the city, casting it in deep winter shade. Metal lampposts stood every few feet, but the frosted glass offered little light on the crowd that had gathered, filling nearly every inch of the pebbled courtyard.

A small dais had been set up before them, a few men already milling atop it, all of them in the black uniforms and masks Loche's men favored. More of Loche's men were posted around the square, their uniforms stark against all the white, and there were groups of nobles scattered here and there, their cloaks a mix of muted green and rich purple.

Ardow shifted his arm from her shoulders to grab her hand, and gently dragged her through the crowd, leading her right beneath the raised platform. Excited whispers surrounded them, people discussing who would nominate themselves and who could stand a chance against Loche.

Lessia did her best to tune them out, keeping her eyes trained on the graying man who approached the dais. One of Loche's men helped him up, and when the crowd quieted, the entire square falling silent, nerves began swimming in her gut.

"As the Guardian of the Law in Ellow, I am happy to welcome you all today."

Before continuing, the old man—whose name she vaguely recalled being Frayson—glared at a few people who continued whispering. "Today marks our twentieth election in Ellow. The twentieth time our people will choose who will represent them. Who will vow to keep them safe and keep Ellow prosperous."

People around her began cheering, the clapping and whistling hammering against her temples.

But when Frayson held up his hands, everyone quieted once more.

"One hundred years ago, a greedy king was the reason for thousands of people in Ellow perishing, through war or hunger or heartbreak following their loved ones' deaths. Liaising with the shifters to win more land in Havlands, he tricked our people into war with the Fae. It wasn't until an unlikely alliance formed by one of our people, a lowborn fisherman, with the Fae king that the bloodshed ended. After the war, we decided as a nation to give control to the people of Ellow, to every far-reaching island, to allow each individual a say in their future. To ensure our nation never again falls because of the greed of one man or woman. To ensure we keep the peace that has allowed us to thrive."

More cheers rang out, and it was all she could do to keep hold of Ardow's hand as her body tensed, her knees nearly buckling.

There was so much hope and excitement pouring from the men and women around her.

And she was about to make a mockery of it.

She'd make them think she wanted to challenge the man who'd brought so much joy to the people who'd had nothing, as if she didn't respect and care how he'd pushed and fought and won for them.

Her shoulders hunched.

This was going to be torture.

But the thought of the fates she held in her hands kept her

feet planted instead of sprinting back to the safety and familiarity of the warehouse.

She lifted her eyes to Frayson when he continued. "Today we will once again give you that choice. I will now ask those who deem themselves worthy to step up and nominate themselves. Please make your way up here and declare your name if you believe you should have a say in Ellow's future."

Ardow grabbed her hand tighter when a strangled sound escaped her throat, and her eyes flew to his. Shaking his head, he nudged her forward, but before she could get a hold of herself, a man stepped onto the dais.

"You all know me," he drawled. "Loche Lejonskold. I've been your regent the past five years, and while I've accomplished a lot, I have more to give to Ellow. I have more to give to all of you. And I won't stop until you have it."

The cheers were deafening.

The crowd tightened around her as they chanted his name, several men yelling that they didn't need an election—there wasn't a question who should continue leading Ellow.

Loche flicked his dark hair, a smirk on his face as he offered the people a shallow bow before stepping back, leaving the front of the dais empty.

Lessia wasn't surprised when Zaddock jumped up, following Loche and taking the spot beside him, his gaze sharp as he swept it across the people.

She shifted her eyes to Loche.

He stood unyielding and with a straight back, his expression unreadable as he glanced out over the crowd.

Lessia's brows pulled as she took in his face.

He was so young.

Somewhere in his late twenties, Loche was the youngest regent Ellow had ever known. She had seen him before, of course. But only from a distance, and up close like this, it was difficult to comprehend how a man only a few years her senior had accomplished so much already.

"If he wasn't so terrifying, I might have pursued that. Lethal and beautiful. Makes me want to see if there is any softness under all that muscle," Ardow whispered, his eyes glittering.

While Ardow was impartial in who he invited into his bed, she knew he only made the comment for her benefit, to try to take her mind off what she was about to do.

She gave him a grateful smile, but as she opened her mouth to respond, another man stepped onto the platform, not as gracefully as Loche, but with his chin lifted high.

"I'm Craven Bernedir. My family have been farmers in Ellow for generations, and while I haven't been regent, I have experience that *younger* men don't."

Craven spun on his feet, not bothering to bow to those who clapped—far less than for Loche, but still enough that it made Lessia nervous for the current regent.

"Farmer," Ardow spat. "His family is one of the richest noble families—they exploit the farmers, pay them far less than their worth, but because his family owns so much land, they don't have a choice but to work for them."

Lessia clenched her jaw as Craven took up a spot next to Zaddock. She'd heard of his family, had purposely not used them as a supplier for the taverns based on the rumors of how they treated their workers.

A woman, dressed in a navy uniform with shining black hair cascading down her back, mounted the dais next.

A woman Lessia recognized very well.

Stellia Silversvard was a commander's daughter and had led several fleets in the navy herself as a captain. Well regarded within the navy, she was known for her fair but strong leadership. Stellia didn't accept failure, but she also rewarded loyalty, and men far older than herself had followed her into dangerous waters. Stellia and her men had sojourned in Lessia's taverns for years, never causing any trouble, and, according to her staff, tipped very well.

Stellia introduced herself, and cheers, mostly from soldiers, followed as she stepped back with a tight smile on her face.

Lessia drew a breath. "We should probably—"

"I'll be the one accompanying you." Merrick slipped in between her and Ardow, shoving the latter so hard he stumbled back, right into a group of men beside them. "Leave."

As he righted himself, Ardow glared at the Fae, and his eyes widened when the Fae blood running through his veins allowed him to see through Merrick's glamour.

"You..." Ardow trailed off when Lessia managed to shake her head, a chill creeping up her neck.

Nostrils flaring, Ardow snapped his eyes to Merrick again.

"I don't think so," he snarled quietly, readying to get into Merrick's face.

But when Merrick's magic flitted over her shoulders, a warning squeeze brushing her neck, she stepped around the Fae.

"Leave it, Ard," she pleaded.

She'd been lucky the past years. Merrick had seldom shown up when her friends were around, and in the rare instances he did, she was always able to rid herself of him quickly. She wasn't about to risk them getting anywhere near his deadly presence now.

Not when she was close to being rid of him forever.

Ardow grabbed her arm, trying to pull her behind him, but she struggled against his hold, ignoring the strange stares they were beginning to gather.

"Please," Lessia begged him. "I'll be fine, I promise. Go home, and I'll come find you as soon as I can."

Shaking his head, his eyes frenzied with rage, Ardow made a rush for Merrick.

The magic instantly tightened around her neck, and Lessia gasped for breath, stopping Ardow in his tracks.

"What's happening, Lia?"

When she couldn't respond, her lungs empty and eyes glazing with panic as she struggled for air, he spun to face Merrick.

"You're attracting attention," Merrick purred. "I'll take good care of her as long as you all behave, *I promise.*"

"You—"

"I'd think you'd want her to behave as well, Ardow. Otherwise, who knows what secrets might come out?" There was no mistaking the threat in Merrick's quiet voice.

Ardow blanched, and Lessia was certain her coloring matched his—and not because of her empty lungs.

She wasn't surprised he knew Ardow's name—he'd followed her for years, after all—but did he know of the children? And if so, how? He'd never come by the house, at least never when she was around, and none of their night guards had mentioned him sneaking around either.

Swaying as black spots began dancing before her eyes, she grasped at her throat.

"She's about to pass out. Not that I particularly care, but I believe she was about to nominate herself, so that might prove challenging." Merrick yawned.

Ardow desperately met her eyes again, but when she narrowed hers at him, he threw his hands in the air.

"Fine, just let her go. I need to see her breathe," Ardow hissed.

The pressure loosened, and Lessia nearly fell into the Fae when she was finally able to draw a breath.

Merrick reached out as if to steady her—or perhaps keep her from running—but she caught herself at the last minute, recoiling from his touch.

"Leave," she got out.

"If you hurt her..." Ardow glared at Merrick.

"She said leave." With that, Merrick wrapped his hand around her arm and forced her to spin around to face the dais.

When she glanced over her shoulder, Ardow was nowhere to be seen.

She sucked in another shaky breath.

It was for the better.

Now he could help Amalise, and if the elections were as dangerous as he believed, it was better he was safe at home.

No need to risk both their lives.

But even so, loneliness snaked its way into her heart as she stared at the platform, where another man had just nominated himself while they'd argued.

"I guess it's you and me now, Elessia." Merrick pushed her a stumbling step forward. "Time to shine."

CHAPTER ELEVEN

Her heart beat a frantic rhythm, and Lessia pulled her black cloak tighter around herself as she ascended the three steps leading onto the stage.

As if some fabric might protect her from what was to come.

Unrelenting eyes tracked her every move by the time her foot reached the second step, and whispers rippled through the crowd.

"What is she doing?"

"She's a damn halfling..."

"The one behind her must also be part-Fae. Look at his hair."

Lessia nearly turned around then, but Merrick's magic still danced across her skin, forcing her feet to keep moving—to take the final step. She held back a shudder—even though his lethal powers were invisible, she felt as if they would permanently mark her skin unless he released her soon.

Her insides twisted as she made herself turn around to face the now-seething crowd.

You're doing this for your freedom. You're doing this for your friends. You're doing this to protect Ellow. She repeated the words to herself as she fixed her eyes on the icy building before her, ignoring Merrick hovering behind her like a deadly shadow.

Lessia cleared her throat. "I'm Lessia. Some of you might know me from frequenting my taverns. I'm officially nominating myself for regent."

The crowd was silent for a beat, and she nearly blew out a breath of release even though no applause followed her declaration. But as she was about to join the rest of the nominees, a wave of shouts shattered the silence.

"This can't be legal!"

"She's Fae. She has no business leading anything in Ellow!"

"Get her off that stage!"

"Better yet, arrest her!"

Someone threw something onto the stage. The object hit her square in her chest, and the pain that stabbed at her heart wasn't from whatever had struck her but from her mistake of glancing down—of seeing the turmoil and the faces flushed with rage glaring back at her.

A hand wrapped around her arm, pulling her back as more objects landed on the dais. She let whoever it was drag her backward, her eyes cast down.

"Keep your head up," Merrick growled in her ear. "Don't let them see it affect you."

Clenching her fists, she forced her eyes up, not letting them focus, trying to keep the crowd before her blurred.

She needed to keep up appearances, needed to pretend she wanted this, but when familiar faces—regulars in her taverns—came into view, her face scrunched at the disgust contorting their features.

She'd known this would happen, but she was still surprised at how quickly people she'd served for years turned against her.

Another hand clasped her shoulder, and she met Frayson's pale blue eyes.

"Head on back to the others," he said softly.

Frayson surveyed her for a moment, his eyes inquisitive as they trailed her face and then behind her over Merrick. Nodding, almost as if to himself, Frayson approached the roaring crowd.

Merrick's hair glittered like the frost lining the houses around the square as he led the way toward the back of the dais, and Lessia made herself keep her eyes on him instead of meeting any of the stares from the nominees.

Drawing deep breaths of chilling winter air, she finally took a spot beside Stellia, who glanced at her with narrowed eyes. But when Lessia shot her a look, only curiosity filled Stellia's gaze before she offered a brief head tilt and shifted her eyes forward again.

Merrick seemed to vibrate beside her, but her shoulders loosened slightly when she realized he'd released the death grip his magic had held her in.

"What are you doing?" she whispered through her teeth when his body continued thrumming, his power rolling off him in silent whispers.

She didn't dare glance at the others beside them.

Even if humans didn't have magic themselves, there was no way they wouldn't notice the deadly energy crackling in the air.

Merrick didn't bother with a response, but the buzzing quieted just in time as Frayson got the crowd under control.

The old man threw out his hands. "While it's unconventional to have half-Fae participate in our elections, the law clearly states that any member of Ellow's society is eligible. And many of us know Lessia. She's lived here for years and has always paid her dues."

When the grumbling returned, Frayson raised his voice. "Enough! She shall be allowed to partake. This is an election, people. And as every other year, *you* will vote in the end."

Remember why you're doing this.

She tried to focus on Ardow's and Amalise's faces, on Kalia and Ledger and everyone else back at the house, when the weight of hostile stares pressed down on her like a dark cloud.

You cannot let them down.

Glares and cruel words were a small price to pay to keep her loved ones safe.

Lessia lifted her chin an inch when eyes burned into the side of her face and she couldn't stop herself from glancing their way.

Loche stared at her with unnerving scrutiny, raising the hair on the back of her neck. Her senses blared with warning when he openly dragged his gray gaze over her black cloak, her simple black tunic, and the leathers she wore underneath.

When his stormy eyes met hers again, his dark brows rose in challenge.

Biting her cheek, she kept his unwavering gaze for another moment before tearing her eyes away, focusing on Frayson again.

Loche was clearly trying to unsettle her.

But if she'd just survived what she hoped would be the worst part of the election, a man was the least of her worries.

Stealing a glance at the raging Merrick, whose eyes were everywhere but on hers, a shiver snaked down her spine.

She had much bigger problems.

Still, as Loche's eyes remained fixed on her the entire time Frayson spoke, unease roiled in her gut.

She didn't need yet another enemy.

CHAPTER TWELVE

Frayson led them through the icy roads winding toward the castle, and even though guilt still burned her cheeks, she couldn't help but admire the proud building.

Pure white, as if it were made of the snow that covered the ground before them, it sat upon a high cliff with four tall towers facing the dark sea.

It was one of the few buildings in Ellow that hadn't been burned or damaged in the devastating war. The royal family had hidden there when it was clear the war wouldn't be an easy win and assigned an army of men to cover its front while a large part of the naval fleet protected it from the sea.

Warmth trailed over her face, and she snapped her gaze to the side when a looming presence near her made her skin tingle.

"Can I help you?" She scowled at Loche, who walked two steps behind her with those steely eyes still fixed on her.

Zaddock hovered by his side, his posture tense as he surveyed the alleys and people around them with a hand on the sword on his hip. Lessia followed his midnight gaze, but the dimly lit alleys were empty; only wisps of snow swirled in the wind between the stone homes.

When she shifted her eyes back to Loche, he still glowered at her, a wrinkle between his brows.

"What do you *want*?" she hissed.

His eyes hadn't left her since she stepped onto that dais, and she couldn't understand why.

He couldn't know the real reason she was here, and he'd been aware of her and her friends' businesses for years. Zaddock had been at her house only a day earlier, for gods' sake.

His jaw twitched, the only sign that he'd heard her, and without a word, he stalked up to the front of the group, falling in step with Stellia and Frayson.

What was his problem?

Staring daggers at his broad back, Lessia grumbled to herself.

It's not like she was the only one who'd nominated herself. From the small talk he made with Stellia, he didn't seem to have a problem with the naval captain.

"He's just trying to figure you out." Zaddock offered her a small smile. "And honestly, so am I. Why are you partaking, Lessia? Running taverns and gambling rooms is quite different to running a nation."

"And what do you know of that? Aren't you just a foot soldier?" She couldn't help the edge that laced her voice.

She'd not expected her nomination to go down well, but if they already suspected her, were already this hostile, her mission would be more challenging than she'd thought.

Cursing to herself, she pulled at her cloak as they walked through the imposing metal gates surrounding the castle courtyard all the way to the cliffs leading into the vast sea.

If she ever wanted to get any information, she needed to figure out a way to make them, if not like her, at least not openly show their disgust.

Releasing a breath, she gave Zaddock a weak smile. "I apologize. That was uncalled for. It's been a long day."

Zaddock dipped his chin, eyeing her once more, then rushed his steps to join Loche on the shoveled stone path to the castle doors.

"You could make this much easier for yourself. Just use that little gift of yours, and they'll be eating out of the palm of your hand in no time." Merrick's whisper brushed her ear, and it was all she could do to hold back a grimace when his power thrummed against her skin.

"Back up," she snarled.

It wasn't like he could kill her right there.

Or even threaten her by taking her breath.

Not unless he wanted everyone to know who he was—that the Death Whisperer himself walked amongst them.

When he still lingered behind her, she turned her head over her shoulder.

Merrick's eyes were cast down, but the threat in the hard lines of his face, the surging power that whispered over his shoulders, was impossible to ignore.

Still, a faint smile curved her mouth. "You know, it will be much more difficult for you not to meet my eyes if you plan on staying around. It will look quite suspicious for my company to never look at me directly. And rest assured, death boy, I will be ready when you do."

His lips lifted to let out a hiss through sharp canines that glinted like the icicles hanging from the metal lampposts lining the path to the castle, but he finally took a step back.

Lessia smiled to herself as she walked through the wooden doors leading into the castle.

It had been a gamble, one that might have cost her her life.

But apparently, Merrick had been instructed not to kill her.

At least not yet.

And she wasn't about to have him order her around when he couldn't hold her life over her head.

She'd use her magic if she had to.

She wasn't beneath that, if it might save her life or keep her friends safe, but until she knew what her king was really after, she wouldn't force Loche and his men to tell her anything.

Not when she'd been ordered to share every detail with King Rioner.

CHAPTER THIRTEEN

The double doors opened to a massive hall framed by an arched ivory ceiling lined with gilded beams. A chandelier dangled in the middle, hundreds of lit candles casting soft light onto the marble floor and the plush chairs and couches spread out beneath.

A dais decorated the back of the room, and Lessia imagined this was where the previous royals held court before they were overthrown. She could almost see the gilded thrones that had stood proud upon the dais, where the king and queen had sat in their finery, jewels, and crowns.

Of course, all the castle riches had been distributed after the war, sold in exchange for material to rebuild Ellow, to restore the towns and islands where only ruins and burned roofs remained after the devastating Fae magic had been unleashed upon them.

Although Lessia's gift was lethal in its own way, the elemental Fae's powers were catastrophic, and the humans had severely underestimated just how much destruction they were capable of wreaking.

Goose bumps rippled over her skin when she thought of how the humans had been tricked into taking on the Fae while the shifters stayed back and watched, biding their time until both sides were weakened.

If it hadn't been for that brave fisherman, this realm might have looked very different.

"Welcome, everyone." Frayson gestured for them to sit in the leather chairs placed in a circle by the large fireplace.

Lessia slipped into one close to the fire, enjoying the heat that licked her freezing body.

A scowl hardened her features when Merrick chose the one next to her, and she moved her arm off the armrest when his nearly grazed hers as he stretched out.

"I assume most of you know what the election process entails, but the law still dictates that I inform you." Frayson shot her a look, and she swore amusement flickered in his eyes.

"The people of Ellow will cast their votes in two months' time, and after that, one of you will be elected to lead Ellow for the next five years. In the time leading up to the vote, you will have to prove that you are fit to lead this country—that you are willing to suffer for your people. We will host debates and give you opportunities to showcase why the people of Ellow should elect you—what you may offer them."

Lessia's eyes widened, and she cast a glance at the other nominees in the room.

None of them seemed surprised by Frayson's declaration. Loche even smirked to himself where he sat opposite her, casually resting his chin in his hand as he listened to Frayson.

The nominee she didn't know—a blond man, perhaps in his early thirties—met her eyes briefly before shifting his gaze back to Frayson.

Lessia frowned—there was something familiar about him, but she didn't think she'd seen him in one of the taverns.

A cloak similar to her own was cast over his broad shoulders, and he wore a simple white tunic with dark breeches held together by a thick leather belt underneath.

Nothing that could betray his occupation.

When Merrick cleared his throat beside her, she snapped her eyes back to the Guardian of the Law.

"To ensure none of you will give in to greed and risk another conflict, you will all be subjected to the hardship the people of Ellow experienced during the war. Hunger, torture, loss. And while you will not face mortal danger, this is not for the faint of heart. You may bow out anytime, but that means you forfeit your nomination. Stellia, you experienced something similar during navy training, and Loche, I'm afraid to say you must go through it again."

Frayson glanced between the two, and as they inclined their heads, Loche's sly smile didn't falter for a second.

Craven's mouth set into a thin line. "I assume it will be adapted to each individual?"

"You scared, Bernedir?" Loche mocked. "All that time sitting around in your mansion didn't prepare you for this?"

Craven flew out of his chair, stalking up to Loche. "Watch it, boy. I can make life very ugly for you."

Loche didn't bother angling his head to look up at him. "Your face is already enough to make my life ugly, old man."

Lessia couldn't hold back a snort when Craven huffed angrily before storming back and throwing himself down in his chair so hard it squeaked backward.

Loche's eyes flew to hers, and he offered her a lazy smile. "Why are you laughing, darling? I thought the only thing you were good at was frolicking in those taverns of yours. If you thought being regent would entail free wine and festivities, you're in the wrong place."

Heat rose on her cheeks, and a growl made its way up her throat.

Who did he think he was?

Anger mixed with the guilt weighing down her shoulders.

She might be here under false pretenses, but that didn't mean she needed to deal with snide comments from this bastard.

Before she could snarl at him to keep his big mouth shut, Frayson held up a hand.

"Save it for the debates. I think that's enough excitement for now. You'll all be shown to your rooms shortly. You're to stay in the east wing throughout this process, but you can leave during your free time should you need to. However, I'd advise caution. While we have brought in a large part of the navy and have stationed guards around the castle and throughout Asker, the elections are always a tense time, and we've had... accidents before."

Lessia tried to quench the anger as she took in Frayson's words.

She was surely most prone to falling victim to any *accidents*, given the people's reaction to her. But she was happy to learn she could leave; she had been afraid she'd be locked up here for as long as she remained in the election.

Frayson rose from his chair. "Please ensure you join us for dinner tonight. You'll be given more information about the next few weeks."

When Loche and Zaddock shot up and made to stalk off, Frayson called out after them.

"That goes for you as well, Loche. Things will change this year, so don't expect the same process as last time."

Loche's face remained impassive as he nodded.

Flicking his eyes to hers, he winked before spinning around and leaving the room.

"He is nice to look at, but he has a mouth on him. And I'm used to soldiers." Stellia elbowed her as Lessia rose from her chair. "I've heard he bites as hard as he barks, too, so I'd refrain from going all Fae on him."

When Lessia scowled at her, the raven-haired woman grinned and gestured to Merrick. "Your man looks like he can bite quite hard, as well, though."

She let out a sharp breath. "He is most definitely not my man."

Stellia grinned wider. "He's not? Well, I might jump on that, then—he's gorgeous. And I imagine the castle can get quite cold and lonely."

A hiss escaped Merrick when the captain brushed her fingers over his arm before wiggling her brows at them. "See you later."

Stellia walked off with the soldier she'd brought as company, the man's stern face displaying no emotion as he followed her out of the room.

"Not a word," Merrick growled as he gripped her arm hard enough to bruise.

Rolling her eyes, she let him drag her out of the hall, where a guard waited to bring them up a spiraling staircase.

CHAPTER FOURTEEN

"Absolutely not."

Lessia glared at the open door between her and Merrick's adjoining rooms. "Go find another room. I refuse to have a doorway to death where I'm supposed to sleep."

Merrick threw his cloak on the bed, then stretched his arms over his head as he turned his back on her. "No."

Then she would find another room.

There was no way she'd be able to sleep knowing he could walk in at any moment.

There wasn't even a lock!

Grumbling to herself, she started walking toward the other door, the one that led into the long hallway the guard had shown them through, when a hand wrapped around her arm and Merrick pulled her flush against his chest.

"Don't you think it will be a bit suspicious if you don't trust your *company* to stay beside you? I'm guessing everyone else has the same setup for safety and socializing," he hissed against her hair.

"Get off me," Lessia spat, trying to get him to release his hold. "I know you can't kill me, so you can stop with these intimidation attempts."

But Merrick was too strong, and he only held her closer, reminding her of the bruises lining her back and stomach as she struggled.

"You and I will have to pretend to get along for this to work, Elessia. And while the king might want you alive, *for now*, you know there are other ways for me to keep you in line."

His hot breath blew strands of hair into her face, and his magic flitted over her skin, making her ears buzz as he let some of his control slip. The oily whispers made bile rise in her throat, and she forced herself to still.

Lessia glared at the closed door before her.

She'd been so stupid in shutting it.

If she hadn't, he couldn't have stopped her from leaving, not with the hawkeyed guards that stood every few feet of the dimly lit hallway.

"Fine! I won't switch rooms if you let me go."

She blew out a breath when Merrick stepped away, keeping her back turned until she heard him walk through the door between their rooms. Whirling around, she ran for the door and slammed it shut, hopefully hitting him in the back of his head.

"And stop calling me Elessia!" she yelled through the closed door.

It wasn't her name.

Not anymore.

Not when all it did was remind her of the parents who gave it to her.

Spinning around again, she leaned against the door should he try to break it down, but when nothing happened, she lifted her gaze to take in the room she'd been given, trying to distract herself from the memories that threatened to take over her mind.

A bed stood in the middle of the room, and under the large window to her right was a small chair, silvery light from the moon that hung over the sea spilling onto it. To her left there was a small bathing chamber, and beside it gaped an empty closet where the guard had dropped her satchel.

Her stomach churned when she realized there was only a small fireplace in the corner, and only a single lantern stood on the bedside table.

She'd have to go look for more lanterns, at least two more, to ensure she'd have light throughout the night.

But first, she needed to go back to the house to let Ardow know she was fine and check in on Amalise to see if she would speak to her yet.

Holding her breath, she tiptoed across the floor and quietly twisted the doorknob.

When Merrick's door didn't open, she thanked whatever god was looking out for her and made her way down the hallway, nodding to the guards standing at their posts with shoulders back and heads held high.

After getting lost twice and somehow ending up outside the kitchen, she finally found her way to the hall they'd first gathered in and slipped out the creaking wooden door into the chill night.

Lessia pulled the hood of her cloak over her face as she walked through Asker, keeping her eyes down not to attract attention. Without any trouble, she soon pushed open the door to the warehouse.

Soft voices traveled down the staircase, and she nearly sprinted up to see a friendly face. Pausing at the top of the stairs, she reveled in the familiar smells of food and leather—the smells of her home—and a smile pulled at her lips as she watched Amalise wag her finger at Ardow.

He looked up first when she cleared her throat, and his shoulders lowered before he ran over and pulled her into his arms.

"Gods," he whispered against her hair. "I was so worried, Lia. Who was that back there?"

Before she could answer, Amalise dragged her into her arms, hugging her so tight she could barely breathe. "I heard what happened! I'm so sorry I was such a bitch when you said goodbye."

Amalise's lip trembled when she pulled back, and Lessia gently smacked her shoulder as she swallowed the lump in her throat.

"Carefree, remember, Amalise? You're fine. I am sorry I have to be so cryptic, but see, I'm already back. Well, at least for an hour. Apparently, there is a dinner I need to attend."

Amalise shook her head, but no tears fell when she let go to sweep her blonde hair over her shoulder.

"Come on, I don't have much time, and I need you"—Lessia glanced at Ardow—"to tell me what I can expect. I'm hearing I'm to be starved and tortured?"

Lessia tried for a smile, but it fell as dread stirred in her gut.

She'd thought there might be more public humiliation, debates where she'd make a fool out of herself, but not physical challenges.

Not that she was new to starvation.

Or even torture.

But she'd hoped those dark moments in the king's cellar were far behind her.

Her blood chilled as the sound of rattling chains filled her ears. She'd tried to hide in that inky black cell, crawling into a corner and making herself as small as possible whenever the creaking metal door opened.

It never worked.

Ardow winced as his eyes flitted between hers, and he motioned for her to follow him into the kitchen. Lessia tried to let the homely scents settle over her, but her hands still trembled as she walked over the threshold.

More steaming fresh bread lay on the counter, and she shared a look with Amalise as they sat down.

The meeting with Merrick must really have unsettled Ardow.

Ardow rested his elbows on the table, leaning forward as he eyed her. "I tried telling you it's not a game, Lia. Why do you think they bring in so many soldiers? Whatever they'll put you through will make you weak and vulnerable, so the soldiers are there to protect the soon-to-be regent. Loche looked near death when he accepted the position five years ago."

Shit.

This wasn't good.

Especially with the people of Ellow likely coming for her, she'd need to be very careful.

But she'd survived worse.

She'd figure it out.

"All right." Lessia nodded, trying to keep the apprehension out of her voice. "So I'll be weak. What else can I expect?"

Ardow sighed. "There will be debates, of course, so you'll need to prepare for those. Based on how the people reacted, it won't be pretty, Lia. And then there are events. Even the Fae came last time to meet with the nominees, and you'll be evaluated based on those interactions as well."

Terror opened a black pit inside her, and she shakily asked, "Who came from the Fae?"

She realized her entire body trembled when Amalise wrapped her arm around her shoulders and squeezed softly.

"It wasn't the king. A few of his emissaries. I don't know their names, but they were highborn Fae."

Lessia closed her eyes.

She knew who they were—the same men her king always sent. But perhaps she'd be able to leave the election before that. She was only there for information, after all. If she was able to gather whatever he needed before they arrived, she could be free, could be far, far away from the castle when their boat docked in Asker.

"Lia—" Amalise started, but a soft voice interrupted her.

"Amalise, I need your help." Kalia made her way into the kitchen, and when her brown eyes fell onto Lessia, her shoulders loosened.

"Lessia! I didn't think you'd be back for a while."

She offered the white-haired girl a small smile. "Me neither. I won't be able to be here as much as I'd like, but I'll try to come as often as I can. Can I help?"

Kalia nodded. "Ledger and one of the other boys got into a fight. I was able to break it up, but I think it would be helpful if you could speak to them."

Lessia immediately got to her feet.

It wasn't uncommon for the children to brawl, especially when they'd just arrived. They often had little trust in others the first few months, and usually, someone misplacing—or in rare cases, someone stealing—something caused trouble.

Ardow and Amalise followed her as she descended the stairs two steps at a time to keep up with Kalia. Casting a glance over her shoulder as they walked through the hidden door, she jerked her head for Amalise to follow her into

Ledger's room. Ardow glanced at her before he slipped into the sitting room opposite the bedrooms, where a few children were studying.

Lessia paused by the threshold. The two boys sat on their beds on either side of the room, one of them holding a red-stained cloth to his face. He looked up as Kalia bent down to check on his nose, meeting Lessia's eyes over her shoulder.

"He started it!" Harver pointed at Ledger, who refused to look her way and only stared blankly ahead.

Lessia raised her brows. "Look at how the tables have turned, Harver. I remember someone who fought every day for weeks when he first arrived. Do you?"

Amalise squashed a giggle beside her as Harver scowled, but when Lessia smiled at him, the corners of his mouth lifted, a hint of red tinting his cheeks.

"Yes," he mumbled.

Winking at him, Lessia approached Ledger, squatting down before him. "Hey, you. We don't condone fighting here, but you're not in trouble. I know what you had to do to survive in Vastala. You're safe here, though, and we will get you anything you need. You just have to ask."

Ledger shifted his gaze to hers, his lower lip trembling. "I thought he stole my coin."

Lessia glanced at the golden Vastala coin he shifted between his fingers and nodded. "But he didn't?"

Ledger shook his head, his chin dropping to his chest.

Lessia placed a hand on his shoulder. "How about you apologize to Harver? I should think he'd accept it quite easily. I believe you might be very good friends, and you can protect each other—be loyal to each other—instead of fighting."

"I'm sorry," Ledger muttered.

"It's fine, as long as you show me how to throw a punch like that. I saw stars after just one." Harver grinned.

Ledger looked up through his lashes, a small smile taking over his face as he nodded.

Her eyes flitted between them, and when Harver rose to sit down next to Ledger, asking him to tell him more about the coin, a faint smile lifted her lips, and she bid the boys good night.

Amalise elbowed her as they left the bedroom. "I can't believe you're leaving me alone with them. They'll probably tear down the house before you're back."

Lessia snorted. "You handle them as well as I do."

She could perhaps do it better.

While Lessia had come to love each one of them, she couldn't help but keep them all at arm's length.

She wasn't sure she deserved the pure love of a child.

Not with what she'd done.

And every single one of the children loved to spend time with Amalise. She would sneak them out to places Lessia disapproved of—like the woods fanning out behind Asker or to some of the cliffs where it was possible to dive in the summer. The children loved feeling like they were in on a secret, so Lessia pretended not to know.

When she pulled the door shut, Ardow chased two girls who'd sneaked out onto the small balcony to do gods know what into their room, softly closing the door after scolding them, albeit not too seriously.

A mist of wistfulness dimmed her vision as Ardow slung his arms over Amalise's and her shoulders.

This was her home.

This messy group of humans and part-Fae was her family.

What did it matter if every other person in Ellow hated her?

As long as she had this to come home to, she'd be all right.

When Ardow and Amalise pulled her into a tight embrace, a true smile overtook her face.

A smile that remained as she walked out the door to make her way to the castle again.

CHAPTER FIFTEEN

Not even the strong gusts of wind filled with shards of ice could wipe the smile off her face as she walked along the dark cliffs toward the white castle. It was a clear night, and she was grateful for the light the moon and the winking stars provided in the deep winter darkness.

Soft light spilled out of the many windows in the castle, and Lessia wished she could bottle the sense of safety that filled her after spending time with her friends, could take a sip every time Merrick snarled at her or one of the other nominees glared.

When steps crunched behind her, she threw a glance over her shoulder and found two men making their way toward her with their eyes narrowed.

Her stomach lurched when she realized she'd forgotten to pull up her hood. Quickening her steps, she fixed her gaze on the castle but slipped on the slick stone path, wincing when small rocks pierced her hands as she fell.

"Did you get thrown out so quickly, halfling? Guess the others weren't too happy having a Fae in their midst."

Springing to her feet, she spun around.

Her heart began racing when she found the men were only a few steps away.

Lessia backed up—slowly, so she would not fall again—and took a deep breath to draw on her magic.

It proved quite easy with the adrenaline thrumming through her veins.

"No, my guard is just around the corner. He probably wouldn't be pleased finding you here, though, so I'd run along now if I were you."

She didn't think they'd believe her, but when the men peered over her shoulder, she quickly closed her eyes. When she opened them again, they hesitated at the golden glow she knew met them.

Lessia fixed her gaze on the closest man. "You didn't see me here tonight. Now go on home, and don't cause any trouble."

As he spun on his heel, heading back the way he'd come, the other man's mouth fell open.

"You're not allowed to use magic on us, halfling. It's against the law," he snarled.

The man took a step toward her, unwisely holding her gaze, and she flashed her teeth. "I know. But so is attacking someone, so I'd say it's only fair. Now you go home as well and forget all about me and what happened here tonight."

Eyes glazed, the man whirled around, his steps heavy as he followed his friend.

Lessia rolled her neck, blinking a few times to get her amber eyes back, then turned toward the castle only to slam right into a hard chest.

Nearly tripping again, stumbling a little too close for her

liking to the tall drop into the dark waves, she stared right into stormy gray eyes.

Her hand flew to her pounding chest. "What are you doing? You nearly had me fall off the cliff!"

Loche ignored her, his eyes lifting to follow the men's backs, which were quickly disappearing as they turned onto the path leading into town.

"How did you get them to leave you alone?" he asked quietly.

Tilting her head, she tried to calm her frantic heart and keep her features passive. "I can be persuasive when I need to."

It technically wasn't a lie.

Brows pulling close, Loche observed her, his eyes roving over her as if he could see through her cloak—into her very soul.

Narrowing her own eyes, she trailed them over him.

Despite the winter evening, he wasn't dressed in a cloak, only a black uniform jacket that fit snugly over his thick arms. It was coupled with breeches and soft leather boots in the same inky black, not a spot on them, and he looked every bit the powerful regent he was.

Lethally handsome and deadly.

When their gazes locked again, he raised a dark brow, and she had to force herself not to scowl.

She still needed information from him, and ideally without using her magic, so she wouldn't learn more than her king required.

Even if it could potentially get her out of this situation faster, she didn't trust her king one bit, and she wasn't about to share more than absolutely necessary about the leader of the lands she now called home.

Lessia cleared her throat. "What are you doing out here?"

When he didn't respond and only continued to quietly assess her with those piercing eyes, she frowned. "Did you follow me?"

Still no answer, only that unnerving stare.

He must have followed her.

But where she lived wasn't a secret—his men had been at her home at least once a month since she'd bought her first tavern—and there was no way he'd spotted the children. They were allowed out only on the balcony that faced the sea, and its railings were so high it was impossible to see anything from the path behind the house.

"Well, I should head back." Grimacing to herself, Lessia stepped around him, forcing her legs to take long strides to return to the castle as fast as possible.

She was going to be late for this dinner, and Merrick would not be happy.

Not that he ever was.

Her sensitive ears picked up on Loche following her, but not close enough that it seemed he'd bother speaking with her, so she ignored him, keeping her gaze on the metal gates enclosing the castle grounds.

More voices, drunken singing, and laughs echoed between the buildings to her left, and she pulled up her hood not to risk another run-in with angry townsfolk.

As the sounds rang closer, a large hand wrapped around her arm, dragging her into a dark alley. Loche slammed her into the freezing stone wall of the building, his back molding with her body as he covered her.

"What are you doing?" she hissed. "Get off me!"

"Be quiet," he growled as he strained his neck to see how close the people were.

The laughter was louder now, and Loche swore quietly under his breath as he pressed her harder against the wall.

Lessia's chest heaved against his back, her breaths quickening as she tried to shove him off. But Loche pushed six foot four and seemed to be made up of pure muscle.

He didn't move an inch when she tried to shift him.

"Get off me. I don't need you to protect me from anyone," she snarled against his back.

She had her hood pulled up; they wouldn't even recognize her.

Spinning around so he faced her, Loche covered her mouth with his hand, his gray eyes nearly black as he glared at her. "I said be quiet. I can't have anyone see me with you."

She couldn't stop her eyes from dropping, her hands falling limp to her sides.

Of course he wasn't protecting her.

He just couldn't risk his reputation if anyone saw them walking together.

His brows snapped together for a moment, but the voices were right beside them now, and the hardness returned as his eyes warned her not to say another word.

Loche's heart thundered against her chest, his breaths fanning over her cheeks as he glowered at her until the voices were muffled, the people heading farther into Asker.

He didn't remove his hand until the road beside them was entirely silent, only the snow softly blowing across the ground whispering in the dark.

When he finally took a step back, his eyes remained on hers as she brushed off the snow and ice that stuck to her cloak, wincing at the soreness of her limbs. Tiredness seeped into her bones under his scrutiny, and she averted her gaze and pulled the hood more snugly around her face.

How fast the sense of home evaporated under his loathing glare.

"I'll wait here for a moment so you don't risk anyone seeing us together again," she said quietly.

Leaning back against the wall once more, she kept her eyes on her boots, but when she didn't hear him leave, she slowly lifted them.

His searing gaze still lingered on her, and a jolt shot through her at the flicker of...

Curiosity?

Surprise?

But as fast as it appeared, it disappeared again, reverting to haunting steel.

Loche spun on his heel, taking two long strides before he turned his head over his shoulder and lifted his brows.

Frowning, she took a hesitant step forward.

Only when she was nearly by his side did he start toward the castle again, keeping a half step before her the whole way, not uttering another word as they passed through the gates and walked the stony path to the castle.

Lessia shook her head when he slammed open the doors, immediately stalking off somewhere without another glance at her.

They probably weren't off to the best of starts.

CHAPTER SIXTEEN

As soon as she stepped inside the castle, Merrick's deadly presence sidled up beside her.

He'd changed for the evening. Dressed in a silvery tunic that shone as bright as his pearly hair, and emerald breeches that showed off his long legs, he couldn't stand out more amongst the muted colors humans typically wore unless they were attending some type of festivity.

"Are you trying to make it known to everyone that you're from Vastala?" she whispered as they walked toward the music and people milling about.

A scoff escaped Merrick. "Humans are too stupid for their own good. They already know I'm part-Fae. They won't look further."

"I think you're underestimating them," Lessia muttered.

When Merrick didn't say anything else as they made their way through the dimly lit halls, worry coiled in her gut. Lessia halted, hovering outside the room where she expected the dinner to take place.

"Are you not going to ask me where I was?"

Not that she particularly wanted to tell him, but she'd expected him to threaten her or at least yell at her for the disappearing act. This thick silence was almost worse. At least if he did it here, he couldn't kill her. Not without alerting the humans on the other side of the wall.

Merrick's sharp canines glinted in the firelight when his lip curled back in a sneer. "Do you wish to tell me, Elessia?"

Frowning, she turned to him. His eyes were—as always—averted, and his posture tense, as if he were preparing an attack. Or perhaps anticipating one.

His silver hair lay in soft waves over his shoulders like it had been newly washed, and there wasn't a single wrinkle on his clothing.

Lessia couldn't stop a shocked giggle from escaping. She imagined him in one of the small tubs she'd spotted in their rooms. He'd probably have to keep his legs out of the tub to even get that hair wet.

"What?" he growled. "Do I amuse you?"

"Not one bit," she grumbled back.

Gods, he was truly the grumpiest person she'd ever met.

And she'd become very familiar with King Rioner's other guards.

A chill danced down her spine.

Too familiar.

"You're already late, Elessia. You're not off to the best start, and I can assure you our king will not be happy with what I can report. Everyone is questioning your nomination, and if you continue to act like you don't want to be here..."

Grinding her teeth, she glared at him, and when he reached out to grip her arm, she flinched.

"*Don't* touch me," she snarled. "I've had enough of men manhandling me for today. I swear I will cut off that pretty hair of yours in your sleep if you do."

Or she might cut off something else more precious to him.

But she forced her mouth shut before she said it.

He'd surely kill her if she did.

To her surprise, Merrick's hand fell to his side, and he only snarled back, "Then get in there and act like you are a willing participant. I won't ask you nicely again."

Nicely...

Lessia grimaced at his broad back as he slammed open the door, and everyone in the room turned their way. Human and Fae males were more alike than they'd like to think.

Grumpy bastards, all of them.

Forcing a smile to her lips, she slipped into the Lessia the people of Ellow expected. The one they'd gotten used to over the years—the persona she'd perfected with the help of Amalise and Ardow.

Hips swaying softly, she strode in through the room, meeting the eyes of all the men and forcing herself not to let her shoulders hunch at the disgust brimming there.

The blond nominee, whose name she had yet to learn, was the only one who didn't look away, and Lessia wiggled her fingers at him as she approached the table with food.

It was easier to keep smiling when the aromas of boiled vegetables and stew filled her nose. She ignored everyone in the room, including Merrick, who stood brooding in a corner, as she took a plate and filled it, remaining standing, not bothering to seat herself at the long table by the back wall. If she was to be starved, she'd better fill up as much as she could.

She didn't care when she burned her fingers ripping pieces off a loaf of bread, only stuffed it into her mouth and barely held back a groan at the sweetness. It wasn't as good as Ardow's, but it was hot. The stew was amazing, though, and she refilled her bowl twice before finally setting it down.

"You eat like a savage. You're making me sick."

Lessia lifted her eyes to Craven, who filled his goblet with wine beside her.

Licking her fingers, she made herself trail her eyes over his stupidly embroidered jacket, shiny black boots, and silver-peppered hair before setting down the bowl on the table still filled with food.

Meeting his muddled brown eyes, she smiled sweetly. "You make me sick, so perhaps we're even?"

Craven's eyes flared, and he took a step toward her when a snort sounded to her left.

She snapped her gaze to Loche and Zaddock, who leaned against the wall a few feet away, their usual black uniforms contrasting with the white walls.

Loche's sharp eyes locked on hers as he took a sip from his gilded goblet, and it took all her willpower to keep his gaze when Craven stormed after her as she started to walk away.

Drops of spit landed on her face when he hissed, "None of us want you here. No one in Ellow wants you here, you dirty halfling. If I were you, I'd watch what I say. Accidents are not uncommon during the elections."

Loche raised his brows, his eyes darting between her and Craven as the latter moved even closer. Heat crept up her neck, and she tore her eyes from Loche. But before she could smack the old man over his head, Stellia swept in and linked her arm with hers, dragging her away to another table.

Lessia glared at the beautiful captain, but she only grinned back and flicked her raven hair over a shoulder. "He's an old bastard. Everyone knows it. Come on, I've heard so much about you. I want to know what's true and not."

Stellia pushed a goblet into her hand, and Lessia cautiously sniffed it.

"I won't poison you. Not yet, at least." Laughing, Stellia steered them into a dim corner on the side opposite from where Merrick and Stellia's guard stood stiffly beside each other.

Stellia's guard swept his gaze across the room, eyes narrowing as he assessed the nominees surrounding them while Merrick's eyes remained locked on the floor beneath him.

"He isn't the most trusting person," Stellia whispered. "So he's perfect for this. He'd probably kill everyone in here if there was a threat to my life. Seems like your guard is the same. He's quite frightening, I must say. I may retract my previous statement about taking him to bed."

Shaking her head, Lessia whispered back, "I think that's wise. He scares *me*, and he's my guard."

Stellia threw her head back and laughed again, the sound so sincere that Lessia couldn't stop her own lips from curling.

The naval captain was nothing like Lessia had assumed.

Stellia's eyes twinkled with mischief, and there was nothing of the ruthless leader she'd heard about in her soft features.

She eyed Lessia knowingly. "I may look nonthreatening, but don't underestimate me, Lessia. I have killed more than you can imagine. I'm tasked with protecting our western border, and the pirates there are ruthless. They can be quite persistent in their quest for revenge after we and the Fae cut off all trade with them."

Clinking her goblet against hers, Lessia smiled. "I wouldn't dare."

Stellia nodded, then leaned in to whisper again. "So tell me, why does Loche look like he wants to kill you?"

Lessia could feel Loche's burning stare roving over her but forced herself to keep her eyes on the captain. "I have no idea. I've tried to play nice, but he doesn't seem receptive to it."

"That one doesn't play nice. He may be pretty to look at,

but he does not have one ounce of charm in him. And he isn't receptive to it either. Trust me, I tried when I was young and dumb. Although I've heard he never takes any women to bed, or anywhere else for that matter. He might be a good regent—he has done more for Ellow than anyone knows—but he's not good." Stellia shook her head. "I'd stay far away from him if I were you, especially when he looks at you like that."

Lessia let her eyes return to Loche, and sure enough, he glared at her from across the room.

Zaddock lifted his goblet when her eyes moved to his, and she lifted hers back, offering him a small smile. If Loche was determined to kill her, or at least stare her to death, perhaps she could get his second-in-command on her side.

When she glanced back at Loche, he still glowered at her, and something dangerous glinted in the gray. Narrowing her eyes, she kept his stare until Frayson walked into the room, waving his hands for them to gather by the fireplace.

Sighing, she let Stellia drag her to the circle of chairs.

She really didn't want to have to use her magic, but if it continued like this...

She might not have a choice.

CHAPTER SEVENTEEN

As Lessia sat down in one of the plush chairs before the fireplace, Merrick slipped up behind her. He rested his hands on the back of the chair, his fingers brushing her shoulders as if to warn her to play along.

Leaning forward, she rested her elbows on her knees and fixed her gaze on Frayson, who remained standing before the fire, the flames softly crackling behind his gray cape.

"Tomorrow, the election formally begins."

Frayson let his gaze sweep across all of them before he continued. "As per tradition, you will be living in a cabin in the woods, a day's ride from the city, for the next two weeks. Your escorts may transport you there, but they are not permitted to aid beyond that, although they may stay in the guard quarters should they wish. There will be no food provided. Nor are you allowed to bring any. And be prepared for the living arrangements to be uncomfortable, to say the least. Your stay is supposed to symbolize how the people of Ellow had to flee into the perilous wilderness with nothing but the clothes on their backs—to let you experience the hunger and danger they faced."

Lessia tensed as she met Frayson's eyes.

There was a reason they stayed out of the woods, why the people of Ellow ventured to the sea for food. Dangerous animals roamed free there, as they had since the beginning of time. Although they didn't intimidate her nearly as much as being alone in a cabin with these people for a fortnight.

"What if we get injured?" The man she didn't know spoke up, and there was a slight tremor in his voice.

"I'd suggest you do not leave the cabin, but in case you can no longer participate, there is a signaling horn. Should you blow it, you forfeit your nomination, and a guard will escort you back to the city."

"And there will be no guards in the cabin?" Craven asked, throwing a smirk her way that made Lessia flash her teeth at him.

"No guards are permitted close to the cabin unless the horn is blown. But you do well to remember, Bernedir, if you're caught harming another nominee, you will be eliminated. There are no exceptions." Frayson glanced between them, his soft eyes lingering on hers for a moment longer than she was comfortable with.

"When do we leave?" Stellia seemed completely at ease where she rested in her chair, inky hair splayed out over the fabric and swirling a goblet of wine.

"At dawn. If you don't show up, we'll assume you've left the elections," Frayson responded.

When they nodded, Frayson glanced Lessia's way again. "The rules are simple enough. You may bring whatever clothing you choose to wear, but nothing else. No one is allowed to help you, and you may not leave the woods unless you decide to leave the election. If there are no more questions, I shall bid you good night and good luck." Frayson patted the back of Loche's chair before he strode out of the room.

"Perfect!" Stellia exclaimed. "We have a whole night to revel. Come on, boys. I've been at sea for too long. I need one more night of glory before misery begins once more."

Lessia's eyes widened when the entire group rose to follow the captain. Even Craven stretched his limbs, although he seemed less than amused.

"You, too, Lessia! I've heard your parties are legendary and that you can drink three full men under the table. Time to show off." Stellia winked.

Shaking her head, she made to rise when Loche spun around and growled, "No."

Forcing herself not to falter, and with Merrick close behind, she slowly walked up to him until she was only a foot away.

Lessia lifted a hand and poked him in the chest, noting how tense the muscles were beneath his leather tunic, even if his expression painted him as bored.

"What is your problem? I haven't done anything to make you dislike me."

She mentally applauded herself when her voice stayed strong.

Apparently, ignoring or being nice to him wasn't working. Perhaps if she served him the same treatment as he did her, he'd at least respect her.

"Come on, Loche. She won't bother anyone." Stellia placed a small hand on his shoulder.

But Loche ignored her, only kept staring daggers at Lessia. "I said no, and it's final. She's not coming."

She narrowed her eyes, keeping his gray ones hostage.

Loche glared back at her, and the mumbling around them quieted as their eyes battled in silence.

She would not give in.

Loche's face showed no emotion as his eyes burned into hers, and she kept her own features blank, fighting against the thoughts that swirled inside.

What had she done to him?

She had never spoken to him before today, and he acted as if she deeply insulted him by her mere presence—as if she'd committed a grave personal offense.

A small voice in her mind reminded her that she *was* there to spy on him—that her king had her betray all Ellow by forcing her to do this.

A wince twisted her features, and Loche's eyes flared triumphantly.

"Fine!" Lessia snarled as she averted her gaze. "I'm going to bed anyway."

When Loche spun around, she couldn't stop herself from hissing "Bastard."

Turning his head over his shoulder, he smiled, a vicious hint to the curled lips. "I've been called worse, darling."

She balled her hands to restrain herself from slapping him across his smug face.

Peeking around him, Stellia winced. "Sorry, Fae-girl. Maybe next time?"

She didn't have time to respond before Loche dragged Stellia with him out the door, slamming it right in her face.

CHAPTER
EIGHTEEN

Lessia stomped up the stairs to her room, not bothering to check if her evil shadow followed, and threw herself on the bed.

What was Loche's damn problem?

It's not like he had been the obvious choice in the election last time, from what she'd gathered about him.

A bastard-born orphan who'd come out of nowhere shouldn't be the one to judge her this harshly.

She could understand Craven, a noble whose family had influence over Ellow even before the royals were overthrown and who probably still harbored a deep hatred for the Fae because of the destruction they'd caused during the war.

Even though he really should be blaming the shifters—the ones who'd deceived them all, turning Fae and humans against each other before either realized they were being played—she could understand that the Fae had been the reason for so many lives lost.

But Loche?

She didn't understand it.

Groaning to herself, she rose from the bed. It was still early evening, and there was no way she could sleep.

Picking up the lantern from her nightstand, Lessia wandered aimlessly around the castle for hours. All the long hallways looked the same—white, polished stone, small balconies jutting out over the sea, and lanterns that hung on the walls every few feet. It was only the paintings that made her understand she was yet again walking through a hallway close to her room.

One of the larger ones was a drawing of Havlands, and she traced her finger from Asker, the capital and largest island in Ellow's vast archipelago, in the north to Vastala in the south and over the many smaller isles between them—about half of them in human territory and the rest in Fae lands.

In the east lay Korina—the shifter isle—but it was veiled in shadows in this painting. Lessia guessed it made sense. The Fae and humans burned it to the ground during the war, and it wasn't habitable.

When her lantern sputtered, she replaced it with a fresh one from the wall. But she still wasn't tired, so she opened the glass doors to a wide balcony beside the painting, drawing a deep breath of salty air.

The sea was wild tonight, with white froth foaming over the crashing waves, mirroring the snow covering the cliffs beneath the balcony.

After setting down the lantern on the ground, Lessia let her hands glide over the icy railing, tracing the sparkling ice as she lifted her face to the sky. She was glad for the lantern she'd brought, as the thick cloud bank that had drawn in didn't let a single star or any stream of moonlight through, lying like a heavy blanket over Asker.

A whisper of awareness made the hair on the back of her neck rise, and without turning around, she hissed quietly, "I can feel you watching me, Merrick. I know I haven't made much progress, but it's been a day. I'll spend two weeks locked in some cabin with them. I'll find out the information our king seeks before that time is up."

"Brave of you to speak so freely when anyone in this castle could hear you. Or perhaps it's stupidity. You seem to have a penchant for it." Merrick's voice grew louder as he stepped onto the balcony.

She slowly turned around, leaning against the railing and enjoying the wind blowing through her unbound hair.

Merrick lingered by the wall, his legs crossed as he rested against it, but his hands were balled into fists, so tight his knuckles blanched.

"You plan on hurting me again?"

A muscle in his jaw ticked, and she prepared herself for the pain, the cold from the railing biting into her back and the waves crashing onto the cliffs below echoing in her ears.

Merrick shook his head. "Step away from the railing, Elessia."

Narrowing her eyes, she watched him closely. "Why?"

A growl rumbled in his chest, so loud she could almost see it vibrating through him. "Why do you ask so many questions?"

"Because you're so pleasant to talk to, of course. I truly can't get enough." Lessia grinned to herself, glad he couldn't see it.

It felt good standing up to the bastard males who seemed to believe they could order her around and treat her as they pleased.

The election was only beginning, and she was already sick of them.

She had enough guilt and worry and shame to carry.

She didn't need cruel words and vile bullies making it worse.

He growled again. "Just step away, Elessia. It's slippery out here. You wouldn't want to fall, would you? Weren't the warnings of accidents occurring enough?"

"Careful, Merrick. That sounds a lot like caring to me," she purred, her smile widening when his body tensed and his lips twisted into a snarl.

It honestly might be worth him killing her to get under his skin like this.

His voice was glacial when he responded. "I couldn't care less if you fall to your death, but my king made me promise to keep you alive for now. Get. Off. The. Balcony."

She shuddered when his magic whispered over her skin, gripping her by the neck and pushing her forward.

Lessia struggled for a bit—mostly to anger him further—but she was cold anyway, so after a moment, she raised her hands and approached the open doors.

Thankfully, he let her go as soon as she took the first step inside.

"Calm down, Death Whisperer. Wouldn't want you to have a heart attack." She nearly reached out to pat his shoulder before she caught herself.

She'd probably wound him up enough for now.

"Don't call me that." Merrick followed her so close that his breath fanned over her neck.

"Don't call me Elessia, then. I don't go by that name anymore."

"Why?"

"Why do you ask so many questions?" she parroted.

Merrick remained quiet behind her, and she braced herself for his magic. But when the dark magic didn't layer over her shoulders or take her breath, Lessia hesitated, her steps slowing.

"Because Elessia died in Vastala. I'm not the same person anymore." She surprised herself when words left her mouth, and halted outside her bedroom door.

She could feel Merrick behind her, hear the rustle of skin against fabric as he shifted.

With her hand on the doorknob, she quietly said, "My family called me Elessia. I can't stand to hear it from anyone else."

When he still didn't respond, she turned around.

Merrick stood so close that his leathery scent engulfed her. It had a wild edge—as if his entire being was poised to charge—but she didn't back down; she only angled her face up toward him.

If she were full Fae, this might have been the perfect moment to force his eyes to hers, but he was undoubtedly stronger, so there was no point in risking it.

Instead, she pulled on the last bit of patience she harbored, exhaustion sweeping through her like the wintry wind on the balcony. "We're going to be stuck together for a few more weeks, Merrick. How about you keep that scary magic of yours to yourself, and I'll follow your stupid orders?"

She eyed his sharp features until he dipped his chin the tiniest bit.

Lessia let out a breath.

It wasn't much, but she'd take it.

"Great! Well, I'm—"

A scream echoed between the stone walls, and they both tensed before Merrick flipped around and sprinted toward the sound with Lessia on his heels.

When they turned a corner, Merrick halted so fast she nearly slammed into his back.

Before them, two navy guards had Craven pushed up against a wall, one of them holding a knife to his throat.

"Shit," she breathed. "We need to help him."

But Merrick remained frozen, and when Craven screamed again, his eyes flying to hers, she reacted before she had time to think.

Overtaking Merrick, she leaped forward and smacked the two men's heads together so hard they both crumpled to the ground.

Lessia stared at the motionless men with wide eyes, but when she noticed their chests move, she let out a huff of relief.

Craven pushed himself off the wall and stumbled to stand beside Merrick, who'd followed close behind her. The noble clasped at his throat, where a few drops of blood trickled down, and his eyes flared as he flicked them between her and Merrick.

Steps approached them, and soon Loche and Zaddock appeared, followed by Stellia, Frayson, and several guards.

"What happened?" Frayson glared at them. "Why are you bleeding, Bernedir?"

Craven dropped his hand from his neck and pointed to Stellia. "She sent her fucking guards after me. They cornered me as I was going to bed and told me they were going to kill me."

"What? No, I didn't! Frayson, I would never." Stellia stepped around Loche and Zaddock, who urgently whispered to each other, too quietly for Lessia to make out the words.

Frayson's brows drew together. "Are these not some of your closest guards, Stellia? Why would they attack Bernedir?"

Lessia tensed. She also recognized the guards' uniforms and Stellia's company symbol on their chests.

Fear flitted over Stellia's face as she took in the men. "What... They're not supposed to be here. I don't know why they would do this, I swear."

Frayson shifted his gaze to the many guards that now surrounded them and inclined his head.

Two guards immediately stepped up to grab Stellia while a few others picked up the two unconscious soldiers and made their way down the hallway.

"I'm sorry, Stellia. You know the rules: you cannot harm another nominee. You're eliminated from the election."

"No! Frayson, you know me! You've known me since I was a child. I would never do this!" Stellia fought against the guards as they began to pull her away. "Karli!"

Her accompanying guard unsheathed his sword as he stalked closer to Stellia.

"Let her go," he said quietly. "We'll leave, but you will take your hands off her."

Frayson nodded once, and the guards released her into Karli's arms. The guard cradled her against his chest as he started to stalk out of the castle.

Sobs racked Stellia's body as she glared at them over his shoulder. "You will regret this, you know. It wasn't me, Frayson," she got out before they rounded the corner.

When Lessia took a step to follow her, Merrick gripped her shoulder.

"Don't," he hissed softly. "Don't draw attention to yourself right now."

Gritting her teeth, she forced herself to still.

She couldn't believe Stellia had done this—regardless of what Craven might have done to her.

But a small voice inside her whispered that Stellia had warned her against underestimating her.

Lessia didn't know what to believe as she sliced her gaze across the lingering group.

Loche also observed them all with narrowed eyes, and when they met hers, they narrowed further.

Lessia didn't know why, but she shook her head as he continued to eye her, and after a moment, he moved on.

"Will you live, Bernedir?" Frayson asked.

The old man nodded, and without another word, he stalked into his room and slammed the door.

Loche and Zaddock soon disappeared as well, with Frayson following and the rest of the guards taking up posts outside their rooms.

As Lessia made her way to her room, her mind still spinning, she turned to Merrick. "Where were the guards before? I didn't think of it, but I didn't see any of them when I wandered around the castle."

Merrick licked his lips, and her eyes fell on his tongue, flicking one of those sharp canines. "I don't know. Perhaps Stellia had them removed from this wing before she sent her guards after Craven."

He didn't sound convinced, and Lessia's brows drew down.

Opening his door, Merrick said quietly, "No more walks without me, Lessia."

Then he walked inside, shutting it softly behind him.

She couldn't stop her lips from curling.

He'd called her Lessia.

At least she was making some progress.

CHAPTER NINETEEN

The group was quiet as they mounted their horses in the morning, the air filled with unspoken tension after last night. The gray light of dawn mirrored the dark ash mare Lessia had been given, and she stroked the horse's warm neck before hoisting herself onto her back.

As Merrick gracefully swung his long leg over a massive black stallion beside her, she couldn't stop herself from throwing a glare his way, even though he wouldn't see it.

He'd insisted on escorting her when he stormed into her room this morning, making her nearly fall out of bed before she realized it was him.

Screaming at him to leave until she had time to dress, she'd started the day in a foul mood, and the cold snow that began falling as soon as they stepped outside did nothing to help it. Grateful for the horse's warm body, she leaned forward to soak up whatever heat she could as they rode out of Asker toward the dark forest.

She stole a glance at the grave-looking nominees riding through the dimly lit streets.

None of them had spoken to her when she'd entered the courtyard in the morning.

Not that it surprised her. But thoughts of Stellia had kept her up last night, and she wondered if it had been the same for them.

Lessia couldn't put her finger on it, but her gut told her Stellia had spoken the truth when she said she knew nothing of her soldiers' actions.

But why would her soldiers act without orders?

She shook her head as they passed her home. The windows in the warehouse were still dark, and she swallowed against the lump in her throat, thinking about how the people in there would soon wake up to Ardow's freshly baked bread and Amalise's awful morning singing.

What she wouldn't do to be back there.

Lessia wrapped her fingers in the mare's mane.

She couldn't think about them right now.

She would be back there.

She would be back there *and* be free.

She only needed to get through the next few weeks, and she'd be right back in that warm, welcoming kitchen, listening to her friends' bickering and hearing the soft tapping of feet as the children disobeyed the rules and came up to grab whatever sweets they could find.

Tearing her eyes away from her home, she focused on the woods ahead.

Blackwoods, the people of Ellow called it, and the name definitely rang true in the winter.

No light broke through the thick branches of the pines, and only the snow on the ground provided a glimmer of light.

"You're Lessia, aren't you?"

She sliced her gaze to the side, finding the nominee she

hadn't met yet urging his brown horse to fall in step with hers.

A black hood covered his blond hair, the cloak falling softly over the horse's back, but she could still make out his familiar features, and she slitted her eyes as his blue ones surveyed her.

"Do I know you?" she asked when his eyes lingered a bit too long.

The man smiled at her, a knowing, secretive smile that made a chill creep over her shoulders. "I've seen you around. But I mostly deal with Ardow, although I've come to understand you're the one who orders the goods all the way from Vastala."

Lessia's eyes widened, and she cast a glance ahead to where Merrick and the rest of the group rode.

Her Fae guard kept his gaze on the horses before him, but his head was tilted slightly.

He could hear every word.

Stroking her horse to buy herself some time, Lessia swore quietly.

The man was Venko Alkhal, the owner of the largest shipping company in Havlands.

And the shadiest.

They hadn't had a choice but to enlist him to bring over the children from Vastala, as he didn't mind carrying goods that couldn't be declared.

Ardow had assured her his ships carried significantly more dangerous and illegal merchandise than a few orphan refugees and that Venko's men were discreet.

But here he was, the insinuations in his voice as clear as the ice clinging to the trees around them.

Shifting her gaze back to him, she forced a smile. "What can I do for you, Venko?"

He offered her a slow wink. “No need for those fake smiles you offer everyone else, Lessia. Don’t worry.” He flicked his eyes forward before bringing them back to hers. “Your secrets are safe with me.”

Well, now they definitely weren’t.

When she glanced ahead, tension lined Merrick’s shoulders, and she swallowed hard against the knot of worry that tightened in her gut.

But the Fae didn’t turn around; he only nudged his horse, creating more distance between them, until he reached Loche and Zaddock riding before him.

Frowning, she flicked her eyes to Venko once more.

“What do you need to keep it quiet?” she hissed sharply, praying the gust of wind that whipped through the trees would be enough to muffle her words.

A smile played on Venko’s lips as he responded, “I believe I need what you need, dear Lessia. We’re on the same side. You’ll do well to remember that.”

With a final long look at her, he drove his horse forward, falling in between her and Merrick.

Lessia ground her teeth as she stared at his back, anger swirling in her gut when he approached Merrick and the Fae shifted his horse to allow space for his brown mare.

Venko was going to be a problem.

Nudging her horse, she followed them, but neither of the males spoke as they rode beside each other.

She was so focused on watching them that she hit a low-hanging branch.

A mass of snow fell over her, seeping inside her leathers and chilling her to the bone.

While she was brushing it off the cloak and trying to get out the snow that snaked its way into her leather tunic, a snort escaped someone ahead, and she snapped her head up.

The group had stopped, every single pair of eyes locked on her.

Except Merrick's, of course.

His gaze remained on his knee, where his large hand rested, fingers drumming a slow rhythm. Brows pulling, fighting the blush that threatened to spread across her cheeks, she swept her gaze across the group.

She couldn't figure out who had laughed, so Lessia made a smile slip across her lips, arching her brow. "Are we lost?"

Zaddock fought a grin as his eyes found hers. "No. The house you nominees are to stay in is right over there."

He gestured toward a stone cottage ahead, and Lessia barely stopped a choked cry weaving its way up her throat at the boarded windows, the crumbling straw roof, and the worn stone.

She'd known their stay wouldn't be comfortable, but that house would be freezing.

And dark.

"We will leave you now. We'll stay in a house a short ride from here, together with a few guards. As Frayson already informed you, you need only to blow the horn if you wish to leave, and we'll come to escort you back to the capital. Other than that, you're to stay within walking distance of the house, and you may not have contact with your escort or anyone else until the two weeks are up. If we find you do, you'll be eliminated immediately." Zaddock shot a glance at Loche. "It happened in the last election, and it wasn't pretty, so please spare us this year. You may say your goodbyes, then your escort is to take your horse."

With that, Zaddock slipped off his horse, Loche and the rest dismounting a moment later.

A wave of murmurs rippled through the trees, joined by the crunching of boots and hooves on snow as horses traded hands. Venko was the only one who hadn't brought an escort with him, and he shifted the reins of his horse to a castle guard waiting by a tall tree.

Lessia jumped off her warm horse as well, eyeing Merrick as he approached her, his gaze on his black boots as he reached out a hand for her horse.

Shifting the leather reins into his hand, she started to walk toward the cottage when he quietly said, "Wait."

She turned around, and her eyes snagged on a gilded dagger in Merrick's hand.

"You planning on killing me right here?" she purred, her magic vibrating inside her, ready if he made a single move.

Sighing, he flipped it so the sharp blade rested between his thumb and finger, offering her the hilt.

"Why are you giving me this?" Lessia slowly reached out and wrapped her gloved hand around the embellished hilt, the rubies lining it still glinting in the dim light.

It was a Fae dagger, and she swallowed as she remembered another one similar to this but decorated with glittering amber.

To mirror your eyes, her father said when he offered it to her on her twelfth birthday. She forced his own amber eyes out of her mind, burying the memory deep inside her, locking it up in that box she refused to open.

Merrick's jaw ticked as if he could read her even without seeing her, and she schooled her features back to neutral as he responded.

"You're staying with three men, and none of them will have your back. I was asked to keep you alive as long as possible, but I won't be there to save you if they decide to eliminate you on their own. You can't blow that horn, so you need to ensure you don't have to."

Releasing a breath, she realized he was right.

King Rioner had forbidden her to leave the election until he told her so, so even if she was injured, she couldn't leave.

Not unless she wanted the blood oath to kill her instead.

Gripping the hilt tighter, she admitted, "I don't know how to use this."

She'd never been trained in fighting—had never had to resort to violence, since she could just use her gift to have people leave her be.

But she had to be careful here.

None of the men knew of her abilities, and if she was found to have used them on humans, they'd execute her immediately for breaking the treaty between Fae and humans.

The muscle in Merrick's jaw twitched again. "You lived on the streets of Vastala for years, and you don't know how to fight? I know you can use that sweet little tongue of yours, but what if someone sneaks up on you?"

She couldn't stop the shudder that rippled through her body.

That's exactly how she'd landed herself in the king's dungeons.

She'd noticed the guard that followed her, and when he came after her, his intent clear in his eyes, she'd sweetly suggested he fall on his own sword.

But she hadn't noticed the guard behind her until it was too late.

Zaddock called out it was time to leave, and Merrick shook his head. "Use the sharp end on your enemy. Good luck, Lessia."

Chest thumping, she slipped the dagger inside her cloak and started walking through the deep snow toward the house.

CHAPTER TWENTY

A musty stench, thick with neglect, washed over her as she stepped over the threshold into the cottage.

Blinking, Lessia adjusted to the darkness, finding a sitting room with a fraying couch and, behind it, a wooden table with a few wobbly chairs. She blew out a breath at the large fireplace in the room—with all windows boarded, it would be the only option for light.

But her stomach knitted when the box that should be filled with firewood gaped empty beside it, and she didn't find kindling anywhere.

When her hands began shaking, Lessia told herself it would be all right.

She'd made fire with wood and rocks before.

She could do it again.

Following the muffled voices, she made her way up a decaying staircase, jumping over two missing steps until she found herself on the second floor.

The dim light was impossibly darker up here.

Drawing deep breaths to settle the weight on her chest, she peeked through the first door.

No.

Lessia's heart slammed against her ribs at the dirty mattress on the floor, the only thing in the small windowless room.

Her chest compressed further as water dripping onto stone and metal clanking echoed in her ears, and darkness tinged the edge of her vision.

Bracing her hands against the wall, she tried to force air into her lungs.

She couldn't panic.

Not here.

Not when Ardow and Amalise couldn't bring her back from the darkness.

Please. Please, not here, she begged her racing heart and the lungs refusing her air.

"How long were you imprisoned for?"

Lessia whirled around so quickly her back slammed against the wall, and she finally gulped down some air when the impact snapped her out of the terror.

Loche leaned against the wall opposite her, his hands leisurely tucked behind his back as his hawk eyes trailed over her face down to her heaving chest.

When she began shaking her head, he growled softly, "Don't lie to me. I've seen that look one too many times after I let out the poor people the previous regent kept in his cellar."

Pursing her lips, she flicked her eyes to the side where Craven and Venko strolled out of two rooms.

The men eyed them as they passed but didn't stop as they walked down the stairway, taking a seat by the table, judging from the low scraping of chairs that reached her ears.

"They can't hear you now. How long?"

Loche glared at her as he flicked his dark hair out of his face.

She thought of lying, but if she wanted to ever get him to trust her so that she could get the information she needed—and not too much to put Ellow at risk—perhaps telling the truth would help.

Loche was too perceptive for his own good.

He'd surely see right through her if she lied.

"Too long," she mumbled, steeling herself for his reaction and readying herself should she need to undo the words with her magic.

His storming eyes narrowed. "That's why you live in Ellow?"

Nodding, she forced herself to keep his gaze.

It wasn't a lie, not really.

Even if her king hadn't ordered her to come here, she would have.

Would have gladly left Vastala behind and never looked back.

"So you're not here to spy for your king?"

Lessia's spine shot straight, her hand moving toward the dagger poking her thigh. "Why would you ask me that?"

Tilting his head, Loche glanced at the hand hovering outside her cloak. "You came armed. Clever girl. Or perhaps it was that resourceful guard of yours. That makes more sense."

He nodded to himself before his eyes sliced to hers once more. "You don't think I know what's been happening in Vastala? Like your king, I have spies everywhere in Havlands."

She remained quiet, keeping her eyes locked on his.

"I've already informed your king we have nothing to do with the deaths and disappearances. And he isn't unaware of my spies. Like I know of his in Ellow. But if he were to have one infiltrate the elections... Now, that's an act of war, one I wouldn't be able to overlook."

"He is not *my* king," Lessia hissed. "I have lived in Ellow for years. This is my home. I don't know what's happening in Vastala, nor do I care."

Still not a lie.

She didn't consider Rioner her king, even though she might have to do his bidding for a few more weeks.

And she truly didn't care one lick about what happened in Vastala.

But her stomach churned as golden-brown hair flashed before her eyes.

With a low snarl, she forced the images away.

"What a temper you have. Is it the Fae genes, or just part of your charming personality? What I've gathered from the patrons frequenting your taverns, you're typically much more agreeable." Loche quirked a brow as his gaze swept over her tense posture.

Clenching her fists, she couldn't stop herself from growling, "Can you fault me? I've tried to be kind to you, but you seem to hate me for no reason."

"I don't care enough for you to hate you, darling." He smirked. "I just think it's curious that you, of all people, would partake in the election."

"Why? Because I'm half-Fae?" She couldn't stop her lip from curling, her canines rasping against the bottom one.

"No." His eyes flashed. "I have been advocating for more collaboration with the Fae. I believe our kind can benefit from forgetting the old grievances. But it does strike me as odd that a half-Fae, as you say, who has shown no interest in politics nominates herself in our election two days after I met with your king to discuss what's happening in Vastala and informed him we've had ships disappear as well, soldiers who never came back from the borders."

It was all she could do to not let her brows fly up, keep her features neutral.

It was happening in Ellow too?

She hadn't heard anything.

No whispers in her taverns, no gossip from her suppliers.

She needed to ask Ardow, who managed most of the business with the ships, if he'd picked up anything.

If whatever was going on was this widespread, there must be rumors she'd missed.

"What doesn't make sense to me, though, is why Rioner would employ a tavern owner. Someone who's lived here for years with no signs of ever even contacting someone in Vastala."

His eyes swept over her again.

Too perceptive.

Too seeing.

"You don't want to be here. That's very clear. So why are you?"

Guilt nearly made her cringe.

But Lessia made herself think of Ardow and Amalise, of the children they saved.

She was doing this for them.

And she'd make sure she didn't give the king anything that would risk Loche's position—that would risk her home.

Because Ellow was truly her home now, and she'd protect it with all her might.

Forcing her face to remain impassive, she responded quietly, "Because I think there are things that need to change in Ellow. You might have done some good work, I'll give you that, but I think I can do better."

"That was your first lie."

Loche shook his head, his jaw twitching as he glared at her. "We're watching you. If we find a single reason to, we'll take you out. And if we find out you're a spy..." His nostrils flared, a lethal promise in those gray eyes.

Shrugging to mask the shudder that skittered down her spine, she offered him a tight smile. "I wouldn't expect anything else."

"We'll see about that." Loche's tongue darted out to wet his lips, and he offered her an infuriating smirk when her eyes followed.

Turning around, he bent down and lifted a loose floorboard, his smirk widening as he pulled out a bottle of amber liquor.

"I learned a few things after the misery here last time."

Swinging the bottle, he started down the stairs, turning his head over his shoulder. "You plan on staying there all night?"

Sighing, Lessia followed him, glaring at his shiny hair and broad back the entire way down.

CHAPTER TWENTY-ONE

The room downstairs had darkened, and Lessia swallowed as she swept her eyes over the old furniture and weathered walls. Only a sliver of moonlight from the boarded windows whispered across the dusty floor. The rest was veiled in shadows.

Craven and Venko were deep in conversation as they walked in, but their heads snapped up when Loche slammed the bottle on the table.

"These next weeks are going to be miserable, and not just because we're stuck together. There is no food to be found, we'll have to melt snow for water, and it gets cold as shit in this house." Loche slipped onto a chair, pulled the cork from the bottle, and took a deep swig. "I have more of these, and I'll share as long as you bastards behave. You'll come begging for it by day four, when your stomach is aching and you're cold to your bones."

"What about a fire?" Lessia hovered by the stairs, unwilling to move away from the little light that shone through the gaps in the wood beside the staircase.

Leaning back in his chair, Loche eyed her. "Do you see any firewood? They purposely remove it, and whatever you can find outside is going to be drenched by snow. We couldn't make it dry quickly enough last time to light a fire until it was time to leave."

Clenching and unclenching her fists, she stared at the men as they began sharing the bottle.

She could manage two weeks without food, and she'd withstood cold dampness before, but no light?

There was no way.

Lessia started toward the door when Venko waved the bottle her way. "You want a sip?"

She didn't have time to respond before Craven spat, "I won't drink from the same bottle as a *halfling*. Especially one with her reputation. Who knows what she might have picked up from all her vile late-night activities?"

Lessia snapped her teeth together to keep herself from snarling at him.

She might have started and fueled that particular rumor, but Craven was no one to judge. She knew exactly what men like him did when they left their wives at home on their islands and ventured to the capital.

Loche slammed his hand on the table. "Don't call her that! I told you two minutes ago to behave, and you're already spewing your shit, Bernedir."

Eyes flying wide, she looked at him, but his blazing gaze remained fixed on scowling Craven.

"She already roped you in, Lejonskold? I thought you were cleverer than that. She might be pretty to look at, but what Fae isn't? They're still evil beneath that pretty shell. As regent, you should be very careful with who you fraternize with, shouldn't you?"

Loche's lips lifted into a glacial smile. "You needn't worry;

I would never *fraternize* with her. We're working with the Fae now, which you're very aware of, Bernedir, as they supply the steel you need for your little weaponry collection. Calling them repulsive names won't help that collaboration, will it?"

Lessia caught Venko's gaze as the man fought a grin. Biting her cheek, she remained quiet, her eyes flitting between Craven and Loche.

"We wouldn't need as many weapons if we didn't work with them, Lejonskold. If you didn't call for so many of our men to become soldiers so we can keep braving the Eiatis Sea, we could cease the trade altogether. That's what I am here to stop. We need our men at home, where they can work the lands. It's becoming too expensive to hire people now, too few to choose from, and we have to keep raising prices of our crops." Red hues flared on Craven's neck as he leaned over the table.

Lessia couldn't stop her feet from bringing her closer to the men, heat flushing her own cheeks. "So you're here to ensure you can continue with your slave work? Line your own pockets but not those of your people? You're truly every bit of the crook I've been told."

All eyes sliced her way, but she glared right back. "We've refused to purchase your goods for years because of the way you treat your workers. It's vile, and so are you."

A frown formed over Loche's brow while Craven shot upright, his finger pointed her way. "You don't know what you speak of, girl. How old are you? Twenty? Managing a few taverns in the slums makes you no businesswoman. I have thousands—thousands!—of workers, and they'd have nowhere else to work if not on my lands."

She hissed between her teeth, "That's because you won't give up parts of your lands, as you should have under Loche's rule. You cling to your wealth because it's all you have in that lonely, big house of yours, when you should have shared it to ensure everyone in Ellow can live better. And if you must know, I am twenty-five, and while that might be young to you, *old man*, every single one of my workers can pay their taxes, care for their families, and live comfortably."

When Craven took a step toward her, Venko raised his hands. "Folks, we're not supposed to kill each other. How about we follow Frayson's advice and keep this to the debates? There will surely be enough time to rip into each other then. I, for one, would be happy to drink in silence until I pass out, so this time goes quickly."

A red haze tinted the corners of her eyes, and it wasn't the darkness that made it difficult to breathe. But as she glared at Craven in the dimly lit room, she realized Venko was right.

She had more important things to worry about than arguing with an old noble. Craven wouldn't listen to a word she said anyway, and Loche would likely win the election again. At least, he would if she could figure out how to obey King Rioner's orders without learning something about him that would start another war.

Lessia forced her stiff shoulders to shrug. "You're not worth my time, anyway."

As the rage lifted, she realized the room had darkened further, and a prickle of anxiety ran through her, the familiar feeling of panic clawing at her chest.

With a final glare at the men, she made to stalk out of the house but froze mid-step when she caught Loche's eyes.

His usual hostile gaze was nowhere to be found.

Instead, a flicker of something she'd yet to see sparked in them.

Lessia thought it might be curiosity but dismissed it when he drawled, "And where are you going? You're not allowed to meet with that guard of yours."

Rolling her eyes, she spun toward the door again. "I'm going to find firewood."

"There's no point. I already told you," Loche called out behind her.

Ignoring him, she slammed open the door and stepped into the freezing wind.

She wouldn't make it one day here if she couldn't find firewood.

She had no choice.

CHAPTER TWENTY-TWO

She'd never been so grateful for the moon as she was now, walking through the dark forest.

Even if the light was dim, the moon reflected onto the bright snow, and Lessia could clearly make out the trees, although she stayed away from the areas where consuming darkness loomed due to the dense copses.

Thickness clogged her throat when she realized Loche was right. Not a single dry branch, not even a small twig, lay on top of the white drifts, and the branches on the trees, even the lower ones, were weighed down by heavy snow.

Drawing deep breaths, Lessia unclasped her cloak and laid it out on the powdered ground. Her fingers were already stiff as she slipped the dagger Merrick had given her from her waistband, but she gripped it tight and began sawing at a branch from one of the pine trees.

Snow from the tree fell as she worked, seeping into her clothing and causing her entire body to shiver, but she ignored it and continued until her cloak couldn't fit any more wood.

Sinking into a crouch, she carefully wrapped the cloak around the wet branches, her movements jerky, as she could no longer feel her limbs from the cold. Lessia exhaled warm air into her uncooperative hands before trying to lift the bundle, the snow covering the branches already drenching the cloak. All the while, she begged the moonlight to remain as dark clouds yet again rolled in over the starry sky.

When Lessia finally got the firewood into her arms, she began rising but stilled when snow crunched between the trees. Tilting her head, she listened to the woods around her, but the only sound was the trees softly rustling in the evening breeze.

Cautiously straightening her stiff legs, she turned her head in all directions, the sense of being watched running down her spine. Lessia sniffed the chill wind brushing her cheeks, her pulse pounding in her ears when the crisp scent of pine and snow was laced with something wild.

There were wolves and bears in this forest, amongst other vicious creatures that kept the people of Ellow out of these woods.

Especially this far in.

And especially in winter, when those creatures would be starved and desperate for food. The bears should be sleeping, she told herself, but when that untamed scent filled her nostrils again, closer now, her legs began moving on their own accord.

Head whipping from side to side, she sprinted back the way she'd come, the hair on her arms rising when the feeling of a presence remained. Snow crunched again, and she spun around, smacking right into a hard chest, the force of it making her drop the bundle in her arms.

"Venko!" Lessia pushed him back, trying to manage her

erratic breathing and hammering heart. “Were you following me just now?”

Venko’s blue eyes flickered with amusement as he watched her bend down to gather the firewood that had spilled onto the snow. “And why would I do that, dear Lessia?”

Slicing her gaze to his, she narrowed her eyes.

They were the only ones out here, and after the conversation they’d had during the ride, she was certain he was up to something.

Making up her mind, she threw a glance over her shoulder, noting the silence and the dark house.

It was worth the risk.

Leaving the firewood on the ground, she rose, drawing on her magic until the light of her golden eyes reflected in the icicles hanging from the tree before her.

Venko didn’t back down when she took a step to close the distance between them.

He only watched her with mild curiosity, and her brows knitted when he whispered, “I’ve wondered what that looks like.”

Staring deep into his crystal-blue eyes, she asked, “Why would you have wondered that?”

Venko’s face softened as her magic filled his mind, his voice turning monotone as he responded. “Because I’ve been told of your magic.”

A chill, and not from the cold wind, brushed her skin. “Who told you of my magic?”

“I don’t know.”

She searched his eyes, but he was clearly still under her spell, face vacant and eyes locked on hers. “How do you not know?”

"I was told in a letter. I don't know who wrote it."

Lessia's eyes widened. "What did it say?"

"That you'd use your gift on me, and that's all I needed to know for now."

She shook her head, her brows furrowing further. "Why are you here, Venko?"

"To participate in the election, try to win if I can."

She bore her eyes into his, making sure her magic still flowed steadily between them. "And why do you want to be part of it?"

"Because I have a mission."

"And what's that mission?"

"I don't know."

Lessia shifted a few strands of hair out of her face and clenched her jaw.

This was worse than she thought.

He'd been strange when they talked on the way here, but she'd attributed it to him trying to use his knowledge of her against her in the election.

But if he knew of her gift...

There were only three people in Ellow who knew—Ardow, Amalise, and Merrick—and she very much doubted any of them would have shared her secret.

Even if Merrick wasn't exactly her favorite person, he'd been ordered to accompany her by his king, and he wouldn't spill Fae secrets to a human.

Someone else must have.

And she had no idea who it could be.

Lessia glared at him. "Who are you working with?"

"I don't know."

"Do you know who is behind the strange things happening in Havlands?"

"No."

She felt like stomping her foot like a child.

He was working with not just anyone, but someone with intimate knowledge of how her magic worked, someone who'd taken great precautions to ensure she wouldn't get any information from him.

Swearing to herself, she burned her eyes into his once more. "You will forget about my gift, and you'll forget about the children you've brought to Ellow. And you'll always speak the truth to me from now on. You cannot lie to me. Understood?"

Venko nodded. "Understood."

"Forget we had this conversation. You found me in the woods, and you decided you wanted to help me carry this wood into the cottage."

After blowing out a breath, she released the grip on her magic, the reflection behind Venko dimming until it finally vanished completely.

As she blinked a few times, Venko bent down to pick up the wood, and she quietly followed him back into the softly lit house.

When Venko opened the door, she stiffened.

Light poured out of the door.

As they stepped over the threshold, warmth rushed over them from a fire already crackling in the fireplace, illuminating the empty sitting room.

With limbs tingling from the sudden change in temperature, she turned to Venko. "Did you light this fire?"

When he shook his head, confusion creased her forehead. "Do you know who did it?"

"I don't, but I'm not complaining. I'm off to bed." Venko grinned at her, his eyes no longer glassy. "See you tomorrow, Lessia."

She took the bundle of wood from his hands and laid it

before the fireplace to dry it out. Sitting down on the floor, with her back against the couch, she savored each lick of heat, even as her skin stung as it finally warmed.

She wasn't complaining either.

CHAPTER TWENTY-THREE

"Is that how Fae usually sleep?"

Lessia woke with a jerk.

Flying to her feet from where she'd fallen asleep on the floor, watching the fire intently, she made sure it still burned bright. Relieved to find the orange-and-red flames blazing, she turned around.

Loche leaned against the wall beneath the staircase, legs crossed and arms leisurely kept behind his back.

Behind his shirtless back.

A smirk slipped across his face when her eyes froze on his tanned, muscled chest, then trailed down the whisper of hair that led into his dark breeches. Heat crept up her cheeks when she forced them back up to his eyes.

Loche tilted his head, shifting his tousled hair out of his face. "Like what you see?"

She squashed the growl threatening to leave her throat.

This man...

Forcing herself to smirk back, she rested a hand on the

couch. "Just curious as to how you're so tan in the deepest of winter."

Loche started toward the door while keeping that searing gaze on hers. "I have many secrets, darling. And I'm not one to share."

With a low sigh, Lessia bent down to check on the firewood she'd spread out across the floor. When she found it had mostly dried, she smiled to herself.

She'd have to get more.

But as long as she kept the fire going, the house would be lit the entire time.

A biting wind blew through the room when Loche opened the door to scoop up some snow in a broken bowl he'd snatched from the table, and Lessia shifted closer to the fire, keeping her hands hovering over the warmth until he closed it. As he walked up to set down the bowl by the crackling flames, she glanced at him, careful to keep her eyes on his face.

"Did you find firewood and kindling in one of your convenient hiding places?"

Loche shot her sideways stare. "Don't play coy and pretend you didn't use magic to light it. Although it's certainly not allowed, none of us will spill your secret. We'll all benefit from it."

When her brows snapped together, his eyes swept over her face. "Ah. It wasn't you."

He searched her eyes, one of the corners of his mouth lifting. "But you do have magic."

Keeping her face void of emotion, she pushed at a branch with her boot. "Not all half-Fae have magic."

"Evading," he mumbled to himself.

Lessia swallowed, wincing when the sound seemed to echo in the small room.

A smug smile crept across Loche's face. "You do, though. And I bet my breeches you won't tell me what it is. Although from the way you're trying so very hard to keep your eyes on mine, perhaps you'll tell me just for me to lose them."

Lessia dragged a hand through her hair, silently cursing herself when it trembled. "If this is your way of flirting, I'm not surprised you never have any women warm your bed."

Loche raised a brow. "You've asked people about me. Not helping your case."

Groaning, she made to step back, but the couch blocked her escape. "I was volunteered the information. I have *not* asked anyone anything about you. If you haven't heard, I have no trouble getting men to fall at my feet."

Her nose scrunched at the lie.

She loathed keeping these rumors stirring.

She had no interest in men.

Like Amalise, she'd given up the hope of finding love. Didn't see the point in it when all she did was put those she loved in danger.

Apart from Ardow keeping her company on lonely nights, and only because he'd never do anything so stupid as falling in love with her, she hadn't had a single man in Ellow in her bedroom.

Loche drew closer, towering over her with his inhumanly tall frame as he crowded her by the couch. She forced herself to arch her neck to keep meeting his eyes—not stare at those hard muscles glowing softly in the light.

His mouth twitched, and his gray eyes flitted between hers as he leaned in to whisper, "I think you forgot how to breathe."

He let out a raspy laugh when she sucked in a breath, and she tore her eyes away, pushing him aside and ignoring the feeling of soft skin under her hands as she stepped around him. Taking deep breaths was easier now that he was a few feet away, and her shoulders lowered slightly as she walked around the couch, keeping it between them.

Loche slumped down on the worn couch, legs splayed over the armrest, head leaning on the other side. "I'm starting to suspect there is more to you than the rumors around town. Those big amber eyes of yours do not tell the story you're trying to spin."

"You don't know anything about me," she hissed.

"Oh, but I do. You almost make it too easy, wearing all of your feelings like you always do that cloak. And what I don't know, I'll figure out. Trust me."

A current ran over her skin as she tried to blank out her features.

She didn't doubt him.

But she needed to do everything in her power to stop him.

Loche propped his head up with his elbow. "While I work on that, why don't you tell me more about magic? You Fae are so secretive, and I'd like to find out more than what I've read in books."

She shook her head as unease flitted down her spine. "Why should I tell you anything?"

Loche eyed her, and she couldn't shake the feeling he was reading way too much in her face. "If you're here to spy on us, I think it's only fair I get some information on your people. And if you're not... why would it be an issue?"

Groaning silently, Lessia traced the back of the couch with her finger.

She'd rather go out in the chill wind again than speak of this, but if it was what it took to get him on her side, perhaps even make him open up to her...

"What do you want to know?"

"Everything." He grinned.

When she glared at him, he let out a low laugh. "Let's begin with what types of magic there are. I know of the elemental Fae. Your king keeps showing up straight from the ocean, not a drop on him, so he must be a water wielder. And those fire wielders nearly burned down all of Ellow during the war. But there are others, aren't there? Perhaps not as lethal at first glance, but surely worth knowing of."

She shuddered at the thought of King Rioner.

He wasn't just a water wielder—he was the strongest water wielder the Fae had ever seen. Her father had told her stories of how he could make the sea swallow small islands if it pleased him.

Lessia cleared her throat, fixing her eyes on the fire. "The Fae descended from two bloodlines: the elementals, who wield fire, water, wind, and earth, and then the mentals, who wield the mind. Which one a Fae has an affinity for manifests when they become adolescents. Although there aren't many mentals left—they're not too popular."

"Why?"

She felt his eyes on her as she walked around the couch again, crouching down to add more wood to the fire. "Some can read minds, some can speak within your mind, some can control it. King Rioner keeps a court of mostly elemental Fae, and they don't take well to anyone who could challenge them."

Her mouth dried as she thought of the mental Fae he *did* keep.

It wasn't just Merrick that terrified her.

Loche shifted on the couch. "What did they do to the mental Fae?"

She hesitated for a moment, waiting to see if the tattoo on her arm would burn.

When it didn't, she blew out a breath. "Hunted them

down one by one. Only a few who swore their loyalty to the crown were allowed to live."

Not that it was much of a life.

She'd seen firsthand with her...

Lessia clenched her fists when her father's face flashed in her mind.

She would not go there.

It was in the past.

As it should remain.

She'd started toward the door when Loche stalked up to her.

Spinning around, she forced herself to meet his hard eyes, locking down the emotions churning inside.

"Is that why you're here? You're a mental Fae who fled?"

"No!"

Lessia backed up when he inched closer, but he didn't stop, and soon her back was against the door, his face an inch from hers, that wintry scent of his enveloping her again.

"Back up," she snarled.

Loche tilted his head, boring his eyes into hers. "Tell me why you're here."

She placed her hands on his chest to try to shove him back, but he didn't move an inch. "I told you. This is my home. The Fae are not my people. I am equal parts Fae and human, and I like Ellow."

He glanced down at her hands before their eyes collided again.

"Little liar," he whispered.

Her breath caught in her throat when he leaned in until his lips brushed her ear. "I've told you I will find out what you're hiding, and it'll be sooner rather than later."

Nostrils flaring, she glared at him when he finally stepped

back. "I told you what you wanted to know. I'll answer whatever questions you have. So, why do you keep doing this?"

The corners of his lips lifted. "Because when someone is uncomfortable, it's easier to read them. And contrary to this town's beliefs, closeness seems to make you more uncomfortable than threats."

Shaking her head, she reached for the doorknob and savored the cool air washing over her as she spun around, leaving the stupid regent behind.

CHAPTER TWENTY-FOUR

When Lessia finally walked inside after gathering more firewood, she shivered, and her hands had a sickly blue cast. Even though it was a sunny day, the wind was merciless, and swirls of snow had kept layering over her as it blew between the trees.

Venko waved at her from where he sat at the table, but she didn't miss the sour glance Craven shot her when she walked over to the fireplace to set the wood down to dry.

The men were drinking again, and while she rarely drank more than a cup of ale or wine, the sight of the amber liquor intensified the ache that had started in her stomach. Having kept busy for a few hours, she'd been able to ignore it, but now a hungry roar rumbled through her body.

"You should have some. We have you to thank for being able to stay warm." Venko lifted a broken cup, and despite the daggers Craven stared at her, she walked over and snatched it, then settled with her back against the wall.

Lifting the cup with stiff fingers, she sniffed the contents, barely holding back a wince at the harsh smell.

"It's not drugged." Loche stretched his hands over his head, and as she cautiously glanced his way, she was grateful to find he'd slipped into the worn leather tunic he'd worn when they rode here.

Nodding, she took a small sip and savored the warmth filling her gut.

While it would probably feel even worse tomorrow, she knew that anything that gave her a bit of energy would help in the days to come, all too familiar with the pain, then the euphoria, then the numbness that came from starvation.

They remained quiet as they drank, and when the little light the day had brought shifted into darkness, shadows veiling the men's faces, Craven first, then Venko, went up to bed.

"One more?" Loche wagged the near-empty bottle, and despite the cup she'd drunk already starting to go to her head, she nodded.

Rising from his chair, he filled her cup with the rest of the liquor, keeping his eyes on hers but not crowding her space again.

When the last drop trickled from the bottle, Lessia averted her eyes and headed back to claim her spot before the fire. She sat down on the floor and wrapped her arms around her legs, her eyes trailing the sparking flames as they licked the wood.

The warmth from the liquor as she took another sip fueled her gratefulness.

It hadn't been the cold, the starvation, or even the beatings that nearly killed her during the years in King Rioner's dungeons.

It was the all-consuming darkness and choking silence.

They'd forced her to delve into the deepest parts of her mind.

Into the memories she'd do anything to erase, into the

guilt and shame and anguish at what she'd done to her family.

Even though tonight had been quiet—a loaded silence, even—she hadn't minded it.

Keeping an eye on the fire, and an eye on the men, distracted her enough not to start down that shadow-filled path.

"You're sleeping down here again?"

Lessia didn't turn her head around as she responded. "Someone needs to keep this fire going, since apparently none of us know how it was actually started."

Loche didn't respond, so she took another sip from her cup and leaned her head back on the couch, wondering what Ardow and Amalise were doing right now.

She could imagine them in the kitchen or perhaps in the bar area with people they'd brought home, and the ache in her stomach was replaced by one in her heart.

Taking another sip, she forced it away.

She was doing this for them. She needed to ensure Ellow remained safe from King Rioner, and if being here for a few months was the price to pay, she'd gladly do it.

Especially if she could also win her own freedom.

"What is it you think I could do better?"

Lessia jerked when Loche's voice ripped her from her thoughts, the liquor in her cup sloshing, nearly spilling over her hand.

Looking over her shoulder, she eyed him where he stood behind the couch, his hands resting on the back of it. When their eyes locked, his held the same intensity as always, but his face was softer.

Or perhaps the shadows masked his usual stony expression.

"What do you mean?" Lessia turned to rest her arm on the couch, looking up at him.

He tapped his fingers against the couch. "You said I've done good things, but I could do better. So tell me, what would you have me do?"

A frown formed between her brows. "Are you trying to unsettle me again?"

Loche's mouth twitched. "Not at the moment. But don't worry, I will keep at it until I figure you out. I am merely curious. You are a resident of Ellow, after all. I do listen to my residents."

Fidgeting with her cup, she assessed him, but no smirk marred his face.

Lessia coughed when she took another gulp of burning liquor. "I do think you're doing good work. I mean, no one likes taxes raised, but you seem to disperse them to the people who need them. Still, there are people who don't benefit. No one would employ me when I arrived here, and it's been the same for all with Fae heritage. It's as if we aren't also human. My friend is only a fraction Fae, and he still couldn't find work before we bought our first tavern."

She waited for him to make a snide remark, but Loche remained quiet as his eyes traveled across the room.

As she was about to turn back to the fire, he finally responded. "I don't agree with that, but I don't make all the decisions. The council is filled with nobles, and they still hold a grudge against the Fae for everything that was lost in the war. You'd think they'd mostly be concerned with the lives lost, but to them, it was the Fae that forced the royal family off the throne and thus limited their power. They don't forgive easily."

Lessia played with the frayed hem of the couch cushion.

"Most of us weren't even born then, and we still pay for what our ancestors did. I'd like to change that."

Surprised at her own words, she turned back toward the fire, her brows drawing close.

Maybe there was a way to change the future for the children she'd brought here. Make sure they didn't have to work in her taverns or with Ardow in the office but have the opportunity to choose whatever path they'd like to take.

She couldn't do it herself, but Loche would likely win this election.

And he could.

"What was it like for you in Vastala?"

Spinning back to face him again, she raised a brow at the curious expression lining his face. "What's with all these questions?"

He shrugged, his jaw ticking. "I told you, I'm just trying to figure you out."

But his eyes betrayed him, something she didn't fully understand flashing in them before he turned and slowly made his way to the staircase.

When he lingered beneath the stairs, his shoulders tight, her face softened.

"You're lonely."

Right now, he reminded her of Ardow, and a shiver of sympathy danced down her spine. Ardow never wanted to be alone—he would rather sleep on her floor than in his own room. Apparently, the broody regent wasn't looking forward to his room either.

Glancing at her from over his shoulder, he smirked. "I'm not lonely, darling. I have everything I want."

Shaking her head, she watched him scale the staircase until his dark hair disappeared behind the bend.

That was his first lie.

CHAPTER TWENTY-FIVE

The following week, a fierce storm raged through Asker, and Lessia wasn't able to go outside to gather wood, didn't have the energy to wade through the thick snow swirling outside the door. The ache in her stomach and the cloudiness in her mind grew every day, even with the small sips of liquor she allowed herself to try to dull them.

Venko and Craven mostly stayed in their rooms, the latter looking older and frailer every time she glimpsed him. Loche came down once in a while but didn't bother speaking to her, and while she knew she needed to try to get closer to him, she didn't have the energy for that either.

But today, the sun finally broke through the clouds, and as Lessia pushed the door open, the snow before the cabin sparkled where the rays hit it through the trees. Forcing herself to take a shaky step outside, she made her way to the closest copse of trees.

Her hands trembled as she pulled the dagger out and slipped off her cloak to lay it on the ground. Black spots filled her vision as she crouched, and when she reached for the first branch, she could barely grip it.

Settling onto her knees, she swore quietly and started sawing at it, every movement causing jabs of pain to radiate through her arm, her vision blurring further as dizziness consumed her.

"So even halflings are affected by starvation. I thought you were immortal."

Slowly lifting her eyes, she met Craven's brown gaze.

"We are, but not if we don't eat," she mumbled. "Do you need anything?"

Even though he was a bastard, she'd been taught to respect her elders, and Craven looked about ready to drop dead this very moment, his wrinkled skin pale and eyes watery.

He sneered at her. "The only thing I need is for you to leave. You're not welcome here. I suggest you blow that horn and get that Fae soldier of yours to take you home. Preferably back to Vastala."

Gripping her dagger tighter, she shook her head. "I can't do that. I have the same right as you to be here, and I'm not leaving. Besides, Ellow is my home."

Craven took a step closer. "I won't tell you again, halfling. Leave."

Rising to her feet, swaying slightly when blood rushed from her head, she narrowed her eyes. "Or what, Craven?"

Taking another step closer, he lowered his voice. "I might be old, but I still have a few tricks up my sleeve."

He reached within his dark purple robes and pulled out twin daggers, flicking them in his hands. "Leave now, and I won't have to do this. But be sure I will if you don't. I love Ellow, and I won't let trash like you try to ruin it."

Backing up a step, she lifted her own dagger. "I don't want to hurt you."

Craven laughed quietly. "You don't even know how to use that. You're holding it completely wrong. You'll only harm yourself, halfling."

A warning growl left her throat when he stepped into her space. "Back off, Craven. I won't tell you again."

"You can't say I didn't warn you."

Before she understood what was happening, she slammed into the hard snow, with Craven's surprisingly strong legs pinning her arms down, those daggers pressed against her throat.

Snarling, she glared at him as he offered her a vicious smile. "You're no better than a wild animal. Look at those canines of yours."

She'd need to use her magic.

Lessia closed her eyes, beginning to draw it up, when a loud thud sounded behind them.

Whipping his head around, Craven swore, and soon crunching footsteps followed. Quickly repressing the magic now glinting in her eyes, she remained still as Venko and Loche appeared, her breathing shallow as she tried to stop the magic from surfacing.

"It seems we weren't informed we were to roll around in the snow today." Loche's dark hair was stark against the snow around him as he tilted his head and eyed them.

Craven growled, and the sharp blades of the daggers dug harder into her skin. The smell of iron reached her nostrils as warm blood began trickling down her neck.

"This was probably not your brightest idea, old man." Loche's eyes followed the blood she was sure started to stain the snow.

"You don't want her here either. It's not like she'll win.

Let's get rid of her together. No one needs to know," Craven spat.

With a snarl, she tried to shift him off but only succeeded in getting one of the daggers to jab into her shoulder.

Lessia bit her cheek not to cry out at the pain.

She refused to give him that satisfaction—would die quietly if it came to that.

"If you're not scared of her winning, why are you trying to cut her head off?" Loche brushed some snow off his tunic, a bored expression on his face, but when his eyes flicked to hers, a dangerous flame burned in them.

"Because it's not right," Craven bellowed. "She is a disgrace to this election. She is Fae, for gods' sake."

"And you'll be thrown out right after you finish this," Venko said quietly, his gaze warily flitting between her and Craven. "Think about what you're doing. It's not worth it."

"You'd take her side? You're as bad as she is. You all disgust me." Craven turned around to glare at the two men, and she didn't hesitate when his weight shifted.

Throwing her arms up, she pushed him and scrambled away when he fell onto the snow. She used a branch to get to her feet, then bent down to clutch the dagger that had fallen out of her hand.

When Craven stumbled to his feet, she stalked up to him and pulled at his stupid robe to get his face close to hers. "If you ever try that again, I will kill you." Her lips curled back to show the canines he'd mocked. "I'll rip your throat out with these, make sure no more vile words can ever leave that wrinkled old mouth of yours."

He started to respond, but when she slapped him with everything in her, he lunged instead, only to grasp air as she'd anticipated, nearly falling when she jumped to the side.

A chuckle sounded before her, and she switched her glare to Loche.

A soft growl left her mouth when one corner of his mouth quirked up, gray eyes flickering with amusement.

"I am going inside. If any of you bother me again, I promise you... you will regret it."

With that, she stalked back to the house.

CHAPTER TWENTY-SIX

Lessia angrily shifted the fire, energy like she hadn't had for days bristling under her skin when Venko and Craven walked through the door. The old man stomped through the room and up the stairs, but not before she caught a glimpse of his bright red cheek.

Despite everything, she smiled to herself.

He deserved it, deserved even worse, but she wouldn't bother wasting any more time on him. She'd be prepared next time, wouldn't hesitate to use her magic to convince him to use those daggers on himself.

Venko made his way over to her, and her eyes slitted when he chuckled as she bent down to count the branches before the fire.

"That was the best entertainment I've seen in years." Venko slumped down on the creaking couch, patting the seat beside him. "You should sit down. Rest. You might have adrenaline running through those veins of yours right now, but you'll crash soon. You need to preserve your energy."

Shaking her head, she glared at him. "I still need to get more firewood. This won't last us through the night."

"Where do you think Loche is?" Venko grinned. "Your little show must have drummed up some energy in him as well. I nearly saw him smile as he stalked off deeper into the woods."

She frowned. "Are you sure?"

The daylight was already dimming—the sun only stayed up for a few hours this deep in winter—and she didn't want to have to go out in the dark again.

"I'm certain. Come on. I'll get us some water." Venko motioned to the seat next to him again, but Lessia ignored it and eased down in the spot on the floor she'd barely left since they'd come here.

Her eyes trailed Venko as he rose and grabbed her cup to fill it with snow, then set it down together with his own to melt before the fire.

"Why are you being nice to me?" she asked cautiously.

Venko wiped his palms on his tan tunic. "Because we're on the same side."

As he sat back down on the couch, she frowned at his pristine boots and the expensive leather of his breeches.

She needed to figure out why he was here.

Needed to ask the right questions.

"And what side is that?"

"The same one."

She groaned. "What does that mean?"

Venko shrugged. "It just means we're on the same one."

"What would you do if you won the election?" Lessia shifted to be able to study his face.

Venko met her eyes, a spark of surprise flashing in his gaze when he responded. "I'd make sure what's been wronged is made right."

Wrapping her arms around her knees, she asked quietly, "What has been wronged?"

"You should know better than anyone, Lessia."

She ground her teeth. "Stop being vague. Tell me what has been wronged."

"The people who are in power." Venko dragged a hand through his hair. "They're what's wrong."

Lessia cast a quick glance at the door. "Do you mean Loche?"

"I don't know."

"What do you mean you don't know?" Clenching her fists so not to raise her voice, she shifted onto her knees. "You must know if you're here."

"I'm only following the orders I was given."

"And what are they?"

"To participate in the election, win if I can."

She frustratedly pulled at her greasy hair.

He was telling her nothing.

Casting another glance at the door and behind the couch at the staircase, she tugged on her magic, the warmth of it thrumming over her skin, warming her far more than the fire behind her.

"When you find out more, you will tell me. Now, forget we had this conversation."

Venko nodded with glazed eyes, and she pushed her magic deep down.

It wasn't difficult. Without food, even that little bit of magic drained her; the energy she'd gained from fighting Craven had quickly vanished.

With a sigh, she shifted back to lean on the couch, pulling up her legs once more.

After a few moments of silence, Venko yawned. "I think I need to lie down. We don't eat the best out to sea, but going without food like this is truly awful. And after going outside... I feel like I might die. I wouldn't have gone if it didn't sound like the whole ceiling was caving in when all that snow crashed down onto it. Good thing too. You might not have been sitting here otherwise."

Lessia remained quiet when he rose on shaky legs and made his way to the stairs, walking with heavy steps up to his room.

After adding the last branches to the fire, she watched it until her eyelids became heavy as shadows fell across the room.

Forcing herself to straighten, she blinked, stretching her arms over her head.

She couldn't fall asleep yet, not without knowing Loche would actually bring firewood back. Even then, after what happened today, she'd have to be on her guard.

She lifted the cup Venko had left by the fire, took a few sips, and poured the rest over her head.

The cold water immediately snapped her out of her drowsiness.

"I guess that's one way to stay clean."

Lessia turned her head to the door, where Loche strode into the cabin, his arms full of wet branches.

She rose and started toward him to help, but when he jerked his head dismissively, she faltered.

Lessia lingered by the couch, eyeing him as he spread out the wood on the floor. The firelight flickered on the muscles playing beneath his damp tunic, and she couldn't stop herself from trailing her eyes over his large frame.

He really was tall for a human.

Her height rivaled that of most human men, but Loche towered over her. And coupled with all those muscles...

She wouldn't have been surprised if he had some Fae blood in him.

When he cleared his throat, she shifted her eyes to his, her face heating as he raised a brow.

"I was just—"

She swallowed when he started to remove the tunic, leaving his tan chest on full display, all the while keeping his steely eyes on hers.

Loche took a step toward her, and she backed up, placing the couch between them and fixing her eyes on the floor.

"Please," she whispered. "I don't have the energy for your games tonight."

Her muscles tensed when she heard him inch closer.

"Stay back, Loche," she warned, but her voice betrayed her, exhaustion seeping into it and making it waver.

The heat from his body enveloped her as he stepped into her space, but Loche didn't crowd her. Instead, his fingers gently cupped her chin and tipped her head up, his eyes slamming into hers before trailing over her neck.

"You're covered in blood."

She shook her head. "It's nothing."

Despite the warmth from his fingers, goose bumps rippled across her neck as he leaned in to examine the wound, his hot breath fanning over her sensitive skin.

When he tilted her head farther, she sucked in a shallow breath, and his grip on her chin tightened.

"It's not deep," he murmured, eyes colliding with hers again. "But you'll want to clean it so it doesn't get infected. All that sawing has me sweating. I was going to use the snow outside to clean up. You should do the same."

Releasing her, he took a step toward the door.

When Lessia remained frozen in place, he arched one of his dark brows. "You coming?"

Blinking a few times to clear her mind, she took a step toward him.

He was probably right.

They still had a week here, and she could do without being covered in crusty blood.

Or dying from infection.

CHAPTER
TWENTY-SEVEN

As she walked out the door, she left it open, allowing the flames inside to spill onto the snow. Loche stood a few steps away, veiled in darkness, only the outline of his body breaking through the night.

Hovering within the light that trickled from the house, Lessia bent down to scoop up some snow into her hands and carefully rubbed it across her raw neck. Red stained her fingers when she wiped off the melting snow, and she ground her teeth as the coldness stung her wounds.

"You can remove your tunic. I'll turn around to give you privacy."

Turning her head, she glared at Loche.

A jolt shook her as his moonlit eyes found hers, and she looked away.

"Not happening," she muttered and continued to reach within her tunic to remove the blood that had streamed down her chest.

Even if it might be nice to get all that blood off her, she couldn't risk him seeing the tattoo.

As regent, he would immediately know what it meant, and he wouldn't just suspect her anymore.

He would know she was here because of her king.

Snow crunched when he took a step toward her. "Your body does not interest me, darling. No need to worry."

Unable to stop herself from hissing, she straightened. "So why are you trying to make me take my shirt off?"

Amusement flickered across his face as he lifted his hands. "If you prefer to remain bloodstained the next few days, that's fine by me. I'm freezing and as clean as I'll get out here."

Loche stepped around her to enter the house, and as he was about to close the door, she yelled, "Wait!"

With her pulse quickening, she sprinted the three steps into the light of the house.

A small wrinkle formed between his brows. "You still have blood on you."

Forcing air into her lungs to try to calm her racing heart, she shut the door behind her and leaned against the wall. Lessia spread her shaking hands against the cool wood and bowed her head to stop him from seeing her struggle for breath.

"I'm freezing. I'll clean the rest off tomorrow," she got out.

With a sigh, Loche grabbed one of the cups off the wooden table and opened the door again.

After scooping some snow up from beneath the step, he pulled the door shut and walked up to her. "Let me."

She warily eyed him as he closed the distance between them, his bare chest glistening from remnants of snow, small drops running down his sculpted stomach.

Halting right before her, Loche cast her a questioning glance.

For reasons unbeknownst to herself, she nodded.

"Tilt your head for me," he said quietly, and a tingle danced down her spine.

Leaning her head back, she allowed him to brush snow across her neck.

Loche's fingers were careful but assured as they wiped off the blood, and his gentle touch prickled her skin—not just where his fingers touched it but everywhere, and she let out a soft sigh when he tenderly traced her collarbone.

"All done," he whispered.

But his fingers still traced over her skin, and their eyes locked as she bent her head again.

A pang shot through her chest when she realized his eyes were hooded and faint color tinted his high cheekbones.

Slowly shifting her gaze down to his fingers, she watched him draw tiny circles over her exposed skin, his hand leisurely trailing up toward her face.

Apprehension and something else tightened in her gut, but she didn't stop him as he cupped her face and his thumb gently swept across her heated cheek.

A floorboard creaked above them, and Loche cleared his throat, stepped back, and headed for the table to set the cup down.

The thud of metal against wood woke her from the trance, and she made her way to the fire, shifting some branches to ensure it would continue burning.

Sitting in her usual spot, Lessia wiped off the last few drops of snow, but her body tensed when she sensed Loche come up behind her.

"Do you mind? The chairs are so damn uncomfortable."

Glancing at him, she nodded when he gestured for the couch, then shifted her eyes to the fire as he sat in the creaking seat.

Lessia fidgeted with her tunic, unable to keep her eyes focused on the flames.

Loche seemed to have warmed up to her.

At least enough to care that she didn't die from infection.

This might be the best chance she'd get to ask him what she needed to know.

"So—"

"I—"

Loche let out a raspy laugh when they started to speak at the same time, and as he shifted on the couch, she turned to face him, crossing her legs and leaning an arm on the cushion.

"You go first." Lessia needed a little time anyway to figure out how to ask him about the things happening in Vastala without him getting more suspicious.

Dragging a hand through his hair, messing it up more than usual, Loche eyed her. "I won't apologize for Craven. He is his own person and is accountable for his own actions. But I am sorry for what you were called, and I'm sorry that even if we inform Frayson about what happened, there likely won't be any repercussions for Craven because of what you are. It's despicable. And I'm truly sorry it's something you're probably quite used to."

Her brows flew up.

Out of everything she thought he would say, *I'm sorry* hadn't even crossed her mind. Something warm filled her chest, and she offered him a half smile as she threw his own words from a few days ago back at him. "I've been called worse."

Loche's lip twitched. "So have I."

Leaning her head on her arm, she observed him. "Why would anyone call you names? You're the current regent. The majority of people in Ellow voted for you to win."

He rolled his neck. "I wasn't always regent."

Lessia remained quiet, and when Loche met her eyes again, his brows furrowed as if he was surprised he'd said anything, but then he shook his head.

"I was a bastard-born nobody, darling. It was a long road for me to get here. I'm from Islia, one of the remote islands in Ellow, near the Fae border. My mother was a courtesan, and she didn't have time—or money—for a child, so she threw me out on the streets, where I lived until I was old enough to enlist in the navy."

An ache tugged at her heart when Loche's eyes flicked to the window for a moment, and something distant blazed in them, but his face quickly hardened again, his familiar smirk slipping across his lips. "I fought hard to get where I am. And I think I did pretty well."

She almost reached out to squeeze his knee but stopped herself when his eyes narrowed on her lifted hand. Instead, she asked softly, "How did you become regent?"

Loche stiffened for a moment before he leaned forward and bore his eyes into hers. "Are you trying to trick me into spilling my secrets?"

Shaking her head, she began to respond, but Loche interrupted her, his foot tapping the floor. "I told you. I have many secrets, and I'm not one to share, especially not how I became regent with another nominee."

She tried for a smile. "Understood."

When Loche remained silent, she drew a deep breath. "I've been thinking of what you told me earlier... about the missing ships and people. Do you know who is behind it?"

She held her breath, barely daring to cast a glance at him, when his leg stilled.

Loche trailed his gaze over her face, brows pinching. "Why do you want to know?"

Picking at the couch cushion, she mumbled, "I am

running for regent. I think it's important to know what's happening in Ellow and beyond."

Loche continued to eye her, and she thought he might get up and leave when he finally sighed, something she couldn't read flashing across his face. "We don't know. We suspect it might be pirates from some of the isles not under Ellow's or Vastala's rule. They've been a problem for years and continue to get bolder."

As he averted his eyes, a sinking feeling told her he wasn't telling the truth.

Or at least not everything he knew.

The couch creaked as Loche lay down across it, his long legs hanging over the armrest. "I'll sleep down here tonight."

When Lessia frowned at him, he gave her a lazy wink. "My tunic is wet, remember? It's still quite cold in my room, and I helped keep this fire going. I should think it's only fair."

Shifting to sit with her back against the couch, she grumbled to herself.

But as her eyelids grew heavy, a feeling of relief whispered over her skin.

At least Craven wouldn't try anything with Loche here.

CHAPTER TWENTY-EIGHT

As the ache in her stomach intensified, Lessia adjusted her position, curling closer to the warmth she leaned on. When her mind began to clear, she winced at its dullness, squeezing her eyes shut.

If she could only sleep through the next few days, it might not be so bad.

Especially when she was so warm.

"You done using me as a pillow?"

Her eyes flew open, and when she turned her head, she stared right into hard gray ones.

Looking around, she realized she was curled up against Loche's leg, which rested on the floor off the couch.

As she flew to her feet, she swayed, nearly falling over—would have if Loche hadn't gripped her arm to steady her.

"Thank you," she mumbled, braving a quick glance at him.

Loche only glared back, rising from the couch and grabbing the tunic he'd laid to dry. Pulling it on, he stalked right up the stairs without another word.

Lessia stared after him, wincing as his angry gait pounded in her head.

Their truce was apparently over.

For the rest of the day, she lingered by the fire, not bothered by any of the men, each only making his way down to refill his cup of water.

Apparently, Loche's stash of liquor had run out, and the sour mood permeated the entire cabin, sighs echoing between the walls whenever anyone was awake.

Lessia kept herself busy by imagining what she'd do when she was free.

She'd never really had any dreams—whatever she'd wished for as a child was long forgotten.

Living on the streets of Vastala had that effect. And she'd lived there for three years.

And once she'd been thrown into King Rioner's dungeons...

No, she wouldn't go there.

She could actually be free now.

Live a good life.

Help others who might otherwise walk a path similar to her own.

She knew she wanted to stay in Ellow, at least.

Ardow and Amalise were her family now, and their life here wasn't bad. Only the constant dark cloud of her blood oath kept her from being truly happy. But in only a few weeks, she might be rid of it, and she could finally leave Vastala and her memories from the time there forever locked in that box inside her.

Steps rang behind her, and she turned her head to find Loche standing behind the couch, the same hardness from this morning lining his eyes.

He gruffly gestured toward the couch, and when Lessia

nodded, albeit a bit confused, he slumped down on it, slung an arm over his face, and promptly fell asleep.

Listening to his deep breathing, Lessia soon allowed herself to fall back against the couch, careful to keep far away from his legs.

They continued this routine every day until it was finally the last morning and time to return to the castle.

Loche hadn't spoken a single word to her—or anyone else—since that night after Craven attacked her, and even when she tried to get him talking, he'd ignore her, turning away, his back toward her.

Having no energy to push him, she kept to herself on the floor.

But she couldn't stop the small ember of gratefulness that sparked in her chest because Craven never approached them and barely spent any time downstairs.

As she packed up the few things she'd brought, carefully slipping her dagger into her waistband, Venko and Craven made their way down.

Lessia nearly winced at their haggard faces, graying skin, and dull eyes, but she knew she couldn't look much better. Her legs shook as she did a final lap around the room to ensure she hadn't forgotten anything.

She picked up a lock of her hair and brought it to her nose, which scrunched at the foul smell. She was glad she'd gotten used to breathing through her mouth to avoid inhaling her own or any of the men's stench.

When the door slammed open and Zaddock called for them all to go out, she could have cried from happiness.

Even seeing Merrick's sullen face behind him—tilted down, of course, with a tense posture and hands flexing—ignited a small flame of happiness.

Lessia snorted to herself.

"What's so funny?" Venko glanced at her from where he leaned on a chair, his arm shaking as he tried to remain upright.

Loche's hoarse voice broke in. "Our reveler is probably just surprised she survived."

Her smile fell as she snapped her eyes to Loche, and a scowl overtook her face at the sneer that played across his lips.

Even though they hadn't spoken the past few days, she'd thought they'd made some progress.

But when he swept his gaze over her, mouth drawn tight, there was nothing of the man who had helped clean her wounds.

"I'm more surprised you all did. You don't look so hot." Lessia smiled sweetly and stepped around Loche, exiting the cabin into the chilling wind.

Sidling up to Merrick, she patted the ash mare she'd ridden here on, leaning on her for warmth—and, truth be told, support as she struggled to keep her legs straight.

She'd literally kill for a warm bath and food.

"You barely survived," Merrick hissed under his breath as he inched closer. "You were caught by surprise by someone who could be your grandfather."

He gestured toward the door where Craven's company, a massive man who looked like he could carry the older one with a single hand, helped him out of the cabin.

Glaring at the side of his head, she hissed back, "Hello to you too. I'm doing fine, thank you. And I was fine then too. Even if Venko and Loche hadn't come out, I had it handled. How do you know about it anyway? You weren't supposed to sneak around the cabin."

If Merrick could look at her, she was certain he'd offer her a death stare by now, but the Fae only gripped her cloak and pulled her so close his wild scent layered over her. "You need to learn how to fight. From now on, we train every day."

"I don't—"

Merrick's magic snaked its oily tendrils over her skin, and she snapped her mouth shut.

When he slowly—very, very slowly—released her, she snarled, "I thought we decided you wouldn't do that anymore."

Flicking his hair, Merrick turned his back to her and jumped onto his horse. "You were supposed to follow my *stupid* orders."

Groaning to herself, she mounted her own mare, but the sensation of being watched tickled her neck, and when she turned her head to the side, Loche was observing her and Merrick intently.

Her eyes widened, and she quickly averted them.

Had he heard their exchange?

It wasn't exactly the warm welcome one's company should provide.

Unease swirled in her gut the whole way back to town.

Even the hunger dragging its sharp nails inside her did nothing to squash it.

CHAPTER TWENTY-NINE

Bone-chilling sea breeze welcomed them back to the capital, and by the time the white castle came into view, Lessia could barely keep her eyes open, her body slumping over the horse's neck as they rode between the dimly lit stone homes.

She guessed adrenaline and the fear for her life—or, perhaps, of discovery—had kept her energized enough not to pass out the past weeks. But as they rode into the small courtyard before the castle, she wasn't sure how to get off her mare without tumbling to the ground.

Craven had already collapsed on top of his horse and had been tied down a few hours from the cabin. Now Lessia watched with blurry eyes as his guard lifted him off the horse and marched through the castle doors with the old man in his arms.

Venko, the only one who didn't have anyone accompanying him, had to be helped by one of Loche's masked men, his face impossibly pale against the black uniform and mask as the man helped him into the castle.

Wrapping her fingers around the saddle, she tried to talk herself into getting off the warm horse.

There would be food.

And clean clothes.

And warmth.

And once she'd eaten, she could visit with Amalise and Ardow.

Her muddled brain vaguely remembered Frayson mentioning something about having a few days' rest after these weeks.

"Do you plan on stealing that mare and getting out of here?"

Turning her head toward Loche made stars dance before her eyes, and she blinked rapidly to regain her sight.

Standing undeservingly straight beside Zaddock beneath the stairs leading up to the wooden double doors, Loche glared at her while Zaddock cast a strange glance between them.

Shaking her head, she tried to get herself to form words and offer him a snarky response, but as she opened her mouth, nothing came out.

Loche fixed his gaze behind her. "She's about to faint. Aren't you her guard? You might want to help her before she hurts herself."

A snarl, too low for Loche to pick up but loud enough for her Fae hearing, rumbled behind her before strong arms wrapped around her waist, pulling her off the horse.

Merrick's eyes closed when she glanced up at him, anger fighting over his features as he hissed between his teeth, "Look away. I won't warn you again."

Too exhausted to fight with him, she let her eyes close as Merrick easily shifted her into his arms and carried her up the stairs.

"We will never speak of this again," she whispered as the warmth of the castle wrapped around her, light flickering over her closed eyelids.

He didn't respond, only continued carrying her through the hallway leading to their rooms.

As one of his arms released her, she prepared her feet to meet the floor, praying she'd stay upright once he set her down, but he easily kept her tucked against his chest with his other one as he opened the door to what she hoped was her bedroom.

When he set her down on the soft bed, she cleared her throat. "Can I open my eyes now?"

As silence stretched on, she sighed. "I can't see if you're nodding or doing that little chin dip you consider nodding."

When he still said nothing, she cautiously opened an eye, finding her room empty.

Confused, she trailed her eyes across the softly lit bedroom.

The lanterns she'd brought in before they'd left were all lit: one on her bedstand, one on a chair halfway to the bathing chamber, and two on the wall beside the door.

The door to Merrick's room was closed, and she breathed a sigh of relief when she didn't hear him grumbling inside.

Light also trickled out of the small marble bathing chamber. Rising on shaky legs, she stumbled toward the chair, using it to rest for a few moments before she braved the final steps.

Steam rose from the already full tub, and she silently thanked whoever had anticipated her need for a bath. Too tired to remove her clothing, she gripped the side of the bath and stepped in, fully dressed.

A moan escaped her as she emerged, the warm water feeling like a caress from a loved one.

Sinking deeper into it, she fumbled with her tunic and leathers and slowly—so slowly—slipped them off.

A few colorful soaps were lined up on the windowsill next to the bath, and drawing up the last of her energy, she reached for the closest one and poured the purple liquid right into the water until white foam covered the surface.

With trembling hands, Lessia washed off the dirt, blood, and sweat she'd accumulated the past two weeks until reddish-brown residue replaced the foam and the water chilled so much the echo of her teeth chattering bounced off the white walls.

Staring at a thick towel laid out on a chair by the door, she told herself she could walk the three steps it would take her to wrap herself in it.

But her hands slipped as she wrapped them around the edge of the tub, and she swore quietly when her legs wouldn't bend the way she needed to get out.

Glaring up at the ceiling, she cursed again—louder this time.

She wouldn't die in a stupid bathtub.

Not after surviving in that cabin.

Not after surviving the streets of Vastala, for gods' sake.

The muscles in her arms screamed as she used them to pull herself over the edge, and a loud thump reverberated through the room as she fell to the hard floor. Her entire body convulsed with shivers from the cold wood, and she grimaced, as she'd surely left herself with a few bruises from the fall.

Unable to get to her feet, Lessia crawled across the floor, her vision going in and out, until she reached the towel.

Out of breath, she pulled at it, laid it on top of herself as best she could, and rested her forehead against the chipped wooden boards lining the floor as the towel dried her back while water from her hair dripped down between the planks.

Even in the streets of Vastala, she hadn't been without food for weeks at a time.

While she'd refused to use her "gift" during those years—hadn't been able to bear it after what had forced her there—there had been other ways.

Getting into the trash cans outside the more upscale taverns late at night would always help fill a screaming stomach.

And when she couldn't do that, she hadn't been beneath capturing the rodents running between the buildings.

But now...

There was nothing left in her to make her get out of the bathing chamber and into bed.

She didn't even want to think about having to go down those stairs to wherever the kitchen was to get the food she desperately needed.

Closing her eyes, she decided to rest for a while.

Perhaps after some sleep, she'd have more energy.

CHAPTER THIRTY

The smell of meat woke her, bile making its way up her throat, forcing her eyes open.

Steam trailed beside her, and for a moment, she thought she'd imagined the scent—that she still lay in the bathing chambers.

But the cool sheets caressing her body and the soft mattress she lay upon made her realize she was in a bed.

The steam came from a cup of broth on her nightstand.

A big glass of water accompanied it, and some type of grainy bread lay on a small plate beside the soup.

Wincing, she made herself sit up, shifting the pillows to support her.

With shaking hands, she drank from the water glass before lifting the cup of broth and taking a small sip.

Lessia had to set it down when a wave of nausea rolled through her, but after breathing deeply, she tried again.

Slowly, she was able to swallow down half the cup, and her vision became clearer with each sip.

After taking a few bites of the bread, she could think clearly again, the fog of hunger and exhaustion lifting.

She sucked in a breath.

Someone must have helped her into bed.

With a pounding heart, she peeked under the blankets, then blew out a sigh of release when she saw the towel was wrapped tightly around her body.

But as the silver snake winding its way around her arm glinted in the dim light when she lowered the sheet, her pulse picked up again.

A knock had her snap her head to the door, and she shook her head when the motion made the fog in her mind return.

Before she had time to speak, Merrick opened the door between their rooms and stalked inside.

Lessia dragged the covers to her chin.

"Can you stop barging in here? I'm not decent." Her voice was raspy, and her tongue wouldn't fully cooperate, a lisp sneaking its way into her words.

Merrick softly closed the door and leaned his back against it, his head tilted so that his silvery hair fell forward.

He was dressed in human clothing: black leather breeches, a deep green tunic that offset his moon-colored hair, and an even darker green cloak with a delicate golden clasp resting over his chest.

When he didn't say anything, she raised her brows. "What time is it? And since when do you knock?"

His sharp canines glinted in the light of the lanterns when his lips curled back. "It's midnight. I won't force you to train tomorrow; you need to regain some strength first, but Frayson informed us that the council is due to arrive the day after tomorrow. There will be a debate and some kind of social gathering. You need to be prepared."

Her stomach dropped.

"I thought he said we would have time to recover?"

Two days were nothing.

By that time, she'd probably not even be able to eat a normal portion of food.

Merrick shrugged. "Apparently, they decided to come early. I have something to attend to tomorrow, so stay out of trouble, as I won't be around. You should rest. Make sure you can play the part convincingly."

With that, he opened the door again, but Lessia called out before it closed. "Wait! Did... did you help me to bed?"

His back stiffened, but his head tilted ever so slightly before he slammed the door shut behind him.

Lessia stared at the closed door for a moment, her hands gripping the sheets.

Then she forced herself out of bed, grateful that her legs kept her standing.

If she was to meet the council, she needed to see some friendly faces first.

After getting dressed in her usual black tunic, leathers, and black cloak, albeit painstakingly slowly, she opened the creaking door to her room and walked into the corridor.

As before the weeks in the cabin, guards stood every few feet of it, and she nodded to them as she walked by.

Lessia had to grip the railing tightly when she made her way down the stairs, one excruciatingly slow step at a time.

No one stopped her as she grabbed a small lantern and walked out of the double doors, and she drew a deep breath of the chill winter night as she made her way out of the courtyard.

It took her twice as long as it had last time to make her way to the warehouse, as she had to stop several times, leaning against the sides of buildings to catch her breath and make sure the black spots dancing before her eyes didn't take over.

The door was locked when she reached it, and when no one answered her soft knock, she cursed her decision not to bring a key.

Knocking harder, she held her breath until steps sounded. From the staircase, if her hearing hadn't gone with her energy.

Amalise's eyes were wild when she opened the door a fraction, her blues slamming into Lessia's before they rounded, and the door flew wide.

"Lia! I've been so worried!"

Lessia let her friend drag her into the warmth, laughing softly when Amalise pulled her into a crushing embrace.

"I'm sorry," she whispered into Amalise's blonde hair, gripping her with all the strength she had left. "We were in the woods. I had no way of letting you know."

Amalise pulled back, her eyes sweeping over her. "Ardow told me. You look like death, Lia. They truly didn't give you any food?"

Shaking her head, Lessia forced a smile. "It was fine. Nothing I haven't been through before."

But Amalise's sharp eyes homed in on her neck, the ocean blue shifting into midnight. "What is that?"

Before Lessia could stop her, Amalise dragged her tunic to the side, her teeth slamming together as she hissed, "Why do you have a wound here? Did someone hurt you?"

Shifting uncomfortably, Lessia shrugged. "You know people aren't happy I'm participating. And can you blame them? Your family lost everything in the war, and while the Fae didn't instigate it, they caused a lot of damage that hasn't been forgotten."

Amalise clenched her hands into fists. "They can't blame

you for that. You weren't even born! And they always seem to forget you're half-human as well."

Lessia took her hand, pulling Amalise up the stairs. "I know. But please, let's talk about something else. I will be busy the next few days, and I just need..." She swallowed as her voice broke, thickness clogging her throat.

She waited for tears, almost hoped for them to relieve some of the pressure in her chest. But they never came. Instead, the lump in her throat faded until only emptiness remained.

She hadn't cried since she was twelve.

Not since that awful day...

Swallowing again to drown the thoughts, she met Amalise's eyes, grateful for the understanding shining in them.

Offering her a smile that didn't meet her eyes, Amalise led the way into the kitchen upstairs, and Lessia quietly followed her, slumping down on one of the wooden chairs.

When Amalise began rummaging through the surprisingly empty cupboards, Lessia frowned. "Where is Ardow?"

Amalise turned around with some dried meat in her hands and placed it on the table between them as she sat down on the chair opposite her.

A real smile lit her face when she met Lessia's eyes again. "I think he's met someone."

A grin spread across her own face. "Really?"

While Ardow's bed rarely went cold, he'd never been serious about a man or a woman before—not for as long as Lessia had known him, and according to himself, it hadn't happened in the years prior to them becoming friends either.

A wave of happiness washed through her.

Ardow deserved to meet someone. He was the most

genuine, kind, and good-hearted person she'd ever met. It was the sole reason she allowed him in her bedroom once in a while—she trusted him completely and without reservation.

He was also the one of them whom she'd worried most about.

Lessia didn't seek love, didn't see the purpose, and Amalise had made it very clear she'd already met the love of her life and there was no one who could replace him.

But Ardow...

He loathed being alone, thrived on feeling needed, and was always seeking something else.

Something new.

Lessia grinned at her best friend. "How do you know?"

Popping a piece of meat into her mouth, Amalise winked. "He's been more upbeat lately, and he keeps sneaking away day and night and refuses to tell me where he's going. But every time he comes back, he has this energy about him, Lia. I've never seen him like this."

Nibbling on her own piece of dried meat, Lessia smiled again. "I'm guessing he isn't here tonight, then?"

Amalise shook her head. "He's been gone since yesterday. But he's on top of all the orders, and the taverns are doing well, so you don't need to worry."

Lessia rolled her eyes. "I trust you both with my life. You know that, Amalise. But how are the children doing? Anything I should be aware of?"

Leaning back in her chair, Lessia listened to the latest updates.

The warmth inside her spread when Amalise informed her everyone was doing well—that Ledger had joined the last trip to the forest and that he and Harver were now inseparable.

When her eyelids started fluttering, Amalise suggested they go to bed.

Nodding, she followed Amalise into her room, her smile remaining as Amalise slipped into the bed with her.

When she fell asleep, the sense of warmth, happiness, and safety followed her into her dreams.

CHAPTER
THIRTY-ONE

She woke late, finding the bed empty and the afternoon darkness already casting dancing shadows on the floorboards in her bedroom.

Amalise had left stew and a note on her desk—apparently, she'd tried waking her, but Lessia had slept like she was dead, and Amalise had promised to take the children out today and didn't want to break that vow. If Lessia had to leave before she returned, Amalise promised to come by the castle in the next few days, joking that she needed to meet up with a guard she'd spotted in the tavern last night.

Lessia shook her head and downed the cold stew, grateful that her stomach didn't turn and that as she rose from the bed, her limbs didn't feel as if they'd collapse after only a step. After making her way to the large clothing chamber connected to her room, she eyed the sparse collection of clothes.

Lessia picked at the only two dresses she owned, both long sleeved and black, neither risking that a glimpse of her tattoo would peek through. They weren't beautiful, not like the colorful dresses her friends owned, and definitely not in the style most women favored currently.

But she loved the silky material of them, and while they were simple, they fit her well. She'd rarely worn them, but Merrick had mentioned some type of social gathering, and her used leathers and thick tunics would probably be frowned upon there.

The comfort she'd felt being home made way for unease as she remembered the council coming into town.

She knew little of them, only that every member hailed from one of the old noble families in Ellow and that they'd fought tooth and nail to keep whatever power they could when the royals were overthrown.

Sighing, she stuffed one of the dresses and a matching pair of heeled shoes into a small satchel.

Like Craven, these men and women abhorred the Fae, and she didn't expect any of them to support her nomination.

After rummaging through the kitchen and finding little more than stale bread—which she still stuffed into her mouth, as hunger gnawed at her despite the stew she'd eaten —Lessia walked down to her study. All her papers were neatly stacked, and she noticed Ardow had worked away on the pile of orders she'd left behind.

A smile pulled at her lips as she traced her finger over his neat signature.

While she wished he'd been here, as she missed him, she was glad he'd found someone. She promised herself she'd seek him out over the next few days and try to learn more about the mystery man or woman who kept him so busy.

The dagger Zaddock had picked at when she was last here with him glinted in the light from the lantern she carried. Taking out the one she had tucked into her waistband, she compared them.

Lessia frowned when she found them nearly identical.

Only the amber stones in the one her father had gifted her marked the difference between the two Fae weapons.

As if they'd been forged by the same blacksmith.

But it made sense.

Merrick was in the king's employ, and like her father, he would surely have access to the best weapons masters in Vastala—the ones only the king, his court, and his closest guards could utilize.

She braced herself against the table when an onslaught of memories overwhelmed her.

Her father's broad grin as he handed the dagger over, promising her he'd teach her how to use it. Her mother's soft smile as Lessia squealed and jumped up and down, excited to finally be considered old enough to carry a weapon. And her sister's sullen expression when she glared at them all—declaring she was only one year younger and she should also be allowed one.

Squeezing her eyes shut, she drew deep breaths until their faces blurred.

She'd managed to keep these memories at bay for years.

Her family was gone, and there was no need to dwell on the past.

She couldn't change it.

Couldn't change what had happened.

What she'd done to them.

Picking up the daggers, she slid both of them into her waistband, shuddering when the cold blades caressed her skin. Casting a final glance around the room, Lessia made her way out.

Amalise and the rest were still not back. There were no sounds of soft footsteps as Lessia put her ear to the wall where the hidden living quarters lay, so she squared her shoulders and walked out into the cold night.

Few people walked the icy roads as she approached the tall castle, but she still drew up her hood, eager to avoid another run-in with the townsfolk.

When she opened the metal gates to the courtyard, ten guards lined the stone path to the wooden double doors. The light from the lampposts played on the intimidating masks that half of them bore, marking them as Loche's men.

Her eyes lingered on the mask of the guard closest to the gate, the almost birdlike beak jutting out beneath the two dark holes where his eyes must be, and a chill crawled over her skin. When she'd disembarked the ship that first day in Asker and two of Loche's men instantly approached her, she'd nearly gotten right back onto it.

Only the blood oath had kept her feet planted on the human isle.

King Rioner's guards had terrorized her enough during the years on the streets, and when she landed herself in his cellars...

They were the reason she'd caved when the king offered her the blood oath in exchange for freedom.

A few of them were mental Fae, and their ability to inflict excruciating pain by forcing her to relive her worst nightmares, over and over, made her beg for physical torture instead on the days they got bored and entered her cell.

Lessia rubbed her arms as she pushed the thoughts from her mind.

While she'd learned Loche's men, and even the navy soldiers, were nothing like the Fae king's, she still preferred to stay out of their way.

None of the guards spoke as she passed, but she nodded once in thanks when one of them, bearing the golden pin of

Stellia's company on his chest—a gilded sail resting upon his heart—opened the heavy doors to let her in. He briefly met her eyes, a flicker of recognition shining in his brown ones, as he stepped back once more, taking up his post outside.

Voices drifted through the hallway from the dining room, and she hesitated beneath the stairs, wondering if she should brave the other nominees to try to find out more about what to expect tomorrow.

But when Craven's shrill voice rose over the murmurs, she thought better of it and took the stairs two steps at a time.

Still not ready to face her bedroom, Lessia decided to find that balcony again.

It was a clear night, and there had been little wind during her walk, so spending a few moments staring out over the sea would hopefully not deplete her meager reserves of energy.

After a few wrong turns, moonlight finally spilled onto the floor before her, and she drew a deep breath of salty air as she opened the glass doors and stepped onto the balcony.

Taking cautious steps over the slippery stone until she reached the railing, she watched as waves softly caressed the high cliffs the castle was built upon.

"And here I thought you'd finally come to your senses and taken your leave."

With a low groan, she turned around as Loche confidently strolled onto the balcony, making his way to the railing and hoisting himself up, his legs dangling over the steep drop.

"Is there anywhere in this castle where people leave you alone?" Lessia glared at him.

There had been a few guards stationed in the hallways she'd walked to get here, but it'd been entirely quiet in the one leading to this balcony.

Loche swept his inky hair out of his face. "Yes."

When she eyed him to continue, his mouth twitched, and she groaned again.

Lessia debated whether to go back to her room, but she didn't want to lie awake in her bed, staring up at the ceiling, especially after the unwelcome memories that had clouded her mind back in the office and in the courtyard.

She had been here first.

So Lessia moved a few feet away, leaned against the railing again, and fixed her eyes on the silver-painted sea.

"How did you and your blonde friend meet?"

Snapping her head to the side, she met his scrutinizing gaze. "Now you talk to me?"

Loche's jaw clenched. "It would seem so, yes."

"You ignored me for a week. Why talk to me now?"

When his eyes narrowed, hers slitted right back.

She truly didn't understand this man's intentions.

Their eyes stayed locked for a few moments. Loche's features remained hard, and his jaw squared while his eyes burned into hers as if he were trying to read her mind.

Sighing through her nose when she realized he wasn't going to offer her a response, she finally broke their stare off, glancing down at her laced fingers. "We met at a ball."

"Shocking," Loche scoffed.

Lessia shrugged, shaking off the feeling of embarrassment that threatened a blush creeping up her neck.

He was supposed to think she was merely a floozy.

That she continued to feed into it was the only way to keep her private business safe.

"And Ardow?"

She wasn't surprised Loche knew his name. Ardow managed a lot of their tavern business, and he'd met with Zaddock and many other men in Loche's employ when she was busy.

Peeking at him, she found Loche's eyes glued to her as if he wanted to see every thought crossing her face.

She made sure her face remained neutral as she responded. "In a tavern."

"You seem close."

"You seem like you're stalking me." Lessia glared at him.

His eyes trailed over her face. "I told you. I'll find out why you're here."

Lessia ignored the current of apprehension skittering down her spine as she realized he must have been having her watched at all times.

She needed to be careful when she went back home.

Clearing her throat, she forced her voice to remain strong. "Let me know when you do."

Nodding to himself, Loche shifted on the railing.

"It's slippery, you know," Lessia couldn't stop herself from warning, even if a small part of her wouldn't mind seeing fear slip across those hard features.

One side of his mouth quirked up. "I like the risk. Makes me feel alive."

Of course he did.

When his eyes drifted ahead again, the intense warmth from them leaving her face, she blew out a soft breath, shifting her gaze to the stars winking above the castle.

CHAPTER THIRTY-TWO

They remained silent for a long while, and Lessia's shoulders lowered when Loche kept his gaze on the dark horizon.

Quietly contemplating whether she could find a way to lead him into answering more questions on what was happening in Havlands, she jerked when a commotion inside the castle pierced the air.

Spinning around, she took a step toward the door at the same time as Loche threw himself off the railing and sprinted ahead of her.

Lessia followed him toward the ruckus, and several servants and guards left their rooms and posts to fall in step with them as screams and metallic clangs reverberated through the halls.

As Loche turned a corner, he lurched to a stop, and Zaddock came into view, his expression serious as he called out, "The castle has been breached. Turn around and find shelter. Quickly!"

When a few guards and Loche and Zaddock lingered,

Lessia remained in place as well, keeping her eyes on the two men as the servants and other guards ran toward the direction they'd come from.

"Who?" Loche's voice was calm as he addressed Zaddock.

Zaddock's eyes flitted between his for a moment before he mumbled, "Stellia's closest guards. They've killed two of your men and several of the other guards. They've made it into the castle. They went after Craven and Venko, but they're safe."

Lessia's eyes widened as she took in his words.

Why would Stellia attack now?

She wasn't in the election anymore, wouldn't have anything to win.

Unless she wanted to take out every nominee and force a reelection...

Loche's back straightened as he unstrapped the sword hanging by his waist. "Where?"

Placing a hand on his shoulder, Zaddock spoke urgently. "There's a dozen or more of them. You can't afford to be captured or injured. Not now, Loche. You need to go to the safe room."

Loche shook his head, his jaw set. "I won't hide, Zaddock. This is my fight."

"All your men have been called in. They'll catch them in no time. Please, Loche. We need you."

Her eyes sliced between them as Zaddock's face filled with worry and Loche's features twisted with defiance.

But when Zaddock squeezed his shoulder, Loche's eyes shifted down.

Slamming his fist into the wall, he cursed but finally nodded.

Zaddock's eyes found hers. "You need to come too. Is your guard around?"

Lessia shook her head, the whirlwind of thoughts in her mind not allowing words to form.

Bowing his head, Zaddock motioned for the guards surrounding them. “You follow them to the safe room, and do well to remember these are two nominees, including your current regent. You give your life for them if it comes to that.”

After patting Loche on the back, Zaddock hurried off the way he’d come.

Loche didn’t spare her a glance as he followed the guards down another hallway, his movements jerky, as if he was about to turn around at any moment.

Soon they stood outside two thick metal doors, and one of the guards tapped on one of them—some type of code, Lessia guessed, as it swung open seconds later.

Hushed voices clung to the air, but as she was about to step over the threshold, she realized the room was veiled in darkness.

Freezing with her foot in midair, Lessia made to turn around, but the guards behind her ushered her in, slamming the door closed behind them and leaving her in complete blackness.

Her heart began thundering as she listened to the heavy breathing and quiet murmurs around her.

Closing and opening her eyes, she tried to make out anything in the room, but whenever she opened them, there was only impenetrable darkness. Clenching her fists, she tried to draw air into her lungs, but heaviness planted itself on her chest, and only a wheezing breath made its way down her throat.

“I need to get out of here,” she got out, not caring that her voice wavered, nor about whoever was in this room.

“You can’t leave, miss. We’re on strict orders to keep you here until it’s safe.”

She had no idea who the voice belonged to but clung to the arm of the person next to her. "Please. I don't care, I'll tell them I made the decision. I..." She sucked in what little air she could as her pulse roared in her ears. "I need to get out."

"Calm down, miss. It will all be all right."

No.

She needed to get out.

Dizziness began swimming in her mind, her limbs tingling, and she knew she would faint if she didn't get out.

Now.

A chilling chorus of clinking chains, falling water, and rusty hinges filled her ears, and another voice drowned the subdued murmurs in the room.

"You'll wish you were still on the streets soon, halfling. You're never getting out of here." The Fae laughed as the heavy door slammed shut behind him.

She sprinted up to it and banged on the metal. "Please! No! Don't leave me here!"

But he only laughed again, the sound barely distinguishable through the thick metal.

Lessia screamed until her throat was raw, her hands bleeding from slamming against the door, her eyes never finding something to focus on.

But the door didn't open.

"Please!" she cried. "I need to get out!"

"Lessia." Loche's voice brushed her ear. "Breathe."

Shaking her head, she tried to get free from the arms that wrapped around her, stumbling backward.

Other images flooded her mind: the creaking door opening, the ominous sound of something dragging on the floor, her backing into a wet corner, trying to hide with the rodents running over the damp stone floor.

"I can't! Get me..." Her voice broke as the last of the air in her lungs left her, panic clawing its sharp talons into her chest.

"Lessia, you're panicking. Breathe." Loche's arms settled around her chest again, his heart pounding against her back as he held her to him.

"Focus on my voice," he whispered, his warm breath tickling her neck.

As she weakly shook her head, the darkness around her seeped into her mind, and her knees buckled. Only Loche's strong arms kept her from crashing down onto the floor.

You're never getting out of here.

A cry left her lips at the truth of his words.

She might have left that cellar, but she'd never be free of the memories.

As unconsciousness threatened to take over, a loud crash sounded before her, a sliver of light trickling through as the doors burst open.

The last thing she saw before darkness swept her away was a flicker of silver.

CHAPTER THIRTY-THREE

When she pried her eyes open, her throat felt like sandpaper. Thankfully, she found herself back in her brightly lit bedroom—every lantern she'd smuggled in kindled.

Lessia's pulse was still heightened as she sat up, casting a quick glance around the room.

Merrick sat on a chair by the door between their rooms, his usually flowing hair tangled and his hands clenching and unclenching where they rested on his knees.

"That's the second time I've carried you." Merrick laced his fingers, leaning forward so his messy hair covered most of his face.

Her cheeks heated, but Lessia forced herself not to cast a snide remark in his face.

She cleared her throat and mumbled, "Thank you."

Merrick let out a low hum as he rose to light a new lantern to replace one that was burning out. After placing it on the small bedstand, he returned to the chair, his dark boots firmly planted on the wooden floor, hands dragging down his face.

Lessia eyed him. "You're not going to ask me what happened?"

When he lifted his head, her heart skipped a beat, but Merrick's eyes remained cast down as he shook his head.

Frowning, she pushed off the blanket draped over her. "Why not? You must be reveling in this. You've found another way to threaten me—without using your magic and risk being exposed."

Flames of anger licked her heated neck.

She needed to have better control over this—over herself.

It wasn't just Merrick who'd found out her weakness.

Loche's strong arms flashed before her eyes, his voice whispering into her ear as she lost her mind to the darkness.

"I already know what happened."

Her gaze, which had been focused on a small tear in her cloak, snapped up. "What do you mean?"

Merrick raked his fingers through his long hair and seemed to hesitate for a moment before he quietly responded. "I was there that day."

Eyes widening, Lessia shifted so her legs swung over the bed. "What day?"

As if he could sense her movements, Merrick's back straightened. "The day they pulled you out of that cellar."

Every muscle in her body locked, and she couldn't stop the onslaught of memories that washed over her.

A creaking door fully opening for the first time in five years, the useless resistance she'd put up as they dragged her out of there.

She'd thought King Rioner's men had finally decided to execute her.

But when light blinded her and a voice she knew all too well broke through the excruciating pain from the sun, the king offered her a deal.

She'd get out of the dungeons—alive—if she only swore a blood oath to him.

Starved, scared, and desperate, she'd agreed far more quickly than she was proud of.

She'd been on a ship to Ellow less than a day after.

Finally gaining control over her mind, she forced her eyes to focus on the Fae before her. "I don't remember seeing you there."

Not that she had been able to see much.

It had taken days for her eyes to get used to light again.

She'd never let them forget after that.

Only when she closed them to sleep did she allow darkness to fester.

On the bad days, she couldn't even allow that.

"The king wanted me there, so there I was." Merrick rose to pace back and forth before the flickering fireplace.

"Ever the good soldier," Lessia muttered, but when Merrick's hands clenched by his sides, his steps faltering slightly, her brows snapped together.

Before she could ask what was on his mind, a knock had them both freeze. Merrick's sword was already in his hand, and his gaze locked on the door.

Freeing her daggers from where they poked her hips, she rose from the bed and followed Merrick as he approached the door.

He moved like a predator, his steps entirely silent and his body tense as he tilted his head to listen. Lessia perked her ears as well, but whatever had Merrick lower his shoulder didn't reach her half-Fae ears.

Spinning around, Merrick hissed, "Don't let your guard down. I don't wish to save you a third time," before he stalked over to their adjoining door, opened it, and slipped inside so quickly she barely caught his cloak billowing after him.

With her mouth open, she turned toward the door, a curse slipping from her lips when Loche's sharp glare met hers.

She started closing the door, but his hand gripped it, forcing it open.

"Tsk, tsk. That was rude. While the election might be ongoing, I am still regent, and this is my castle."

Loche strode into the room, closing the door behind him as Lessia backed up, tightening her grip on the daggers.

She had no idea why he was here, but she was done taking any chances.

Grudgingly, she admitted that Merrick might be right about making sure she kept her guard up at all times.

Loche's mouth twitched when he glanced at her hands, then let his gaze sweep across the room, lingering on the many lanterns lining the walls, the bedside table, and the small desk.

He pulled out the chair Merrick had just sat on, spun it around, sat down, and rested his arms on the back of it.

Loche flicked his dark hair out of his face. "Scared of the dark. I should have guessed in the cabin."

She didn't respond, only backed up until the cold wood of the wall bit into her back.

His storming eyes swept over her once more, his features softening slightly. "I am not here to hurt you, darling."

Biting her lip, she narrowed her eyes as his gaze focused on the sharp canines she was sure he glimpsed. "Why *are* you here?"

Loche leaned his chin in his hands. "I'm not entirely sure."

A flicker of something she couldn't quite read raced across his features.

"I don't like it," he muttered.

A weak smile spread across her face. "The infamous Loche

Lejonskold isn't sure of something? Now I've seen everything."

Rolling his eyes, he gestured toward the bed. "You should sit down. After an adrenaline rush like you just had, you're probably about to crash any moment."

Her first instinct was to argue, but her limbs felt heavy, so she cautiously made her way to the bed, keeping her eyes on Loche's the whole way.

After propping up a pillow against the wall, she lowered herself down and placed the daggers on the mattress beside her.

Loche continued to eye her, a wrinkle between his brows.

When she couldn't stand the silence anymore, Lessia pulled at a strand of her hair. "What happened tonight? Why would Stellia's guards attack?"

Shrugging, Loche tore his eyes away from hers. "I'm sure there will be a briefing soon where they'll tell us what they think happened."

"What they think—" Lessia started, but Loche interrupted her.

"Why were you a prisoner?"

Her pulse quickened, and she fixed her gaze on her hands, trying to straighten the wrinkles on her cloak from the day's wear.

When she lifted her gaze again, Loche's slammed into hers with so much force she sucked in a breath.

Grinding her teeth, she responded quietly, "I did something bad."

Loche tilted his head. "How bad?"

"Bad enough."

Lessia groaned silently.

She wanted to forget all about her time in the king's cellars and any time before.

Lately, everything seemed to stir the memories she'd worked so hard to bury.

"Did you kill a Fae?"

Understanding glimmered in his eyes when she tensed.

"You did. Did he deserve it?"

She was surprised at herself when she nodded.

But he had deserved it.

He might not have gotten to her, but she'd heard all about his reputation on the streets, what he'd done to Kalia...

No, she didn't regret making him take his own useless life.

"You lived on the streets in Vastala."

Even if it wasn't a question, she nodded again.

"Why?" There was only curiosity in Loche's eyes when she met them.

"I did something even worse." As soon as the words left her mouth, she drew a shaky breath, not understanding what drove her to be so honest with him.

"I tend to have that effect." Loche smirked.

But it wasn't his usual smirk.

It wasn't lined with smugness or even ridicule—there was more of a softness to it.

Rising from the chair, he pointed to the bed beside her. "Do you mind?"

Averting her eyes, she shrugged and moved to the far side of the bed.

Closer to the door, should she need to get out of there quickly.

The bed shifted when Loche sat down, and the scent of him immediately enveloped her.

If Merrick smelled like wilderness, Loche smelled like brightness. Like a cold winter night when the huge moon and millions of stars lit up the sparkling snow.

Wrapping her arms around her knees, she made herself

draw air through her mouth, keeping one eye on the man beside her and one on the door to her right.

"What did you do that was so bad?"

Her teeth slammed together as she refused to let the images pressing at her mind surface.

Still, golden-brown hair, brown eyes full of life, and a heart-shattering laugh made their way through. Her sister's smiling face was like taking a dagger to the heart, and she swallowed hard when her body began shivering.

As Lessia began to shake her head, another knock, harder this time, sounded.

At the same time Zaddock peeked through the door, Merrick stalked into the room.

Flicking his gaze between the three of them, Zaddock waved. "There is a briefing happening right now. All nominees are to attend."

Loche gracefully got up from the bed but shifted his gaze to hers once more. "You got lucky this time."

Then he followed Zaddock out of the room.

With a tense Merrick beside her, Lessia fell into step behind him.

CHAPTER THIRTY-FOUR

As they walked down the stairs to the sitting room, Lessia turned to Merrick.

"Did you hear anything about what happened?"

The Fae shook his head, his eyes fixed on the stone stairway. "I arrived back in time to hear you in that room, but I didn't see any of the guards that breached the castle."

She lowered her voice. "Where were you?"

Not that she particularly cared what Merrick did with his free time, but if he had been out on orders from his king, she wanted to know why.

And he seemed more talkative than usual today.

Merrick rushed his gait, taking the stairs three steps at a time with his long legs. "I had business to take care of."

Sighing, Lessia forced her tired legs to follow him.

Apparently, he wasn't *that* talkative.

Dozens of guards, some dusty and bloodied, stood outside the arched doors to the room they were to gather in.

Lessia eyed them as she passed, but the men kept their gazes straight ahead.

At least those she could see the faces of.

Ten of Loche's men stood on either side of Ellow's guards, their masks glowing in the firelight.

One of the men turned his head when Loche passed him, and goose bumps raced across her skin when the mask snapped to her next. The long beak pointed directly at her as the man inside it sized her up.

She slipped past him, letting out a breath of relief as she walked into the room. Only Ellow's guards were posted here, standing every few feet of the curved walls.

Before the fireplace sat a tired Craven and Venko, and opposite them, Frayson rested in a plush chair, a long nightshirt haphazardly tucked into his dark breeches.

Their eyes lifted when Loche threw himself down in a chair to Frayson's right, Zaddock taking a place right behind it.

Sitting down in the only free chair, Lessia cautiously observed the men around her, very aware of Merrick's brooding presence behind the backrest.

Gods, even when he didn't wield his magic, she could feel it thrumming from him, a constant reminder the Death Whisperer was her companion.

If she'd only known when her father told her and Frelina stories of him growing up...

Her hand flew to her chest as her sister's name slammed into her mind, followed by her squeals of excitement—and fear—as she begged their father to tell them more about the man who'd fought so many wars for the Fae, won against so many enemies.

When Merrick's hand landed on her shoulder, she snapped out of it, realizing all men in the room stared at her:

Craven with a look of disgust, Venko blankly, and Loche with that curious expression again.

As if he needed to figure out every thought passing through her mind.

Merrick removed the hand when Frayson cleared his throat. "As you're all aware, the castle was attacked today. A few of the men got away, and those who weren't killed seem to have brought poison to ensure we couldn't make them speak." Shaking his head, the graying man stared into the orange flames. "But they all bore Stellia's emblem on their chests."

Craven slammed his hands against his knees, his eyes bloodshot. "Well, then she needs to be captured and executed. She clearly had an agenda from the beginning—taking out her competition. They came straight for me when they entered the castle."

Frayson eyed him for a moment, then turned to Venko. "Did you see anything else? Did they say anything when they stormed in?"

Venko shook his head, his eyes meeting Lessia's for a moment before he turned them to the fire.

"They didn't say anything, but they clearly came for me—again!" Craven's cheeks burned as he glared at them. "They know who will win this election. They didn't even bother with Venko; one even pushed him aside."

"I fought him off, Craven." Venko rose from his chair, taking a step toward him. "I didn't run like you, coward."

Frayson raised his hands. "Settle down, gentlemen. There is no point in arguing. We need to figure out who did this and how to stop it from happening again."

Loche turned his head when Zaddock bent down to whisper something, then stalked out of the room after the exchange.

"You're unusually quiet, Loche." Craven waved a finger in his direction. "Anything you'd like to share?"

Loche didn't bother glancing in the man's direction. "Not really."

Frowning, Lessia sliced her gaze between the men.

Loche was unusually quiet.

Some of his men had died tonight, and while she'd seen him affected by it, she was surprised he didn't offer more opinions.

They all turned to the door when a guard walked through it, and Lessia tensed when he bore the dark blue uniform signaling his captain's position in the navy. But the pin on his chest was of two crossed swords, not the sail of Stellia's company.

"You may speak freely, Captain." Frayson eyed them, his gaze lingering on Merrick behind her for a moment before he continued. "There are only friends in the room."

Nodding, the captain straightened, heels slamming together. "Stellia and two of her battleships have gone missing. They were seen close to the borders of Vastala two days ago, but it's like they've disappeared from this realm. We spoke to one of the Fae captains, and they haven't crossed their waters. We will continue searching, but it seems she had this planned for a while."

Lessia's mouth fell open when Loche stormed out of the room, the door slamming shut behind him.

"I guess Loche is informing his own guards to keep an eye out." Frayson tried to smile at them.

"As he should. He is still regent," Craven scoffed.

Lessia rolled her eyes, briefly locking her gaze with that of a scowling Venko.

"Well." Frayson rose on shaky legs, glancing down at his nightshirt. "The council is still coming tomorrow. There will be a debate at noon and a ball in the evening. We cannot postpone it, but we're bringing in twice the number of guards and will keep a close eye on who enters the castle. I suggest you go to bed. We'll ensure your rooms are well guarded."

Muttering under his breath, Craven left the room with his massive guard, who'd been posted by the door. Venko followed soon after, still without a personal guard by his side, but two of Loche's men fell in step behind him as he disappeared around the corner.

As Lessia walked through the doors, closely followed by Merrick, a hand landed on her back. "May I speak with you?"

When she turned around, Zaddock gestured toward a small alcove beneath the stairway. "In private?"

Stepping in between them, Merrick growled, "If you think I'm letting her out of my sight, you're very wrong."

Lessia fought a smile when Zaddock nodded gravely.

Merrick wasn't concerned for her safety out of the goodness of his heart. He was only concerned because of his duty to his king—because they needed her alive.

For now, at least.

"Of course. I wasn't implying you weren't welcome to join." Zaddock waved toward the dim spot by the stairs again. "Could we speak over there?"

"Yes." Lessia glared in Merrick's direction when a low sound rumbled in his chest.

When the Fae reached out for her arm, she slipped away, following Zaddock.

She was curious whether he'd be able to tell them more about why Stellia would attack, and she wouldn't have the grumpy Fae warrior stop her.

As they huddled together, Merrick's large frame towering over them, Zaddock waited until two guards marched past to take up their positions at the castle entrance.

Lessia's pulse quickened in the thick silence.

What could he want to tell them that he couldn't even tell the guards of Ellow?

After casting a swift glance around, Zaddock spoke in a hushed voice. "I don't know what's going on with you and Loche, and usually I would say it's none of my business, but election times are dangerous as it is..."

Her brows flew up.

He wanted to speak about Loche?

Glaring at him, she responded quietly, "Nothing is going on with us, and you don't need to worry about him. He seems to be able to take care of himself."

A frown formed across Zaddock's forehead. "I am not worried about him, Lessia. I came to warn you from getting too involved—"

"Or what? You're threatening her?" Merrick snarled. "I don't take easy to threats."

She was glad Merrick couldn't see her roll her eyes, but Zaddock caught it, the corners of his mouth quirking slightly. "I am not threatening her, I am just looking out for her. I've seen you spend a lot of time with him, and I just..."

Merrick snarled again, his magic thrumming in the air, and Zaddock's face blanched.

Pinching his arm, Lessia tried to snap Merrick out of it before he exposed them both.

Even if Zaddock was human, he must feel the air shifting.

And it wasn't a natural tension filling it.

Slowly the air stilled, no longer sparking from electricity, and Zaddock glanced between them, shaking his head. "I see I am not explaining myself well. I shall leave you to it, but just... remember what I said."

With that, he cast a final look at them, uncertainty flitting across his features before he scaled the stairs.

Lessia took a step closer to Merrick, trying to ignore the deadly magic still vibrating softly around them. “You need to stop doing that. He could sense your magic. They’ll know something is up if it happens again, and I’d prefer to get out of this alive.”

His jaw ticked, but finally, he flexed his hands, his tense posture relaxing slightly. “You need to go to bed. We’re training early tomorrow.”

Turning around, he started up the stairs but stilled when Lessia didn’t immediately follow.

Sighing, she fell into step with him.

What was his problem?

Everyone was on edge because of the election and the attack, but Zaddock’s, Merrick’s, and even Loche’s reactions confused her.

When she went to bed, her thoughts still swirled, but she was no closer to understanding what was going on as sleep crept in.

CHAPTER THIRTY-FIVE

"How are you going to train me if you can't look at me?" Lessia yawned as she followed Merrick down into the lower levels of the castle, where apparently, there was some kind of training ring.

Her body was still exhausted, her clothes worryingly loose from the weeks without food, but Merrick had woken her before dawn, a steaming bowl of porridge in his hands that he made her eat every last bite from.

Shivering, she took the final step onto a dimly lit cellar floor and glanced around.

The room was simple, with smooth curved walls, racks of wooden swords and daggers to her right, and a raised platform lined with thick rope to her left.

Merrick set down the two lanterns he'd carried and hopped onto the platform, waving for her to follow. "I don't need to see you to fight you. Or to teach you."

Hoisting herself up, she ducked underneath the rope. "You fought in the War of Storms, didn't you? You were considered a hero, together with that other male. What was his name?"

There had been many wars between the Fae, especially before King Rioner's family came into power.

The War of Storms was one of the most brutal.

A Fae family that could wield clouds had tried to take control of Vastala—and nearly succeeded—by conjuring raging thunderstorms and electrocuting whole towns.

She shuddered just thinking of it.

Hailing from an island far away, further than anyone in Havlands had ever traveled before, they fought for control over every Fae lineage. They'd made nearly all Vastala bow before Merrick and his band of Fae warriors took them out.

Apparently, they were all formidable, a combination of mental and elemental Fae, and while Merrick and the other leader were the strongest, they were all deadly in their own way.

"Raine," Merrick muttered.

"That's it. And there were more of you, wasn't it? Where are they now? Do they also support the king? I thought you were a brotherhood or something."

"They're gone," Merrick growled. "And we were friends, not a 'brotherhood.'"

A muffled laugh escaped her lips.

"What?" Merrick's shoulders tensed.

Taking a step back, Lessia raised her hands. "I was just surprised you had friends, that's all."

"Why?"

A wave of Merrick's magic wove its way through the room, but she couldn't stop another laugh from bubbling up. "I don't know... Because you're not very friendly?"

He seemed to vibrate from the rumbling in his chest, and the air shifted again, thickening with whispers.

"Sorry, sorry!" Lessia grimaced. "Maybe it's just with me you're not very friendly."

And he was literally called the Death Whisperer, not the most warm and fuzzy nickname.

But given the vibrations rolling off him, she decided not to bring that up.

They were alone down here, after all.

Probably best not to rile him up too much.

Merrick impatiently gestured for her. "Stop stalling and get into position. We'll start with hand-to-hand before we go into trying weapons."

Groaning to herself, she took up a spot opposite him, trying to mimic his squared shoulders and wide stance.

"That's not the right position," Merrick hissed.

"Well, I told you I haven't done this before," she snarled back.

While she was grateful he'd offered to teach her—even if it was for his own benefit—she was still weak and tired from the past few weeks.

And she had little patience with his stupid attitude.

"Feet apart, and plant them firmly. Lower your center, so you're more stable on the ground. And brace your core," he barked. "You need to be steady if you're attacked. If your enemy gets you down on the ground, you're done."

Trying to engage her abs only reminded her of the gnawing hunger that still preyed at her, and she placed a hand on her stomach when the ache intensified. She couldn't eat enough to satisfy it yet, as queasiness would set in after only a few bites.

As Lessia tried to follow his instructions, Merrick sighed loudly, and she stuck out her tongue at him.

"Very mature," he snarled.

"I thought you couldn't see me." She grinned at him.

"I see more than enough even if I don't see your eyes, Lessia. Now raise your arms and be prepared."

Scowling, she raised her arms, the leather tunic she'd pulled on shifting after her weight loss. As she habitually pulled at it to ensure her tattoo was covered, she slammed into the hard ground, the air knocked out of her.

"Don't ever lose focus," Merrick gloated.

Lessia blinked up at the stone ceiling, her heart thumping against her ribs until she finally could draw a breath again. Wheezing breaths whistled down her throat as she cursed Merrick, cursed the stupid elections, cursed King Rioner, cursed all Havlands.

When she could breathe normally again, she shifted up on her elbows, glaring at him.

Not even a lock of silver hair was out of place from his advance.

"Are you not going to help me up?"

If she didn't know better, she'd have sworn he hid a smile when he reached out a hand and easily pulled her to her feet. As she let go of his grip, Merrick spun around and moved a few feet away again.

"Into position. I'll go slower this time."

Biting her cheek, she took up the wide stance again, her eyes fixed on his set jaw as he approached her.

Still, when his arm wrapped around her, she didn't have a chance. He easily swept her legs out from under her, and she once again fell onto the floor, dust swirling around her, layering over her face and clothing.

Scrambling to her feet using the rope around the platform, she swore loudly. "Again."

This time Merrick couldn't hide the crooked smile that spread across his face, and the urge to slam her fist into his face nearly overwhelmed her.

When he approached again, she jumped to the side, shoving her hand out, but Merrick caught it with such force she lost her footing.

Only his hand wrapping around her arm kept her from falling face-first into the stone.

"Better. But you're still not fast enough." Merrick let go of her arm, his finger poking her gut so hard she hissed at him. "And keep your core engaged. You need to have control of every limb and every muscle if you're to stand a chance against me. Or anyone else, for that matter."

Letting out a sharp breath, she clenched her muscles, ignoring the black dots whirling in her vision. Merrick nodded as he paced around her, his lethal movements slow and deliberate.

But when he approached her again, he moved so quickly she didn't have time to spin around before his arms had hers in a lock. Kicking backward, she tried to get free but only managed to allow him a better grip.

Merrick twisted her arms so hard crimson tinted her vision, and when he pulled her close and a low laugh escaped him, she felt her features twist into a sneer. Letting him pull her even closer, she relaxed for a moment, and it seemed Merrick was about to let her go; then she stomped on his foot with all her might.

A hiss blew through her hair, and a tremble shook her shoulders when the air stilled and whispers reverberated through the chamber. But Merrick only muttered "Good" before releasing her.

Panting, she whipped her head from side to side as he stalked around her in a circle, like a predator moving in on its prey. Lessia wiped at her forehead when drops of sweat formed there even in the damp, cool air, and Merrick didn't hesitate as he took the opportunity to strike her with such force she once again crashed to the floor.

They continued this dance until she could barely get herself up from the dusty stone.

When Merrick dragged her to her feet yet again, her body swayed, and he finally took a step back. “That’s probably enough for today. I wasn’t expecting much, but at least you have some control over your body. It’s a start.”

“Is the almighty warrior complimenting me? Why, thank you, Merrick.” Even if he couldn’t see, she exaggeratedly batted her lashes in his direction.

“Don’t push me,” he grumbled, but the corners of his mouth curled again before he stalked off toward the stairs.

As she followed him up from the cellar, she thought he wasn’t so scary after all.

Even with the bruises she’d gained from his deadly skills, when that hardness always etching his face softened, he almost seemed friendly.

CHAPTER THIRTY-SIX

When she got back, a warm meal waited in her room, and Lessia gobbled down the soup and bread so quickly that she was worried it would all come right back up again.

But after sitting down on the bed, her stomach calmed, and she stretched out her aching limbs as she waited for the sun to indicate that it was noon.

There had been lively conversations coming from the sitting room when they'd walked up the stairs, but she wasn't about to spend one more second with those people than she had to, so she hid in her room like a child until the sun peeked over the cliffs outside her balcony.

Merrick stood outside her room when she opened the door, and with a grumbled "Let's go," he led her up the set of stairs the guard outside her room informed them would take them to the debate chamber.

Beads of cold sweat were rolling down her neck by the time they reached a set of white-painted wooden doors, and she wiped her damp palms on the black breeches she'd pulled on.

She wasn't sure what was appropriate to wear to a debate, so she'd settled on her usual black tunic and breeches but took the time to polish her boots and brush her hair until both shone.

She'd left it down, even though elaborate hairdos were the latest fashion, mostly because she didn't have the energy to put it up but also because the thick locks felt like they could help shield her from whatever she was to face.

Rolling her eyes at herself, she hesitated with her hand hovering over the gilded doorknob.

"What are you waiting for?"

Merrick took a step closer, the heat from his body burning into her back.

She turned her head over her shoulder.

He'd also changed, and even though he'd dressed in a simple ivory shirt and dark trousers, his pearlescent hair falling in waves over his shoulders, there was still an otherness radiating from him through his glamour.

Swallowing, she hoped none of the council members were too familiar with the Fae and would assume—like the rest of the nominees and guards—that he merely had a Fae parent or grandparent.

Merrick nudged her, and she realized she'd been staring at him.

"I—" she started, but his hand reached out for her.

For a moment she thought he was about to comfort her, but then he placed his hand over hers and opened the door. "Best to get this over with."

Why she'd thought he might offer her some soothing words, she didn't know, but a rush of disappointment slammed into her like the floor had this morning as she stepped over the threshold.

Forcing herself to keep her features neutral, she took in the room.

It was packed, with two dozen or so people milling about beneath a raised dais where five wooden chairs stood. The grandest chandelier she'd ever seen hung from the ceiling, its light mingling with the white winter sunlight sifting in through the windows lining the wall opposite the dais.

Lessia realized she'd underestimated the need to dress up when she caught Venko's eyes from where he stood conversing with two older men.

They were dressed in elaborate jackets and doublets, with silver and gold embroidery delicately weaving its way up their chests and jeweled weapons hanging by their waists.

The women wore the latest fashion: expensive silk dresses—extremely impractical for winter but hugging their curves meticulously, with white ruffles that caressed their necks and peeked out from their short sleeves, contrasting beautifully with the vivid gowns.

Most dresses were colorful, lilacs and pinks and some beautiful greens and blues that stood out against the white stone walls of the room. Lessia pulled at her black tunic when two men gave her a once-over, disdain twisting their features.

A few more faces turned her way, and her cheeks heated when hushed giggles followed. Spinning around, she was about to hide behind Merrick, but he stalked right past her, joining the other companions by the wall behind the dais.

"You look like you're about to be sick. Still not recovered from the cabin?"

Loche leaned against the wall to her right, and despite his amused expression, she made her way over, grateful that she'd at least have someone to talk to—even if he was planning on making fun of her.

"My guard thought I needed to train this morning, so I am mostly recovering from that." Lessia ignored the soft laughs echoing behind her, keeping her burning face turned away from the crowd.

"Smart man."

Loche brushed some dust off his jacket, and she trailed her gaze over him.

Like her, he hadn't dressed up.

Instead, he wore the same jacket he always did, simple and black, paired with leathers and dark boots, his sword resting across his back and its hilt peeking over his shoulder.

When a particularly loud laugh reverberated through the room, a set jaw replaced Loche's amused expression, and those piercing eyes shifted to his side.

"Would you like to enlighten us as to what's so humorous, Malain?"

Lessia followed his gaze, and her eyes widened when they settled on one of the most beautiful humans she'd ever seen.

Ebony hair cascaded down the woman's back, held away from her delicate face with two gilded combs that shimmered like the golden dress she wore. Thick, dark lashes framed her huge blue eyes, and her mouth was painted in a deep red, contrasting with her fair skin.

The woman clung to an unfairly gorgeous man. His dark hair was peppered with silver, but few lines graced his face, and his dark gaze was clear when he swept it over Lessia, then, with a bored expression, shifted it back to the man he'd been conversing with.

The beautiful woman raised a perfect brow. "Are we forbidden to laugh now, dear regent? You've set out to make life ever so boring for us already, so I suppose I shouldn't be surprised."

Loche offered Malain one of those lethal smirks Lessia hated when directed her way. "From what I've heard, your life is boring because that husband of yours can't seem to stop gambling away your fortune."

The man beside Malain shifted his gaze their way, anger flitting across his features.

"Or am I mistaken, Berhn? My guards reported saving your life when you stumbled out of that tavern, not even wearing the cloak you'd walked in with. And you still owe half the town money. I'm surprised you dared show your face here today—you're braver than I thought." Loche winked at him.

Malain opened her mouth, but her husband's face reddened, and he dragged her across the room into a corner, where they proceeded to cast furious glances Loche's way.

When Loche turned around again, Lessia offered him a small smile. "I don't know if I should be offended or glad you treated me the same way you treated them."

Surprise sparked in his eyes when he snapped them to hers, and when Lessia nervously licked her lips, his gaze flew to her mouth.

She hadn't meant to say that out loud.

But apparently, she'd lost all sense when she stepped into this room.

To her surprise, Loche's lips lifted in a real, blinding smile, and a chuckle escaped him. "I've worked hard on my charm."

She pulled at a lock of her hair to hide the heat creeping up her cheeks. "If that is you working hard, I truly don't want to know what you are like when you are not trying."

When his grin widened, she couldn't help but smile back.

His face turned almost boyish, those gray eyes twinkling in the light and small dimples forming above his strong jaw.

Lessia had the urge to reach out and poke one of them but clenched her hands.

He'd probably bite her finger off.

A whistle behind them quieted the room, and when Frayson scaled the dais, her smile fell.

She had no idea what to expect from this, but she wasn't eager to find out.

Frayson asked all nominees to join him, and as Lessia made her way through the parting crowd, Loche pulled her to him.

With his lips against her ear, he whispered, "They're going to be ruthless, so make sure that mask you've perfected stays on."

A shudder went down her spine.

She wasn't entirely sure if it was unease or from the tingling sensation his lips had left.

Shaking her head at herself, she took the stairs to the stage, two steps at a time.

There was no turning back now.

She just needed to remember why she was doing this—for her family, for Ellow, and for her freedom.

CHAPTER THIRTY-SEVEN

As they sat down in the chairs, Frayson walked up to the edge of the dais and threw out his arms.

"Welcome, council members. As is tradition, you will be able to evaluate this year's nominees. I know many of you come with proposals, or challenges, that you need our regent to act on or resolve. While Loche will be making the final decisions as the current regent, all nominees will get the chance to respond to ensure you understand their stance on different matters. Nominees, as you all know, council members vote for all the people inhabiting their islands, so this is your chance to garner votes outside of the capital."

Lessia's brows snapped together.

She knew each council family led its own island, but she had no idea that they voted on behalf of their people.

While Asker was the largest island in Ellow, the smaller ones made up two-thirds of the population.

No wonder the nobles always won the election.

She couldn't comprehend how Loche had convinced any

of them, especially considering the venomous glares he shot around the room from the chair next to her.

Her eyes left his scowling face when a man who introduced himself as Ludvak stepped forward to begin the debate. Lessia swept her gaze over his expensive navy robe and the intricate silver embroidery of his family crest decorating the chest of the dark shirt he wore beneath it—two half moons overlapping a rose.

Ardow had mentioned each noble family had their own crest, but apart from the few times nobles had ventured to her taverns, she'd had little to do with them and had no idea which family Ludvak hailed from.

Ludvak claimed that the cost of feeding his cattle, which apparently produced most of the milk in Ellow, had gone up so much that he couldn't continue to pay his workers.

Loche snarkily responded that he could perhaps sell some of the family gold he hoarded in his basement if he was so worried, while Craven suggested the workers should work in exchange for free milk.

When Venko cautiously argued they couldn't live off milk, Loche shot him a nod and proclaimed Ludvak needed to start paying them immediately and reimbursing them for what he'd withheld, or his men would come and raid the family treasures, selling them off one by one until he started giving his workers their due.

Remaining quiet, Lessia eyed the men, noting that Venko and Loche seemed to agree on many things, although Venko argued strongly for more soldiers to help protect the waters from pirates that kept attacking any ship they could.

Craven disagreed with every single point the other two men made, his face turning a shade darker every time Loche ruled in the opposite way he would.

Loche fascinated her the most.

He mostly responded to outrageous requests with boredom, but a vein strained on his neck as he glared at some of the people coming forward. He was quietly furious, and she made a mental note to learn how to control her emotions like he did.

"Lessia, what do you think?"

She shifted her gaze to Frayson, pink tinting her cheeks as he raised his brows.

Clearing her throat, she sat straighter in the chair. "I'm sorry, what was the question?"

A low growl behind her told her Merrick wasn't impressed that she'd gotten lost in her thoughts, and so did Loche's disappointed expression when she glanced his way.

Her stomach sank at the look in his eyes—as if he'd expected more of her—and the shame that settled on her chest made her cheeks burn brighter.

"Hawker"—Frayson gestured to a younger man with dark eyes who refused to meet Lessia's—"is concerned about the trade slowing down because of the threat of pirates. Fewer merchants are willing to brave the sea, so prices are increasing, and it's getting more difficult to acquire certain goods."

Nodding, Lessia kept her eyes on the man, who still wouldn't look at her.

She'd experienced the same thing with her taverns. For the past few months, they'd had to pay far more for the same goods so that the captains of the ships could employ mercenaries to protect them.

She laced her fingers together, forcing her voice to stay strong and ignoring the unfriendly faces before her.

"I have the same concerns for my business. But since we're employing more soldiers, couldn't we find a way for the warships to collaborate with the trade ships? Perhaps even have them join forces, reevaluate the trade routes so that ships could protect our borders while also transporting goods."

It was quiet for a beat, and she dared steal a look at Loche. His face remained impassive, but something in his eyes made her continue.

"It would also allow more opportunities for the people. I know many are forced to become soldiers because there are so few other options, but perhaps they could be offered a choice after they've been trained—become either a soldier, a merchant, or even a ship captain."

Hawker's jaw clenched, his gaze still fixed somewhere above her head, but some of the other nobles glanced at each other and nodded.

"I like it."

Her eyes widened when Loche spoke, and his features softened for a moment as their eyes locked.

"While we allow women in our ranks, many aren't willing, so this would also allow more opportunities for them outside of working the farms or moving to the capital in search of employment. I will speak to our admirals and see how we could go about setting this up." Loche shot her another glance before shifting his eyes to the nobles again. "Who's next?"

"What about the Fae?" Another man stalked forward, a sneer on his face beneath his neatly combed golden hair. "They drive up the prices by bringing their goods here. We should seal the borders from them, should have never opened them in the first place!"

Lessia schooled her features into a mask of neutrality at the disgust that twisted the man's face when she cleared her throat. "Don't the Fae and humans trade different goods, though? We have never purchased any produce or liquor from Fae vendors. My understanding is that they mainly provide steel for weapons, or even finished weapons, if you can afford it. And building material, of course."

She made the mistake of glancing out over the crowd. The blond man wasn't the only one staring at her with outright loathing. Most of the people closest to the dais averted their eyes when she met them, one woman even hiding behind the man closest to her and shuddering.

The blond man's lip curled. "We only have to purchase the building material because the Fae burned down most of our forests in the war. It takes centuries to get those kinds of forests back. They should be giving it for free as payment for their destruction."

"But it was also humans who started the war. The Fae lost almost as many, and they depend more on trade now, as they can't reproduce as fast as humans can." She tried to keep her voice even as more faces turned her way, stares of pure hate burning into her skin.

While she wasn't the biggest fan of the Fae, she knew they relied heavily on trade, since they had fewer Fae able to help produce food and clothing. And despite all the bad seeds, there were good Fae too.

Lessia winced when people around her started screaming in outrage.

"She is on their side!"

"Of course she'd defend the Fae. She is a halfling. She's one of them!"

"She shouldn't be allowed here. She'd probably put Ellow under Fae rule if it was up to her!"

She shot a quick glance at Loche, but his face was turned away, his foot nonchalantly bouncing up and down. Steeling the emotions churning inside her, she made sure not a lick of the pain those words caused reflected in her features.

"Quiet!" Frayson barked, breaking through the chaos.

Before anyone else could speak, Lessia sucked in a breath and rose from her seat, hiding her shaking hands behind her back.

"I understand why you might not trust me. Believe me, I've seen firsthand how cruel Fae can be. But like humans, Fae differs from Fae, and I am also half-human—one of you. I consider Ellow my home, and I've made sure to contribute to society during my years here. I have no ill intentions in this election."

She bit her cheek not to grimace at the last bit.

It wasn't a lie.

Not really.

She might have been forced to be here by King Rioner, but she was doing everything she could to ensure Ellow remained safe.

Even if the people here treated her like an outsider, she knew Ellow was safer for someone like her, for someone like Kalia or Harver, than Vastala would ever be.

And she needed to make sure it stayed that way.

Make it better if she could.

The only way to do that was to show them they had nothing to fear from half-Fae like herself.

It was quiet for a moment, but then someone called out, "You're not one of us! Go home, halfling!"

The room erupted in more shouts.

Sitting back down, Lessia tried to shrink into the chair, making herself as small as possible.

It took Frayson a long time to calm everyone down, and when the debate continued, no one asked for Lessia's opinion again. Not even Frayson looked her way as they discussed taxes, how to feed everyone until the end of this long winter, and how to fill the ranks of soldiers while keeping enough men and women at home to manage farms and stores.

When the debate finally ended, Lessia walked right off the dais, keeping her head down until she reached the stairs.

She felt Merrick follow closely behind her, but the Fae didn't speak as she bolted up the stairs and didn't enter her room when she walked in and threw herself on the bed.

CHAPTER THIRTY-EIGHT

Lessia stared up at the ceiling for what felt like hours until a soft knock interrupted her thoughts.

She didn't bother responding, but Merrick opened the door between their rooms anyway.

Keeping her gaze on the wooden beams, she said, "I'm not going."

She'd had enough of name-calling and cruel glares for the day.

She didn't need to endure a whole night of it as well.

"I didn't think you'd break that easily."

Merrick walked up and, to her surprise, sat down on the edge of the bed. His large frame shifted the mattress, so she nearly rolled into him, and Lessia braced herself with her hands against the soft bedding.

"They don't want me there, and I don't believe it's actually mandatory for the election, so what does it matter if I stay here."

She almost wished she would cry then, shed at least one

tear to relieve the lump that seemed to have taken up a permanent position in her throat.

Merrick tapped his fingers against his knee. "Don't let them win, Lessia. You have every right to be there."

She shot up, staring at the side of his head, at the silvery lashes dancing across his high cheekbones. "Do I? I am literally here to spy on them, Merrick. They *should* be outraged with me. I'm a traitor. They wouldn't just call me names if they found out. They'd execute me. And who could blame them?"

When he tensed, she realized what she'd just done.

She'd just told the king's right-hand man that she considered herself a traitor to Ellow.

That she considered this her home enough to feel guilty.

If he told the king, Rioner wouldn't stop at the loose instructions he'd given her when she saw him last. He'd give her detailed instructions for how to spy, what to ask, how to ask for it.

But Merrick didn't storm out to immediately send a message to the king.

Instead, he sighed and leaned his elbows on his knees, resting his head in his hands.

"You don't need to feel guilty, Lessia. You're only doing this because you are loyal to your real king, isn't that right?"

When she remained quiet, he asked again, "Isn't that right?"

Lessia nodded but realized he couldn't see her movement from the way he was facing, so she got out a croaked "Yes."

"Good. I'll send the king an update that while you won't be the next regent, you're doing everything you can to find out information. You are, aren't you?"

"Yes."

At least everything she could while keeping Ellow and her friends safe.

Merrick lifted his head from his hands and nodded. "Now, put on whatever nice thing you have in that closet, and let's go down. I don't believe some crude humans can break you, not after everything you've been through."

"Will you come with me?"

She didn't know who was most surprised, herself, at the words that left her mouth, or Merrick, whose brows flew up so high they almost reached his hairline.

He rose from the bed, offering her his hand.

"I'll wait outside your door."

She let him drag her upright, and her eyes tracked his broad back as he left her room.

When the door closed behind him, she walked up to the rounded mirror beside the clothing chamber and stared at the dusty reflection.

Her cheeks were hollow, eyes slightly sunken in.

But that was to be expected after two weeks without food.

She pulled out a small cosmetic pouch and dabbed a bit of color onto her cheeks and pale lips, then grabbed a brush and dragged it through her hair a few times.

She picked up a silvery comb Amalise had gifted her, then pulled her hair back and fastened it. The ornament wasn't as elaborate as Malain's gilded ones, but it complemented her golden-brown hair and comfortably kept it out of her face.

Merrick was right.

She wouldn't break because of the council's—or anyone else in Ellow's—reactions.

They were justified, after all.

Although she was doing everything she could to ensure these people remained safe while spying on them...

She was still spying on them.

As she pulled out the black dress, her mind replayed the debate, the matters that had been discussed.

Even if they had included her, she wouldn't have known what to say. Many of the concerns discussed were foreign to her, and she wasn't even sure what her opinions on them were.

Slipping out of her breeches and tunic and pulling the dress over her head, Lessia promised herself that she would read up on each one.

Not for a chance to win this election.

But if she was to stay here, she should be more informed about the land's issues. She might have opinions on how people like herself and the half-Fae she brought over should be treated, but if she didn't know how society worked, she could never change it.

After a quick glance in the mirror, wincing at how plain she looked, Lessia squared her shoulders, made sure her sleeves safely covered her tattoo, and walked out the door.

As promised, Merrick waited right outside in the same clothing he'd worn to the debate, even if she knew he had other, much more elaborate pieces.

She doubted it was for her benefit—to make her feel more comfortable—but regardless, it lifted her spirits.

Surprise made her brows pop when he offered her his arm, but she still took it.

Even if he was hardly a friendly face, she could pretend for tonight.

"You look like you're going to a burial. I suppose it's fitting."

She threw a glare his way and snarled softly, "If you had to hide the lovely tattoo your king graced me with, you would also have to be careful with how you dressed."

His jaw flexed, the arm she was holding tensing, and she

wondered if she'd gone too far. But Merrick only rushed his steps, nearly having her fall in the stupid shoes she'd paired the dress with.

Like many women, she loved beautiful clothing and would have done much to be able to wear one of the fashionable dresses other women did.

But the shoes she could do without.

She didn't mind the additional height they gave her—she had come to terms with the fact that human women would almost always look dainty next to her—but did they have to be so damn uncomfortable?

As they took the final steps down to the sitting room, delicious smells that made her mouth water washed over them. Lessia picked up the smell of bread, of meat and vegetables, but it was the sugary scent of cakes and pastries that made her stomach rumble loud enough for Merrick to scoff.

"What?" she hissed. "I am starving. I didn't eat anything but snow for two weeks, and you wore me out this morning. My body needs the energy."

Shaking his head, he dragged her toward the sitting room.

Lessia couldn't stop her mouth from falling open when they entered through the double doors, where dozens of guards stood posted outside.

The room had been completely transformed.

Gone were the couches and plush chairs; instead, the room was filled with table after table of food and drink. The walls were covered in sparkling silvery tapestries, and a circular rug in the same material decorated the center of the room.

To their right, there was a whole orchestra, the music softly weaving its way through the room. Couples already braved the dance floor, their bodies swaying gently in rhythm with the melody.

She gripped Merrick's arm tighter when he made to step away.

"Let's get some food. Even the mighty Fae must eat sometimes," she whispered.

A sigh escaped him, but he led the way toward the overflowing tables.

Warmth trailed over her face when they navigated through the crowd, and she searched the faces, expecting a hostile glare from one of the council members.

But her eyes met Loche's with a jolt, and she raised her brows at the thunderous look on his face. When Merrick pulled at her so she wouldn't bump into a dancing couple, she tore her eyes away, still sensing his glacial eyes tracking her movements.

As they reached the tables, she suddenly wasn't so hungry, trying to understand why Loche, yet again, looked like he wanted to kill her.

She let go of Merrick, picked up a beautifully decorated cake, moved to lean against the wall, and took small bites, barely tasting anything of the sugary decadence.

Merrick took up the spot beside her, and she rolled her eyes at how awkward his "casual" stance looked. Even resting against the wall, every muscle in his body shifted under his clothing, his head subtly tilting to pick up conversations in every corner of the room.

She let her eyes drift toward Loche again.

He'd moved his gaze to Zaddock, with whom he was holding a passionate, whispered conversation. A frown slipped across her face when Zaddock threw his arms out and Loche took a step toward him, hardness lining his jaw.

When Zaddock placed a hand on his shoulder, Loche threw it off. The former shook his head and stormed out of the room, his black cloak trailing behind him.

Leaning against the wall opposite her, Loche lifted his face, and Lessia snapped her eyes to the dance floor, where more couples now filed in.

The music shifted to a slower song, and she watched Craven offer his hand to a woman who seemed to be his wife, her long hair sparkling with silver. Venko also pulled a beautiful blonde with him, spinning her expertly around the circular dance floor.

People at all the tables around her began pairing up, men bowing to the women, who giggled and let them lead them to the already dancing couples.

She glanced at Merrick, who hissed, "Don't even think about it. I don't dance."

Sighing, she watched couple after couple join, the laughter from the women as the men spun them humming softly over the beautiful music.

A wave of wistfulness washed over her.

She'd always loved dancing and music.

There hadn't been a day growing up when her mother hadn't been singing in the kitchen until her father pulled her into his arms and swung her around. And they'd always let her and Frelina join; Frelina, who sang as beautifully as their mother, who'd tried to teach Lessia to sing until they figured out it was hopeless.

She could dance, though. Her father had let her stand on his feet before she could even walk, and after that, he'd practiced with her whenever she wanted.

Lessia tilted her face to the floor and ground her teeth as the lump from earlier returned in full force. She should be grateful she'd had such a beautiful childhood, but there was only pain whenever these memories surfaced.

She'd ruined everything.

"May I have this dance?"

Her eyes flew up, and her mouth fell open when Loche bowed before her.

CHAPTER THIRTY-NINE

Loche's mouth twitched when she only stared at him.

Was this a game?

Another way for him to unsettle her?

"You're asking me to dance?" she got out.

Amusement brightened his eyes. "It would seem so. I am certainly not asking that grumpy guard of yours."

Merrick snarled softly beside her, and she quickly offered Loche her hand when the Fae seemed about to say something.

Or perhaps to knock Loche out.

He clearly didn't take well to being humored.

As Loche led her onto the dance floor, she tried to ignore the glares they received.

He seemed completely unfazed as his arm circled her waist. Pulling her close, he guided the hand she'd placed on his shoulder to his chest and gripped the other one tight.

"Why are you doing this?" she whispered.

His heart thumped steadily against her hand, and when she glanced up at him, his eyes flared for a second before he offered her a smirk. "I enjoy riling up these stiff nobles. And what better way to do it than dancing with the person they hate more than me."

She frowned at him and moved to step away, but Loche didn't allow it; he only pulled her closer.

Bowing his head, he brushed his lips against her cheek, lowering his voice. "You wanted to dance, and I think you've had enough of a bad day."

Goose bumps whispered across her skin where his lips grazed it, and she cleared her throat. "You could have helped me."

He pulled back, slamming his eyes into hers. "You can help yourself, darling. But there is something holding you back from doing so, and I haven't figured out what it is yet."

Although I will was implied in his tone.

Lessia forced herself to roll her eyes, forbidding guilt to seep into her features.

They stayed silent for a moment, and as furious whispers reached her ears over the music, she stiffened again.

"Don't let them get to you. They're bastards, every single one. Besides, they're not just angry that you're here. I mightily angered every person in this room today." Loche grinned at her, the boyishness from earlier crinkling his face and embers of pride filling his eyes.

He was *enjoying* this.

Lessia tilted her head. "How can they hate you so much? They elected you."

His grin widened. "That's exactly why."

The music picked up speed, a surge of energy pulsing through the room, propelling the soft tunes into faster ones.

Loche wiggled his brows. "Come on, let's give these bores something to talk about the next few weeks. I assume you actually *can* dance, given the pining look on your face when you watched the floor."

She didn't have time to nod before he spun her out in a wide circle, and a shocked giggle escaped her when he followed with a low dip.

Tuning out the gasps around them, she let herself become one with the music and let Loche glide, spin, and dip her until she was out of breath.

The couples around them gave them a wide berth, many halting their own dancing to watch, but she didn't care as the music ran through her veins. Her lips lifted into a real smile as Loche lifted her, spinning around in a circle, her silky skirts flying around them.

As he set her down, the music shifted again, an alluring melody seeping through the room.

He didn't hesitate as he pulled her close, guiding her arms to wrap around his neck and securing his own around her waist.

Loche's eyes glittered when she lifted hers, and a current ran over her skin when his thumb gently caressed the exposed skin on her back. She really should tear her eyes away, but when his darkened and he pulled her impossibly closer, until his heart hammered against hers, she let her hands weave into his dusky hair.

Loche shifted her away from the center, every deliberate movement of his hard body sending a tremor down her spine and the little space between them crackling with electricity.

His hands continued to roam over her back, flooding her veins with warmth, until they reached a dimly lit corner, where he positioned her out of sight from the rest of the people.

As they swayed from side to side, his eyes burned into hers until it felt like every nerve inside her was on fire.

When a glass clattered behind him, Lessia jerked, and she instinctively went to take a step back.

Her eyes widened as Loche stepped with her, his hands still caressing her back, eyes locked on hers.

What was she doing?

Lessia's heart nearly stopped when Loche leaned in, so close their breaths mingled.

A smile spread across his face, but surprise filled his eyes when he whispered, almost as if to himself, "You want me."

A blush threatened to creep up her neck, and she stuttered, "Wha— No, I don't."

His eyes flitted between hers, his smile faltering. "Tell that to your eyes."

She averted them, becoming acutely aware of how every inch of her body aligned with his.

When she took a step back this time, he let her.

Cautiously lifting her gaze, she found his face steeled, his features once again etched with hardness.

"You should stay away from me, Lessia."

With that, Loche bowed and spun on his heel, leaving her feeling more confused than ever.

"Do you know what you're doing there?" Merrick sidled up beside her, and she quickly closed her gaping mouth.

Lessia drew a breath, trying to calm her racing heart. "Dancing?"

"That wasn't just dancing." Merrick rubbed his neck.

She glared at him. "I am just trying to gain his trust."

"Don't forget I can smell you, Lessia. And I know very well what that scent is." Merrick's teeth snapped together before he started off in the direction where Loche had vanished.

Feeling as if her face might melt right off, she followed the Fae out of the room.

She had been attracted to him.

But it was only because of the dancing—because she'd felt free—had fun.

She argued with herself for hours, but even the cracked window in her room didn't help the fire that continued to lick her skin as she thought of the dancing.

Of Loche.

CHAPTER
FORTY

Lessia's legs ached as she walked up the stairs from the training room, where Merrick had once again made her feel like a fumbling child.

Gripping the railing when her tired legs wouldn't obey, she cursed Merrick and his stupid belief that she needed to learn the hard way, otherwise, she wouldn't learn quickly enough.

When he'd woken her at dawn, she'd glared at him and asked what was so urgent. They weren't to return to the cabin, and Craven hadn't bothered her since they'd been back. As he enjoyed doing, Merrick only barked at her, "Listen to my stupid orders," and once they'd gotten down to the musty cellar, he proceeded to slam her into the floor what felt like a thousand times.

But by the end, she'd been able to avoid him for a whole ten seconds, and when she grinned from where she lay on the ground, she swore he turned away to hide his own smile.

A soft laugh bubbled out of her.

She'd made the Death Whisperer smile.

"What's so funny?" Merrick placed a hand on her back, pushing her upward from where she'd taken a break.

"Nothing," she mumbled, too tired to deal with the grumpiness that would follow if she told him.

When she slowed once more, Merrick snapped at her, asking if she needed to be carried again. That gave her the final energy to ascend the stairs, and when she reached the ground floor, a familiar laugh floated toward her.

Rushing her steps, Lessia walked toward it, a smile breaking out across her face when she caught Amalise's blue gaze. She leaned against the wall beside the entrance, twining her blonde hair and flirting with one of the guards. When Ardow's sullen face popped up behind Amalise, Lessia started running, the tiredness long forgotten.

"What are you doing here?"

Lessia dragged them to her, ignoring the tremors running through her arms as she wrapped them around her friends.

Amalise pulled back, grinning at her. "I told you; I have a very good friend here."

She winked at the guard, wiggling her fingers as he walked out to his post outside, his face reddening.

"And here I thought it was me you were coming to see." Lessia mock-frowned at her.

"A welcome addition." Amalise laughed.

"Well, I, for one, am here to see you, Lia." Ardow dragged her into his arms again, and she drew a deep breath of his familiar smell. "You look thin, but I was worried you'd look worse."

She playfully punched his arm. "What a compliment. Thanks, Ard."

Rolling his eyes, he glanced behind her.

Lessia stiffened but then turned to introduce them to Merrick. Ardow had already met him, of course, and not under the best circumstances, but hopefully, he'd play nice if she explained they'd come to a strange truce.

But when she turned around, Merrick was nowhere to be seen.

Instead, Loche and Zaddock walked down the stairs, and her heart began beating faster when her eyes collided with his gray ones.

She spun back to her friends, cursing when Amalise's brows shot up.

"Why are you so flushed, Lia?" Her friend threw a look over her shoulder. "Is it because of the delicious regent that is heading straight for us? Or perhaps his handsome friend?"

Lessia flashed her teeth at her. "I am not flushed. I just came from training—I am hot."

Elbowing Ardow, Amalise giggled. "She's hot for something, that's for sure."

"Amalise, Ardow, I believe we haven't had the chance to meet."

Clenching her teeth, Lessia turned around, plastering a smile on her face as Loche and Zaddock joined them, praying he hadn't picked up on Amalise's insinuations.

Ardow offered Loche and Zaddock a nod. "Regent. Zaddock, good to see you again."

Waving to the two men, Amalise gave them a blinding smile, flicking her blonde hair over her shoulder and suggestively licking her lips.

Lessia felt like stomping on her foot, but while Loche looked bored, Zaddock couldn't seem to take his eyes off her friend.

It was quiet for a beat, then Lessia cleared her throat. "So, these are my friends. I believe we're allowed to socialize during our free time?"

She had no idea why Loche lingered, especially after his warning to stay away from him yesterday.

Zaddock made more sense—he seemed transfixed by Amalise, his eyes trailing her hand as she brushed some hair off her neck.

When she spoke, Loche shifted his gaze to hers, and the intensity of it jolted through her. Lessia stepped closer to Ardow and Amalise to keep herself grounded.

A voice interrupted the tense silence. "Why are you looking at her like that?"

Everyone's faces snapped to Amalise as she glared at Loche with crystal eyes narrowed.

His infuriating smirk played on his lips. "Like what?"

Amalise waved her hand Lessia's way. "Like you either want to eat her or kill her."

Ardow coughed beside her, and she did stomp on his foot when laughter broke through the fake cough. A shocked laugh escaped Zaddock as well, and he took a step toward Amalise, who gracefully slipped away from him when she caught the look of awe in his eyes.

Lessia eyed him regretfully.

He'd ruined any chance between them.

Amalise didn't spend time with men who showed any care for her other than for her body.

"She does look tasty. But I neither want to eat nor kill her. I just want to learn all her secrets." Loche grinned at Lessia when she looked his way, then dragged a mesmerized Zaddock out of the castle with him.

Staring after him, Lessia wanted to stomp on his foot as well.

Or perhaps punch him in the face the way Merrick was teaching her.

He must have done what he did yesterday to get under her skin—to try to figure her out.

The happiness she'd felt seeing Ardow and Amalise faded into something she hadn't felt for a long time.

Disappointment.

"Well, that was fun. Are you going to show us around?" Amalise dragged her toward the staircase as if she knew the way.

Shaking off the unwelcome feeling, Lessia smiled at her friends, leaning into Ardow when he wrapped an arm around her shoulders.

They spent the rest of the day in her room, trying to pry information from Ardow about his secret lover, and Lessia retelling what she'd experienced during the election so far, leaving out most of the debate and what had happened with Craven.

Her friends couldn't do anything about it, anyway, and she didn't want them to have to worry more.

By the time she waved goodbye, the disappointment she'd felt earlier had been replaced with joy and a sense of home.

CHAPTER FORTY-ONE

After eating a quick dinner in her room—alone, since Merrick hadn't returned from wherever he'd taken off to—Lessia walked around the castle searching for the rumored library hidden within its towers.

She'd promised herself she'd learn more about Ellow's politics, and where better to start than the history books?

Of course, she knew the gist of everything that happened during and since the war, but she'd never truly applied herself to understanding the shift in Ellow's dynamics that happened because of the war and its aftermath.

After taking the wrong spiral staircase—twice—she finally found a guard who showed her up to the empty library.

Stepping over the threshold, she glanced around in wonder at the seven levels of the curved tower, each lined with thousands of books. Beautifully carved handrails adorned the stairs up to each level, each one telling its own story of the different creatures living in realms outside Havlands.

She trailed her finger over one with sea wyverns and

water serpents, wondering if the creatures still swam the waters beyond the horizon like in the children's stories her mother had told her or if they'd disappeared, as many of the other magical creatures had centuries ago.

After too many wars between the Fae, shifters, and humans, either against each other or between their own races, all other creatures had left, not wishing to be caught up in the power struggles.

Shaking her head, she went to the third floor, where a wooden sign indicated the history books were kept.

While the shifters were long gone, humans and Fae seemed to have learned little, still engaging in spying and mistrust.

A large table stood in the middle of the half-moon room, six comfortable chairs set around it, and she cautiously placed the lantern she'd carried down on top of it. Making sure the glass was secured—so she didn't risk burning down the entire place—she walked along the shelves, picking up a book here and there.

When she couldn't carry more, Lessia brought them back to the table, sorted them in the order she wanted to read them, and got comfortable.

The first book outlined how the Fae had chosen Vastala as their home, the humans Ellow, and the shifters Korina.

The Fae had wanted the island closest to the next realm, where another lineage of Fae lived—where they'd migrated from.

The humans had wanted the land with the most space, and the thousands of islands that made up Ellow suited them.

Already outcasts back then, the shifters were content with Korina, the most secluded island, with cliffs as high as the clouds skirting the whole island.

The book didn't explain how the shifters traveled in and

out of their island, but since they could change their human form to anyone they wanted, animal and human and Fae alike, Lessia guessed they'd shifted into something with wings and flown in.

The next book she picked up depicted the war, how the shifter ruler convinced the human royals that the Fae were plotting to take over their lands—that their population had outgrown Vastala and wanted to claim all Havlands for themselves.

The humans sent out covert ships to take down Fae ones, with the goal of destroying their entire fleet before they could take over Ellow.

The Fae didn't respond kindly.

King Rioner's father sent out his water wielders to drown hundreds of human ships as revenge.

The human king retaliated by bringing over his entire army to Vastala, targeting innocent families, children, and whoever they came across.

That prompted King Rioner's father to send out every offensive magic wielder, the fire wielders spearing the operation and burning down most of the fields, forests, and towns in Ellow. Only Asker remained relatively unharmed because most of the fleet and guards were brought back to protect the royal family and the nobles who left their people and islands to fend for themselves.

Thousands upon thousands perished, and in the end, even King Rioner's father was captured and brutally murdered.

It wasn't until a lowly fisherman overheard the shifter ruler urging the human king to take out all Vastala and approached King Rioner, who'd just inherited the throne, that humans and Fae realized they'd been misled.

The shifter ruler had wanted all Havlands for himself and

his people, and he was patiently waiting for the humans and Fae to destroy each other before he made his move.

Instead, they joined forces, hunting down every single shifter and killing them until no more remained in Havlands.

More humans and Fae died, and the book depicted how thousands of bodies floated across the Eiatis Sea, staining its crystal surface crimson.

There had been so few survivors to rebuild the lands that humans and Fae had no choice but to collaborate—share the resources of their lands—to persist.

"That's a lot of books."

Lessia looked up to find Loche leaning his hands on one of the chairs opposite her.

She'd been so engrossed in reading she hadn't even heard him approach.

Closing the book, she eyed him. "What are you doing here?"

Loche dragged out the wooden chair and sat down, resting his elbows on the table and leaning his head in his hands as he eyed her right back. "I am here a lot. I find reading soothing after a long day. I tend to prefer the fictional works, though. Those look quite boring." He waved toward the thick leather-bound history books before her.

Lessia narrowed her eyes. "Seriously, Loche. I don't have time for your games. I know what you're trying to do."

Tongue darting out to wet his lips, Loche leaned forward. "And what am I trying to do?"

She refused to let her eyes follow his tongue as it slid over his exposed teeth, clenching her hands into fists by her side. "You're trying to seduce me into *telling you all my secrets.*"

Lessia wasn't sure what she had expected, but Loche breaking out in a loud, real laugh wasn't it.

His entire face lit up, eyes sparking like gray diamonds,

and his curved mouth made him look even more handsome than he usually did.

Scowling, she patiently waited for him to catch his breath, refusing to let her own lips curl when he gulped for air.

When he finally calmed, she glared at him. "What's so funny?"

Loche shook his head, the smile still brightening his dark features. "Zaddock said the same thing about you."

A frown formed between her brows. "That I was seducing *you*?"

Loche winked at her. "Your reputation precedes you, darling. But don't worry, I set him straight. I am confident it's one of the masks you wear, especially after your friend's little show for Zaddock. I can't wait to learn what you're hiding behind it."

Swallowing, she shot him an icy stare. "And what makes you so confident you're right?"

He lazily leaned back in his chair. "You're too innocent. You blush just at the mention of something between us. I haven't seen you approach a single man, not even that guard of yours that all the women in council were fanning over—even with his Fae heritage."

Loche's eyes trailed over her face as he nodded to himself. "You're too caring to be taking every man in Ellow who glances your way to bed. A woman like you wants to be loved, deeply and without constraint, by someone who knows the true you and adores you all the same."

Heart racing, she forced herself to draw a breath and raise an unbothered brow. "I am not innocent, Loche. And I don't want or need love."

"Your mask is slipping, little liar. You may have done bad things, but you're not a bad person. I know how to read people, and while you're still hiding something from me, I know you're good. And you crave love more than anything, I think."

Heart pounding more rapidly than it should in this stupid library, Lessia made to leave but stilled when Loche raised his hands.

"Don't let me stop you from your research." He picked a book from the pile. "I'll be here reading, but I won't bother you anymore. The castle isn't safe, if you haven't heard."

Shaking her head, she waited for him to say something else, but Loche only made himself comfortable in the chair and glued his eyes to the book. Lessia stared at him, but when he remained quiet, she picked up the book she'd started on and began reading again.

They stayed like that for the next few hours until Lessia rubbed her blurry eyes, a yawn shattering the quiet rustling of pages.

Loche immediately shot up to help her put the books back in place and, without a word, followed her back to her room.

CHAPTER FORTY-TWO

"Where did you disappear yesterday?" Lessia took the hand Merrick offered to get up from the training floor.

She'd done better today.

Perhaps gobbling down several plates of food after returning from the library had given her more strength.

Or she was learning something.

Merrick released his grip as soon as she was upright and turned his back to her. "I had some business to attend to."

With a scoff, she followed him up the stairs, grateful for the two lanterns he carried, as evening was already falling and not a sliver of the moon shone through the thick cloud bank surrounding the castle.

Merrick had been nowhere to be found when she woke, and as a snowstorm had raged since last evening, Lessia had spent the day holed up in her room. Mostly to avoid Loche and the other nominees, but also because she'd woken to dreams that hadn't plagued her sleep in many years.

Not nightmares.

No, she would have preferred to dream of King Rioner's dungeons instead of her family, her sister, and the warm home she'd grown up in. The devastation of waking up had nearly paralyzed her with guilt, so spending a day in bed trying to lock it down had been a relief.

When Merrick barged in, she'd been sitting with the balcony doors open, listening to the roaring storm and relishing the biting cold that kept her mind from wandering.

Lessia was grateful he hadn't questioned what she was doing. The Fae had only waved for her to follow him.

Trailing her eyes over his thick winter leathers, she wondered what other missions the king had him undertake in Ellow. She sighed as she nearly lost sight of him around a spiraling bend of the staircase and made her tired legs take two stairs at a time.

Perhaps she needed to figure out not only Loche's and the rest of the nominees' intentions.

But also Merrick's.

Lessia tapped his shoulder, or as close as she could come from the step below him. "Would you like to join me for dinner?"

Stiffening, he made to turn around but appeared to catch himself at the last minute and instead took the final step into the castle's entrance hall. "I have more business in town I need to see to."

"Is it for our friend?" she dared ask.

"It relates to him, yes." Merrick started toward the door but tensed again, halting his steps. "Stay in your room tonight. The storm is bad."

Frowning, she watched him stalk out of the castle while throwing on a thick dark cloak that had been hung to dry right inside the double doors.

When the door slammed shut behind him, she glanced

toward the dining room, where Craven's voice carried across the rest.

With a scowl, Lessia started walking over, trying to convince herself she could stand being around him for the few minutes it would take her to fill up on food. But when a server passed with a tray of something that smelled delicious, she stopped him, asking if he would bring her food into the library.

Offering her a shy smile, he promised to bring something from everything they served tonight, especially the desserts. When he winked at her, her face heated, and Lessia quickly thanked him and made her way to the library.

The server didn't disappoint.

Lessia had to move the books she'd spread out across the table to the chairs surrounding it when he put down more dishes than she could eat in two days.

Intoxicating smells filled the rounded tower, and she paused her reading—on how the islands in Ellow had rebuilt the crop fields that had been destroyed in the war—to eat as much as she could of the vegetable soup and bread, finishing with pieces of both chocolate and vanilla cake.

As she picked up the book again, her stomach nearly bursting, the words on the pages blurred. Not even finding out how they had managed to transport cattle across different islands to help fertilize the crops could keep her focused.

Yawning, Lessia put all the books back into their places and gathered the food, carefully placing the plates on the trays to bring them down.

"The servers will take care of that."

She whipped her head up to find Zaddock leaning with crossed arms against the railing of the staircase.

Blowing out a breath of relief to calm her racing heart, she offered him a weak smile. "I don't mind. The poor man carried it all the way up here; the least I could do is bring it down again."

Shaking his head, Zaddock said quietly, "I can see why he's intrigued by you."

"Who?"

A loaded silence followed, and Lessia rolled her eyes. "He's intrigued because I am not the cold, heartless Fae he expected?"

"No. Because you're up here reading about crops."

Her eyes widened. "How long have you—"

The smirk Zaddock offered her made her squash a snarl.

That smug grin must be a prerequisite to join Loche's terrifying group of men.

That and showing up without her noticing.

"Why are you here?" She bit her cheek not to growl at him.

A scowl replaced Zaddock's smirk. "To walk you to your room, since your guard was seen leaving the castle hours ago and it appears he hasn't returned yet."

Brows pulling, she picked up the trays. "Thank you, but I don't need you to walk me to my room. I am sure you have more important things to do."

His shoulders tensed. "Lessia, put those down. I've already asked a new server to pick them up, and Loche pays them handsomely for their work. It's not like the old days. They earn more here than in your taverns."

As if conjured, a server popped up behind him, wearing the customary stark white uniform and a wide smile on his face as he took the trays from her and whispered, "He is right, miss. Although I've heard good things about your taverns, as well."

They watched the server carry the trays down the stairs, and when his soft steps were silenced, her eyes shifted to

Zaddock again. “As I said, I am perfectly capable of getting to my room by myself.”

He glared at her. “It was an order, Lessia. Now, if you don’t want to get me in trouble, please come with me.”

Grinding her teeth, she followed his rushed gait down the stairs.

Zaddock’s speed prevented her from admiring the beautiful carvings on the railings; she had to hurry more than she liked with a full stomach to keep up with him.

Was Loche using Zaddock to keep an eye on her?

Or was this a new tactic to get her to spill all her secrets?

Her lips lifted into a smile.

Two could play that game.

“So, Zaddock. How long have you known Loche?” Lessia tilted her head when Zaddock’s eyes moved to hers.

“Since we both enlisted.” A smile softened Zaddock’s sapphire eyes. “I was never a great soldier, but Loche refused to leave me behind when he rose in the ranks.”

“So, more than a decade, then? You must be very close.”

Zaddock’s smile widened. “We are. I owe him everything.”

Nodding, Lessia made sure her smile remained. “So, what’s your role? I mean, I know you collect taxes and ensure we proprietors follow the law. But you don’t wear a mask like the rest of the men.”

A frown formed between Zaddock’s brows, but he still responded. “Everyone knows me already.”

“What do you—”

A clang of metal interrupted her, and her eyes flew wide when Zaddock unsheathed the sword at his side, his eyes snapping ahead.

Following his gaze, she froze.

Three men approached them, each of the three bearing

Stellia's symbol on his chest and holding a sword in his hands, his eyes fixed on her and Zaddock.

They hadn't yet reached the lower levels of the castle, where the sleeping quarters lay and where guards were stationed every few feet, and Lessia realized the thick stone walls would not carry either screams or the sounds of fighting.

Apprehension whispered over her skin, and as she grasped for the daggers she should have tucked into her waistband, she swore quietly.

She'd left them in her room when she joined Merrick in the training chamber.

Taking a step back, she hissed, "Do you have another one of those?"

Zaddock's eyes sliced to hers, his face grim. "No. Get behind me."

When a man lashed out, she followed his advice, her heart hammering against her ribs as Zaddock parried his blows.

She took another stumbling step backward when a man rounded them, his eyes locked on hers.

Shooting a glance at Zaddock, she realized he was too close for her to use her magic, so she backed up farther until cold stone pressed against her back.

The man slowly approached her, his sword glinting in the firelight from the lanterns lining the white stone walls around them.

Holding her breath, she waited for him to come into range so she could sweetly ask him to leave.

But a few steps away, he hesitated, his eyes sweeping across her features and snagging on her ears.

The man took a step back.

Chest heaving and forehead creasing, Lessia watched him

turn toward Zaddock instead, sneaking up on his unguarded back as he fought the other two men.

Her heart skipped a beat.

"Watch your back!" she screamed.

Zaddock had a second to spin around, but he caught the man who'd backed away from her by surprise, and with one blow to the chest, the man crumpled to the ground, the sound of his body hitting the hard stone echoing around them.

Zaddock didn't waste any time.

As quickly as he'd turned around, he was back fighting the other two, but they were skilled at wielding their swords, and soon they'd driven him into a corner.

Clenching and unclenching her fists, Lessia watched a strike hit true, and blood from Zaddock's arm began to pool on the floor beneath him.

When one of the men grinned and lifted his sword again, she didn't think; she just sprinted toward him and threw herself into him.

Lessia went down with the soldier, her head slamming into the ground with a crack, sending excruciating waves of pain through her body.

Shaking it to drive away the dizziness that fought to take over, she forced her eyes to fix on the man's and urgently pulled on her magic.

"You don't want to hurt me. Give me your sword, but make it look like I won it," she whispered when the familiar warmth of her magic sparked in her veins.

The man's eyes glazed over, and with a scuffle that almost had her vomit from the pain that shot through her head, his sword was in her right hand.

Making her way to her feet and pushing her magic back down, she pointed it to his heart.

Lessia didn't dare turn around as the scuffling behind

them went quiet, and she nearly flew into the air when a hand landed on her shoulder.

"Thank you, Lessia."

Zaddock's voice was low, and there was a hint of surprise in it. "You saved my life."

Arm shaking from holding on so tightly to the hilt, she turned to him. "Surprised yet again that I am not as cold-hearted as you believed?"

Zaddock offered her a sheepish grin. "I guess I deserved that one."

As she returned his smile, steps thudded in the stairway ahead, and they stiffened again, but it was the two guards who were usually stationed outside her room that came into view.

A gurgling sound had her shift her gaze back to the man at the same time as Zaddock yelled, "No!"

White foam formed around the attacker's mouth, his face paling so fast Lessia thought her eyes might be fooling her.

With a final wheezing rise of his chest, his eyes closed.

The sword in her hand clattered to the ground as she backed away, guilt and anger swirling inside her: she hadn't thought to ask him what Stellia was after.

Swearing loudly, Zaddock followed her, his arm wrapping around her back as he barked at the guards to take care of the bodies, then quickly guided her to her room.

Inside, she sank down on the chair she'd been sitting in all day and once again opened the doors to the chill night. Her head still pounded, stars flickering before her eyes, but her mind wouldn't let her rest.

These men hadn't just come after nominees today.

And why had the man let her be when he realized she was part-Fae?

CHAPTER
FORTY-THREE

Banging had her pry her eyes open, and she flexed her frozen fingers, realizing she'd fallen asleep in the chair.

Lessia groaned as the pain in her head pounded with each knock on the door, and she quickly shouted "Come in" to make it stop.

Merrick stalked across the threshold, still wearing the leathers he'd had on yesterday.

His posture was tenser than she'd ever seen before, and he seemed to glare at the now-clear sky when he slammed the balcony doors shut.

Shuffling to her feet, she took stiff steps toward the chair where she'd left her cloak and wrapped it around herself.

With chattering teeth, she glared at the Fae. "I don't think I can train today. I must have gotten a concussion last night. There was another attack while you were gone."

Merrick's canines reflected the pale winter sunlight when he hissed, "I told you not to leave your room. You agreed to follow my rules, Lessia."

"I only went to the library." The words came out clipped as she continued shivering.

He dragged his hands through his silvery hair, causing it to fall in tangled waves across his shoulders. "Did they hurt you?"

She shook her head even though he couldn't see it. "I might have slammed my own head against the floor when I jumped one of them. But you'd be proud of me. I used my whole body, as you taught me, and he went down immediately."

Merrick huffed something that could have been a laugh if she hadn't known him by now and turned toward the door again.

She eyed his back, debating with herself whether she should tell him what had happened before she tackled the man.

It didn't seem like anything that could harm Ellow if Merrick told the king, and regardless, if the king asked her, she'd have no choice but to share it.

"Merrick," she mumbled. "Something strange happened. The man I fought saw I was part-Fae when he was about to attack me, and it was as if he changed his mind. He... he backed away from me."

He spun around again; his gaze focused on her black boots. "Perhaps he was afraid you had magic?"

She chewed on her lip.

It hadn't been fear in the man's eyes when they widened as they recognized her pointed ears for what they were.

It was something else.

"I don't think so. It was almost as if he knew me."

"Of course he knows you. You're one of the nominees." Merrick adjusted the curved sword hanging by his hip. "Everyone in Ellow knows who you are by now."

She followed his fingers as they trailed over the rubies decorating the hilt. His sword was the sister to the dagger he'd given her, she realized.

"But why would he hesitate, then? It seems they've been going after nominees?"

"Maybe that's not what they're after. But we need to hurry up, Lessia. We're going to be late." Merrick whirled on his heel again and opened the door leading out into the hallway.

"I told you. I can't train today." Lessia rubbed her hands over her arms, casting a longing look at the bed.

She could do with another day in it, getting warm and rested.

Tapping the doorframe, Merrick spoke quietly. "If it were up to me, I'd let you stay here, but they're making you go through the next part of the qualification today."

Her stomach sank, and she clutched the folds of her cloak to her body as if it might protect her from whatever they'd put her through.

Swallowing, she took a step toward him. "What are they going to do?"

A muscle ticked in his jaw as he stepped aside to let her out. "They're going to make sure you're here for the right reasons and that you don't have anything to hide."

Fear rushed through her veins, the adrenaline from it driving away the lingering tiredness.

She had been tortured before; King Rioner's Fae guards didn't take well to finding out she'd killed one of their own, but they'd typically beat her too hard, too quickly, not realizing she wasn't as strong as a full Fae, allowing her to float into blissful oblivion sooner than they'd expected.

Exactly like Merrick had done when the king ordered him to show her what awaited if she failed.

But if she was to be questioned, and by humans at that, she had little doubt they'd do it in a way where she'd stay awake, feel every moment of pain.

As she walked with hesitant steps toward the stairs, Merrick's large hand closed around her wrist.

She glanced up at him, his face tilting over her shoulder as he whispered, "Don't be afraid, Lessia. They are not allowed to kill you, and while there will be pain, you are stronger than you think. Remember why you are doing this."

Her cheek brushed against his as she nodded, and her brows flew up when Merrick's hand wrapped around her own. He led her down into the cellars, taking a path different from the one to the training room.

When voices hummed between the polished stone walls and light flickered ahead from a burning fireplace, Merrick squeezed her hand, and it was as if some of his conviction flowed into her.

Squaring her shoulders and lifting her chin, she told herself she was strong enough for this.

She'd survived five years in a dark cellar, had survived moving to Ellow not knowing a soul. Had even survived what she'd done to her family and when she'd left for the streets of Vastala.

She could do this.

As they entered a large oval room with a huge marble fireplace and several lit chandeliers hanging from the low ceiling, Merrick had to bow his head not to hit the hanging lights as he walked over to join the other companions, taking up a spot next to Zaddock.

When she met his eyes briefly, Zaddock smiled at her before shifting them ahead to where Loche, Venko, and Craven stood huddled together with Frayson.

Loche's eyes flew to hers, and a current ran over her skin when a half smile overtook his face.

Flicking his eyes between her and Zaddock, he inclined his head.

Confused, she bowed her own before sidling up beside him, facing Frayson and trying to ignore the electricity that crackled between them when Loche's hand brushed hers.

She shifted an inch away from him, blowing out a deep breath as Frayson began to speak.

"I know this isn't the best timing." He threw Lessia an apologetic look. "I heard you were injured yesterday, Lessia. But we have only two weeks until the commoners' debates, and you will need time to recover. We have brought in more guards after the attack yesterday to ensure it won't be repeated. There will not be a single room in the castle unguarded while you rest up."

Lessia cast a quick glance at Venko, whose face paled at Frayson's words, and then at Craven, who stared straight ahead, only the vein throbbing in his neck betraying his fear.

Loche moved closer to her again, and when she stole a glance at him, his steely gaze slammed into hers.

"How badly are you hurt?" he whispered while Craven demanded more details on what happened last night.

"I'm fine." She shrugged. "I just overdid it a bit when I tried to fight one of them."

The need to avert her gaze when his hardened nearly overwhelmed her.

Icy rage burned in his eyes as they swept over her body, then back to her face, and his hand brushed hers again when his clenched into fists.

"If he hadn't already taken care of it himself, be sure he would not have lived to draw another breath once I got to him."

Frayson cleared his throat. "Loche, are you finished?"

Loche continued to stare into her eyes as he nodded and waved for Frayson to go on.

Finally tearing her eyes away, she tried to focus on Frayson, not on the waves of anger that rolled off the most confusing man she'd ever met.

"This year, we'll do this part a bit differently, I'm afraid. As I hope you've been informed, you will be interrogated today, and the means will be unpleasant. Our law dictates that we need to ensure our regent wants to rule for the right reasons, and this is part of that process. But while we usually have our guards do the interrogation, it's been decided this year that your companions will do it."

Gasps reverberated between the walls, and Craven's eyes widened as they moved to the enormous man who was his companion.

Venko's eyes fell to the floor, and Lessia eyed the man next to Zaddock, whose features twisted with unease.

She vaguely recognized him as one of Venko's closest men; he'd been in their office before. Venko must have been directed to bring someone in, as he hadn't had a companion before, and it was clear he hadn't been given the reason why.

Zaddock's and Merrick's faces remained stoic, and Lessia drew a trembling breath as she studied the Fae's hard features.

He knew exactly what the worst way of torturing her would be.

"I know this isn't what most of you expected. But in war, friend turns on friend, and you need to understand the implications of not just the physical pain but the emotional one as well."

Frayson met each set of eyes before he continued. "You will be going one by one, and no one is allowed to leave until the last of you has been interrogated. We have healers here that will tend those of you that go first, and one will stay with you during the night should you wish."

His kind eyes shifted back to Lessia. "I'm afraid to say it's ladies first."

CHAPTER
FORTY-FOUR

Merrick stalked forward, and Lessia took a shaking step as well.

Frayson started toward a dark hallway where no light betrayed what lay at the end, but as she was about to follow him, Merrick by her side, a hand wrapped around her arm.

When Lessia turned her head over her shoulder, Loche stared at her with a wrinkle between his dark brows, eyes darting between hers.

"What is it?" she asked quietly, acutely aware the whole room watched them.

Loche's nostrils flared, but when he opened his mouth, no sound came out.

Releasing her, he stepped to the side and approached a wary-looking Zaddock.

Brows pulling, she cast a final look his way, but Loche's eyes remained on the ground, his shoulders tense and hands behind his back, so with a shrug, she followed Frayson and Merrick into the darkness.

Merrick grabbed a lantern off the wall, and he slowed his stride until she reached him a few steps into the hallway.

Casting him a grateful look, she kept Frayson's slow pace until only their soft breaths and the sound of water dripping bounced off the curved walls.

After a while, the hallway opened to a murky chamber without windows, where a large wooden chair with chains wrapped around the arms and legs was placed in the middle. To her side, a large, corroded tub stood, and the smell of stale water hit her like a wave.

Guards lined the white walls, standing almost shoulder to shoulder, and large lanterns had been placed on either side of the opening.

Still, an ember of gratitude settled within her chest when Merrick placed the one he'd brought right by the chair, as little light reached the area.

Frayson cleared his throat, eyeing them both but avoiding Lessia's gaze. "Please know I take no pleasure in what comes next. We will ask you a number of questions, Lessia. They may not be easy ones, so forgive us for any pain they might bring. As we would in a normal interrogation, we will ask Merrick to give you..." Frayson winced. "To give you a little encouragement to tell us the truth."

Two guards stepped forward, each taking a place on one side of the chair, and tingles of unease shot down Lessia's spine when they fixed their eyes on her face.

With a nod, Frayson continued. "These men are trained in detecting lies, the best in our armies. They've interrogated spies for years and will be the ones asking you questions. Please do not try to lie, Lessia. We see it every year, and it will make this more uncomfortable for everyone."

She tried hard not to grimace.

Frayson meant well.

But the only one who would be uncomfortable soon was her.

Merrick wasn't a stranger to torture; he'd done it before, and he'd do it again.

Based on the gilded shield-and-sword symbols on their black jackets, signifying high rank, the soldiers in the room must all have received similar training.

Straightening her spine, she offered Frayson a forced smile. "Shall we get on with it?"

Best to have it over with.

The anticipation of pain was almost equally torturous as receiving it.

Frayson waved toward the chair. "Merrick, please help secure her."

She made her way over to it and sat down on the solid wood, keeping her face a mask of neutrality as Merrick pulled the clasps of the icy chains into place: one wrapped across her chest, one around each of her wrists, and two around her ankles, to ensure she could barely move an inch.

Before he stepped back, he checked the chain by her chest again and breathed, "I will do my best to make this as painless as possible. Remember that you're stronger than you think."

She eyed him as he backed up.

At least they weren't at risk of being discovered because he wouldn't meet her eyes. Everyone here believed she'd brought him as a trusted companion, and as such, it wasn't strange that he shouldn't want to look at her as he inflicted her pain.

As long as she told the truth as much as possible and lied convincingly when she had to, they would hopefully both get out of this in one piece.

Even if hers might be a bit more broken.

The two soldiers didn't bother introducing themselves as they took their places on either side of Merrick. Both men wore dark hoods to veil their faces—probably to instill more fear—and while neither was as tall as Merrick, they were both massive.

Probably chosen for this very purpose, because they were intimidating enough, even without the theatrics.

The man on Merrick's left pointed to her. "Break her finger."

Merrick hesitated.

And Lessia could have kissed him for it.

When he slowly took the step needed to reach her, she lifted her chin, and the smile that spread across her face wasn't forced.

Somehow, she and Merrick had formed a strange kind of truce.

Perhaps even the beginning of a friendship.

And while it wasn't necessary, having him on her side might aid in the little progress she'd made in finding information for the king.

Unless the truce remained only while the king was back in Vastala.

She drew a deep breath when his hands gently wrapped around hers.

"I'm sorry," he whispered.

The crack of her finger bending backward until it snapped echoed through the room.

Lessia hissed through clamped teeth at the pulsating pain, staring straight ahead.

Forcing her mind to think about her friends and the children she needed to protect kept her breathing.

In and out.

In and out.

"Good."

She raised her eyes as the man who'd commanded Merrick spoke again.

Merrick remained by her side, his shoulders hunching as he stared at her hand, where the middle finger stood at an odd angle.

"Elessia Gyldenberg, we do not think you've joined this election purely for selfless reasons. Why are you truly here?"

She fixed her eyes on the hooded man. "I am here because I want to make Ellow a better place for everyone."

"Punch her."

A low growl escaped Merrick as he lifted his fist, but Lessia didn't tense because she braced for impact. She tensed because hushed whispers reached her ears when Merrick's magic roiled in anger, oily vibrations rolling off his large body.

"Do it *now*," the man ordered.

Merrick's breathing became labored, and the whispers grew louder.

"I said now!"

"Merrick." Lessia tried to reach out for him, but she couldn't move her arms enough, the rattling chains restricting any movement.

Shifting so she could look up at him, she tried to make her voice soothing. "Merrick, it's all right. You know why I am here; you know I want this."

Another growl rumbled in his heaving chest.

"Merrick. Please," she whispered as fear—not only of the guards and Frayson realizing who was amongst them but of what would happen if she was eliminated—danced over her skin.

"Fuck," he snarled and finally reined in the magic that, judging from a glance behind him, it didn't seem the others had noticed.

Then her head flew to the side, a spark of pain radiating through her cheek, down her neck.

Blinking, she tried to focus her eyes on the Fae, clenching her jaw as the dizziness from last night returned, only slivers of silver dancing before her eyes in the dark cellar.

"Elessia Gyldenberg, how did you get to Ellow? We have no records of your parents nor of your ancestry."

She shook her head, trying to get her eyes to focus on the man approaching her and Merrick.

"Punch her again."

She didn't have time to close her eyes before her head snapped to the other side, her vision going entirely black for a moment.

"M—" Her voice cracked when a whimper escaped at the white-hot pain exploding in her head.

Bending her head forward, she forced out the words. "My mother was from Ellow."

"We don't believe you. Punch her again."

Her head slammed into her shoulder this time, bile rising in her throat as stars continued to blaze before her eyes.

Lessia's panting was in sync with Merrick's, the barely controlled rage vibrating around him the only thing keeping her conscious.

"It's all right," she croaked when his hand squeezed hers. "I know... I know what you're doing."

He tried to aim his blows not to hit the same spot, to cause as little damage as possible, and he was definitely not using his full strength, barely that of a human man.

If he'd gone full Fae on her, the first blow would have already knocked her out.

"What was your mother's name?" the man behind him screamed.

She wasn't prepared for the emotional onslaught of pain,

the chains clinking when her body slumped forward, trying to cave in on itself at the pain in her heart.

"You will look at us when we speak to you! Punch her stomach this time."

Lessia was almost relieved when the pain from the blow in her gut made her lose her breath, forcing her mind to block out her mother's golden-brown hair and kind blue eyes.

"Her name!"

"Miryn." Lessia squeezed her eyes shut as she spoke her mother's name for the first time in years, but she felt Merrick tense further beside her.

"Bring her to the water."

Lessia's eyes flew open as footsteps joined the buzzing in her ears, and guards left their posts by the wall to lift the chair she sat upon. She breathed heavily through her teeth when the movement as the men lifted the chair sent another wave of pain washing over her.

Merrick growled as the guards set her down and loosened the chains she was bound in.

Glancing from his blanched knuckles to the muddy water sloshing in the tub, she swallowed.

"What are you waiting for? She looks a little dry to me."

The chair shook as Merrick's wild scent filled the space, and she couldn't help but let a small whimper escape before he pushed her face underwater.

She hadn't had time to draw a breath, and she futilely tried to push back at the large hands gripping her shoulders. Bubbles boiled in the water when her eyes opened in panic, and she cried out when memories flooded her mind, like the water now filling her lungs.

"You stupid halfling bitch!" The Fae ripped a chunk of hair out of her scalp as he pulled her face out of the bucket. "Did you think you'd get away with killing him?"

Before she had time to gasp for air, his fist slammed into the side of her head, and she must have lost consciousness because when she woke, she was strapped to the standing contraption this particular guard favored.

"Not so cocky now, are you?" he taunted as he dragged a table with tools across the floor.

He did it slowly, letting the metal legs scrape across the stone floor of her cell.

"Please," she begged. "Just kill me!"

She wanted to die.

There was nothing left inside her that wanted to fight anymore.

He let out a low laugh, and the sound convulsed through her body, making her bones shake.

And when he pulled up a blindfold, her mouth opened, and she screamed, and screamed, and screamed.

Cold air struck her face, and a gentle hand tilted her face up when it lolled down to her chest.

"Breathe. Please, breathe," Merrick whispered as she coughed up the dirty water.

"Back away from her!" someone yelled.

She couldn't breathe.

Couldn't see.

Flashes of King Rioner's cellar mixed with flickers of a dimly lit Fae, and she flinched when the Fae crouched down before her.

"I said get away from her!"

"Fuck you," Merrick snarled as one of his hands cupped her chin, the other squeezing her shoulder.

"Lessia. You're not there. You will never go back there. I won't allow it," Merrick urged.

Pinching her eyes closed, she focused on his deep voice as he repeated, "You will never go back there."

Her erratic heart slowed.

"You will never go back there."

Air started traveling down her lungs.

"You will never go back there."

She finally drew a full, shaking breath.

"She will be eliminated if you don't comply, Merrick."

Frayson's voice sounded as if from far away.

As if only Merrick's voice existed in this version of her world.

"Lessia, if you want to bow out, you only have to nod."

A sharp pain snaking its way up her arm jarred her out of the daze.

"Merrick," she pleaded.

"I know." He tucked her wet hair behind her ears before he straightened. "She will continue, but no more water."

Lifting her dripping face, she took in the room.

Despair lined Frayson's wrinkled face as he ordered the guards to bring her back into the middle of the room.

The guards who once again lifted her chair showed no emotion, though.

Not one of them met her eyes as they dragged her chair back into place.

The two hooded men gestured for Merrick to take his place before her again.

He shook where he stood, muscles beneath his clothing locking and unlocking, and the guards took a step back from their spots beside him.

The one to her left brushed his hand over the hilt of his sword. "Are you conspiring with the Fae to take over Ellow?"

Her mouth fell open as she stared at the faceless men.

Merrick snarled softly as he also turned his head toward them.

"Answer me!"

Lessia started shaking her head, but her blood chilled when the guard ordered, "Break her ribs."

"Now!"

She blew out a choked breath.

Then she moved her arms so the snarling Merrick would have better access.

His hair hung in his face when he lifted his fist, and his canines drew blood from biting into his lip.

"It's all right," she whispered.

She couldn't hold back a scream when a loud crack confirmed Merrick hit true.

Losing control over her body, she slumped down as much as the chains would allow, pain pulsating through every limb, and every breath she drew feeling as if a knife cut through her.

"Again!"

With a roar, Merrick spun around. "Give her time to breathe! You're supposed to be doing this to ask questions, not for the enjoyment of hurting her!"

Drawing shallow breaths, Lessia gasped, "I am not conspiring to take over Ellow."

"Why not? You're half-Fae. Punch her again."

"Perhaps we ought to give her a little more time," Frayson cautioned.

"No! Do it now!"

She braced herself as much as she could, but Merrick didn't approach her.

He stalked to tower over the two men. "What is wrong with you? One more, and she'll be out. Look at her!"

"If you don't do it, we will."

Merrick leaned down to glare into the man's face, and Lessia was almost relieved he couldn't look into her eyes when the man immediately cowered, stumbling back several steps.

But the other guard slipped around him.

He sprinted toward her with a large wooden stick in his hand, and before she realized what was happening, the man slammed it into her chest.

Lessia let out another scream as more ribs cracked.

Her vision blurred, shadows creeping in.

The last thing she heard was a man's groan before everything went dark.

CHAPTER
FORTY-FIVE

"I am not going next. I don't care if you eliminate me. You bastards broke her! This did not happen to anyone last time. What was it, a way for the guards to get back at the Fae?"

Lessia pried her eyes open, meeting Loche's feral ones where he towered over one of the guards that had stood along the walls in the cellar room.

Loche's eyes widened when they found hers, and he pushed the guard out of the way to stalk over to her, ignoring him as the guard argued that it was his turn.

"Stay back. I will not warn you again, regent."

Shifting her gaze up, she realized Merrick's furious face was inches from hers and that the comfortable place she rested was in his arms.

Blinking hard to clear her blurry vision, she glanced around.

A healer sat crouched down beside her.

Merrick sat against the wall, and her body lay atop his lap.

"I don't take orders from you, Merrick. You're the one

who did this!" Loche's eyes were black as he dropped down on the other side of the healer and cupped her chin with his hand.

Her eyes followed his fingers as they shifted a strand of wet hair away from her face, then traced her aching jaw, a shiver running through her when his finger trembled.

A warning growl vibrated in Merrick's chest, and Lessia winced when it shifted her body and jolts of pain shot from her ribs.

"You men need to stop this right now. She is hurting, and you are making it worse," the healer ordered.

"It is your turn, regent. You must come at once, or you will forfeit your participation." The guard Loche had screamed at eyed them cautiously.

Ignoring both of them, Loche leaned in farther, eyeing her surely bruised face, then trailing his eyes down her body, his hard features twisting.

But when his eyes met hers again, only concern flared in them.

Lessia cleared her throat. "I'll live, Loche. You need to go."

He really did.

Because if he wasn't elected, she feared Craven might be the one to rule Ellow.

And there would not be a place for her or her friends here then.

He stared at her with those all-too-knowing eyes. "I won't let them get away with this, Lessia."

When she nodded, he touched her cheek, then rose and walked into the hallway, not responding to either the guard or Zaddock as they tried to speak to him.

"How are you feeling?" Guilt lined every word of Merrick's question.

She forced a smile, even if he wouldn't see it. "I'm fine. A few broken ribs and fingers aren't the worst things that have happened to me."

"You're going to be fine, dear. But you need to rest." The healer glared at the guards in the room. "She is not to stay here. I demand she is to be taken to her chambers."

The snarl that left Merrick when a guard dared to argue that all nominees were to wait until the last one was finished made a shiver skitter down her neck.

When the guard backed away, Merrick carefully rose, keeping her steady in his arms as he spun around and headed upstairs.

His power thrummed through him and over her body with each step away from the cellars, anger, guilt, or perhaps both keeping his magic close to the surface.

"Perhaps I needn't ever walk again. You're becoming quite good at carrying me. What is it? The third time?" she tried to joke when low growls continued to stir in his chest.

Merrick didn't respond.

He only scaled the stairs, taking three or four steps at a time.

His arms remained steady, though, his grip on her never wavering, and even when he kicked the door to her room open while snarling at a guard to bring food and wine immediately, he didn't hurt her further.

More gently than she could ever imagine the Death Whisperer moving, he set her down on the bed, checking on the bandages the healer had wrapped over her black tunic—another reason she was grateful he was there—and lit every lantern in her room, then went to the fireplace.

Roughly shifting some of the firewood, he lit the fire faster than she'd ever seen anyone do, and her eyes widened as the hot flames licked the sooty stone.

"It was you," she whispered.

Merrick froze, crouched down by the white fireplace.

"You lit the fire in the cabin."

"You don't seem to do so well in the dark," he muttered as he rose to walk back and forth in the room, dragging his hands through his hair.

"Thank you," she whispered.

While she had no idea why he'd done it, why he'd been looking out for her already then, before they'd formed whatever kind of friendship this was, she was grateful.

She wouldn't have survived those weeks in the woods without it.

"Why are you thanking me? I hurt you today, and it's not the first time, nor is it likely the last. You should despise me. Or at least be frightened of me." Merrick slumped down on the chair before the balcony door, covering his face with his hands.

"You don't scare me, Merrick. At least not anymore." She pressed on a sore spot on her cheek. "I know you tried not to hurt me today. You could have done much worse. And you've helped me as well. I wouldn't be here if it wasn't for you."

"Why are you defending me!" Merrick raised his voice, and she jerked, holding back a groan when pain spiked from her ribs.

"I am evil, Lessia. I'm the Death Whisperer, for gods' sake." He lifted his head and gestured to her chest. "I did that!"

"Merrick..."

Lessia's brows rose when he hid his face in his hands again, his shoulders slumping.

She couldn't even comprehend being frightened of this Fae anymore.

He was nothing like the rumors.

Nothing like what he had been the times they'd interacted before the election.

When he began shaking his head, she cleared her throat. "You do not need to feel guilty. I am a bad person. I have done horrible, horrible things. This, and whatever else the king has planned for me... I deserve it. I deserve every single moment of pain life brings me."

His hands muffled his voice when he responded, "You are *good*, Lessia. Remember that I have watched you for almost five years. You treat every person you meet with kindness and respect. You rarely use the gift you've been given by the gods, even though it could make your life so much easier, and even me—even the Death Whisperer—you treat with compassion. What could you have done that's so bad?"

"I killed my sister." She sucked in a sharp breath as the words left her mouth.

She hadn't meant to blurt them out, but she couldn't stand seeing the guilt lining his shoulders.

Not when every broken bone, every bruise she was dealt was deserved.

A dry sob escaped her when Frelina's beautiful face slammed into her mind, the memory of what she'd done to her flashing before her eyes.

When Merrick remained quiet, she forced herself to continue. "My *gift,* as you call it. It's no gift. It's a curse. Like everyone else who's half-Fae or more, I couldn't wait for my twelfth birthday to see what gift might manifest. A few months after my birthday, nothing special had happened, and I was growing surlier by the day. Frelina, my sister, was my constant shadow, like I guess most younger siblings are. She annoyed me to no end, and this particular day, I wanted to ride alone in the woods by our home, and she kept following me. I got angry and..."

She drew a shaky breath, her voice barely a whisper as she continued. "I... I told her to jump off a roof or something, and her eyes glazed over. I didn't think much of it then, but when I returned that evening, my parents were distraught. She'd jumped off the roof of our house."

"Lessia..." Merrick shifted toward her.

"I couldn't bear the look on their faces when they realized it was my fault. I was terrified, and I didn't know what to do. So, I told them to forget about me, forget I'd ever been their daughter. And then I left for Vastala. I suppressed my magic for years. Until that night..."

A humorless laugh escaped her. "I used it once—one time—in Vastala to kill a guard that kept attacking the female half-Fae in the streets, and then I was thrown into King Rioner's cellars. I guess it serves me right."

Her father had worked so hard to keep her, Frelina, and her mother safe. Keep them all hidden from King Rioner and the rest of Vastala so they'd survive. Even live a good life.

And she'd ruined it all.

"Don't tell me anything else. Please." Merrick rose and walked over to her, cautiously sitting down on the bed.

"I'm sorry. I didn't mean to unload on you."

She drew deep breaths through her nose when it felt as if her chest would burst.

But no tears came.

Like no tears had come since that night she walked through the forest, crying so hard she lost her way a dozen times. By the time she'd finally found a carriage that would take her to Vastala, the tears had dried.

She hadn't cried since.

Placing a hand on her leg, Merrick said quietly, "You were a child. I don't think your parents would have faulted you. You didn't mean it."

She slammed her hands against the mattress, grateful when the physical pain from her broken finger lessened the one in her chest. "But I did! My magic only works if I truly mean it. I am as evil as my magic."

"I guess that makes two of us."

She peeked at him through her lashes. "Was... was that a joke?"

Her heart nearly stopped when a crooked smile spread across his bent-down face.

"You must have rubbed off on me."

She shook her head, not able to muster a smile as exhaustion and guilt and pain lay heavy on her limbs.

But when the servant knocked on the door, bringing food and wine, and Merrick moved the blankets on the bed so they could dine together in comfortable silence, a sliver of warmth settled in her broken chest.

At least she wasn't entirely alone.

CHAPTER FORTY-SIX

After Merrick bid her good night, she stared up into the ceiling, the pain from her broken ribs and the memories she rarely spoke of keeping her awake.

She hadn't meant to tell him, but the guilt he carried was mirrored inside her, and she didn't wish that feeling upon anyone.

In Vastala it had taken her months to even dare interact with other children on the streets, as she'd been terrified she might hurt someone else.

Only by refusing to leave her alone had Kalia managed to break through the walls she'd put up.

As Lessia wrapped her arms around her broken body, another dry sob escaped her.

She missed Ardow, Amalise, Kalia, and the rest more than ever.

Ardow and Amalise were the only ones—outside Merrick now—who knew what she'd done, and they'd done everything in their power to convince her she wasn't at fault.

Even though she was.

But perhaps if she could continue to save other children, save Ellow, she could redeem a small part of herself.

Do something good to make up for the horrible things she'd done.

Her door flew open, and Lessia straightened, clenching the blanket to hold back a cry at the pain in her ribs.

She wasn't sure who she'd expected, but Ardow peeking his tan face through the opening wasn't it. A small smile spread across her face, and she waved him in. "What are you doing here?"

Ardow grinned at her as he strode through the room, wearing a beautifully intricate green tunic and breeches in the same shade. "I heard you got yourself injured again, and I thought you might want some more fun company than the stiff people we encountered here last time."

Reaching out her uninjured hand toward him, she rolled her eyes. "I had no part in getting myself injured, thank you very much. How did you hear about it, anyway? Does castle gossip truly spread that fast?"

Ardow sat down on the bed, taking her hand in his and squeezing.

"You know I have my sources." He winked, but his smile fell when he searched her face and then shifted his gaze to her bandages. "You're more hurt than I was informed."

Nostrils flaring, he pulled at the blankets, revealing her bandaged chest.

"Those bastards," he hissed. "This isn't right, Lessia. This shouldn't be allowed. This is everything that is wrong with our world."

She made herself smile at him again, trying to keep the light atmosphere a little bit longer. "You know as well as I do that I'll be healed in a few days. Perhaps the only perk of our

Fae blood. So, who is this mystery informant? The secret lover you've yet to tell us about?"

Ardow's face remained hardened with rage, but when she eyed him pleadingly, he let out a choked laugh.

She loved him for it.

Even if it didn't reach his eyes.

"Perhaps, perhaps not."

Sticking out her bottom lip, she pulled at his hand. "Come on, Ard. I probably must lie in bed for a few days. Give me something fun to think about."

Ardow moved closer, wrapping his arm gently around her shoulders. "I can't yet, Lessia. But he..."

His eyes widened, and Lessia giggled when his cheeks heated.

Groaning, Ardow leaned his head back on the wall.

She poked him in a burning cheek. "All right, you don't have to tell me yet, but Amalise and I will want to meet him at some point, especially if he makes you blush like this."

"I promise." Ardow squeezed her shoulders. "Now tell me about you. Is the regent still giving you a hard time?"

It was Lessia's turn to blush, and Ardow laughed when she playfully shoved his shoulder.

But when he eyed her, she realized he wanted an answer.

She shrugged. "I don't know, Ard. He seems like a good person, but he is as hot as he is cold. He is extremely perceptive, and he seems to like playing on my emotions to figure me out."

Ardow tensed, his smile falling off his face. "He doesn't know about you, does he?"

Lessia shook her head. "But I am worried he might figure something out."

Even though she couldn't tell Loche even if she wanted to, she had a feeling he read way too much in her silence.

"Be careful, Lessia. While he might have done some good for Ellow, he is not a good man." Ardow bore his eyes into hers. "You only have a few more weeks of this, and then you're free. Be smart, and do not let emotions get in the way of what you're doing."

Frowning, she observed him.

A deep wrinkle lined his forehead when he stared back at her.

She tried for another smile. "There are no emotions involved."

A knock at the door caused them both to turn toward it, and when Loche walked inside, Ardow shot her a stare.

"Am I interrupting something?" Loche's jaw ticked as he stared at Ardow's arm over her shoulders.

"No!"

Lessia snorted when she and Ardow spoke in unison.

But the laugh faded when Ardow's face remained tight as he glanced from her to Loche.

"I was just leaving." Ardow slowly got up, turning his back on Loche as he mouthed, "Be smart."

A frown formed over her brow at the hardness in Ardow's eyes as he spun around.

"Regent." Ardow offered Loche a nod as he slipped out of the room.

She shifted her eyes back to Loche when the door closed behind Ardow.

He had a deep purple bruise over his cheek and a cut lip, and when he walked to pull up a chair to the bed, he limped slightly.

"Are you all right?" Lessia didn't miss the slight wince that slipped across his features when he sat down.

Flicking his hair out of his face, he smirked. "Zaddock and

I have had some disagreements the past few days. I believe he quite enjoyed himself today."

His searing gaze swept over her body when she nodded, and Lessia pulled up the blanket when it lingered on the bandages over her tunic.

"How are you feeling?" His eyes softened when they met hers again.

"I'm fine. The broken bones will heal in a few days, probably faster than that cut on your lip." She moved her gaze to the darkening evening outside when the air between them filled with crackling electricity.

It was a clear night, and the large moon was nearly full as it hung over the calm sea.

She wished she could open the doors to let the brisk air in and relieve some of the tension Loche had brought with him.

"The guards who did this to you are gone."

She snapped her eyes back to his. "What do you mean, gone?"

"They will never bother you again. Nor will any others, unless they want me to pay them a visit." Loche's gaze refused to leave hers. "This isn't what my Ellow stands for, Lessia. We do not mistreat anyone based on where they come from or what legacy they might bear."

She tilted her head, her face pinching when pain stabbed through it. "I know you like to think so, but there is still a ways to go, Loche. You don't think the election is the first time someone like me gets called names or is assaulted?"

Loche leaned forward to grasp her hand, the one without a broken finger, and his eyes clouded when a shiver ran through her.

"I know that now. If I win again, I'll ensure that it never again happens. I promise you, I take this extremely seriously."

She'd counted on it, but it was still nice to hear him say it, especially since there was no chance Venko or Craven would ever prioritize Fae concerns.

It was quiet for a moment, but as she cleared her throat to tell him they should probably sleep, Loche squeezed her hand. "Do you mind if I stay here for a bit?"

Her brows snapped together. "I thought you wanted me to stay away from you?"

The question came out softer than she'd meant, but she didn't know what to do with all this buzzing energy or the unsettling intensity of his gaze as his gray eyes burned into hers.

Loche's jaw clenched, and his eyes darted to the door for a moment before he sighed. "I never said I wanted you to. I said that you *should* stay away from me."

"Why?" she whispered.

Something dangerously close to hope twisted in her chest, and a shadow of apprehension crept up on her.

She wasn't sure if she wanted the answer.

Not when it wouldn't be one she could keep to herself.

Not when anything he said would be relayed to her king.

"Why do I want to stay here? Or why should you stay away from me?"

Lessia swallowed, but she couldn't stop herself from responding, "Both."

Loche offered her a half smile. "I told you. I don't share my secrets."

Letting out a frustrated breath, she pulled her hand from his, annoyed at herself when a feeling of emptiness washed over her.

His eyes trailed her hand as she tucked it under the blanket. "Zaddock is in the room next to mine. I can't promise I won't beat him up if I go back right now. He took today's trial a lot more seriously than he should have."

The air between them lightened, and she drew a deep breath when some of the tension rolling off him lessened.

Forcing her lips to curl into a smile, she joked, "You can't handle that he roughed up your handsome face?"

Loche grinned, leaning back in the chair. "I was right."

"About what?"

"You think I'm handsome."

Groaning, she waved toward the couch. "Go sit over there before I kick you out."

Loche laughed all the way to the couch, and he thankfully didn't mention all the lit lanterns as Lessia shifted her gaze to the ceiling.

They talked for a while about the things Loche hoped to do for Ellow, and as Lessia's eyelids grew heavy and she stopped asking questions, Loche continued telling her of the plans he had to ensure everyone would survive until summer.

As she listened to his deep voice, sleep came quickly.

CHAPTER FORTY-SEVEN

When she woke in the morning, Loche was gone.

The next few days, she didn't see him or anyone else except Merrick, who barely spoke a word to her when he brought in food three times a day.

Lessia passed the time reading after forcing Merrick to bring her books from the library, trying to prepare as much as possible for the commoner's debate that was due sometime in the next week.

When her broken bones finally healed and she could leave her room, Merrick made her continue her training, although he didn't slam her down as hard as he used to the first few days.

He remained quiet during their training sessions, and even when Lessia tried to rile him, he responded with only a few muttered words. His mind seemed elsewhere, and after his reaction to her confession, she thought it best not to push him too hard.

In the evenings, she'd venture to the library, and every night, she scolded herself for hoping to run into Loche.

But he was nowhere to be seen.

Neither was Venko or Craven when she made her way down into the dining hall.

Although that wasn't too surprising. As humans, they needed more time than her to heal, even though she'd heard neither of them had walked away with broken bones.

After a week on her feet, she was nearly climbing the walls, and when Merrick announced he had more business to attend to, she sent a note to Amalise and Ardow, asking to meet.

Amalise had written back that she was planning on bringing the children out to the woods to let off some steam, as Ardow had some deliveries to attend to, so Lessia slipped into her usual black tunic and breeches, pulled her thick wool cloak over her shoulders, and left the castle.

It was a beautiful winter day, the snow sparkling under the rays of sunlight dancing over it, and she filled her lungs with crisp, salty air.

Her shoulders lowered as she walked the familiar streets of Asker, making sure her hood covered her face whenever she passed any townsfolk.

It felt as if she'd been inside forever, and she hungrily took in the glittering ice-covered buildings, the bustling taverns packed with soldiers, and the fishermen heading to the harbor to make the most of the sunny day.

When she reached the edge of the town, she walked south toward a thick copse of trees on a rock formation jutting out over the sea, watching her steps on the narrow, glassy path.

Few people in town ever came out here. The area was rocky and uneven, and the farther she walked, the narrower the path became—until there wasn't a path at all. Lessia had to wade through snow, following the small footsteps that marked the white ground.

It was the safest place they'd found to bring the children when they wanted them to feel comfortable expressing their Fae side, whether by practicing their magic or just running around and playing.

Lessia heard them before she saw them, trickles of laughter drifting toward her over the chill breeze, and she smiled when branches around her rustled in welcome as Fiona noticed her. Waving, she walked into the meadow, then ducked when Fiona made a branch beside her snap down instead of the wave back she'd planned.

At least Lessia hoped that's what she'd meant to do instead of nearly slamming it into her face.

"Lia!" she squealed, running up to her, snow swirling around her feet before she jumped into her arms.

Burrowing her face into Fiona's auburn hair, Lessia let out a sigh.

They could be a handful to deal with, but she loved each and every one of them.

Even if they reminded her of her sister.

A dull ache spread in her chest at the thought of Frelina, and as she set Fiona down, lifting her eyes to find Kalia and Amalise approaching her, she tried and failed to muster a smile.

"What is it?" Kalia searched her face, the pain inside Lessia mirrored in her eyes.

"I'm sorry, Kalia." Lessia pulled her into a hug, trying to shake the guilt and sorrow.

Kalia could sense and influence emotions, and like Lessia, she hated her gift.

When she was younger, she couldn't shut it off and was constantly overwhelmed by what everyone around her was feeling.

When Lessia realized, she'd tried to help her. Kalia's

magic was similar to her own, and she'd been able to show Kalia how to lock it down. But here in the meadow, Kalia typically didn't bother, especially since most of the children were overjoyed by being outside without the restrictions of having to hide a part of themselves.

Pulling back from the embrace, Lessia finally managed to curl her lips into a smile. "I just miss you, that's all."

Amalise placed a hand on her shoulder, blue eyes rounded. "And here I thought you were too occupied with that handsome regent of yours and had forgotten all about us."

Lessia's cheeks heated. "I am not occupied with anyone."

"But you want to be." Kalia's brows rose. "You're disappointed that you're not."

Amalise threw her head back and laughed. "Elessia Gyldenberg! I was only teasing, but the regent has truly caught your eye?"

"Don't call me that." Setting her jaw, she eyed two of the boys as one melted the snow around them and the other quickly froze it into clear ice.

Amalise winced. "I'm so sorry, Lia. I didn't think."

Blowing out a breath, Lessia made herself smile at her. "I know."

Kalia flitted her gaze between them and took a step back, gesturing toward Fiona, who'd wrapped a branch around another girl and appeared to be yelling at her. "I'll give you some space. I'll deal with them."

Lessia's eyes trailed Kalia as she walked over, urgently trying to convince Fiona to let the poor girl go. Over the whistling wind, Fiona argued that the girl had said something mean and that she deserved it. But when Kalia explained that she was now the one doing something mean, Fiona grudgingly released her.

Lessia offered an encouraging smile when Fiona's eyes flicked her way.

Fiona had been in rough shape when she arrived in Ellow.

Mistrusting, all skin and bones, and with a penchant for lashing out whenever she was told to do—or not to do—something. It had taken months for Lessia to get her story out of her, and when she did, she almost wished she hadn't.

Fiona, like herself, had grown up hidden, with parents who loved her and would do anything for her. But one day, someone spotted her, and the village banded together and killed her parents before her eyes.

Fiona was only six years old when they left her to die in the woods.

Somehow, she'd managed to get to the harbor in Vastala, where one of Lessia's men spotted her as they rescued another child.

He'd nearly lost an eye dragging the small girl onto the ship.

But in the year she'd been in Ellow, she'd blossomed—had become the kindest and most caring little girl. Even if she still had a temper.

Lessia let out a sharp breath.

She couldn't let King Rioner destroy the home—the safe place—they'd built in Ellow.

Her eyes darted toward the castle.

If Loche was true to his words, they might even be able to do more.

Bring more children over.

Give them a chance at a normal life.

"Daydreaming about the regent?"

Snapping her gaze to Amalise, Lessia scoffed, "Not in the way you're thinking."

Amalise wrapped an arm around her. "It's all right to

want him, you know. From what I could tell, you've caught his eye too."

Lessia rolled her eyes. "I don't want him. He frustrates me, is all."

Amalise eyed her. "Lessia, you need to let go of the guilt at some point."

She moved to stand before Lessia, her blue eyes glossing as they met Lessia's. "You deserve love. Promise me if there is a chance you find it, you will. I will never regret loving Karich. Not for one moment. Not for all the pain in the world."

Lessia grabbed her hand, thickness filling her throat. "I will if you promise me the same. He wouldn't want you to be alone forever, Amalise."

When Amalise began to shake her head, Lessia lifted her chin.

Amalise, if anyone, deserved to find love again.

She loved fiercely, wholly, and she had so much more to give.

Groaning, Amalise let go of her hand to twist a lock of her hair but finally fixed her gaze on Lessia's again. "I promise. Once I've seen you fall in love, I will try too."

Lessia grinned at her. "What about Zaddock? He seemed quite spellbound by you."

With a snort, Amalise turned around to join some of the children in the snowball fight that had broken out, but not before Lessia caught a glimpse of the pink creeping up her neck.

A smile overtook Lessia's face as she followed her, a giggle escaping when a snowball hit an unsuspecting Amalise right in the chest.

CHAPTER FORTY-EIGHT

Wet from all the snow the children had managed to get in under her clothing, Lessia walked through the forest back to the castle.

Her ears buzzed from the delighted screams they'd all let out as they played and from Kalia and Amalise telling her of everything she'd missed the past week.

Two of the boys had begun working with Bren in her favored tavern, and so far, it had gone well, apart from a small mishap when a soldier had gotten a little too rowdy and one of them had punched him out cold.

Despite that going against the rules Lessia set for them—no fighting, especially with humans—she smiled to herself.

The boys' success had prompted one of the girls to see if she could get work in one of the weaponry shops. While the owner had been hesitant at first, when she'd worked a day for free and he realized how skilled she was at molding the iron, she'd been offered three full days a week.

Lessia pushed away the sense of wistfulness that traced

across her skin upon realizing many of them might leave the house soon.

It was a good thing for them to integrate into Ellow's society.

Even if it might mean the house would be a bit emptier when she returned.

She rushed her steps when shadows danced over the rocky path before her.

It was still early afternoon, but the sun was already on its way down, and she wanted to be back at the castle before darkness fell.

When she rounded an especially sharp turn, the lights from the capital finally breaking through the tree line, the hair on the back of her neck rose.

A sense of being watched pricked her skin, and she whipped her head around, holding her breath as she listened to the forest.

Snow crunched to her left.

As silently as possible, she slipped behind a tree, unsheathing the two Fae daggers from her waistband.

Leaning her back against the tree, she planted her feet like Merrick had shown her, breathing deep to keep her rising pulse in check.

Snow crushed again, closer this time, and Lessia risked a peek around the trunk.

A cloaked figure approached her, the height indicating it was a male if it was a human. Pulling off her hood to ensure her eyes were visible, she reminded herself of everything Merrick had taught her.

Keep your center low so a swing to your face or chest doesn't make you fall.

Take them by surprise if you can.

Don't bother being gracious. Go for a kick between the legs or a hit to the stomach—anywhere where it'll hurt the most.

Merrick's voice echoed in her mind, and she quietly promised him that she'd make him proud—that the training sessions had taught her something valuable.

When the person's soft breaths broke through the silence, she steeled herself and leaped out from behind the tree. Daggers raised, she launched herself at the figure, but he anticipated it, fingers wrapping around her wrists as the force of her attack slammed them both into the snow.

Snarling, she tried to free her hands but stilled when low laughter erupted beneath the hood.

"Are you trying to kill me, darling?"

Lessia groaned as she tried to free her hands once more, but Loche wouldn't let go; he only pulled her closer until she could make out his amused expression beneath the black wool.

"Let me go," she growled.

The corners of Loche's mouth curled. "If I do, will you try to stab me again?"

"That depends on why you're following me."

Lessia's heart slammed against her rib cage as she realized he'd come from the direction of the meadow.

"I told you I'd find out your secret." Loche winked.

Her pulse roared in her ears as she stared back at him.

She'd have to make him forget.

He'd send them back.

They were here without papers, breaking one of Ellow's fundamental rules: all Fae, part- and half-Fae alike, needed to report their ancestry to ensure they weren't related to the ones responsible for the destruction during the war.

Most of them were younger than sixteen, the age of adulthood in both Vastala and Ellow, when they were brought over, so they were also required to be accompanied by a parent or guardian. Since the children had either dead parents or parents who didn't want them—parents who would more likely kill them if they knew they were still alive—that wasn't possible.

Instead, Lessia smuggled them over on Venko's shady ships. Hiding them in the provisions hold, she got around having to inform anyone in Vastala or Ellow about their existence. But it also required her to keep them hidden until they were of age and they could forge papers for them, allowing them to work and contribute to Ellow's society.

Loche's eyes bounced between hers, and his features softened. "You're doing this for them."

Swallowing, she began pulling on her magic, even as everything inside her told her not to, that if she did this, she'd ruin everything between them.

Her nostrils flared at the thought.

There was *nothing* between them.

And even if there was, she couldn't risk the people she loved.

Not for a man.

Not for anyone.

Familiar waves of warmth began rolling through her when Loche released her wrists. Muscles tensing, she sucked in a breath when his hands cupped her face instead, and he forced her eyes to his.

"I won't tell a soul."

She narrowed her eyes, her magic buzzing over her skin.

Loche didn't seem to notice as his thumbs stroked her cheeks. "I knew there must be something behind you joining the election. You clearly weren't doing this for yourself—I've never seen anyone be so reluctant. Now I understand why. You're saving those children, trying to make their lives better.

And you can't do that without them being fully accepted in Ellow."

"Loche..." she started, but Loche interrupted her, a shadow crossing his face.

"I won't tell a soul because what you're doing is not wrong, Lessia. It's admirable. It's right. If you don't win, I will make sure you and all your friends, and anyone else who comes from Vastala, are taken care of. That no one will endure what you have had to experience during this election."

She didn't know what to say.

Gratefulness and guilt tangled within her as she pushed the magic deep down.

Lessia shook her head. "Loche, I..."

The tattoo on her arm burned, tightening its grip on her throat.

Her daggers slipped out of her hands, landing on the snow with a soft thud.

"Are you hurt?" Loche's brows knitted, his eyes searching hers.

"J—just a bit sore still."

She bit her lip at the lie, hating that she couldn't tell him that it wasn't the reason—or at least not the only reason she was doing this.

He didn't deserve this.

King Rioner was wrong.

Loche had nothing to do with what was happening.

She must have read Stellia wrong. It was her soldiers who kept attacking, and the captain had disappeared without a trace.

It wasn't fair for Lessia to continue this.

She couldn't hold back a wince as another stinging pain shot up her arm.

"Perhaps you should get up if your ribs are still sore?

Unless you plan on lying on me all day. Although thinking of it, I might not mind that too much."

Loche's eyes twinkled when she met them, and her breath caught in her throat when she realized she was still lying on top of him, his chest moving with hers as they filled their lungs with air.

Shifting her eyes down, she scrambled to her feet. Lessia picked up the daggers and tucked them into her waistband again while trying to block out Loche's low chuckle.

"Come." Loche reached out a hand as he got to his feet. "I want to show you something."

When she glanced at his hand, he pulled back his hood and smiled at her.

A smile that made her face heat despite her cold and wet clothing.

Her eyes flitted between his, and she hesitantly took the hand he offered, following him as he guided her west—the opposite direction of the castle.

CHAPTER FORTY-NINE

"Where are you taking me?"

Lessia cautiously surveyed the wide streets of the western part of Asker.

She wasn't too familiar with this area; the neighborhoods here were more upscale than where her home, taverns, and gambling rooms lay.

Loche nudged her with his shoulder, his face once again shrouded from view by his hood. "Do you trust me?"

Pulling at her own hood, she shrugged. "I don't know yet."

A laugh escaped him. "Fair enough. I'm taking you to my house."

Her steps faltered. "I thought you lived in the castle? Isn't that what regents do?"

"Officially, yes. Unofficially, I live right there." Loche gestured toward a white three-story building before them, where a large glass-encased balcony jutted out from the top floor.

The glass was black, impossible to see through, and she

wondered whyever someone might choose to do that when they had the opportunity to have a clear view of Asker, given the hill the house was embedded in.

Dragging her with him, Loche pulled the hood from his face when they neared a large steel door with two of his masked guards posted outside.

The men bowed their heads as they recognized him, opening the squeaking door to reveal a beautiful foyer with light gray walls and glass lamps lining the entire ceiling.

Soft music flowed through the house as she stepped over the threshold, and muffled laughter and conversation reached her ears as Loche led her up a black spiral staircase.

When they reached the third floor, Lessia's eyes widened.

On a table to her right, a dozen of those frightening black masks were lined up, and farther in, several couches and chairs stood before a massive stone fireplace.

More than twenty men turned their heads as they approached, the conversation falling silent, and as her eyes met Zaddock's where he leaned against one of the pillars lining the walls, his mouth fell open.

Zaddock made his way over to them, his wide eyes shifting to Loche. "What is she doing here?"

Loche plucked two goblets of wine off a side table, barely sparing Zaddock a look as he pressed one into her hands. "I invited her."

Zaddock's face tightened, and he turned his back on her, not realizing Lessia heard every word he whispered into Loche's ear. "Did she do something to you?"

Muscles tensing, Loche glanced at her from over his shoulder before he responded. "I'm pretty sure she can hear everything we say, so why don't you ask her directly?"

Zaddock's eyes flew to hers, and he cleared his throat. "My apologies, Lessia. We don't usually bring anyone here."

She fixed her gaze on his. "I didn't do anything to him, Zaddock."

"I'm pretty sure you do more than you think," he mumbled but then excused himself, returning to the conversation he was having with a man clad in the black uniform Loche's men always wore.

Sweeping her gaze across the room, she realized every man in here was one of Loche's guards.

She'd never seen any of them without the masks.

Hadn't even heard of anyone who had.

"This is our safe space." Loche squeezed her elbow, steering her toward the balcony she'd spotted from the outside. "They don't need to hide here."

She turned to him, a wrinkle forming between her brows. "What do you mean, they don't need to hide?"

Pausing for a moment, he sipped from his goblet. "I just meant they don't need to be guards. They can just be themselves."

Loche motioned for her to continue walking, and as she stepped onto the marble floor of the balcony, she sucked in a breath.

The impenetrable glass she'd seen from the street was completely clear, offering them a breathtaking view of Asker, of every single person walking the streets beneath them.

"It's amazing, isn't it?"

When her eyes settled on his face, the genuine smile that graced it threatened to take her breath once more, and she could only nod.

It was amazing.

She could see all the way to the castle, the harbor to the east, the forest to the north, and every building in between.

Loche directed her to a small couch facing the glass.

Taking the seat beside her, he clinked his glass against her own before leaning back and releasing a sigh.

"I had this built when I was elected." Loche's steely eyes collided with hers. "There is so much scrutiny when you're regent, people tracking your every step, so I wanted a place where I could do the same. Anonymously watching and evaluating and judging."

Lessia glanced at the people below, every expression and movement clear to her as they walked the streets. "I can see why that would be appealing."

"I thought you might."

Leaning over her knees, he pointed to an older couple walking on one of the dimly lit streets. "See how she turns away from him? They're in an argument, but they're waiting to get home before they start yelling."

His face was an inch from hers when he turned back to look at her.

Fighting the instinct to lean back, to get some space between them, Lessia made herself stare right back into those storming eyes, biting her lip not to blush under his piercing gaze. "So, this is where you learned how to read people so well?"

Loche's eyes remained locked on her mouth as he smirked. "You'd be surprised how much you can learn from studying your enemies in secret."

Her brows rose. "Your enemies? I thought they were your people."

"You know as well as I do the people who live here aren't my people. These are Craven's people, and they hate every moment of my reign."

Loche offered her another devastating smile, but it was replaced with hardness as he continued. "I'm sorry that you must live with so much hate from them, Lessia. It's not fair, but if you're to trust me with anything, know that I will dedicate my life to ensure no one else of your kind has to."

A weak smile overtook her face as she nodded.

"Unless *you* win, that is." Loche grinned.

Lessia snorted, shifting her gaze out to the night again.

Nobles and wealthy merchants walked in and out of upscale taverns and music rooms, the laughter and boisterous voices brushing her ears.

A soft sigh escaped her as she wondered if there would be a time when she, or any of her kind, might walk into those establishments and be greeted with warmth instead of glacial stares and hostile whispers.

A tiny seed of hope took root in her heart.

Perhaps if she succeeded in what her king wanted, and if Loche kept his grand promises, she would live to see it.

Loche's hand gently cupped her chin, shifting her gaze to his again. "What thought just crossed your mind?"

Holding his stare, she asked, "Do you know what it's like wanting something so badly, believing you can never have it? And suddenly, it might be within reach?"

Loche's eyes flared as they traced over her. "More than you can imagine."

Her cheeks heated, but she whispered, "That's why I have to do this, Loche."

He nodded. "I understand."

Her eyes fell to the goblet she held in her hands.

"I do, Lessia." Loche's fingers brushed her cheek, his eyes darkening as he leaned in closer. "I know what it's like to risk everything for what's right."

"I..." Her tattoo burned again, the pain rippling through her arm, sparking every nerve inside her.

No.

The goblet clattered to the floor, wine splashing her legs,

and she couldn't stop herself from rising, an invisible tether pulling her.

"Where are you going?" Loche's dark brows knitted.

"I... I must go. I'm sorry."

He called out for her as she nearly sprinted out of the room, but she couldn't even turn her head over her shoulder as the force of King Rioner's command overpowered everything else.

CHAPTER
FIFTY

Snow began falling as she walked through the streets, and when she reached the cliffs leading to the place where she'd last met the king, her teeth were clattering so hard she worried one might break off.

Lessia's ears remained trained, worry that Loche might once again be trailing her lying heavy in her gut, but no soft steps echoed behind her on the packed snow.

"Were you followed?"

Merrick slipped up beside her, his steps nearly silent, but his power surged through the air, and she drew a shaky breath, unsure whether the anger he radiated was because of her or something else.

"I don't think so. But I was with Loche," she admitted.

Nearly paralyzing dread gripped her heart.

If Loche followed...

If he found out who she was meeting...

She didn't doubt he would confront them.

And there was only one way that could end.

Forcing her head to turn over her shoulder, she swept her gaze over the dark path.

No shadows walked behind them.

But Loche had sneaked up on her before.

She stumbled when her foot hit a rock, and only because Merrick gripped her elbow did she not tumble over the steep cliffs right into the freezing water.

"Watch where you're going," he growled.

Nodding, she drew a steadying breath.

If he didn't allow her to fall to her death, perhaps the king's visit wasn't too alarming.

"Why is he summoning me?" Lessia peeked at him under her hood.

Merrick's shoulders tensed. "I am not sure."

"How are you not sure? He must have let you know to meet him." Her eyes fixed on the cliffs before them, where King Rioner had last stood and waited.

They were empty for now, only the forest standing tall behind them, no cloaked figure perched atop.

"I told you. I am not sure. Now be quiet," Merrick snarled.

Apprehension pricked her skin at his tone—so similar to the one he used before the election.

As they came to a halt beneath the cliffs, her tattoo no longer burned her skin, and she angrily swallowed the lump in her throat.

It didn't matter if Merrick wouldn't honor their truce now that his king was back.

She shouldn't have been surprised.

He'd been loyal to the king for centuries, and not in the way she was through her blood oath.

They remained quiet as they waited, and as snow slowly covered her black cloak, she almost wished it would fall more heavily so it would fully coat the wool and provide a little bit of warmth.

When water sizzled beneath the cliffs, a thick stream forcing its way up, she squared her shoulders.

King Rioner stood steadily atop the rushing torrent, a burgundy cloak, held together with a thick gilded chain, covering his face. He gracefully stepped off when the waters reached the top of the cliff, and the stream immediately fell into the wild sea, drops of it trickling over her and Merrick.

Straightening his robe, the king took a step toward them.

Merrick dropped to one knee, and when Lessia didn't immediately follow, his magic wrapped around her neck, forcing her stiff legs to bend in a deep bow.

"I'm surprised you haven't killed her yet, Merrick. Although I'm pleased to know you still follow me blindly." The king's shining boots came into view as he stepped closer.

"You may rise."

As Lessia lifted her head, her lips curled back in a hiss when Merrick didn't let go of his grip on her neck.

A low chuckle escaped the king's hood. "I thought the lesson my dear Merrick taught you last time would be enough, Elessia, but clearly, you still don't understand the respect you ought to offer your king."

She huffed breath through her nose, writhing under the oily vibrations playing across her skin. "I do understand, my king."

"I doubt that." The king brushed something off his cloak, the chain clinking as it shifted. "What have you learned so far, Elessia? And do not leave out any important details."

Grinding her teeth against the stinging on her arm from the command, she struggled to keep her voice steady. "The regent seems to have nothing to do with this, Your Majesty. It seems Stellia, a former captain of the navy, is behind it all. Her soldiers have been attacking us during the election, and her ships have vanished near where I heard others have."

King Rioner clicked his tongue. "'Seems to have nothing to do with this'... Say, Elessia. Did I ask you for speculations?"

As she opened her mouth, Merrick's magic pushed her head down.

"Stop it," she hissed.

"Are you asking your king to stop?" The king's voice was lethal as he advanced toward her.

"No, Your Majesty," she got out, the sting from her arm mingling with pain from Merrick's magic as it forced her head further down.

King Rioner turned toward Merrick. "Is she following the orders I gave?"

Merrick straightened beside her, but his magic still wouldn't release her. "She is doing what she believes she must."

Lessia bit her cheek to keep the shock off her face.

He was protecting her.

"And what is it she believes she must do?"

"Find out what it is you seek to earn her freedom," Merrick responded, his hold on her easing.

When Lessia continued to keep her head down, it lessened further.

Peeking at them through her lashes, she watched the king step closer to Merrick.

"And is she doing everything she can to do so?"

Lessia stiffened when Merrick's loud swallow seemed to echo in the moment of silence.

"No."

Her stomach sank when the cloaked king inclined his head.

"I should have known I needed to be more prescriptive. I

thought the promise of freedom would be enough, but you're a strange one, aren't you, halfling?" The king let out a deep sigh. "Elessia Gyldenberg, you must do everything in your power to find out what the regent hides. You will use your magic on him, you will threaten him, you will hurt him if needed. Do you understand?"

A gasp left her when she tried to fight the oath burning through her veins.

Shaking so hard that the snow beneath her cracked, she tried to remain silent—grasp at every ounce of control left inside her.

But when another wave of fiery pain crashed through her veins, she whispered, "Yes."

CHAPTER
FIFTY-ONE

After pulling Merrick aside and holding a hushed conversation Lessia couldn't make out, the king disappeared as quickly as he'd come, leaving a freezing drizzle washing over them in his wake.

Spinning on his heel, Merrick stormed toward the castle, and Lessia stumbled after him, her limbs numb from the cold.

"Merrick," she got out through shivering teeth as they neared the dimly lit town. "Merrick, wait."

The Fae halted so fast she smacked into his rigid back, and Merrick had to catch her once more when she slipped on the snow-covered cliffs.

Lessia tried to back up when he trembled from barely restrained anger, but he didn't release the strong grip on her arm, forcing her close to his side.

"You need to give the king the respect he demands," Merrick hissed under his dark hood. "It's not that difficult, Lessia. You bow, you don't talk back, and you follow the orders he gives you."

She ground her teeth, trying to keep her voice steady. "But

he is wrong, Merrick. Loche has nothing to do with this. You must see it too. He is a good regent. He doesn't deserve this!"

"A good regent?" Merrick snarled. "Tell me, was he not regent the past five years you lived here? How was that life, Lessia? I've seen how these humans look at you. How they talk to you."

She shifted her eyes down and fixed them on Merrick's black boots. "He didn't know. He promised me it'll be better if he wins this time. He'd make sure me and my..." She snapped her mouth shut as icy fear gripped her heart.

While Merrick had protected her back there, he had still told the king she wasn't doing everything in her power to figure out what Loche knew. And she couldn't risk those children more than she already had with Loche now knowing of them.

She cleared her throat. "He promised that those like me would be welcome here, that we won't be disrespected anymore, and that we'll be able to live like any other resident of Ellow."

Merrick threw his head back with a growl, his grip on her arm tightening. "You're making excuses for him! Exactly like you did for me! When will you understand that this world is ruled by power-hungry, evil, and ruthless males who should not be forgiven? All Havlands is full of them. Making excuses won't change that!"

Glaring at him, she growled right back, "Tell me what else I can do! I won't win this election. I have no power. I am at the mercy of the king you hold so dear, and whoever will rule Ellow. At least Loche isn't threatening to kill me every time I see him."

"Do you truly think Loche would let you live if he knew what you were? Why you're really in the election?"

Her nostrils flared. "He wouldn't hurt me. He..."

Merrick let out a cold laugh. "He likes you? He certainly seems intrigued by you. But that man is not good, Lessia. He wouldn't hesitate to have your head if he knew you were here to spy on him."

Clenching her jaw, she swallowed the words threatening to burst out of her.

Merrick was wrong.

She wasn't sure what Loche thought of her, but she couldn't believe he'd actually have her executed if he found out about her.

At least if she found a way to tell him herself.

Tell him it wasn't a choice she made but one she was forced into.

That she was trying to protect Ellow.

Protect him.

Merrick pulled her flush against him, his hood twitching as if he was struggling against boring his eyes into hers. "You will *not* find a way to tell him, Lessia. I can see you've softened to him, but this is not wise. You and him? It will never work."

She'd opened her mouth to respond when commotion sounded behind them, and as she spun around, her eyes widened upon finding several black-clad figures sprinting through the streets, heading the same way they were.

"What..." she whispered, but her words cut off as Merrick pulled her behind him.

He released her and gripped his sword in one hand, the other pulling off his hood.

Unsheathing her daggers from her waistband, Lessia peeked around the stiff Merrick, watching several of the men close in on them. She widened her stance, clutching the hilts tightly, when the men faltered, one of them pulling back his hood.

A gasp escaped her when her eyes slammed into walnut ones. "Ardow?"

His rounded eyes flicked between her and Merrick before he stalked over, waving for the two other men to walk off back into the icy alley behind them.

Ignoring Merrick, Ardow reached out for her, a smile pulling at his lips when he realized both her hands were occupied by daggers.

"Look at you." His smile widened, but it didn't reach his eyes, and when he shifted them to Merrick, his features hardened again.

The Fae turned his back on them, moving a few steps away but not far enough that he wouldn't hear every word they exchanged.

Slipping the daggers back into her breeches, she pulled off her hood. "What are you doing here, Ardow?"

He grinned at her again.

But there was something off about it, and her brows snapped together when he hesitated for a moment, his eyes shifting to Merrick.

"Ardow?"

He shook his head, his shoulders loosening. "There's another attack on the castle. I was on my way to our home with a few *friends*"—he wiggled his brows—"when people started screaming. I feared for you, so I was about to play white knight and come rescue you."

His eyes moved to Merrick again. "Seems I was too late, though."

Unease thrummed over her skin. "Did you hear anything from the castle? Did someone get hurt?"

"I don't know. I only just heard of it." Eyes narrowing, he swept his gaze over her. "You look like you're one minute away from turning to ice, Lessia. What were you doing?"

She opened her mouth, nearly choking when the blood oath constricted her throat. Ardow's eyes trailed her hand as it flew to her neck, a flicker of recognition igniting within them.

"He's here again?" His gaze sharpened, and he snapped it behind her as if the Fae king could somehow have been hiding there all along.

"We should get going." Merrick closed the distance between them, shoving Ardow out of the way and nudging Lessia until she took a stiff step toward the castle. "They'll be wondering where we are, especially if there's been another attack."

Turning her head over her shoulder, she mouthed "I'm sorry" when Merrick forced her to walk in front of him with one hand wrapped around her arm.

Ardow's face remained hard, his eyes locked on the two of them until shadows veiled his features.

Torn between wanting to reassure Ardow and worrying about what they might face when they entered the castle, she hesitated, but Merrick's grip on her arm tightened, and he made her continue the brisk walk toward the lights in the towering white castle.

"You don't have to be so rude," she hissed when the Fae growled at her for slowing the pace.

He stilled, then turned toward her, forcing them both to a stop.

Jaw twitching, he leaned in, his voice low but laced with such cold she shivered for a different reason than the roaring winter wind.

"You don't seem to realize how serious tonight was, Lessia. You are blood-sworn to follow our king's orders, and while I have been trying to let you do it your way, it's now out of my hands. You will need to use that silver tongue of yours, and it will put both of us at risk, not to mention the regent you apparently hold dear."

Lessia swallowed, looking out over the dark sea behind him. "He didn't say when."

A snort escaped Merrick, and he shook his head. "Always looking on the bright side."

Waving for her to follow him into the light of the metal lampposts lining the pathway to the castle, he continued. "You know as well as I do that it doesn't matter. Our king will come back, and if you haven't done it by then, he will tire of your disobedience."

Silently cursing, she fell in step with him.

Merrick was right. There was no escaping it now.

She would only have to hope whatever she found out wouldn't damn them all.

CHAPTER FIFTY-TWO

Frantic guards paced back and forth outside the tall gates of the castle, letting Lessia and Merrick pass only after a thorough interrogation of what they had been up to.

Lessia mumbled something about drinking in a tavern, squaring her shoulders and keeping her face impassive as the guards' brows rose upon noting her blue lips and pale complexion.

But when Merrick backed her up, stepping in close, they averted their eyes, a shiver running through the nearest one as he gestured for them to walk through.

Still, eyes burned into her back as they walked the foot-worn stone path to the large double doors.

Merrick opened them for her, and when she stepped over the threshold, she nearly walked right into a bloodied Zaddock. His eyes flew to hers, immediately narrowing, and he blocked her path as she tried to take another step inside.

Her gaze snagged on the bloody trail that snaked down

his face from his temple, then moved to his heaving chest. "Are you all right?"

"Where have you been?" Zaddock's nostrils flared as his eyes sliced between her and Merrick.

Forcing herself to keep his stare, she said, "I had some business to attend to."

Brows pulling, Zaddock shifted closer. "And what *business* was that?"

Lessia shrugged, casting a glance at the empty hallway behind them. "Just tavern business. You can ask Ardow when you see him next. I just left him."

Ardow would catch on quickly if Zaddock asked.

He always did.

Her pulse quickened when Zaddock didn't back down, his face remaining stony.

"Why don't I believe you?" He wiped at his cheek with his dark cloak when more drops of crimson trickled down his face. "Seems a bit convenient that you storm out of our house, luring Loche to follow you back to the castle only to find you weren't there. Instead, there was an ambush waiting for him outside your room."

Lessia had opened her mouth to respond when Merrick placed a hand on Zaddock's chest, easily driving him two steps back.

"I suggest you back off. My understanding is that she saved your life during the last attack. And now you're implying she might have something to do with it?" Merrick snarled.

The two males glared at each other, and Lessia imagined the chilling glint in Zaddock's eyes was mirrored in Merrick's.

Pulling at the Fae's cloak to get him to step back—without any success—she cleared her throat. "We're on the same side. There is no point in fighting each other when we should find out why Stellia and her men are doing this."

"She's half-right, you know," Loche drawled as he limped into the room, his black jacket and breeches ripped and blood marring his face from a split brow.

Something stirred in Lessia's chest as he came closer, and she clenched her hands when a whisper of fury danced over her skin. Even if his usual smirk graced his face, shadows clouded his eyes when they met hers.

"What do you mean?" Merrick growled with eyes still fixed on Zaddock.

"We're on the same side. But Stellia is dead. She is not the one doing this." Loche grimaced as he shifted his weight to his right foot.

Lessia's mouth fell open.

"What?" she whispered.

A frown formed between Loche's brows as he trailed his gaze over her, from her snow-covered leather boots to her still-clenched fists, slowly lifting it to meet her eyes.

Hesitating for a moment, he seemed to be debating with himself but finally set his jaw. "You'll find out soon enough anyway. Frayson is calling a meeting with all nominees any minute now."

"Loche—"

Loche's eyes left hers to bore into Zaddock's, and his guard's lips tightened into a thin line when Loche glared at him.

Moving to lean against one of the white pillars in the foyer, Loche turned to her once more, ignoring Merrick as he stepped up right behind her.

"My men found parts of Stellia's ship floating around one of the small islands just across our borders. When they ventured onto land, her body was the first one they found.

Most of her company was found dead with her. They'd fought hard—there was too much blood for it to have come from just her soldiers. But whoever they fought cleaned up after themselves."

Merrick stiffened behind her, and Lessia cast a quick glance over her shoulder.

While Merrick's eyes remained on the floor, every muscle was locked, his tan hands twitching by his sides.

Turning back to Loche, she caught the quick glance between him and Zaddock as she asked, "Do you think her own men betrayed her?"

Loche's eyes didn't meet hers as he responded, "We don't know."

The low huff that escaped Merrick made her realize she wasn't the only one who didn't believe him.

Her gut twisted as Zaddock took a step back.

His face was still hardened with anger, but it was the slight flare of worry in his eyes when they accidentally met hers that had the hairs on the back of her neck rising.

"There you are!"

Frayson stalked into the room, followed by several guards, including a few of Loche's, all bearing those dark masks that somehow seemed even more ominous now that she'd seen the men behind them.

"Lessia, I'm glad to see you in one piece. We looked all over the castle for you." Frayson offered her a tight smile before gesturing for them to follow. "I'm calling a meeting regarding the election and the news we received tonight. We need to make some fast decisions."

Loche glanced at her and opened his mouth, but after another look at Zaddock, he closed it and followed the older man into the dimly lit hallway.

"You need to find out what he knows. And soon."

Merrick's whisper brushed her ear as he stepped up beside her.

Wringing her hands, she followed him as they walked toward the throne room, where hushed voices drifted toward them.

She wasn't sure she wanted to find out.

But if they were targeting the nominees, they were targeting Ellow.

And she'd made a vow to protect it with all her might.

Lessia was still deep in thought when Merrick moved to the side, allowing her to enter the room first.

"It must be her! She is the spy! Throw her into the dungeons or banish her—I don't particularly care."

Whipping her head up at Craven's shrill voice, she took in the room.

Craven walked back and forth before the crackling fireplace, his muddled eyes venomous, while Venko sat in one of the chairs, his face pale and hands gripping the plush arms.

Guards stood rigid by every wall, and several were posted by the windows—one row facing out and the other watching the room with sharp eyes.

"What are you waiting for?" Craven waved his arms. "It's clear that there is a spy in the castle, and who could it be if not the halfling? She must be feeding them information about where we are and what we're doing to allow them to sneak in undetected. Not a single guard saw them come in or stumbled upon them while they waited in the shadows."

The anger from earlier returned with full force, and Lessia couldn't stop herself from stalking up to the man, jabbing a finger into his chest. "I have no idea how or why they keep attacking. Or who is behind it, for that matter. I wasn't even here tonight, Craven."

A sliver of guilt rushed down her neck as she spoke.

But she wasn't behind this, and she doubted King Rioner had anything to do with it.

Not if the same things were happening in Vastala.

While he was shrewd and vicious, what did he have to win by messing with the human election?

Craven's bloodshot eyes narrowed, and she pushed him backward, cringing as the musty scent of his breath washed over her when he opened his mouth. As she took a step back, she slammed right into a hard chest, and a strong arm snaked around her to steady her when she stumbled.

She almost thought she imagined it when his grip tightened around her for a moment before he snarled over her head, "This is why you'll never win, Bernedir. You're a fool if you think Lessia has anything to do with it." Loche took a step toward the graying man, leaving a wave of coldness washing over her as his arm dropped to his side. "And if I hear you call her that vile name one more time, I will personally make sure you need a healer ship to bring you back home."

Lessia bit back a grin when Craven sighed loudly, then slumped down into a chair, his arms crossed over his chest like a child.

"We have much to discuss tonight, and it's already late. Let's end the fighting, shall we?" Frayson also seemed to be hiding a smile as he gracefully sat down.

With a glance at Merrick, who hovered beside her, Lessia took a seat in the closest chair, with Frayson on one side and Loche sitting on the armrest of the one on her other side. Loche's leg bounced as he fixed his gaze on Frayson, the fabric of his ripped breeches flapping with each movement.

Drawing a breath, Frayson glanced around the room. "It appears everyone knows Stellia is dead. We're waiting on a detailed report, but she fought bravely until the end." The old man clasped his hands together, his chin dropping an inch.

"We do know she's been dead for a while, which means she's likely not behind this. We don't know yet who is—if it's some of her own men or someone else entirely. But whoever it is, they have intimate knowledge of the election and of each one of you."

Frayson paused for a moment to shoot Craven a sharp glare. "While I don't think any of you nominees has anything to do with it, we do believe there must be a spy in the castle. We have employed every single soldier available to find him or her. And trust me, we will do so quickly."

The fire roared in Lessia's ears in the silence that followed, and she had to fight with everything in her to keep a mask of indifference when Loche's stare burned into the side of her head.

Lifting her eyes to his, she forced a shrug, then crossed her legs, trying to get her muscles to focus on anything other than the apprehension that lay heavy on her chest.

Frayson cleared his throat. "While we will find the spy, it's becoming too dangerous to prolong the election more than we must. Ellow will not be safe without a fully committed regent. With that, we've decided to move up the next elements. The commoners' debate will happen tomorrow, and the last trial in the days following. After that the vote will open. There will be a final ball, where we'll invite our allies from Vastala to meet you, to ensure you're comfortable managing the relations with King Rioner's emissaries. I realize this gives you less time to rally votes, so I strongly suggest you inform your people to speak on your behalf with voters as soon as possible."

Lessia frowned when the hope that fluttered in her chest at the chance of being free within weeks, perhaps even days—even if she had to face the Fae—mingled with wistfulness.

Her eyes collided with Loche's again, and her cheeks

reddened when his stormy gaze already waited for her, flaring when she continued to meet it.

"You should rest up before tomorrow. From now on, guards will follow you wherever you go in the castle, and if you need to venture out, please inform us so we can ensure your protection then as well. If there are no more questions, I shall bid you good night."

Lessia didn't break Loche's gaze while Frayson spoke, nor when he, together with Craven, rose and swiftly left the room, followed by a large number of guards.

"Lessia?"

She forced herself to look away from Loche as Venko's hand landed on her arm.

"May we speak?"

Concerned to find Venko's eyes glazed, she got to her feet, dragged him to the fire, and positioned him with his back to the others.

Casting a quick glance behind him, she found Loche staring at them intently and Merrick's entire body turned their way.

She cursed softly.

Loche probably couldn't hear over the wind hitting the windows on either side of the fireplace, but Merrick wouldn't miss a word.

"You told me to tell you if I found out more."

Lessia hushed him, burning her eyes into his, but she did not dare draw on her magic.

"You need to whisper," she hissed between clenched teeth.

Nodding once, Venko lowered his voice. "You're no longer off limits."

Her brows pinched. "What do you mean?"

"I don't know. I was just given a letter that said you're not off limits."

Lessia threw another quick look over his shoulder, the knot of fear in her chest tightening when Merrick moved closer. "Off limits from what? What did it say exactly?"

Venko's empty gaze stared into the fire. "Elessia Gyldenberg is no longer to be exempt."

Following his gaze, she pulled at her hair.

Was it a warning?

Had whoever Venko worked with figured out she'd gotten to him?

A chair scraped the floor when Loche also shifted closer, his eyes glued on hers, and Lessia quickly squeezed Venko's shoulder. "Thank you. Go to bed."

With a nod, Venko spun around and walked out of the room.

Lessia followed, keeping her eyes on the floor as she passed Loche, but she couldn't escape Merrick as he fell into step with her. The Fae didn't say a word as they were escorted to their rooms, only quietly bid her good night and slammed the door to his bedroom.

As she lay on the bed, unease gnawed at her.

Whoever Venko was working with had known of her, and had known of her abilities.

They must have known she'd get the information.

Was whoever he was working with connected to the attacks that kept happening?

She moved to lie on her side, and her eyes followed the heavy snow that fell outside her window.

But they'd gone after Venko as well.

Fear pricked her skin.

There might be more people than Stellia's men and King Rioner she needed to look out for.

CHAPTER FIFTY-THREE

Lessia woke late the next day.

She scrambled to dress in her favored leathers and fastened her messy hair into a simple updo, with a few golden ringlets framing her face, when a guard outside her door knocked and shouted that the debate was to start.

She'd gotten used to Merrick storming into her chambers at dawn, waking her by throwing open the balcony doors to let in the freezing winter air. But it was quiet when she listened by his door, and when she opened it to peek in, the room was empty, the bed untouched.

Frowning, she opened the door to the hallway, allowing the horde of guards outside it to lead her to the same debate chamber they'd used when the nobles were in town.

While she hoped the commoners—many of whom she'd likely met in her business endeavors—would be less hostile than the nobles, she still steeled her spine as she walked into the crowded room.

"Lessia!"

Her eyes found Amalise's blue ones across the room, and a

smile spread over her face when her friend waved excitedly, nearly smacking the woman to her left.

Beside her stood a tired-looking Ardow. Even from a distance, Lessia could make out the deep circles under his eyes, the slump of his usually straight shoulders, and how the smile gracing his face did not brighten his dark eyes.

"You took your time. I was almost worried you might have run from the debate like you ran from me last night."

Ripping her eyes from her friends, she met Loche's.

She couldn't stop her smile from widening when his eyes twinkled, the corner of his mouth lifting as his gaze snagged on her lips.

Loche raised a brow. "Perhaps you're more afraid of me than being ripped apart before a crowd."

She groaned when a blush threatened to creep up her neck, and Loche let out a deep chuckle as he stepped closer.

His scent invaded the space, and she sucked in a breath of mint and something wintry, like the smell of a fresh layer of snow on salty cliffs.

Shaking her head, she took a step back and tucked one of her free locks of hair behind her ear.

"Perhaps I find them better company." She raised a brow when the fog that overtook her mind had lifted.

"You continue to tell yourself that." Loche smirked.

She rolled her eyes and had moved to walk toward the stage when he offered her his arm.

Eyeing it, she hesitated.

Leaning in until his warm breath fanned over her, blowing a piece of hair across her face, he whispered, "I would say I don't bite—but I'm not a liar. Although I prefer to do it in private."

A shiver danced across her shoulders, and a nervous laugh bubbled up when his lips grazed the skin just below her ear.

"I don't think they'll wait for us all day."

She snapped her eyes to his, realizing he'd stepped back, still with his arm in the air.

An amused smile played across his full lips when she finally took it.

Lessia scolded herself as they walked toward the dais and she threw another look toward her friends, finding Amalise grinning wide. Ardow's mouth, though, was set in a straight line, his thick brows pulled down and eyes wary.

She raised her own brows when their gazes locked, but he subtly shook his head, eyes darting ahead of her.

As she followed his gaze, she realized she was already by the stairs.

Letting go of Loche's arm, she walked ahead of him, taking up the seat in the hard chair next to Venko. The blond man offered her a tight smile when she sat down, and she nodded back, briefly glancing at Craven. He didn't meet her eyes, keeping his straight ahead, his back rigid, and his features tense as he stared out over the crowd.

It was a lot bigger than that of the nobles—to be expected—but Lessia hadn't quite realized just how many would attend today.

It seemed like every merchant, fisherman, and store owner in Asker was attending the debate. Every chair beneath the dais was filled, and several groups of people, including her friends, lined up by the back wall, some pushing forward to get a better look.

When Frayson ascended the dais, the people immediately fell silent.

"Welcome, people of Ellow. For those of you who haven't attended before, this is your chance to evaluate the nominees for the next regent of Ellow. You will all have the chance to ask questions and raise concerns that are keeping you up at night. Please don't be shy to ask what you think is necessary to decide who you will vote for to lead Ellow. But I do ask that you do it one by one. This is a debate—not an opportunity to pick a fight. If you'd like a specific nominee to answer your question, please address them directly."

Loche coughed beside her, and when she peeked at him, she realized he was laughing.

He smiled at her when he caught her staring, then moved his eyes forward.

"Well, I guess there is not much more to say. Please raise your hand, and I will choose the speaker." Frayson clasped his hands behind his back and stepped to the side, hovering beside Loche's chair.

A man in the front immediately shot his hand into the air, and as Frayson nodded to him, the door into the room slammed open.

Every head turned toward Merrick as he stomped inside, eyes cast down as he gruffly leaned his back against a free spot by the side wall amid the many soldiers standing guard.

Flickering her gaze over him, Lessia realized he wore yesterday's clothing, and her brows furrowed as she wondered what task King Rioner might have assigned him that had him out all night.

As she shifted forward again, Loche's eyes struck hers with such force her stomach surged.

Thankfully, the man Frayson had allowed to speak rose at that moment, clearing his throat.

"I'd like to address Lessia."

Blood rushing in her ears, she focused on the man.

He was a regular in her taverns. Gerdho was a successful fisherman and a good man, judging by their interactions. His gaze didn't waver as it met hers, but she found no hostility in it as he continued.

"I believe we were all surprised when Lessia nominated herself. And from what we're hearing in town, she has not had the easiest time with it. I often visit her establishments, and from what I've seen, she treats her staff and her vendors exceptionally well."

"Do you have a point?" Craven spat.

Gerdho snapped his eyes to Craven, contempt twisting his features as he beheld the noble.

"I thought the rule not to interrupt also applied to nominees, but perhaps our dear nobles are exempt?" he asked Frayson.

"It does. Craven, you will speak only when asked."

Shaking his head, Craven clamped his mouth shut, but Lessia could smell the loathing in his scent, even with Venko seated between them.

"As I was saying. I have seen the good Lessia can do, and while I've heard the angry whispers about the risks of her Fae heritage, I'd like to take another angle instead: Lessia, how could your connections to Vastala help Ellow?"

Lessia swallowed.

She'd prepared for any and all questions about trade and taxes and even cattle.

But working with the Fae?

Every second that passed in silence seemed like an eternity.

What could she offer?

Crossing her legs, she leaned forward. "I can offer information that could facilitate better collaboration. I consider Ellow my home, and if working with the Fae can help us, I will share whatever I can to make that happen."

She waited a beat to see if the blood oath would punish her, but when no pain seared through her arm, she continued. "I will be honest. I am half-Fae. We're not particularly popular in Vastala, either, but I lived there for years, and I know the customs and traditions that might aid in fostering better relationships."

"And you're willing to share those with us?" a woman asked.

Lessia recognized her too.

She had worked in one of Lessia's gambling rooms before she became a mother, and she'd even spent a few nights at their house when Ardow had caught her eye.

Shooting a quick glance at Merrick, she nodded. "I am willing to share whatever I can."

Gerdho dipped his chin. "With these attacks we keep hearing of, we might need more weapons, perhaps even a stronger alliance if they grow worse—stop being limited to the nominees."

"But what if the Fae are behind them?" a woman toward the back shouted.

"We've seen no such indication. All who attacked were human." Loche flicked his hair out of his face. "I think you have a good point, Gerdho. I've been working to build a better alliance, and I think it's wise to see how Lessia could aid in that—see how her differences can benefit Ellow, as her businesses have."

She threw Loche a surprised glance.

While she'd warmed to him, as Merrick had so rudely stated, for him to defend her, even speak up for her during a debate, when she was technically his opponent, was entirely unlike him.

Loche grinned at her when Gerdho thanked them and sat down again.

A red-haired woman in a worn brown coat stepped up next, and her voice quivered as she started to speak. "My husband was a fisherman, and he provided for our entire family. But he..." She drew a shaky breath. "He never came back from sea last month. None of his crew did. I have four young ones, and I can't leave them to take up work. We have no coins left, and food is becoming scarce. I fear we'll end up on the streets if I don't find a solution. Is there... is there something you can do to help us, especially with the sea becoming increasingly dangerous, risking more families end up like mine?"

Lessia had never heard Loche's voice be so gentle as when he leaned forward, resting his hands on his knees. "Syvvie, we'll not let you or your children end up on the street. I have had to raise taxes already, but I will do so again to benefit the fishermen and any other families who struggle. You will be provided for by me and my men."

"We can't afford higher taxes!" several people grumbled, and ripples of assenting whispers rose across the room.

"We allow our employees to bring their children to the taverns, should they like. Perhaps there is a solution other than taxes," Lessia offered.

When the crowd remained quiet, she fidgeted with her cloak, but when Loche met her eyes and inclined his head, she continued. "I think most people prefer to provide for their own family, not rely on others. So, what I've offered one of our widowed cooks is to bring her children with her. It's worked out well—they even help sometimes, carrying smaller plates and cleaning. It keeps them entertained, and their mother can work in peace, knowing they're taken care of. Perhaps more businesses could do the same. At least in the taverns and shops."

One of Asker's bakers rose from his seat. "I'd be happy for the extra help, and we also have our young ones running around—they'd enjoy the company, if you'd be interested, Syvvie?"

Syvvie nodded, her flaming hair shining in the light of the chandelier hanging from the ceiling. Drops of tears streaked down her cheeks as she wrapped her arms around herself. "I'd like that. I'm a quick learner, and my little ones are good children. They would help if they could."

As she took her seat again, warmth clawed its way into Lessia's chest.

It wasn't much, but it felt good to be able to offer something.

When she dared a look at Loche, pride glittered in his eyes, and he leaned back in his chair, waving for her to continue as another man stepped forward.

CHAPTER FIFTY-FOUR

A smile pulled at her lips as she stretched her arms over her head before getting off the dais.

Lessia waved to a few people she recognized as they filed out of the room, then caught Amalise's eyes and started to make her way across the room.

It took longer than she anticipated, as several people stopped her, real smiles on their faces as they congratulated her on a good debate. Even if she spotted a few frosty glares and backs that turned on her as she passed, she didn't care.

It had been a good debate.

She'd spoken to nearly every topic: from how to involve the smaller isles in Ellow's business more, to how to ensure the harvest didn't suffer too hard from the harsh winter and how to build better ships to guarantee the safety of the fishermen.

To her delight Craven had said little more than a sentence, and Venko had also been unusually quiet, speaking up mostly when it came to trade—as it directly impacted his own ventures.

Loche had been in his element, and Lessia hadn't been able to tear her eyes away when he spoke to the townsfolk.

The kindness and care that radiated from him as he walked off the dais and hugged a widow whose husband had been one of Stellia's men, telling her he wouldn't stop until whoever did this was hung from the gates of the castle, was unlike anything she'd encountered.

He patiently listened to even the smallest of complaints about loose stones in the road outside a resident's house, never once raising his voice or dismissing a concern.

She could see why the people had elected him.

Why he'd likely win again.

Lessia was grinning from ear to ear by the time she reached Amalise and Ardow.

Although the attack and what Venko told her last night lingered in her mind, she had too much to be happy about.

The election would soon be over, and so, hopefully, would be her entanglement with the king.

Loche would surely be elected again, and she believed him when he said life would be better.

And her friends were here—had seen her success during the debate.

Dragging them both into her arms, she let out a deep breath, the constant tension in her body easing.

When she pulled back, Amalise patted her arm. "You did amazing. I knew you would, but I had no idea you knew so much about harvest or taxes."

Lessia wiggled her brows. "I may have done some homework."

"Ever the overperformer." Ardow chuckled. "You might even win this whole thing."

Lessia batted him away. "You know as well as I do that I

won't. But Loche did great, didn't he? I think the next five years will be quite good under his rule."

Ardow's features darkened, and he lowered his voice as he glanced behind them. "He's really got you under his spell, then. I wondered, but I thought you were cleverer than that, Lia."

She shared a look with Amalise.

When Amalise only shrugged, she frowned at Ardow. "What do you mean?"

Dragging them both with him into a corner, a safe distance from the people who lingered in the room and from the guards who hadn't yet started following people up into the sitting room where food was going to be served, Ardow spoke urgently.

"He is not good, Lessia. I don't know how you cannot see it, but he's dangerous. You need to stay away from him."

Apprehension churned in her gut, and as she turned her head over her shoulder, she caught Loche's dark eyes from where he stood by Zaddock's side in the doorway.

His mouth lifted when their gazes locked, and she couldn't help but offer him a small smile in return. Averting her eyes, she forced herself to keep the smile as she turned back to Ardow and Amalise.

Like Amalise, Ardow was protective over her.

He had been ever since he'd figured out her backstory.

But he was wrong about Loche.

Loche was many things, but her instincts told her she could trust him to care for Ellow.

Perhaps even care for her.

"You sound like Merrick," she joked. "Are you two conspiring?"

When Ardow stiffened, her eyes widened. "*Are* you two talking?"

He shook his head. “Of course not. But if he’s warned you against Loche, he’s right. It’s dangerous to spend time with him, Lessia. And based on your interaction earlier, it seems you’re spending more time together than I thought.”

“You almost sound jealous, Ardow,” Amalise scoffed. “If Lessia has found someone to keep her interest, leave her be. I, for one, think he’s perfect. Handsome, powerful, and clever? And interested in our Lia. I’m supportive.”

“You don’t understand—” Ardow started, but Lessia interrupted him.

“I don’t know what you have against him, Ardow. But he’s a good man. He might be frustrating and annoying and impossible to figure out, but he’s good.”

“I’m going to take that as a compliment.”

Her heart stopped, and she spun around, finding her face one inch from Loche’s amused one.

“We—we—uh,” she stuttered.

“Were just talking about me? I’m flattered.” Loche grinned. “If you’re finished, there is a whole dessert table waiting for you upstairs. I’ve heard you can’t turn down delicious cakes.”

She let out a low laugh. “Keep track of me much?”

“Always.” Loche chuckled, offering her his arm. “Come on.”

Reaching out a hand for Amalise, she took Loche’s arm, ignoring the hard look from Ardow as they ventured upstairs.

Zaddock fell into step with them, trying to get Amalise to talk about the debate, but she promptly ignored his questions, only grimacing at Lessia when she raised a brow.

Merrick was nowhere to be seen when she looked for him as they walked up the stairs, but given he seemed to have been out all night, Lessia guessed he might have retreated to his chambers.

When they entered the hall, she realized Loche hadn't exaggerated about the abundance of food.

As he slipped away to talk to someone who called out for him, she took in the room.

Several long tables had been brought into the ballroom, one entirely dedicated to desserts, with cakes and candies and whatever else Lessia could imagine. It seemed as if everyone from the debate had decided to join, the room full of people eating and mingling, some sitting down in the chairs spread out across the space and some taking to the small dance floor that formed to the left.

After stuffing her mouth full of everything she could find, Lessia slumped down into one of the plush chairs by the fireplace while Amalise sat on the armrest.

Ardow mumbled something about having business to attend to, and Lessia thought for a second about convincing him to stay. But she was still annoyed he'd ruined her buzz after the debate, so with a quick hug—that held none of the warmth they typically entailed—she offered him a quiet goodbye.

"So... Loche?" Amalise grinned.

Lessia peeked at him out of the corner of her eye.

He stood together with Zaddock and a few other of his guards by one of the drinks tables, but as soon as her eyes landed on him, he looked her way, and her stomach flipped at the magnetic pull of his gaze.

Looking down at the cup of water in her hands, she shrugged. "I don't know. Maybe Ardow is right. I probably should stay away from him."

Her friend placed a hand on her shoulder. "Stop overthinking this. I've never seen you like this. Look at you. You're blushing!"

Amalise leaned in closer. "And he's still staring."

Lessia dared a quick glance his way, and sure enough, his eyes clashed with hers again.

Squeezing her shoulder, Amalise got to her feet. "I'll go see what's up with Ardow, and I suggest you go over there and talk to the man. The Lessia I know isn't afraid of anything, least of all a man. Have some fun tonight—you deserve it!"

When Amalise left the room, once again ignoring Zaddock, who tried to stop her, Lessia sucked in a breath. Every nerve inside her sparked as she turned Loche's way, a fire igniting inside her when she found him already on the way over.

As he reached her, he jerked his head toward the bustling dance floor. "Will you join me for a victory dance?"

Nodding, she let him pull her onto the dance floor, allowing herself to stop thinking as he spun her around, even letting herself rest her head against him when the music slowed, melting against his broad chest.

CHAPTER FIFTY-FIVE

By the time she pulled out of Loche's arms, sweat dripped down her back. As they headed to the drinks table for refreshments, Zaddock intercepted Loche, his expression tight as he whispered that he needed to speak to him immediately.

Her eyes trailed them as they walked out of the room, and she wondered what had raised Zaddock's shoulders so high and turned his expression so serious. The anger coiling his muscles reminded her of Merrick, and she realized she should probably check on the Fae.

He'd seemed exhausted when he came to the debate, and she doubted he'd eaten.

Grabbing a plate and heaping it with meat and potatoes, Lessia ventured out of the room.

As she was about to take the first step up the stairs, angry whispers reached her ears. Her name drifted over the muffled music, and she spun around, searching the dimly lit hallway.

The voices came from one of the alcoves beside the spiraling stairs down to the cellars.

With a hand on the railing, she hesitated, but when her name was mentioned again, she tiptoed over and hid behind one of the white pillars beside it.

"Loche, this is serious! You can't be seen with her like this! What are you thinking?"

Zaddock's low voice was urgent, and he must have slammed his hand on the wall, given the loud bang that followed.

"Calm down, Z. We danced, so what?" Loche drawled.

A groan followed, and Zaddock hissed, "*So what?* You're risking everything, and you know it! You can't do this—not when we've gotten this far."

A guard walked out into the hallway, and Lessia slipped farther into the shadow of the pillar, staying out of the flickering light from the chandelier. A dusty gold tapestry tickled her nose as she pressed herself against it, and she held her breath until the guard disappeared up the stairs.

Her heart thundered in her chest when Loche raised his voice and an icy edge laced it. "Remember your place. I have it under control. She means nothing to me, and everyone knows it. I have been vocal about the need to collaborate with the Fae, and I need to show leadership in accepting them. She is just the means to that end."

A sharp pain jabbed her heart, and Lessia stumbled out from behind the pillar.

In her rush toward the stairs, her foot snagged on the thick carpet covering the stone floor. As she tried to catch herself, the plate slipped out of her hands, clattering to the floor, the sound piercing the stone-walled space.

Steps rang behind her, and she abandoned the plate and the stairs. Spinning around, she slammed open the castle doors without daring to look behind her.

Lessia was met with a bone-chilling breeze that blew

straight through her wool cloak as she stormed down the castle courtyard, but she barely felt it as a hollow ache spread in her chest.

With the wind roaring in her ears, she sprinted away from the castle toward the towering cliffs and the meadow where she'd last met Kalia and the rest. Swearing to herself as she slipped every few feet, she ignored the darkness that loomed ahead, fixing her gaze on the moon hanging low over the upset sea.

The crashing waves mirrored the turmoil inside her, and she cursed again as she thought of how stupid she'd been to read into her interactions with Loche.

Ardow was right.

She was cleverer than this.

Pretty promises and heart-stopping looks shouldn't have her act like a mere child.

Still, it was like her heart had cracked in two, every breath she drew feeling like a shard of ice making its way down her lungs.

"Lessia, wait!"

A growl left her throat, her top lip curling back to display her canines as she spun around, finding Loche a few steps behind her.

"Leave me alone," she snarled.

"Lessia, let me explain." Loche slowed his long strides, his eyes searching her face.

She frantically scanned the area for a way to escape him, but there was no way she could enter the dark woods behind her or to her right, and to her left, there was only a steep drop into the dark sea.

Although the cold water might be preferable to spending one more second in his presence.

"Listen to me. It's not what you think."

She snapped her eyes to his, her hands shaking by her side as she tried to manage her breathing. "There is no need, Loche. I get it—it's just business."

A small part of her truly understood him—understood that he needed to do everything in his power to do right by Ellow.

But it did little to soothe the betrayal.

"It's not. Please, come back with me, and I'll explain everything."

Shaking her head, she turned around again, starting toward the woods anyway.

Maybe the anger would keep her fear of the dark at bay.

A branch snapped somewhere behind her, but she didn't turn around, only continued walking over the slippery cliffs, grinding her teeth against the snow the wind swirled into her face.

"Lessia!"

She stilled at the urgency in Loche's voice.

As she turned her head over her shoulder, her muscles locked.

Loche was still a few feet behind her, but it wasn't his shadowy figure that caused icy dread to fill her veins.

It was the twenty or so black shapes that filed out of the trees beside them, the glinting swords in their hands.

She froze as the figures closed the distance between them, and it wasn't until Loche spoke again that she snapped out of it.

"Darling, come to me." Loche's voice was soft, beckoning, and it was all she could do to take a faltering step toward him when something glimmered in his eyes.

He was scared.

And that made her terrified.

When she didn't move fast enough, Loche bridged the

space between them with three assured steps, pulling her behind him.

The figures were only a few steps away now, and goose bumps rippled across her skin when she realized they were all cloaked, dark hoods shrouding their features.

And most importantly—their eyes.

There were too many for them to take on alone.

Especially if she couldn't use her magic.

Her nostrils flared when they slowed to a stop before them, and she unsheathed the daggers she had tucked into her waistband. Loche cast her a quick glance as he gripped the sword hanging by his side, and while the flicker of fear in his eyes remained, resolve sharpened his features.

His free hand cupped her chin. "Don't let them get you closer to the drop."

When she nodded, his eyes moved forward again, and Lessia's body thrummed with adrenaline as one of the men let out a low chuckle before ordering "Get them."

Two of the cloaked men were instantly upon her, but she planted her feet wide, and turning her body sideways to throw them off, she lashed out with a dagger, grimacing at the sickening sensation of it burrowing into soft flesh.

The man she'd struck tumbled to the ground with a stifled cry. The other gripped her arm, and as she tried to elbow him, he stepped out of the way, twisting her arm at a painful angle behind her back.

Remembering Merrick's lessons, she bent down, driving the hilt of the dagger in her free hand between his legs. When his grip loosened, she ripped her arm free, spinning around and closing her eyes as she slammed the dagger deep into his chest.

Yanking it out, she turned around again, kicking at another figure to keep him back.

But he continued advancing, and when his sword whistled through the air, she wasn't fast enough.

The blade sliced her wrist, and the dagger she'd held clattered onto the cliffs.

"Lessia!"

She caught Loche's gaze as he fought off four men, and his eyes widened as he screamed, "Watch out!"

Whirling around, she found three more men stalking toward her, crowding her against the steep drop.

Lessia cursed loudly and tried to jump to the side, but the man that struck her blocked her way, laughing when she snarled at him.

"Not fast enough, little Faeling," he taunted.

"Take off that hood and tell me to my face," she growled.

He laughed darkly again. "I don't think so."

She prepared to lunge at him, but as she took the first step, arms wrapped around her chest, and another hand gripped her wrist so tight she had no choice but to let the other dagger fall to the ground.

Kicking and twisting, she tried to get free, but the men behind her locked her arms against her body, their sharp breaths brushing her cheeks as they pressed against her.

"Throw her off the cliff," the man before her ordered.

"No!" Loche screamed.

Pushing off the men he was fighting, he sprinted toward them, but they caught up with him, and he had to stop to continue parrying their blows, spinning, lunging, and dropping low so not to get impaled by the long blades.

The men started dragging her toward the sea, and Lessia continued to desperately kick to get out of their hold, but it did little to stop them from soon reaching the edge.

As they shifted her to face the wild waves, she thought of Amalise, Ardow, and all the children, praying that Loche would make it out alive so he could keep the promise he'd made and give them a chance at a better life.

Just as they were about to push her off, the air stilled.

A rush of ancient, wild magic tinged the whistling wind, and harried whispers boomed in her ears. Oily vibrations tangled with the icy winter night, softly layering over her skin.

The men around her screamed, their hard grips releasing her as their shrieks cut off midway. The whispers softened, drifting away with the salty squalls from the sea, leaving a deafening silence in their wake.

Shakily taking a step back from the icy drop, she spun around.

Merrick stood tall amongst the fallen bodies, the air surrounding him rippling and whirling and his silvery hair blowing wildly around his hard, bent-down face.

Loche also stood straight amongst the men on the snow beneath him, his eyes wide and snapping back and forth between her and Merrick. Emotions raced across his features as understanding—too much understanding—filled his gaze.

A wave of fear rushed through her when he didn't lower his sword but gripped the hilt tighter as he faced Merrick. The Fae ignored him as he stalked up to Lessia and bent down to pick up the daggers, shoving them into her hands.

She remained still as he looked her over, careful not to meet her eyes, before he leaned in close. "You need to erase his memory."

When she started shaking her head, Merrick hissed, "Look at him! He is about to fight me. Perhaps you as well."

Lifting her eyes to Loche, she nearly stumbled back at the flames burning in his gray ones.

"Loche..." she started but trailed off when his eyes snapped to Merrick.

"You're the Death Whisperer," Loche growled. "King Rioner's right-hand man."

His gaze shifted back to Lessia, and she swallowed at the hurt twisting his features.

"So, you are a spy, after all." He started pacing back and forth, his sword ready in his hand. "Does he want war? Is that what your king is after? I can't ignore this. Ellow can't ignore this."

"Loche—" she started again as she slipped one of the daggers into her waistband, but he interrupted her.

"No! I thought I'd figured out your secret, but you keep many, don't you? Fuck! I don't want another devastating war. Why is he doing this?"

When Lessia and Merrick remained quiet, he screamed, "Tell me! You owe me that much."

"I... I can't," Lessia got out, her voice strangled.

"You won't. That's what you mean!" Loche dragged a hand through his dark hair. "You need to come with me. I'll have to take you to the dungeons. I'll try to make sure they don't execute you, but I need time to figure this out."

Merrick gripped her arm. "If you don't erase his memory, I have to kill him."

His magic whispered through the air again, and Lessia bit back a cry.

She didn't want to do this.

She couldn't do this to him.

But as she desperately scanned the area around them, a sharp pain coiled its way up her arm.

Loche knew about them now, and even though the king hadn't given her a timeframe for when she needed to use her magic, he'd told her she couldn't share anything about him or her mission.

Beside her Merrick shook from restraining his magic, the

oily whispers snaking over her shoulders, and a whimper worked its way up her throat when the pain in her arm intensified.

Her feet moved of their own accord, making her take a step toward Loche.

"I'm so sorry," she whispered as she pulled on her own magic.

"What are you sorry for?" Loche snarled, eyeing her as she took another step.

"This." Her voice barely carried over the wind as magic rushed through her body, her eyes shifting into a molten golden glow.

Loche's hard eyes widened for a second before they glazed, every line of his face softening into a mask of obedience.

She huffed a breath as her heart cracked at seeing him like this.

Completely unrecognizable from the strong, lethal, alluring leader he was.

Placing a hand on his heated cheek, she gently caressed it with her thumb.

"I'm so sorry," she whispered again before dragging up every ounce of magic within her.

Her voice lowered into a seductive murmur. "You will forget that Merrick has magic, forget that he's the Death Whisperer and full Fae. You will forget that we are spies. You will forget I did this to you, forget that we had this conversation. The only thing you will remember is that we were attacked, and we fought them bravely. Merrick thankfully showed up before we were overwhelmed, and he helped take them down."

As she began to pull away from Loche, Merrick spoke behind her. "Give me a minute."

She didn't dare avert her eyes from Loche's, but out of the corner of her eye, she caught Merrick unsheathing his sword, driving it into the lifeless bodies on the ground, backing up her story.

Her throat went dry as she stared into Loche's vacant eyes, and she continued to brush her thumb over his cheek—as if the touch could somehow make up for what she was doing.

"Ask him what King Rioner wants to know," Merrick ordered as he made his way to them.

Lessia stiffened. "No. This is enough."

Merrick stepped up behind her, placing a warm hand on her shoulder. "He ordered you to. This is the best chance we'll get, Lessia."

"No! I can't do this."

Merrick's hand brushed her arm, but she found no comfort in it.

"You don't have a choice. You'll fulfill his orders if you do this. Think about what you have to lose. If you don't care for your own life, think of your friends."

Lessia stared up into the gray clouds above her, only seeing Amalise's and Ardow's faces before her eyes.

Drawing a shaky breath, she opened her mouth, clasping at her chest when it seemed to cave in on her. "What do you know of the attacks in Havlands?"

A dry sob left her throat as the words tumbled out.

Loche's voice was monotone as he spoke. "They're retaliation for what I did."

She blinked but couldn't stop herself from asking, "What did you do?"

"Betrayed the people who helped me become regent."

"What... what do you mean?"

Not a muscle moved in Loche's face. "Everyone thinks it's

a miracle the lowly bastard rose so quickly in the ranks and then was able to win the election. It wasn't. I was offered money for my campaign and information that allowed me to blackmail the nobles into voting for me. All in exchange for them having a say in how Ellow should be ruled. But I'm not someone you can control. I took the money and information, won, and then stopped all correspondence with them. I want what's best for Ellow, and those people are not it. They've been attacking me and my men ever since then, trying to get me to fall back in line."

Her stomach dropped.

She'd thought it strange he had been able to get as far as he had, but after getting to know him...

She'd thought she'd understood why.

This, though...

This was information her king really shouldn't have.

"Who are they?" Merrick asked behind her.

"I don't know." Loche continued to stare blankly into her eyes. "I've never met them. We communicated through letters."

"Enough!" Lessia cried.

She couldn't hear more.

She didn't want to hear more.

Not like this.

Not when she would have to relay this word for word to King Rioner.

As she forced her magic down, Merrick let out a grunt behind her, and she was about to snarl at him when his hand dropped from her shoulder and he fell to his knees with a thud.

Pulse thundering in her ears, she tore her eyes from Loche, slamming into dark ones under a hood. Pulling the cowl back, the man spat on Merrick's body as it crumpled to the ground.

"Traitor," he hissed, raising the sword again and angling it to Merrick's heart.

Blood dripped from the sword, pooling on the ground beneath the Fae, and a mirrored crimson hue filled her vision. Anger like she'd never felt before overwhelmed her, and without thinking, Lessia lifted the dagger she still held on to.

With a bloodcurdling cry, she jumped over Merrick and drove it right into the man's heart, the cracking of his ribs as she broke through them echoing in the night.

CHAPTER FIFTY-SIX

"Merrick!"

Lessia dropped down beside the unmoving Fae, using two fingers to feel for a pulse on his neck. Blowing out a breath after finding a heartbeat, she searched him for injuries, wincing when she found a deep, bleeding wound in his back.

"Is he all right?"

Loche dropped down beside her, flicking his head to get his hair out of his face.

She stared back at him with guilt sloshing in her stomach, but there was no hurt in his eyes, only relief and worry for her guard.

Swallowing the lump of despair in her throat, she responded quietly, "He's alive, but we need to get him back to the castle."

Nodding, Loche rose to his feet. "I'll help you."

Together, they lifted him off the ground and dragged his body between them as they slowly made their way back across the dark cliffs.

Merrick's large frame was heavy to carry, and Lessia tried to focus on keeping him upright instead of on the knot of shame that tightened in her gut every time she caught Loche's eyes over his head.

They were both out of breath by the time they reached the light spilling out of the gates from the courtyard, and as Loche kicked open the creaking metal wicket, guards sprinted up to them, shifting Merrick's arms over their shoulders.

"Take him to the healer wing," Loche ordered.

"No." Merrick regained consciousness, head slumping forward between the two men but voice surprisingly strong. "Just take me to my room. I'll heal quickly."

"Merrick, you need someone to look at your wound. It's deep," Lessia argued.

"Please, Lessia," he begged, his voice quivering as he sucked in a breath.

She stared at the Fae.

Not once had she heard him sound like this.

Hadn't even imagined he ever could.

The vulnerability in his plea tugged at her already broken heart, and when he whispered "Please" once more, she nodded reluctantly.

"Take him to his chambers. I will take care of him."

When Loche opened his mouth, she shot him a dark glare, and he finally bowed his head, gesturing for the guards to follow her command.

She walked behind them while they half carried, half fought Merrick as he tried to walk by himself to his chambers, shaking her head when the Fae snarled at the two men as they tried to lift him.

After what felt like an eternity, they reached the door to his room, but as the guards were about to walk through with him, Merrick hissed, "Only her."

Rolling her eyes, she thanked the guards and slipped under Merrick's arm, ignoring his grumblings as she led him to the bed.

After walking back and kicking the door shut, she sat down next to him and started pulling at his cloak.

Merrick let her slip it off, but when she pulled at his tunic, he shoved her hands away.

"We need to clean it, at least," she grumbled. "Stop acting like a child."

He tried to push her off again, but when she didn't give up, he eventually resigned, his head slumping even farther forward than usual as she peeled the blood-soaked tunic off his muscled back.

"Lift your arms," she ordered.

Merrick hesitated for a moment but finally raised his arms over her head.

"Good male," she joked as she pulled the tunic off. "Now—"

Lessia sucked in a sharp breath.

A silver snake tattoo twisted around Merrick's forearm, coiling its way up his large bicep, the dark eyes of the snake glaring right at her.

"You're—you're—" she stuttered.

His head fell to his chest.

Merrick was blood-sworn to the king.

Lessia stared at the tattoo, and couldn't help but trace it with her finger.

It was identical to hers, with the same twists and turns, a vicious reminder that the king had them in his grasp.

The mark of a Fae traitor.

But Merrick had been in the king's service for centuries. Surely he couldn't...

"How long?" she whispered.

His head tilted slightly, but no words left his lips.

As no words would have left Lessia's lips if she'd been asked the same question.

"The entire time?" She almost didn't want the answer.

But the small twitch of his jaw told her everything she needed to know.

"Oh, Merrick," she whispered as she moved closer, wrapping her arms around his neck and hugging him tight.

He stiffened at first but then leaned into her embrace, his heart hammering in sync with hers as the air turned thick with grief.

No wonder he understood her so well.

He was living the same life.

Had been living it for hundreds of years.

They sat like that, quiet and holding on to each other for a long time.

It was only when Lessia remembered his wound that she got up and cleared her throat. "I will get some water and cloths to clean you up."

With heavy steps, she made her way to the bathing chamber, where she picked up a bucket already filled with water and a soft cloth hanging off the side of the bath. As she made to walk out, she caught a glimpse of herself in the mirror and winced at the paleness of her face.

Staring into the lifeless amber eyes, she ground her teeth.

She should have figured it out.

The fact that Merrick not once had mistakenly looked into her eyes was surely a result of King Rioner's orders. His insinuations about the evil men in Vastala. His attempt at protecting her from the king by choosing his words so carefully.

She dragged a hand through her damp hair, her finger getting stuck where the tips had frozen from the chill wind.

How had he ended up like this?

He was so powerful.

Not weak, like she'd been.

Lessia sighed.

He wouldn't be able to tell her.

Averting her eyes from the mirror, she walked out into the softly lit chamber again.

Merrick had lain down on his side on the bed, blood dripping onto the pale blanket. Streams of moonlight danced over his bare torso, the silver in them mockingly mirroring the silver tattoo wrapped around his strong arm and the pearly hair splayed out across the covers.

She eyed him as she approached, and the tension lining his shoulders eased slightly as she sat down.

After dipping the cloth into the bucket, Lessia carefully cleaned his wound.

It was deep but had started clotting, his Fae blood already working hard to heal him.

Merrick barely seemed to notice, and once she finished, his breathing had slowed, his eyes closed, and his features softened.

She tiptoed to the closet, pulled out a thick blanket, and covered him with it.

Lingering by the side of the bed, she gently stroked his face, letting her finger travel from his high cheekbones to his strong jaw, pushing a strand of hair behind his pointed ear.

"What happened to you?" she whispered as he shifted in his sleep.

Merrick continued sleeping, his face seeming so young without the tension and contempt that usually lined it, and something tugged at her heart as she wondered whether this was what he'd looked like before he'd fallen into the king's grasp.

How had King Rioner snared the Death Whisperer?

Merrick was one of the strongest Fae in Vastala—in all Havlands.

His face twitched, and as she smoothed out the wrinkle between his brows, she realized there was somewhere she could potentially learn more about him.

With a final caress, she sneaked out of the room.

Several guards stood posted outside, and as she started to walk down the hallway, two of them quietly followed her as she made her way up the spiral staircase to the library.

Outside the library doors, she managed to convince them she needed some time alone after allowing one of the guards to search the tower first. When he came back, assuring her no one was lying in wait, she thanked him and walked inside.

She hadn't bothered with the books about the Fae when she was here before.

She'd seen them but hadn't thought they would be very helpful in learning as much about Ellow as she could.

She made her way up toward the top floor, pausing on the final staircase to eye the beautiful carvings of Fae decorating the broad wooden railings.

The carved stories were of battle and fighting but also of love and friendship, one depicting Queen Trista, the original queen of Vastala, and her consort, Melekh.

Their love had been epic.

Lessia's father had told her stories of how Trista had been promised to another Fae of royal blood but had fallen in love with a foot soldier and had refused to leave him, even as the noble Fae threatened her crown.

Lessia smiled at the defiance in the queen's eyes, clear as day even in the wooden carving.

She'd hoped for that kind of love when she was younger.

Tearing her eyes away, she mounted the final steps onto

the crescent-shaped floor, where she browsed the shelves until she reached one about the Fae battles.

Lessia sat down on the wooden table, as there were no chairs on this floor, placed the book in her lap, and flipped it open.

The first pages depicted the many wars fought in the early days after the Fae moved to Vastala—the power struggles between the elementals and the mentals.

Then Merrick was named for the first time.

His brotherhood had famously squashed a devastating war by killing an entire army of Fae that threatened Vastala.

Together with Raine—rumored to be the most powerful mental Fae ever to walk any realm—and the rest of their brotherhood, Merrick had stood against thousands upon the beaches of Vastala.

And came out victorious.

But nowhere did it mention why they fought for King Rioner's family—why they'd stood against their own kin, the mental Fae.

Lessia slammed the dusty book shut when she didn't find any more mentions of Merrick and was about to jump to her feet to look for another when she caught movement out of the corner of her eye.

Whipping her head up, she found Loche leaning against the railing, his eyes thoughtful as he observed her. She couldn't stop a shiver jerking her shoulders, and a smile pulled at his lips as he followed the tremor running through her.

"I didn't mean to scare you."

Loche made his way over until he stood right before her. She tilted her head to continue meeting his eyes, forcing herself to hold back a wince at the rush of guilt that tightened her chest.

He glanced at the book in her hands, and she quickly set it on the table beside her.

Placing her hands on her knees, she tried for a shaky smile.

Loche took another step.

Nudging her knees apart to make space for him, he erased the final distance between them.

"What are you doing?" She stared at his strong legs, leaning against the table between hers.

"Do you want me to move?"

Yes.

No.

Her heart skipped a beat at the storm raging in his eyes when she met them again.

Loche leaned in close enough for the heat of his body to envelop her. "I need to tell you something."

She bowed her head, but Loche's fingers gently lifted her chin, forcing her eyes to his.

"Lessia, I… I haven't been truthful with you, but I need to be. Especially after what happened tonight."

She started shaking her head. "Loche, you don't owe me anything—"

He interrupted her. "But I do. I've put you in danger, and you don't even know it."

"Loche…"

"Lessia." He placed both hands over her cheeks. "Please, just listen to me."

Swallowing, she finally nodded, even as she struggled to breathe from the shame that seemed to permeate every inch of her body.

His eyes bounced between hers before he cleared his throat. "Years ago, I was starting out in the navy. I was doing well—exceptionally well. They promoted me to captain within my first year and talked about making me commander of the whole fleet. People noticed."

He ground his teeth. "One day, I got a letter with information on one of the other captains, who was making life miserable for the soldiers. I was able to use it to blackmail him into leaving, never to return. Then, more letters started to come in, full of information on the most powerful men and women in Ellow. I used it for good—to help people get out from under their tyranny. So, when another letter came, offering to help me become regent, I accepted. I was young and dumb, and I thought I was in control. But once I'd won, they started making demands—demands that I couldn't agree to. So, I didn't. I thought I was strong enough to take them on. But then they started attacking anyone close to me. First my family—not that it mattered much to me—I never cared for them. But then they came after my men."

Loche's eyes left hers for a moment, and he drew a deep breath as his hands dropped to his sides. "They killed one of my best friends. Nearly got to Zaddock too. That's when I came up with the masks. If they don't know who they are, they can't come after them."

His eyes clashed with hers again, and the gray filled with the same guilt she was trying hard to keep out of her own.

Lessia reached out and gripped one of his hands. "It's not your fault. You couldn't have known."

He laced their fingers together, glancing at them for a moment before lifting his silver eyes again. "But it is. Everyone who comes close to me risks their lives. And now I've risked yours too. I've been so stupid, but I can't seem to stay away from you."

He let out a sharp breath as he moved their hands to her lap, slamming his other one on the table beside her. "I don't want to stay away from you!"

Trailing his eyes over her face, Loche continued in a lower voice. "They must have learned that. Must know how I feel. That's why they came after us tonight. I'm so sorry."

Her skin burned when he leaned in closer, jaw ticking. "I have every man in my employ looking for them. And we're close—we finally have a lead. We'll catch them any day now, and I promise you that they won't come near you again."

Nodding, she fought against leaning into him.

"Lessia," he rasped as he tilted his head down.

Her breath hitched when he stilled with his lips an inch from hers.

"I don't want to stay away from you," he whispered again.

A tremble seized her body when his hot breath hit her mouth as he continued. "Tell me. Tell me you burn for me like I burn for you. Tell me your heart stops when I walk into a room like mine does for you. Tell me you can't stop thinking about me like I can't go a waking second without thinking about you. Tell me you don't want me to stay away."

Loche's gaze consumed her, hope and desire and vulnerability flaming in the gray.

She opened her mouth, but no words came out.

Eyes flitting between his, she willed herself to be strong.

What she'd done to him tonight was unforgivable.

He wouldn't be here if he knew.

She wouldn't be here if he knew.

She'd be in the musty cellars beneath the castle, chained to the wall in wait for a death sentence.

"Lessia."

She saw the resolve in his eyes just before his mouth crashed against hers.

A low moan escaped her when his hands wrapped in her hair, dragging her to him, and heat erupted in her core when he responded with a growl.

Loche's lips were anything but gentle as they hungrily, possessively, explored hers, his teeth scraping against her bottom lip until she let his tongue dance with hers.

As he went to shift her down onto the table, she forced herself to snap out of the fog that filled her mind.

Mustering the last strength within her, she placed a hand on his chest.

"Loche," she whispered.

He pulled back, and their eyes collided, a flame shooting down her spine at the heat surging in his gaze.

"Loche, I need to tell..." She let out a huff at the agony searing through her arm, gripping Loche's biceps to restrain herself from reaching down to rub it.

"I..." she tried again. "I'm not good."

Electricity crackled over her skin as one of the corners of his mouth lifted.

Leaning in again, he spoke against her mouth. "Neither am I, darling."

His lips brushed hers. "Let's be bad together."

When his warm mouth sought hers again, she had no fight left.

Pushing the self-loathing deep down, she let Loche kiss her until the only thing she could think about was his hard body pressing against hers, his strong hands exploring her neck, and his skilled tongue playing with hers.

CHAPTER FIFTY-SEVEN

Loche's lips didn't leave hers when he lifted her off the table, shifting her so she straddled his lap as he took her place. His hands found her hair again, and he wrapped the golden strands in one of his fists, tilting her head backward.

When his mouth left hers, a muffled complaint left her throat, and Loche's low laugh fanned over the sensitive skin of her neck as he trailed his lips down. Shivers racked her body as his hot breaths ignited every nerve, and she wrapped her legs around his back, her arms locking around his neck, forcing their bodies closer.

Her chest rose and fell with his, and Loche growled again as he unfastened her cloak.

A sharp exhale left her as it fell to the floor, and he hooked a finger inside her tunic, pulling it off her shoulder to let his mouth explore more of her skin.

But when he went to pull it farther down, fear stabbed at her like a knife, breaking through the clouded heat scorching her mind.

Lessia shifted, gripping his hand.

Stilling, he pulled back, eyes searching hers.

The desire swimming in his steely ones made her cheeks flush, and Loche grinned—that boyish, playful grin that lit up his entire face—as he released her hair and lifted his hand to trace the crimson blooming across her face.

"I love it when you blush like this."

His husky rasp was full of promises, and without thinking, she leaned in and kissed the corner of his mouth.

"I love it when you smile like this," she whispered as she straightened.

Their eyes locked, and Lessia couldn't breathe as emotions raced across his face.

"Come away with me."

Her eyes widened, and for a second, she thought about nodding.

Letting go of all her responsibilities.

Being utterly selfish and taking him somewhere they could never be found.

But then her gaze snagged on the arm wrapped around his neck.

As she began shaking her head, Loche's hand cupped her face and gently stopped the movement, his thumbs brushing over her lips.

"We have a few days between the final hardship and the election, and trust me, it won't be pleasant. Let's go away—just you and me. Forget all of this for a while."

A chasm of ice opened in her chest at the hope in his eyes, and she averted her own, fixing them on his heaving chest.

"I can't," she whispered.

"Why not?" His voice was soft.

Curious.

As if he truly didn't understand.

Swallowing, she forced her eyes to meet his. "Merrick is injured. I need to take care of him. And I have duties here. My friends..."

Loche gave her a crooked smile. "I'll have our best healer tend to him. She can even move into your room while we're gone. Although something tells me Merrick would be quite opposed to that. And Zaddock can check on your friends. He'd be happy for it. I think he might have developed a small obsession with the blonde. As for your duties—it's only a few days, Lessia."

Amalise's words echoed in her mind.

You deserve love.

Promise me if there is a chance you find it, you will.

She'd made that promise.

And while she wasn't sure if this was love, she'd never before felt the warm feeling coursing through her veins as she met Loche's eyes.

Hadn't ever had her heart skip a beat like it did when Loche smirked at her.

But chilling guilt mingled with the warmth, and she winced as the memories from earlier flooded her mind.

If she went with him...

If she was this selfish...

Eyes narrowing, Loche leaned forward. "I've learned the hard way not to feel guilty over doing something selfish once in a while. It gets lonely at the top, Lessia. And I have a feeling you've been lonely for a long time."

She rubbed her neck, suddenly very aware of how close they were. How strong Loche's legs were beneath her. How hard the chest she rested against was. How soft the skin at the base of his neck was.

Goose bumps raced across her skin when he grinned at her, pulling her other arm around his neck and leaning his forehead against hers.

"I'm not the begging type, Lessia. But if you need me to, I'll get on my knees. I'm already risking everything. I don't mind throwing my pride into the ring as well."

Despite everything, a giggle bubbled up her throat, and Loche's mouth twitched.

"You think that's funny, darling?"

Raising a brow, she grinned at him, grateful that some of the tension in the room eased. "You just surprise me, is all."

Loche winked at her. "You don't know me as well as you think you do. Besides, I can think of some very good reasons to get on my knees before you. And I promise you won't be laughing then."

She thought her face might melt off, and Loche chuckled softly. "There's that blush again."

His eyes wandered over her face, and he shook his head. "You're so beautiful."

Shaking her head back, Lessia shifted, creating some distance between them. "I'm Fae. We're all beautiful."

Loche moved his hands from her face to wrap them around her waist, pulling her to him and erasing the space again, and his eyes bore into hers. "You're Lessia. And you're the most interesting woman I've ever had the honor to meet. You're beautiful, and kind, and caring, and intelligent. And somehow, you seem to have an inkling of interest in me. I am not known to let opportunities pass me by, and I won't do it with you. If I am lucky enough that the feelings I sense from you are true, I will always cherish them. I'll do anything to keep them, fuel them, make them burn bright even in the darkest of winter."

A lump formed in her throat as a small piece of the walls she'd built around her heart shattered, each pulse echoing in her ears.

She hadn't known how much she needed to hear those words.

That he saw her for Lessia.

Not half-Fae or half-human.

Just...

Lessia.

His eyes flitted between hers, something soft settling in his gaze. "How about you speak to Merrick to see what he thinks of you going away?"

A sigh escaped her as she burrowed her face into his neck, drawing deep breaths of his minty smell.

How did he know that was the right thing to say?

There was no way Merrick would approve, but at least then she could blame her guard, and even if she could feel that Loche wouldn't fault her regardless, she didn't have to be the one to let him down.

His large hands stroked her back, and when she pulled away, he brushed his lips against hers before lifting them both off the table.

As he set her down on the floor, Loche reached out a hand, and she didn't hesitate as she took it and allowed him to lead her out of the library.

The soldiers who had followed her there still stood guard outside, and while they shared a look when they noticed their joined hands, neither said anything.

They remained quiet as they all followed her to her chambers, and outside the door, Lessia hesitated.

Loche didn't.

Without a glance at the guards, he pulled her to him, kissing her until her breath caught in her throat. When he finally pulled away, her lips ached, and a deeper ache burned in her core as he remained outside until she opened the door, slipping inside.

Leaning her back against the door, she caught her breath.

Lessia trailed her fingers over her lips, and she couldn't stop the smile that spread across her face.

"Where were you?"

She tensed, and her eyes rose to the brightly lit room.

Merrick sat fully clothed on her bed, his bent-down face paler than usual but his back straight and shoulders squared.

No sign that he'd been grievously wounded earlier in the evening.

For the first time, a twinge of envy tightened in her chest at his full Fae blood.

While half-Fae healed quicker than humans, she wouldn't have survived if it had been her.

Fear crawled up her spine as she realized that getting more involved with Loche would likely put her in more situations like that of tonight.

When Merrick cleared his throat, she opened her mouth to speak, but he was faster.

"I can smell him on you. Spare me the details."

Face burning, she opened a window, letting the winter breeze cool her skin.

And hopefully diluting whatever Merrick could smell on her.

With her back to him, she said quietly, "He wants me to go away with him for a few days. I said no, of course."

It was quiet for a moment, and she turned, pulling the chair by the window around to face Merrick.

The Fae gripped her blankets tightly, his face strained as he spoke. "Why did you say no?"

She shrugged, biting her cheek at the guilt threatening to take her voice. "Because I can't do that to him. It's not fair to him when he doesn't know everything about me."

"But you want to go?" Merrick's voice was barely carrying over the strong wind roaring in the room.

Shrugging again, she glanced down at her hands. "It doesn't matter what I want. I can't."

He drew a shaky breath through his nose, knuckles gripping the blanket blanching. "I think you should."

Lessia's eyes flew wide.

"You think I should?" she echoed.

With a nod, Merrick rose from the bed, his movements jerky as he used the bedpost to steady himself. "It will be good for you. Our king won't come back for a while, and you have a few days off."

She blinked. "You don't think it's too dangerous?"

Making his way to his room, Merrick lingered by the door, his fingers tapping the wooden frame. "Everywhere is dangerous right now. But perhaps the castle is the most dangerous of all. Go, Lessia. I have some matters to tend to anyway, so I won't be around. And while he is human, I believe the man can protect you. Perhaps better than I can."

Her mouth still hung open as the door closed behind him.

As she lay down in the bed, anticipation danced across her skin, and a stupid smile wouldn't leave her face even as sleep took her.

She had no nightmares that night.

CHAPTER
FIFTY-EIGHT

A demanding knock on the corridor door woke her, and Lessia yawned as she wrapped a thick blanket around herself against the freezing air in the room and made her way over to open it.

No light trickled in through the large windows as she unlocked the hatch, but Loche was fully dressed in dark clothing, with a thick fur-lined cloak clasped atop his chest, a satchel slung over his shoulder, and a grin gracing his face.

"I heard you were free to go."

A wrinkle formed over her brows as she tried to smooth out the hair she was sure was tangled around her face. "How?"

Loche grinned wider. "I've told you before; I get what I want."

Her frown deepened.

With a wink, Loche gently nudged her backward, opening the door farther. "I might have had Zaddock pay your guard a visit while we were spending time in the library."

Lessia shot a look at the door leading into Merrick's room.

Had he known all along Loche asked her to leave?

She glanced from Loche to the darkness outside her windows. "Is it even morning?"

Chuckling, Loche walked into her room. "No. But I'd prefer not to have anyone see us or try to stop us. Now get dressed, and let's leave."

She was already dressed in her usual tunic and breeches, so Lessia laced up her worn leather boots and made her way to the bathing chamber. A shiver danced across her shoulders when Loche's hand brushed hers as she passed him.

She threw him a glare, but he only chuckled again, his eyes glittering in the dim light.

Closing the door behind her, she drew a deep breath.

Nerves tangled in her stomach, and she wished she'd had time to speak to Amalise or Ardow before leaving.

Not that she had never been alone with a man before, but Loche...

There was something about him that unsettled her, shook her to her core.

And she couldn't help but worry what would happen once they were alone again. She'd nearly gotten carried away yesterday. Had almost forgotten about what she kept hidden beneath her long sleeves.

Lessia splashed some cold water on her face and picked up a brush to try to tame her unruly hair. The amber eyes looking back at her in the scuffed mirror as she worked were wide, and there was a rosiness in her cheeks she couldn't attribute to the cold.

She groaned to herself.

He was just a man.

Straightening her dark tunic, securing the sleeve over the silver snake, she shook her head and walked out into the room again.

Loche stood in the same spot, his eyes immediately finding hers. When he offered her her cloak, she let him place it on her shoulders and clasp it shut.

His fingers lingered by her neck, and when she glanced at them and then back up at him, he grinned at her. “All ready?”

“Where are we going?”

Gesturing for her to walk ahead, he said, “You’ll see.”

She still wondered whether this was a good idea as she walked out the door into the brightly lit corridor.

Especially when there wasn’t a single guard in sight.

Loche’s eyes followed hers, and he whispered, “Zaddock is creating a little diversion.”

She frowned. “I thought he wasn’t supportive.”

“He was only looking out for us. But after last night...” Loche’s eyes hardened for a moment. “There’s no point in hiding now. Not when they already know.”

Grabbing her hand, he pulled her with him down a corridor she hadn’t been before and lifted aside a dusty tapestry, revealing a rickety staircase that looked like it had been placed there temporarily and then forgotten about.

When she hesitated, Loche walked ahead, confidently gripping the rusty railing and stepping onto the first creaking stair.

“It leads to the stables. It used to be a stable boy entrance, but since we don’t force the people who work here to live at the castle anymore, it hasn’t been in use in a long time. Come on. They’ll be back any second, and while this might be a secret passage, this staircase is loud.”

Lessia scowled at him, but Loche only raised his brows and started down the stairs. As she reluctantly followed him, she was grateful he’d grabbed a lantern off the wall. And when he made sure to remain close to her, never allowing the darkness to creep in, her shoulders lowered another inch.

Loche was right about it being loud.

For every step Lessia took, the staircase creaked and whined—as if it might fall into a heap of dust at any moment. But soon enough, more light trickled over their boots, and the comforting smell of horses and hay washed over them.

When their feet finally found solid ground, they stepped right into the pen of an already saddled horse. It was a beautiful gray stallion, the coat's color eerily similar to Loche's eyes, with a long, almost pearly mane.

"This is Reks. Reks, meet Lessia."

The horse neighed softly when Loche approached, and when he urged Lessia forward, she lifted her hand to stroke Reks's head. Reks nudged her hand with his muzzle, and she giggled when his wet lips nipped at her in search of a treat.

"I may have spoiled him, but he's a good horse. And he'll easily carry us both, even in winter." Loche patted the horse before reaching for her as if to lift her up.

She shifted away, placing her foot in the stirrup and pulling herself up.

"He may be tall, but so am I." She grinned.

Loche's eyes glinted as he mounted the horse, pulling her body flush against his and reaching around her to grab the reins. "That you are."

His lips brushed her cheek. "But I've come to like throwing you around, so please refrain from denying me the pleasure in the future."

Goose bumps rose in the wake of his warm breath, and she had to stifle a groan when her cheeks heated. "I'll be deciding when and if you're bestowed that pleasure, thank you very much," she grumbled when she gained control over her features again.

A snort whispered over her skin. "I'm well aware."

Fabric rustled behind her.

"Pull up your hood. We've probably been loud enough to alert every guard in the courtyard, so we'll need to ride fast. The gates will be open, but they'll try to stop us."

As she pulled up her hood, she glanced over her shoulder at Loche's covered face. "Aren't you still regent? I assume you have the authority to do as you please."

His arms tightened around her. "But this is much more fun, don't you think?"

She raised a brow, and as if he could see her expression even with the hood covering her face, he continued. "We have a lead on the spies in the castle, but I am not sure if they are working alone. I'd prefer no one sees us."

Facing forward again, she nodded.

But as Loche urged the horse forward and a low laugh rang under his hood as the stallion's heavy steps launched into a gallop even before they burst out of the open stable doors, she couldn't help but think he also enjoyed this.

Shouts sounded around them, mingling with Reks's hooves crunching the snow, and she kept her face down, fingers tangling in Reks's long mane to hold steady as he increased his speed.

The gates—as Loche promised—were open, but her stomach surged when the guards called for horses.

As Lessia tried to turn around, Loche's arms held her in place.

"I hid the saddles and reins." He laughed, unconcerned, as they passed a few more guards stationed outside the castle walls.

Reks's gait increased further, and Loche steered him toward the woods, the sound of the guards fading with each stride.

When the sound vanished completely and only the wind and crackling snow whistled around them, Reks slowed but still kept a steady gallop, each step keeping to a narrow path, far away from the cliffs to their left.

Lessia released a breath, her eyes following the white puff, and allowed herself to lean into Loche's warm chest. Even with the layers of clothing between them, the heat from his body cloaked her, and electricity pulsed through her when Loche's breathing deepened.

They rode quietly beside the forest for a while, but as Loche steered the horse onto another path, even slimmer than the previous, she stiffened.

Loche had left the lantern in the stable, and until now, the light from the town had illuminated their path, but the direction in which Reks now set off was entirely cast in shadows.

Loche rested his chin on her shoulder as he pulled on the reins until the stallion came to a full stop.

"I have something for you."

He gently pulled off her hood, and as she turned her head over her shoulder, a gasp left her.

Loche smiled as he weighed the sparkling stone in his hand.

Luminous, silvery light burst out of the hand-sized rock, casting a glow that radiated like millions of tiny diamonds, brightening the snow beneath them in a wide circle.

"What is this?" she whispered as he offered it to her.

When she didn't immediately take it, Loche's hand gripped hers, gently opening her palm and placing the rock in it.

As her fingers wrapped around it, she realized it was warm, as if the glow somehow not only shone like the sun but also provided the same warmth as a beautiful spring day.

His mouth lifted in a one-sided smile. "I found it in the regents' vault. Apparently, not all treasures were distributed amongst the people. I gave away everything else, but somehow I couldn't make myself get rid of this. Now, I'm glad I didn't."

She stared at the stone in her hand, extending it toward him. "I can't take this. It belongs to Ellow."

Loche's large hand wrapped around hers, closing her fingers over it. "It belongs to the Fae. I don't know how it ended up here, but that is no stone of Ellow. From what I've understood, King Rioner has enough riches for a million lifetimes. You, on the other hand, need something bright to light up the darkness."

Swallowing, she traced the smooth rock with her fingers.

She'd never seen anything like it.

But she hadn't seen much of Vastala either. Being hidden away in her youth and then living in squalor on the streets didn't allow her much insight into whatever treasures the Fae kept.

When Loche wouldn't budge, she sighed, promising herself she'd give it back once they returned.

But for now...

She held on to the stone the entire ride through the woods, not once losing her breath within the thick darkness.

CHAPTER FIFTY-NINE

It was a cloudy day, and by the time they reached a small village, Lessia realized it must be early afternoon.

Even though it was still dim outside, the little light there was came from the southwest, gray rays dancing between the snow-covered mountains that towered there.

After Loche dismounted, Lessia let him help her off Reks, and she winced at the stiffness in her legs as they hit the hard-packed snow.

"We have a short walk still, but Reks cannot follow where we're going. I'll take him to a trusted friend in the village, but it's probably best if you stay here. While they won't mind, they'll know who you are as soon as they see you."

Patting Reks's warm neck, she nodded.

She sat down on a small boulder, keeping an eye on the satchel Loche left behind and remaining alert to any sound from the dark forest surrounding them.

Nothing happened in the short time Loche was gone, and she jumped to her feet when he made his way back through the deep snow.

As he once again reached out a hand for her, she folded her arms over her chest. “You need to tell me where we are going.”

While she somehow trusted him, she didn’t like not having all the information, especially in a part of Ellow that was entirely foreign to her.

Loche huffed and gripped her hands, unlocking her arms and pulling them around his waist.

He glowered down at her. “So nosy.”

She raised a brow, ignoring the tingling sensation in her gut as his body pressed against hers. “Tell me.”

His gaze drifted upward for a moment before he sighed. “It’s the winter solstice. I’m taking you to my favorite place to celebrate.”

Her brows shot up.

She’d forgotten about the winter solstice, one of the most important holidays in Ellow. On this one day a year, no one worked, so families and friends came together to celebrate the seasons shifting into brighter times.

Of course she loved it.

Loved knowing the consuming darkness would soon be replaced with midnight sun, with warm wind and flowers and leaves and greens.

When a smile spread across her face, Loche’s eyes flashed, and he bent down, claiming her mouth.

His kiss was urgent and possessive but gentle all the while, and she lost herself in his soft lips.

“Smile like that again,” he mumbled against her mouth.

She couldn’t help her lips curling, and he growled, fusing their mouths together again.

When he finally pulled back, they were both out of breath, and Loche dragged a hand across his face. “You drive me to the brink of insanity.”

She giggled and immediately wanted to smack herself in the face for the airy sound.

What was this man doing to her?

Pursing her lips, Lessia tried to ignore the unease that swirled in her gut as she righted her left sleeve, which had slid down, only looking up when Loche let out a low laugh.

"What?" she muttered.

"Nothing." Loche shook his head, took a step forward, and gripped her hand. "Come on, we want to get there before it's too late."

She thought about asking him yet again where they were going but decided against it when a smile played across his lips as he led her through two towering snowbanks.

Fresh snow lay across the ground, and she was grateful for it when Loche rushed his steps, heading toward a snow-covered hill where glittering ice slithered along the bottom.

As they came closer and she spotted a dark opening at the base, her stomach flipped.

Even with the glowing rock in her fist, that darkness seemed all-consuming.

Loche dragged her all the way to the opening, and she cautiously sniffed the air, expecting some sort of musty smell to rise from it. A crease formed over her brow when instead the smell of food and wood wafted through, and she glanced at Loche.

"We're going down there, yes. It will be fun, I promise." Loche let go of her hand, took a few steps to the right, and brushed some snow off what looked like a small boat.

As he pulled it free from the heavy snow covering it, she realized it was some kind of sled. The townsfolk in Asker would use similar ones to drag goods across the snow, and the children had versions they used to go downhill in the winter.

This one was curved at the bottom, though, and made of smooth wood that looked as if it would sail right across the snow.

Her eyes snapped between Loche and the opening.

"No." Lessia took a step back. "You can't mean we're getting into that thing, going down *there*."

Her lips curled back when Loche snickered, and a warning hiss involuntarily left her throat as he took a step toward her.

Loche's eyes rounded with innocence. "The other option is sliding down yourself, and while I've tried it, I can't recommend it."

She backed up another step, shaking her head.

Absolutely not.

The abyss before them was pitch black, and based on the other paths he'd taken her on, she didn't expect this one to have much better upkeep.

"Darling." Loche's lips twitched as he tracked her retreat. "Do you trust me?"

Her eyes narrowed.

Perhaps.

But refusing this was just common sense.

Setting down the sled, Loche leaned against the wall. "We can go back to the village if you prefer, but I promise it will be worth it. There's food, and I've been promised music and entertainment. And... I'd like you to meet some of my friends."

Her eyes narrowed farther when something soft—vulnerable—flashed across his face.

As she took another step back, Loche nodded and pushed himself off the icy wall, the playful expression vanishing.

Clenching the sparkling stone hard, she eyed him as he approached, and when he reached for her hand again, she groaned, "Fine! But you'll have to explain yourself to Merrick if I die."

His eyes dropped to her mouth. "I'd gladly let him rip me apart if I ever cause you harm."

The words slammed into her heart, and she fixed her gaze on the ground as she walked up to the black pit.

"What do we do?"

"I'll show you." Loche's arm snaked around her waist as he guided her into the sled.

As soon as she was positioned, he sat down behind her, his legs snugly sitting outside hers in the narrow seat and his arms clasped around her.

Once they were seated, Loche pushed something on the wall, and the scream ripping from her throat echoed between the ice-covered walls as the sled angled down and accelerated deep into the hill.

She wasn't proud of it, but she couldn't stop screaming, feeling as if her stomach would fall out of her body until the sled finally skidded to a stop.

"Took you long enough."

Lessia looked up, right into the bluest eyes she'd ever seen.

They belonged to a beautiful middle-aged woman with gray-streaked auburn hair.

She smiled at Lessia as she caught her breath. "Everyone screams the first time. And now everyone knows you're here too. Loche likes to sneak up on us."

Lessia tried to smile back, but as she drew a deep gulp of air to settle her pounding heart, a strangled noise escaped her.

Eyes wide, she stared at the woman, slamming into Loche's chest as she shifted backward.

"You're a shifter."

CHAPTER
SIXTY

Her blood chilled in her veins, and Lessia dropped the stone as she grasped for the daggers tucked into her waistband, wondering if it was worth risking her magic.

Before she had a chance to unsheath them, Loche's fingers wrapped around her wrists. "She's a friend, Lessia."

Shooting him a wide stare over her shoulder, she wrangled her arms free and got out of the sled, putting it and Loche between her and the woman.

If she even was a woman.

Lessia didn't know much about the shifters.

They were all supposed to be dead.

But that scent...

The scent of constant change, of mystery, of winter and summer and snow and grass at the same time...

There was no mistaking what stood before her.

She crouched down, the memory of Merrick's lessons burned into her muscles, and Lessia sliced her gaze between Loche and the laughing woman.

"She's feisty, Loche." The shifter offered him a hand to get out of the sled. "Not that I'd expect anything less from you."

"Geyia..." Loche shook his head before turning to Lessia. "Lessia, it's all right."

Muscles locked, she glared at him, unable to control the adrenaline pulsating through her and the low growl vibrating in her throat.

While she knew little about the shifters, she knew they were not to be trusted.

Lessia had heard enough about the destruction they'd caused during the war.

When Loche let out a low chuckle, she snarled at him, "Why did you bring me here?"

"I told you, I wanted you to meet my friends," Loche said, taking a step toward her, the smile on his face never faltering. "She is a shifter, yes. But you, out of anyone, should know what it's like having people judge you because of your heritage."

Drawing a shaky breath, Lessia moved her eyes to the woman again.

Geyia remained in the same spot, her posture relaxed and her eyes kind as they watched her.

"There is more to our shared history, Lessia. The books have some facts right, but not all." Loche closed the distance between them, reaching out for Lessia.

She flexed her hands.

She usually tried to keep an open mind.

Some of the children she brought over had definitely engaged in questionable behavior while on the streets.

But it was because they were forced to.

Geyia's people had been greedy—ruthless.

Had sacrificed so many humans and Fae in their attempt to take control over Havlands.

And now, one stood right before her.

"Not all of the shifters agreed with our king."

Lessia's eyes snapped to Geyia.

The woman offered her a sad smile. "The books don't tell of those who fought back against our own. They lost, and those who weren't killed were imprisoned, forced to work as slaves."

Lessia glanced from her to Loche. "But how did we not hear of it? I've heard nothing of a resistance."

It was Loche who answered.

"Because the shifter king was clever." Loche scratched the shadowy stubble on his chin. "He made everyone think those who stood against him sided with the Fae. That they wanted *them* to rule Havlands. With their own kind and humans against them, they lost their voice."

Geyia nodded. "They did. My ancestors rebelled against him, wanting nothing to do with his plans. The only thing I have him to thank for is that they escaped the slaughter that ensued when humans and Fae caught on to what he was planning. They were left to die in the cellars he put them in, but once the king and his followers were dead, they managed to break out. Some died, of course—they were starving and sick already—but the rest of them escaped. We've been hiding across Havlands ever since."

With her brows furrowed, Lessia straightened, but still held on tight to her daggers. "How many of you are there?"

Geyia shrugged. "I'm not sure. My parents died when I was quite young, and the ship we'd been living on dropped me off in a harbor, as they had too many mouths to feed."

Geyia's eyes moved to Loche, and the love in them strained Lessia's chest. "I ran into Loche here when he was just a small, angry boy. But apparently, he didn't forget about me. He brought me here a few years ago. Told me of a place with a bunch of misfits that wouldn't mind a shifter in their midst."

Loche smiled at her. "She's being modest. She saved my life when my mother forced me onto the streets. And while the people here might be misfits, they're a great bunch."

Lessia stared at the two of them.

A bunch?

How many people lived here?

Geyia rolled her eyes, then fixed her piercing gaze on Lessia again. "If you're not going to kill me, we should probably head over. Since hearing Loche was bringing a woman, they've been cooking up a storm."

The shifter spun on her heel, her long curls bouncing with every stride she took into a glittering, arched hallway.

Lessia stared after her, then back to Loche. "What is this place?"

Wrapping his hand around hers, Loche leaned in and whispered, "I'll tell you everything. But I promise you, she's nothing like the shifters you've heard of in the books. She's good. Every person here is good."

Her mind still spun, but something in her gut urged her to trust him.

Like he'd trusted her when he'd found out about the half-Fae she'd smuggled into Ellow.

So Lessia nodded, and after bending down to pick up the sparkling stone she'd dropped and putting it in her pocket, she allowed him to tug her with him into the passage.

A few feet inside, Loche halted, turning toward her.

"Thank you," he said softly.

Her heart leaped when their eyes clashed.

Pride and something else flashed in Loche's dark ones, and a thrill raced across her neck.

When she managed to nod again, he smiled wide.

She couldn't help but smile back.

Loche stared at her for a moment, and she waited for him to say something else, but he only shook his head almost imperceptibly, his lips lifting higher as he continued walking.

Lessia stared in wonder at the ice-covered walls of the hallway he and Geyia led her through, the simple beauty of the sparkling ice illuminated by torches attached every few feet.

Murmurs and the rattle of dishes drifted toward them as more light spilled onto the stony ground and the passage opened wider until a massive arched chamber came into view.

Geyia skipped out right into the arms of a beautiful man. He was short, with wild red curls tumbling down his back and piercing green eyes that found Lessia's the moment she stepped into the chamber.

The man grinned at her, giving Geyia a quick kiss before running up and pulling Loche into a tight embrace. As Lessia backed up a step, the man released Loche and turned to her. Wrapping his arms around her, he enveloped her in the smell of fire and food.

Lessia stiffened, but when the man barked a laugh, she made herself return the greeting.

As he pulled back, Loche glared at him, pulling Lessia to his side.

The red-haired man winked at her, flashing a row of large white teeth. "Welcome! I'm Steiner."

His eyes trailed over her face and body, zeroing in on where her hand was joined with Loche's, and his green eyes glinted with mischief. "You're even more beautiful than I imagined. How did Loche manage to snare you? Or did he kidnap you?"

"Steiner..." Loche warned, his grip on her hand tightening.

She could only sense pure sincerity from the man, so Lessia gave him a faint smile. "He did, actually."

Steiner threw his head back and cackled. "I like her already."

With a groan, Loche tugged her closer, his arm snaking over her shoulders. "I'll show Lessia to our chambers, and then I expect some of that food Geyia talked of. But tone down the insinuations. Remember who brought you all here."

As Loche dragged her with him, Steiner's laugh echoed behind them, and Lessia let out a surprised snort when she overheard Geyia scold him, telling him not to scare her away.

"This is where the nobles and part of the royal court hid during the war," Loche explained as he led her up a wide stone staircase. "It's a cave, but the king took great measures to make it comfortable. There's room for hundreds of people, although there's only about thirty or so living here now. I came here a lot during my first year as regent—when I needed a break from all the politics."

Lessia nodded as her eyes swept around the space.

They'd entered a large circular room where several fires burned bright. Groups of people huddled around each hearth, some cooking and some seemingly only mingling and socializing.

Around them, a great number of benches and chairs were arranged, and a few long tables stood closest to the grandest fireplace. Barrels of what she guessed was stored food and wine were placed around the walls, and everywhere flickered lanterns and candles that cast the room in a warm glow.

By the stairs where they now walked were rooms every few steps, rounded openings exposing comfortable bedding on the floor, smaller dining sets, and a fireplace in each.

"The people living here are outcasts. Some I knew living on the streets back home, some I met during my time in the navy, and then there is Geyia, of course. They don't fit in society—some don't even want to try, but they still deserve a safe place to live."

Her eyes briefly met his in understanding, and she bit her lip to hide a smile.

Loche's gaze shifted to her mouth, and he lifted his hand to her cheek, his thumb freeing her lip from her teeth.

"Don't," he whispered.

So she didn't.

Lessia let her lips curl into a broad smile, and Loche exhaled sharply.

Dragging her with him, he took two steps at a time until they reached the top floor, where another small chamber lay. In the middle of the room stood a large bed with white bedding and a thick fur blanket, and in the corner crackled an already lit fireplace with a plush couch before it. On the other side of the bed was a desk with a few books and papers strewn out across it.

As Loche set down the satchel he'd been carrying on the desk, his head whipped back and forth from the room to the rounded opening, and his brows snapped together.

"What is it?" she asked.

Loche dragged a hand through his hair. "I didn't think this through."

She raised a brow.

He bridged the distance between them and pulled her to him, pressing her body against his hard one. His lips whispered over her mouth, barely touching, before shifting to her ear.

"I want you alone. And there is not even a door in this damned place," he rasped.

A shiver of anticipation traced a path over her shoulders, and her breaths quickened as she breathed, “I’ve heard you’re quite resourceful.”

A growl rumbled in his chest, and Loche crashed his lips against hers.

CHAPTER SIXTY-ONE

"Dinner is served!"

Steiner's voice had them both sigh as they reluctantly pulled away.

When she looked up at Loche, her stomach fluttered at the softness in his hard features, and she almost wished he had picked somewhere else.

Somewhere far, far away from any people.

Another small piece of the wall around her heart broke down when Steiner called out again and Loche's gaze drifted toward the opening, a hint of a smile touching his lips.

He'd wanted her to see this place because it and the people within it were important to him.

From their first real conversations, she'd felt that he read her better than anyone she'd met before.

She'd thought it was because he was so perceptive.

But perhaps it was because he wasn't so different from her.

Lessia touched her aching lips, and a small part of her was also relieved that Steiner had interrupted.

If he hadn't, she would have had to.

She cast a quick glance at the large bed.

She couldn't let herself get carried away.

But when she briefly met Loche's eyes, her mind muddled with the promise that flared there, and she cursed herself silently as she turned toward the opening.

As she started toward the staircase, limbs weak from the fever Loche ignited inside her and heart thumping in her chest, he caught her hand. "Ignore him."

Lessia snorted. "You were the one who wanted me to meet your friends. I won't be rude when they've apparently been cooking all day for us."

Throwing his head back, Loche groaned, but when she started to walk again, he followed her.

The scents that rose from the communal area made Lessia's mouth water, and she realized she hadn't really eaten since last night. The hunger clawing at her gut drove her forward, even as twenty or so pairs of eyes tracked them as they descended.

Warmth crawled across her skin when Loche wrapped an arm around her shoulders, and curious whispers reached her ears. Fixing her gaze somewhere above the faces staring at them, she drew a steadying breath.

There were people of all ages spread out across the stone floor.

A few younger ones, perhaps in their early twenties, but also older—like Geyia and Steiner.

When they reached the bottom, the people swarmed them, pulling Loche into their arms and offering loud and excited greetings. A few embraced Lessia as well, and while some stayed back, the smiles on their faces were genuine, and she didn't catch even a glimpse of fear or distrust in their eyes as they took in her pointed ears.

Geyia ushered them to a table in the middle of the room, next to the largest fire, and as Lessia began to pile food onto her plate—steaming vegetables, newly baked bread, and lots of fish—the heat from the fire and from the warm welcome settled in her chest.

Loche was seated next to her, and he seemed to be unable to stop himself from touching her.

Even as he shuffled food into his mouth, his other hand rested on her leg, stroked her back, and played with her hair, and wide-eyed stares were thrown their way when he lifted her hand to kiss it.

Her skin buzzed, and the air around them crackled with electricity and unspoken wishes whenever Loche's eyes found hers. Struggling to focus on anything other than his playful fingers whispering over every bit of bare skin he could find, Lessia mostly listened as Loche caught up with his friends, leaning into his chest when he snaked an arm around her waist.

After making sure everyone had gotten at least a second serving, Geyia slipped into the spot on the wooden bench beside her, and Lessia eyed the woman curiously.

"Ask away." Geyia grinned at her.

"Is this your real form?" Lessia tried to soften her voice, but something stirred within her upon not knowing if the warm older woman she saw was only a facade.

Geyia clasped her hands over the table. "It is. It's exhausting for us to keep a shifted form. We can only do it for so long."

Nodding, Lessia tried for a smile. "I must apologize for how I reacted earlier."

Loche's hand traced small circles on her back.

When she peeked at him, he was deep in conversation

with two young men, but he shot her a small smile, and a thrill ran through her at the tenderness of it.

The shifter grinned as she glanced at Loche. "Don't be. You accepted me much quicker than others have."

"Still... I'm sorry. I... I know how it is." Lessia's eyes dipped as a twinge of guilt joined the warmth in her chest.

She knew exactly what it was like to be judged based on what you were.

Geyia placed a wrinkled hand on her shoulder. "I know. I can see it in you. But you haven't let it fill you with hate." She sighed. "Many of my kind have, and I've met a few half-Fae who have as well."

Lessia smiled at her again. An easier smile, as there was no contempt in the shifter's blue eyes.

When they'd eaten everything on the large plates and Lessia had said no twice to more food, wine was served, and a few of the humans took out drums and other instruments.

While Lessia didn't usually drink, when Steiner pushed a goblet of wine into her hands, she took it and sipped as music filled the arched cave. Loche clinked his goblet against hers, and she wasn't sure whether the wine immediately went to her head or if it was his presence that made her mind hum in tune with the music.

People started to get up to dance, and she laughed when Geyia dragged Loche with her, making him perform some sort of intricate step. His usually hard face was free of lines as he concentrated on following Geyia's fast movements, and his eyes twinkled when they met hers over the crowd forming before the table.

When he kept her gaze over the crowd, the warmth inside her seeped into every muscle and limb, and she couldn't tear her eyes away when his gray ones flared, an ache starting deep inside her.

One of the younger men bowed before her, asking her to dance, and she smiled at him as she took the hand he offered.

Thankfully, he didn't make her try to follow Geyia. Instead, he spun her around in a clumsy version of a waltz, dipping and lifting her until her stomach hurt from laughter.

When the music slowed, a strong arm wrapped around her waist, and the man before her grinned and backed away.

As she whirled around, her breath caught in her throat at the look in Loche's eyes.

Pure adoration shone there, the heat in them making the flames within her burn hotter.

He pulled her flush against him, his fingers whispering over her back, teasing, grazing her neck as he swept her hair over one shoulder. As he bent down, Loche's lips softly trailed across her sensitive skin, up to her ear, and he whispered, "I want to show you something."

Unable to form words, she nodded, and he led her away from the crowd to a narrow passage beneath the staircase. Lessia told herself to breathe as the air charged, and she didn't dare look up at Loche when his breathing became ragged.

They walked in silence for a few moments until a sharp turn finally led them into a dimly lit chamber.

"What is this place?" Lessia gasped as her eyes flew around the circular cave.

The chamber was filled with large formations of ice shaped like trees, a forest of sparkling sculptures, with black glittering flowers growing straight out of the ice around them.

Above them, an oval opening let the nearly full moon in. Thick dark clouds danced around the moon, but they didn't cover it.

As if this place wouldn't allow the darkness that would follow.

"They call it the Lune." Loche gently tugged on her hand until she stepped onto the hard ice. "These flowers only grow under moonlight and only in the winter. I know Ellow doesn't hold magic the way Vastala does, but there is something magical about it, anyway."

She couldn't even nod.

The magic in her veins thrummed in here, not as if it would burst out of her but as if it were saying hello to an old friend.

It was peaceful and energetic at the same time, a tingling sensation brushing her skin.

Lessia bent down to touch one of the flowers, and a shudder ran through her when the buzzing inside her intensified.

Straightening, she turned to Loche, unable to stop her hands from shaking.

"Thank you for bringing me here," she whispered. "Not just to this place, but to meet your friends."

His eyes burned into hers, and when he stepped closer, another quiver racked her body.

They reached for each other at the same time, the urgency in their kiss making her mind go blank.

Loche shifted her so her back was against the cold wall, but it did nothing to soothe the wildfire in her core. His warm tongue slid across her bottom lip, and she let her own play with it until he groaned into her mouth.

Locking her arms around his neck, she jumped up on him, wrapping her legs around his waist, desperate to get closer. Her fingers sought any soft skin they could, and when his neck wasn't enough, she pulled at his tunic, forgetting her strength and tearing a wide gash that left his entire chest bare.

Her eyes widened, and she made to pull back when he growled, “Rip them all to threads if you like. Just don’t stop.”

Her ears buzzed when his eyes bored into hers, the desire coursing through her veins mirrored in his steely ones.

She hesitated for a moment, but when he burrowed his face in her neck, nipping at her skin, she gave in.

Lessia moaned as she let her hands explore his sculpted chest, and she kissed the goose bumps that rose across his skin from the soft wind that blew through the chamber.

Setting her down, Loche trailed his hands down her body, his eyes following them as they slowly moved across her shoulders, down to her chest, and farther, until a finger hooked in her breeches.

“I want to see all of you, but it’s too cold in here,” Loche rasped. “These need to go, though.”

A small ember of worry whirled in her gut, breaking through the cloud of desire.

She could never be bare for him.

Not without him seeing her tattoo.

The brand that would destroy whatever it was they were doing.

But as he slipped one of her daggers out from her waistband, letting it fall with a soft thud to the ground, and then the other, the worry was replaced with a consuming need.

Loche took his time to lower her breeches to the ground, kissing and caressing every bit of skin he exposed.

When only her silky underwear remained, he lifted his gaze to hers.

She dragged him to her, crashing her mouth against his while ripping his own breeches to shreds in her urgency to get them off. Loche growled into her mouth as he lifted her again, one of his hands slipping between them, dipping into her silky underwear.

She let out a cry when his finger slid between her folds, biting down on his shoulder to quench it.

"Fuck," Loche breathed, pulling back to look at her. "Is this all for me?"

He lifted a glistening finger, and she could only nod, so close already to seeing the stars the clouds above them were hiding.

"I want to take my time," he growled. "But it's freezing here, and I need you."

"I need you," she whimpered when he pressed against her, his hardness crushing against her hip.

"Fuck," he rasped again, his chest heaving against hers as he freed himself.

Eyes locked on hers, he pulled her underwear aside, and her breath choked when he nudged at her entrance.

"Loche, please," she moaned when he teased her with the tip, his fingers digging into her back.

His mouth found hers as he slammed into her with his full length, both crying out as he filled her, pushing her up against the cold wall.

"So warm," Loche growled. "So perfect."

She held on to his shoulders as he slowly—deliberately—pulled out, then plowed into her again.

Lessia's head fell back to the wall as Loche increased the pace, urgently slamming into her, filling her completely. Light flickered behind her closed eyelids as her back scraped against the ice while Loche's warm, hard body pushed against her.

A deep need built inside her, fueled by Loche's heavy breath fanning over her chest, his hard, assured strokes, and she leaned forward, biting down on his shoulder as she screamed his name.

He called out hers as well as he drove into her one final time, and their bodies shook in rhythm as they reached release together.

Loche's head fell forward against the cold wall as they caught their breaths, and as her muscles softened, he tightened his grip, not allowing any space between them.

When she could finally think clearly again, she lifted her head, and Loche straightened as well.

A satisfied smirk lifted his mouth as he lazily kissed her.

"I thought I was clever sneaking off in here, but since I'll have to walk back half-naked, I'm pretty sure no one will buy that we only looked at the Lune."

Lessia giggled as Loche set her down, swatting at him when he winked at her.

They got dressed in whatever clothing was not ripped to shreds, and she pulled at his hand to make their way to the fire when goose bumps continued to rise across his bare torso.

But as she was about to drag him into the passage, Loche stopped her, pulling her into his arms again.

"I've wanted you for a long time, Lessia," he whispered. "Longer than you can imagine."

She nodded into his chest, a wave of emotions washing over her at the tenderness of his voice.

Holding him tight, she winced at the guilt that surged within her.

She'd wanted this as well.

But she'd known it was selfish when he didn't know everything about her.

When he didn't know she was deceiving him, deceiving everything he stood for.

Swallowing, she pulled out of his embrace and walked

quietly beside him as they tried to sneak up to the chambers without anyone noticing.

Lessia couldn't muster a smile even as people shouted playful quips at them as they ascended the stairs, even as Loche gently pulled her with him into the bed and wrapped his strong arms around her, even as he whispered the sweetest words in her ear as they fell asleep.

CHAPTER
SIXTY-TWO

She woke to an empty bed.

Frowning, she turned over and found the sheets where Loche had lain already cold.

When she listened to the large cave, no voices broke through the soft snoring and breathing from sleeping people.

Glancing out of the small window beside the fireplace, she realized it was still dark outside.

Lessia pushed the sheets off, shivering as she stepped onto the cold stone floor.

After lacing up her boots and pulling her cloak around her, she tiptoed down the stairs.

Only one of the fireplaces still burned from last night, and before it, Loche sat with his head in his hands. Beside him, one of his guards from the castle snored softly in a plush chair, a black mask resting beneath him on the floor.

Loche didn't look up as she approached, and her frown deepened when she made sure her steps could be heard and there was still no reaction from him.

Coming to a stop right before him, she reached out and placed a hand on his shoulder.

Finally, his head lifted, and her stomach flipped at the hardness of his face, his cold and distant glare.

"What's happened?" she whispered.

His eyes trailed over her face, and his jaw clenched as uncertainty flashed in the gray. "They caught the spy. Found him conspiring with one of his accomplices."

Loche eyed her as she nodded, and apprehension made her shoulders rise when his gaze filled with the same scrutiny it had during their first times together.

"Who is it?" she asked cautiously.

"Did you know?" he blurted out, his dark brows narrowing.

"Know what?"

She couldn't read him.

Didn't understand what was causing the turmoil within him.

It was good they'd caught the spy, right?

Loche's jaw flexed, his eyes boring into hers, but when she only eyed him back, he released a deep breath.

"Venko is one of them."

Lessia's eyes widened.

But it made sense.

"I should have known. He..." She swallowed as her heart skipped a beat.

She'd nearly told him she'd used her magic to figure out what he was hiding.

But Venko had known so little...

How could he be the one behind this?

And she'd asked him to tell her if he found out more.

Loche watched her quietly, and she tried to gain control over her features.

"I just mean… he said some strange things to me. I should have figured out he was up to something." Her voice shook a little, and she glanced down when Loche flexed his hands.

She was not convincing him.

But then Loche threw his head back and sighed. "I'm sorry."

Lessia remained quiet even though all she wanted was to tell him he had nothing to be sorry for.

His intuition was right.

She did know more than she let on.

But the blood oath wouldn't allow her to tell him, invisible fingers wrapping around her throat even at the thought of trying.

Loche reached out for her and pulled her onto his lap.

Nestling his face into her neck, he spoke softly. "We need to return immediately. They've decided to speed everything up again. The Fae delegation is coming tomorrow already, and the votes will be counted the day after that."

An icy hand squeezed her heart at the thought of the Fae.

But King Rioner wouldn't send his best men.

Not for mere humans.

Drawing a shaky breath, she nodded. "At least it'll be over soon."

Loche tensed beneath her. "They'll make you go through the last ordeal today, Lessia."

"What do you mean? How do you know?" She pulled back to look at him.

His eyes bounced between hers, then moved to the still-sleeping guard beside them. "He came to bring you back."

Her chest tightened, but she forced herself to pull air into her lungs.

It was fine.

She'd managed the other ones.

One last trial before she got her freedom back.

"What about you? And Craven?"

Loche's arms wrapped around her, one of his hands stroking her back. "I've already gone through mine."

She didn't like the look in his eyes.

Not one bit.

And when the scent of sorrow washed over her, she swallowed audibly.

"What was it?" She forced the words out—wasn't sure she really wanted the answer.

"A deep loss. One I'll live with for the rest of my life."

His head slumped forward, and Lessia's mouth went dry at the guilt lining his shoulders.

Leaning into him, she wrapped her arms around his neck and held him tight.

They sat like that until the guard stirred, his mask falling over with a loud thud as he accidentally kicked it, making them both jump.

"You ready?"

The guard glared at her for a moment before shifting his gaze to Loche. His eyes trailed her arms around his neck and narrowed as he noted the conflicting feelings twisting Loche's features.

When Loche didn't say anything, Lessia got to her feet, making herself meet the guard's hostile eyes. "I'm ready."

The guard continued to glower at her the whole time they packed up their things, said goodbye to Geyia and Steiner, and started walking toward a tunnel.

Within the tunnel, wide steps snaked their way up the hill, and as Lessia took the first one, she offered Loche a small smile. "So there was another way in?"

He gave her a crooked smile back, but it didn't reassure her at all.

His eyes remained hollow, with anger and something else flashing in them.

Glancing from him to the guard, she wondered whether she was missing something.

She didn't understand the hostility radiating from the guard, nor did she understand whatever was going on in Loche's head.

Fixing her eyes ahead, she tried to clear her mind.

Two more days.

Then she could be free.

CHAPTER SIXTY-THREE

The ride back was quiet, and when she tried to strike up a conversation, neither Loche nor the guard answered with more than one word.

Loche's arms held on to her as if she would disappear if he released his grip, and every so often, he'd lean in and rest his chin on her shoulder.

But she didn't miss the way his muscles locked, the sound of his teeth grinding as he stared off into the distance.

When they finally reached the town, she was exhausted from trying to understand what was going on and from trying not to force Loche to speak to her.

As they entered the castle courtyard, more guards than she'd ever seen filled it: rows and rows of soldiers mixed in with Loche's own masked men and some in uniforms she'd never seen before. Based on the old family crests sewn onto their jackets, she guessed they were the nobles' own guards.

With wide eyes, she let Loche help her off Reks, and she didn't even have time to pat him before one of Loche's men led him off.

Merrick and Zaddock stood right outside the large double doors leading into the white castle, and her heart began pounding when the Fae immediately gripped her arm, pulling her into one of the alcoves.

"We don't have much time."

She'd never heard his voice like this.

It wasn't the soft pleading she'd heard when he was injured and feared being found out for what he was.

There was real terror in it.

Merrick pulled her close, urgently whispering in her ear. "You need to remain calm. Whatever happens, remember why you are here. Two more days, Lessia."

"Merrick..." she started, her blood rushing in her veins.

"I'm so sorry. I can't come with you," he interrupted. "But you need to promise me to stay calm."

"What—"

He raised his voice. "Promise me!"

"I..."

The grip on her arm tightened.

"I promise," she whispered.

Merrick nodded. "I'll find you after."

Then he stalked right up the stairs, leaving her standing there, feeling colder and more alone than she ever had before.

"Lessia. You need to come with us." Zaddock gestured for her when she left the alcove.

And when he wouldn't meet her eyes, his head remaining bent as he led the way into the cellars, dread stabbed at her chest, thrumming in rhythm with their soft steps as they descended the stone stairs.

Loche walked behind her, his eyes slamming into hers when she turned her head over her shoulder, and when he reached out to squeeze her hand, a wheezy breath finally made its way into her lungs.

He wouldn't allow anything bad to happen to her.

Loud voices echoed between the polished walls when they reached a part of the castle Lessia hadn't been to before. While lanterns also lit this part, pressure laced her chest when she realized it was the dungeons.

Rows of cells lined the walls on both sides of her, and when a familiar sound of dripping water and the musty smell of wet stone and decay reached her, she stiffened, fighting the urge to sprint back the way she'd come.

"What... what are we doing here?" Her shaky voice barely carried over the shouting ahead.

Neither Loche nor Zaddock responded as they continued walking.

More light flickered ahead, and soon Frayson came into view.

He was surrounded by twenty or so guards, all standing before a brightly lit cell.

But it was the familiar blue eyes that locked on hers, the blonde hair reflecting the flames on the wall that had her gasp for air.

Amalise stood beside one of the guards, her face a mask of fury as she pulled at the arm he was holding on to.

"Get off me, you stupid bastard," she screamed.

"Amalise!" Lessia rushed her steps, running up to her best friend. "Let her go!"

She shoved the guard so hard he took a stumbling step backward, but he still held on to her friend, nearly making her fall from the movement.

The guard glared at her. "She is no prisoner, but she has tried to fight every man in here. If you can get her to calm down, I'll let her go."

"I won't stop until you let him go!" Amalise's cheeks burned as she spat at the man.

"Amalise." Lessia reached out for her, gripping her free hand. "We'll figure this out. Please, just calm down."

Amalise's eyes burned into Lessia's. "You don't even know, do you? They just stormed into our house last night and took him! They're mad!"

Tensing, Lessia searched her face. "Took who?"

Amalise jerked her head toward the cell behind them. "Look for yourself."

Turning around, her pulse roaring in her ears, Lessia fixed her eyes on the cell.

A strangled noise escaped her when Ardow's defiant brown eyes found hers.

Blood trickled down his temple. His face was beaten and bruised, and his body must have been, too, based on the way he leaned against the wall, keeping his weight on one foot.

On the dusty floor beside him, Venko lay unconscious, his pale hair spilled out over the dark stone.

When she took a step toward them, several guards stepped into her path.

"Get out of my way," she snarled, her fear from earlier giving way to rage.

Lessia's nostrils flared when the guards didn't move, and her hands balled into fists, but as she lifted them to slam them right into their stupid faces, Loche leaped in between them.

With his back to her, he ordered the guards to get out of her way, pushing one aside when he didn't move fast enough.

Stepping around him, she sprinted up to the metal bars and reached in through them. "Ard!"

When he offered her a crooked smile, a dry sob lodged in her throat. "Oh, Ard. Are you all right? Is anything broken?"

He shook his head. "They dragged me here so quickly I

lost my footing. I think I twisted my foot. The other stuff is just pretty decorations, don't you think?"

She could have slapped him for trying to be funny right now.

But instead, she wrapped her fingers around the bars, trying to keep her voice level. "What happened?"

The smile fell from his face, hard lines taking over, and he squared his jaw as he glared behind her.

She followed his gaze, locking eyes with Frayson.

There was nothing kind in the old man's eyes as he stared at her. "He's a traitor, Lessia. We overheard him and Venko conspiring about another attack. And you better not have known about this or you will join him in that cell."

"She didn't know!" Ardow limped to the bars. "I worked alone. I didn't tell Lessia or Amalise. Please just let them go."

Her head whipped between the cell and Frayson.

There was no way.

Not Ardow.

What would he have to win by attacking nominees?

But when she met his eyes and guilt filled the brown, her stomach dropped.

"Why?" she whispered.

Ardow just shook his head, his shoulders dropping.

Staring at his matted hair, the bruises blooming across his face, she thought back to their conversations the past weeks.

Ardow urging her to stay away from Loche.

His conviction that he was a bad man.

The first attack, when the soldier backed away from her upon realizing who she was.

Venko knowing of her gift.

A stifled cry tore from her throat.

Ardow had challenged her to use her magic on him.

Not once in the past five years had he ever worried she'd

use it on him. Not even when they'd had heated arguments about how to manage the children or the businesses.

But he had when he learned she was joining the election...

A warm hand slipped into hers, and her eyes flew to the side.

Loche's face was full of sympathy, and she couldn't help another whimper from escaping as she tried to comprehend what was happening.

When his gray eyes flickered with pain, she sucked in a breath.

"You knew," she hissed.

That's why he'd been so strange this morning.

Why he'd barely been able to meet her eyes all day.

She dropped his hand as if she'd burned herself. "You wanted to make sure I didn't know. That I wasn't working with him."

"Lessia..."

She backed away from the cell—away from Loche. "Stay away from me."

Frayson cleared his throat. "Thank you, Loche. I wasn't sure you'd follow my orders, but I'm glad to see your feelings haven't clouded your dedication to Ellow."

Loche's eyes pleaded with her, but she averted hers, hissing a breath through her teeth.

She couldn't look at him.

He hadn't even warned her what she would walk into.

"You bastards!" Amalise snarled in the back of the room.

As Lessia took a step toward her, Frayson ordered, "Silence!"

Frayson waved his hand toward Lessia. "Now that we've cleared you from suspicion of being an accomplice, you will go through your final trial before the election."

Lessia stared at him.

Perhaps they'd beat her again.

Hopefully they'd do it until she passed out.

Oblivion seemed like a blessing right now when the pain from Ardow's admission and Loche's betrayal felt as if it would tear her apart.

Frayson eyed her. "The final hardship is loss. So many lost their family, friends, their loved ones during the war. Becoming regent means that you will need to go through the same loss to ensure you won't put your people through that again."

He fidgeted with his gray cloak before he continued. "We had difficulty figuring out what choice we'd offer you, but your friend's betrayal of Ellow made it clear. Your task is simple: you need to decide whether to execute Ardow today or banish Amalise from Ellow forever."

CHAPTER SIXTY-FOUR

Each beat of her heart slammed in her ears, mocking her with its vigor.

Lessia backed into the wall, agony ripping at her chest as she stared from Amalise's stricken face to Ardow's white one.

She couldn't do this.

As she started to shake her head, opening her mouth to tell them she was leaving the election, the tattoo on her arm pulsed, and she had to brace herself against the wall not to bend over.

Panting, she tried to come up with a way around the oath she'd been forced to take.

But there wasn't one.

"Lessia, it's all right." Ardow's voice was gentle. "I knew this was the risk."

"No!" Amalise cried behind him. "I'll go! I'll go!"

Her eyes sliced frantically between her closest people.

Her friends.

The first people who'd accepted her for Lessia.

Who loved every broken piece of her.

"Can... can I talk to him alone before I decide?" She forced the words out.

Frayson started arguing that he was a prisoner, but Loche interrupted him. "She will be allowed to talk to him. I was allowed time to make my decision, and she will be as well."

"Loche..." Frayson started, but Loche stalked up to him, his eyes glacial as he glared down at the man.

"I am still regent, and this is an order, Frayson."

With a clenched jaw, Frayson finally nodded, gesturing for the guards to leave the room.

Amalise burst into tears as two guards started to drag her toward the tunnel, and Lessia had to fight with everything in her not to cover her ears as her friend's heartbreaking cries reverberated between the walls.

Zaddock stalked up to her side, and shoving the two guards out of the way, he held Amalise up when her body nearly slumped to the ground. Whispering something into her ear, he managed to stop the worst of the crying, but tears still spilled down her cheeks when she stepped into the darkness of the passage.

Loche was the last one to leave. With a pained expression, he hesitated for a moment. "I can't buy you much time, so get to the important stuff right away."

She nodded once, and Loche finally followed the others.

When she could no longer hear any footsteps or Amalise's sobs, she walked up to the cell again.

Her eyes lingered on Venko's body on the floor. "Is he alive?"

Ardow inclined his head. "They roughed him up quite badly, but he's breathing. He'll live. At least for now."

She stared at her friend. "Why, Ardow? Why would you do this?"

His gaze flitted to the dark passage for a moment before returning to hers. "Why do you think? You know better than anyone that we'll never be treated right here or anywhere in Havlands. It's time for new leadership—a new world where everyone is welcome."

"But it's changing. Loche is changing Ellow!"

Ardow's eyes narrowed. "It's not just about Ellow. It's about every oppressed person and creature in Havlands! And while Loche might be a lesser evil, he used blackmail to win last time, Lessia! Blackmail made possible by someone who wanted to control Ellow through him! He's not a good man."

She shuffled her feet. "He didn't do what they wanted, though. He's following his own path."

"You knew!" Ardow growled. "I can't believe this! You knew he only won because he blackmailed people into voting for him! That all that comes out of his mouth are lies! And you still trust him to lead Ellow? Have you lost your mind? You, out of all people, I thought would understand... especially after what your king did to you! What he continues to do!"

"Loche told me about it. He trusted me with it," she mumbled as heat burned her cheeks.

Ardow slammed his hand against the wall, and she jerked at the sudden movement. "You're in love with him."

She started shaking her head, but Ardow interrupted her. "You can't trust him! You can't! This will end badly for you, Lessia. Mark my words."

"And I can trust you?" she snarled, unable to contain her anger. "You kept this from me! Loche is at least truthful. How long has this been going on?"

Ardow glared at her. "Longer than you think. But I wish it had been longer! This was in the works for decades. We just needed the numbers before we acted."

She glared right back at him. "And what do you think

you'll accomplish? You've killed people, Ardow! They came after me!"

His eyes dipped. "They weren't supposed to. But you weren't supposed to become friendly with anyone. You should be on our side, Lessia!"

"And whose side is that?"

Ardow snapped his mouth shut.

She laughed hollowly. "You're not going to tell me."

He reached through the bars for her hand, but she shied away from him. "Lessia, you know why I can't."

Biting her cheek, she drew a breath through her nose to calm the simmering rage. "I can't believe this."

"I'm sorry," he whispered. "I didn't want it to come to this. But you need to decide whose side you're on. This is bigger than me. Bigger than any of us, Lessia. It goes far beyond Ellow. And when the next phase starts... those that stand against us... it won't be pretty."

"Who are you working with, Ard? And what do you want?" she cried. "You can't ask me to stand with you when you won't tell me anything!"

"I'm sorry," he mumbled again.

Pacing back and forth outside the cell, she covered her face with her hands. "You need to stop this. You need to promise you'll work with Loche and Frayson and the rest. Maybe they'll spare you if you agree to spy for them."

"I can't do that." Ardow's eyes glossed when she looked up at him.

"They'll kill you!" she screamed, not caring if the sound traveled to wherever the rest had gone.

"Then they kill me," Ardow said gently. "I am happy to die if it will allow others like me—like you—to lead a better life. Think about Kalia, Harver, Fiona, and the rest. You convinced me we needed to help them, and that's exactly what I'm doing. Trust that, if nothing else."

"There must be another way!" Lessia stared up at the stone ceiling, the cracks weaving their way through the white stone mirroring those splitting her heart open. "Loche has promised to make it better for us here. I believe him, Ard. Please!"

"And what about those not in Ellow? We can't rescue every single half-Fae from Vastala. Especially not if it becomes common knowledge what we've done."

She wrapped her arms around herself when his words cut deep into her heart.

There was truth to what he said.

But Ardow would die.

"Please, Ardow. Please don't do this," she begged.

When he remained quiet, she shook her head. "I can't let them execute you."

"Lessia—"

Steps reached her ears, and she steeled herself, hardening her shattered heart.

"No! I am so angry at you right now. So. Damn. Angry. But I can't live without you. I'm sending Amalise away. And once I can, I will get you out. We'll have to find somewhere to go after that—all of us."

Ardow stared at his boots. "I'm sorry it's come to this."

"Me too." Lessia breathed a shaky sigh as exhaustion crept into every single one of her limbs.

Voices drifted toward them as the group returned, and she forced herself to reach in and squeeze Ardow's hand.

"I'll get you out," she promised under her breath when the first guard walked into the cellar.

Loche's eyes sought hers when he made his way inside, but she kept hers on Amalise's bloodshot ones.

Walking up to her friend, she gripped both her hands with her own.

Amalise stared straight into her eyes, and her chin dipped at whatever she saw there.

"I'm sending Amalise away." Lessia continued holding Amalise's blue gaze as she spoke, and her friend squared her shoulders.

"Very well. She may stay until after the vote closes, but after that, she is banished from Ellow forever." Frayson clasped his hands over his stomach. "Let's retire for today. The Fae delegation will be here tomorrow afternoon, and then this mess will finally be over."

Without looking back, Lessia dragged Amalise with her up the stairs, heading straight for the doors and into the cold winter night.

CHAPTER SIXTY-FIVE

She could barely look at Amalise as they made their way back to the warehouse—the only home Lessia had known in the past thirteen years.

When the familiar shape broke through the darkness, Lessia forced her eyes not to linger on the warm light pouring out of the windows, on the door where she'd laughed when she'd walked through it the first time, or on the balcony where the children always tried to sneak out—until they realized the drop was hundreds of feet down into the wild sea.

They'd have to leave it behind.

She stiffened her spine.

They'd all be together again.

She'd make sure of it.

And that was the most important thing.

As Amalise opened the creaking door, Lessia lifted her eyes to the sky, praying that the plan she'd started formulating would work.

"What do you need?" Amalise eyed her as she lingered inside the door, nervously twisting a blonde tress.

Lessia drew a deep breath. "I need to speak to you and Kalia."

Nodding, Amalise turned toward the hidden door.

Lessia thought of following her but decided to mount the stairs instead.

Making her way to the bedroom she'd slept in the past five years, she continued breathing in and out, trying to calm the apprehension that rolled in the pit of her stomach.

As she opened the door, the smell of soap and firewood filled her nose, and she stared at the fire burning bright in her fireplace.

Sitting down on the bed, she splayed her fingers over the soft blanket, remembering how proud Kalia had been when she gifted it to her.

It wasn't the most beautiful blanket, but Kalia had paid for the fabric on her own and then convinced one of the seamstresses in town to show her how to make it.

Lessia braced herself as more memories of those early days flashed in her mind, and she realized she'd experienced true happiness here.

They'd have that again, she promised herself.

All of them.

"Lessia?"

Kalia's voice wavered slightly as she walked into the room, her eyes filling with confusion at the emotions she must have picked up from her.

Lessia waved for her and Amalise to come into the room, patting the bed beside her. When they'd made themselves comfortable—Amalise taking a corner and tucking her legs beneath herself, with Kalia squeezing in as close to Lessia as she could—she cleared her throat. "Kalia, I'm going to need you to be strong for me."

Kalia's chin quivered, but she nodded.

"We need to leave. I know of a place where you and the children will be safe, but Amalise and I cannot follow you there. Not yet."

A soft whimper escaped Amalise, but when Lessia glanced at her, she nodded, reaching out a hand to grip Lessia's.

"I promise we'll come for you when the time is right, but I need you to get the children there as fast as you can. Amalise will transfer the ownership of the taverns and gambling rooms to you, and you can use the money from them to ensure you have everything you need. I'm hoping I will be able to convince someone to accompany you, but if not, I will draw you a map."

She squeezed Amalise's hand. "Amalise, I need you to get horses tomorrow, when everyone will be busy voting. You can use the emergency funds in my safe. There is only enough to ride two and two, but there will be some left over to ensure you can pay for food and anything else you might need."

Kalia stared straight ahead when Lessia turned toward her, and she softened her voice. "Kalia, look at me."

Her half-Fae friend turned to her, her eyes glossy.

"You are stronger than you think." Lessia smiled at her. "You're ready for this. And where you're going isn't bad. The people there are kind. When you get there, ask for Geyia and tell her Lessia owes her a favor if she lets you stay."

"But what about you two? And Ardow?" Kalia's lip trembled.

"We will be all right." Amalise shifted on the bed, wrapping her arms around them.

"Lessia and I will free Ardow, and then we'll come for you. Won't we?" Amalise stared defiantly into Lessia's eyes.

She nodded. "We will."

Kalia still seemed uncertain, but after Lessia and Amalise convinced her that they'd be safe and Lessia promised her again that she'd see her soon, she left the room to make sure the children started packing.

"What a mess." Amalise crawled to Kalia's spot, draped an arm around Lessia's back, and leaned her head on her shoulder.

"I know." Lessia sighed.

They remained quiet for a while, just staring into the flames in the fireplace before them.

"Amalise?" Lessia whispered after a while.

"Lia?" she responded with a yawn.

"If something happens to me, I need you to go with Kalia. I think Loche will help keep you hidden, and I need to know you'll be safe."

"Stop it, Lessia. You will be fine. Ardow will be fine. I will be fine. I won't hear it."

Lessia picked at a loose thread in the blanket as she nodded.

There was no point in arguing.

She knew Amalise would do it if it came to that.

After hugging her friend tight, she made herself walk out of the house.

She needed to talk to Loche.

CHAPTER SIXTY-SIX

The number of guards in the courtyard seemed to have doubled during her absence, and she spent fifteen minutes explaining where she'd been before she was let through the gates.

Eyes trailed her the entire time she walked the path to the castle, as she ascended the stairs, and when she finally reached Loche's room.

Lessia pulled at her tunic before she lifted her hand to knock on his door.

She almost wished he wouldn't be there, but as soon as her knuckles touched the wood, the door flew open, and Loche's shoulders seemed to drop an inch when his eyes locked with hers.

"Did you think I would run away again?" she tried to joke.

Neither of them smiled.

With a glance behind her, Loche grabbed her hand and pulled her inside, softly closing the door behind them.

She glanced around the room.

She hadn't been here before, and she was surprised by how tidy it was.

A few books lay on a table by the window, and his sword, with polishing material beside it, lay on the bed. Clothing was folded atop a dresser by the fireplace, and several lanterns were placed around the room and in the windowsills.

Loche walked up to the bed, picked up the sword to lean it against the bed frame, and swiftly packed up the cleaning supplies. As he gestured for her to join him, he dragged a hand through his hair, and there were purple crescents under his eyes as he tracked her approach.

She sat down next to him, trying to keep some space between them, but the mattress was too soft, and soon his leg rested against hers. Glancing out the window at the clouds building over the sea, Lessia wrung her hands, unsure how to start this conversation.

"I'm sorry." Loche shifted so he faced her, his bent leg still touching the side of hers. "I should have told you, but I realized immediately you weren't involved, and I worried that if your reaction wasn't real, others wouldn't see it as clearly as I did."

She searched his eyes, the cloudy gray mirroring the brewing storm outside, worry and caution simmering in them.

Lessia didn't know why she trusted this man so easily, but she believed him.

And even if she hadn't...

She needed him.

She drew a shallow breath. "I know. I understand why you did what you did."

Loche nodded and placed a hand on her knee, his fingers absently drawing small circles that awoke that yearning in her veins again.

She pushed the thoughts aside. "You showed me that cave because you suspected something like this might happen."

His jaw twitched. "Yes. I wasn't sure who the spy was, but Zaddock told me that the guards who attacked you seemed to hesitate when they realized who you were. I guessed it must be someone close to you unless you were involved yourself."

Unease roiled in her gut.

She hadn't thought Zaddock noticed.

Swallowing, she gripped his distracting hand. "I need to get the children out of here."

"They can go to Geyia and Steiner."

She released a breath.

She had trusted that he would say that, but hearing it relieved some of the weight pressing on her chest.

Loche tugged on her hand until she moved closer, shifting her onto his lap.

"Amalise will be taken care of." His eyes burned into hers, a flicker of pain shining in them. "Zaddock will also be banished, and he's promised to ensure her safety."

She stiffened in his arms. "Why?"

Loche offered her a sad smile. "You weren't the only one who had to make an impossible choice."

She was about to ask what his choice was, but the way his eyes trailed over her face, as if he was memorizing every single one of her features, told her everything she needed to know.

"It was me or him."

Loche crushed her against his chest, his whisper barely audible. "If I won, I could banish either you or Zaddock. I couldn't bear for it to be you. Not just for myself, but for you to once again not be welcome."

A lump formed in her throat at the shudder that ran through him.

She couldn't believe he'd chosen her over Zaddock.

She didn't deserve it.

She'd need to leave anyway.

And Loche would have no one.

The guilt that overtook her nearly made her scream.

She wanted to crawl out of her own skin.

Erase the person she was and every action that had led her here.

Loche pulled back to look at her, a wrinkle forming over his brow. "It was my choice, Lessia. Do not carry my guilt."

She huffed a breath.

It wasn't his guilt to carry.

He didn't even know.

But those invisible fingers had her in a death grip, and not a word left her lips to convince him to change his decision.

Loche's hands stroked her back as she caught her breath, his eyes worryingly flitting between hers.

When she could finally speak again, she whispered, "What about Ardow?"

His eyes hardened. "He will be put on trial after the election. I will do my best to convince them not to execute him, but he will remain in the cellars, Lessia."

Biting her lip, she just stared at him.

She couldn't even nod.

Couldn't tell him another lie.

"I should probably sleep," she mumbled.

As she rose, Loche stood with her. "I'll follow you back to your room. We don't think Ardow and Venko worked alone. Someone else with intimate knowledge of the nominees and the election has been helping them."

She was too tired to argue, so she let Loche take her hand and lead her back to the room.

Outside, he brushed his lips against hers, lingering for a moment, but she needed time alone.

Loche seemed to read her mind, and with a final kiss that, despite everything, madc her skin tingle, he bid her good night.

When she walked inside, Merrick's door was closed, and she thought for a moment to knock, but exhaustion swept through her.

Without even removing her clothing, she climbed into bed and fell asleep within seconds.

CHAPTER SIXTY-SEVEN

"Lessia!"

She pried her eyes open to find Merrick sitting on her bed. A muscle in his jaw ticked as he flipped a dagger between his hands.

Lessia threw an arm over her eyes. "If you're not here to kill me, I need a few more hours of sleep."

"It's early afternoon already. The Fae delegation and those vile human nobles arrived a few hours ago, and the festivities are about to begin." Merrick mercilessly pulled off the blanket. "You need to hurry."

She flew up, staring with wide eyes at the dim light shining in through the windows.

How had she slept this long?

As her mind woke, everything that happened yesterday slammed into her, and her grouchiness at being awoken was replaced with nagging dread and nearly overwhelming guilt.

Here she was, sleeping the day away when there was so much she needed to do. When Ardow had slept on a cold stone floor, when the children she'd promised would be safe had to pack up their lives once again, when her best friend had to prepare to leave the only home she'd known.

Sprinting to the closet, she started pulling out the black dress she'd worn last time, all the while thinking about how she would find time to figure out how to get Ardow out, when Merrick cleared his throat.

"Loche dropped off a gift for you last night."

Her brows snapped together as she stared at the beautiful package on the desk Merrick gestured toward. It was wrapped in silky paper, and as she cautiously removed it, her mouth fell open.

It was a dress.

The material was pure gold, shimmering slightly in the gentle winter light. The dress had a boned bodice with darker gold bands holding it together, and the skirt was layered so that it would fall beautifully from her waist.

But her shoulders slumped when she realized there was no way she could wear it.

The flowy sleeves were capped in the latest fashion to show off her arms.

Lessia draped it over the chair, swallowing against the thickness clogging her throat.

"I thought this might happen," Merrick muttered. "One second."

Her eyes followed him as he stalked into his room. A moment later, Merrick emerged with another package, this one much smaller and wrapped in brown paper.

He ungraciously threw it to her. "Here you go."

Tearing it open, she pulled out silky white fabric.

"Merrick..." she breathed.

It was gloves that would reach far beyond where her tattoo stretched up her arm.

"Thank you," she got out as more tightness constricted

her throat.

Merrick only grumbled as he turned his back to her. "Now get dressed so we can go down. I have some business with the Fae."

Despite the beautiful dress and the unexpected thoughtfulness from Merrick, dread once again whirled in her stomach.

As she slipped it on, lacing up the bodice and fluffing the skirts, then pulling on the gloves, she asked quietly, "Who is here?"

Merrick's shoulders tensed. "No one you will know. A few Fae nobles and emissaries. And King Rioner's brother."

Her hand froze midair with the brush she'd planned to use to tame her hair. "Which brother?"

"Alarin."

The brush clattered to the floor as black spots danced before her eyes.

No, no, no.

This couldn't be happening.

Not with everything else that was going on.

It was too much.

"I can't. I can't. I can't," she whispered as devastated amber eyes etched into her mind.

Lessia crouched down with her hands over her face as if the darkness could purge the memory, and it wasn't the bodice she'd laced up that constricted her breathing.

"Lessia." Merrick's hand landed on her shoulder. "What is it?"

She lifted her head, for the first time wishing she could meet his eyes so he could read her, not so she could send him away.

But while his brows pulled, Merrick's gaze remained averted as he gently dragged her upright.

"What happened?" he asked again, his hand remaining on her shoulder as her body racked with shudders.

She thought about telling him.

She wanted to tell him.

But she couldn't.

Not as long as he was blood-sworn to the king.

Instead she removed his hand, forced her shoulders back, and picked up the brush again.

She had no choice but to get through this evening.

Keep it together for a few more hours.

There were more lives at stake than her own, and after tonight, she'd be free to save them.

When she'd gotten all the tangles out, albeit with a shaky hand, she glanced in the mirror, trying to light up her face to match the dress.

But her eyes remained wary, and with a deep sigh, she took the arm Merrick offered, allowing him to lead her out and down into the common room.

Merrick was tense as he walked beside her, and she could sense he wanted to ask again what had happened, but thankfully, he kept his mouth drawn into a thin line as they reached the double doors.

She'd kept her gaze down as she passed a few groups standing around the hallways, but when Merrick came to a halt, she lifted her eyes and found Loche leaning against the wall outside the doors to the ballroom.

Releasing her arm, Merrick took a step aside just as Loche's eyes found hers.

His mouth quirked as he dragged his gaze over her body, and he shook his head as he closed the distance between them.

"I don't know what to say," he mumbled as he pulled at her hand for her to spin before him.

"That would be a first," Lessia joked weakly, trying to push away the mounting feeling of panic that roiled inside her as a guard opened the door for them.

Loche snorted, his fingers laced firmly with hers.

She glanced down at their joined hands and then back up at him. "Is this a good idea? I don't think they'll like you walking in with me."

Loche smiled at her, his eyes glittering. "Fuck them."

A small smile pulled at her lips.

He was right.

Fuck them.

After tonight, this nightmare would be over, and she'd never have to see these people again.

But her smile fell as she glanced at Loche, at how his broad grin wavered not once as they strode into the room and conversations quieted as people noticed them.

She'd never see him again either.

Merrick followed closely as Loche led her toward a table with wine, and Lessia tried to tell herself it was for the better.

Not just for her but for him.

She took a deep sip from the goblet Loche pressed into her hands, then turned toward the room.

It looked spectacular. Deep purple tapestries decorated every wall, and large chandeliers had been strategically placed to shine soft light over the many humans and Fae mingling in the room.

Well, the humans mingled with humans while the Fae stood by themselves to her right, seemingly whispering about the humans that dared walk by them and laughing at whatever they found amusing about their kind.

She looked away when she caught one of the Fae's eyes, shifting to stand a bit behind Loche.

Craven was nowhere to be found in the crowd, though,

and she frowned at Loche. “Where is Craven?”

“He couldn’t go through with the final challenge.” Loche smirked. “He didn’t even have the courage to tell us in person. He just left a note in his room that he’d decided to bow out.”

Lessia offered him a faint smile back.

She didn’t blame Craven for opting out.

Had she had a choice, she would have as well.

As she let her eyes sweep across the room once more, she caught a glimpse of golden-brown hair and quickly spun around, facing Merrick, who leaned against the wall. Picking up a goblet from the table, she offered it to him, trying to pretend that was her intent all along.

But the crease between Merrick’s brows deepened as he accepted it, and his head tilted slightly as he repositioned himself to see behind her.

“They’re coming over,” he mumbled.

Lessia froze.

You can do this.

You can do this.

He doesn’t remember who you are.

She repeated the words to herself as she turned back toward the room.

Loche’s hand found hers, and she pretended to fix something with her dress with the other, keeping her gaze down.

Merrick stepped up behind her, so close that his breaths blew through her hair, and the leather of his tunic scraped against her arm.

You can do this.

He doesn’t know you anymore.

Lessia trembled as she drew air into her lungs.

Unlike Merrick, Loche seemed entirely at ease when a group of four Fae reached them, keeping hold of Lessia’s hand while reaching out the other in greeting.

The first male accepted it, then turned to Lessia.

She knew he could hear her racing heart when she lifted her eyes to meet his silver ones, but she kept her face blank as she gave him a nod. "Nice to meet you."

The Fae quirked a dark brow, letting his lips curl into a lethal smile. "And you, Elessia. I've heard such very interesting things about you."

She held back a grimace at the icy implications in his tone, but Loche released the hand he'd just shaken and turned their way.

"You are in my lands right now. If I am informed that one of you so much as glances at her the wrong way, this will end very ugly." Loche's glacial tone mirrored the frosty smile of the Fae male, and Lessia stiffened when they continued to stare daggers at each other.

But then a golden hand landed on the Fae's shoulder.

"Riven, the regent is right. You will not disrespect the people of Ellow, or I have orders from Rioner to make sure you do."

The Fae stepped around Riven, and she hadn't thought her heart could beat any faster, but when kind amber eyes fixed on hers, each beat thrummed in her ears, drowning out all other noise.

"I don't think we've had the pleasure of meeting before." He bowed to her and Loche. "I am Alarin Rantzier, King Rioner's brother."

Loche nodded back, but Lessia stood paralyzed, unable to utter a word as he straightened.

Alarin's eyes found hers again, and his mouth fell open. "You look so much like..." He shook his head. "Forgive me; I am forgetting my manners. What is your name?"

She couldn't help but stare at his familiar face, and a wave of memories washed over her as she noted the stubble on his chin, the one spot where hair never grew. Some of the creases by his eyes had deepened, but otherwise, he looked exactly the same as the last time she'd seen him.

A deep ache spread inside her, and she had to bite her tongue not to jump into his arms, telling him how much she'd missed him.

Her father.

Loche cleared his throat beside her, and she quickly snapped out of it.

He didn't remember her.

Didn't know he'd lost two daughters that day.

"I'm Lessia Gyldenberg," she mumbled.

Her father smiled at her, and the sight crashed right into her chest, before he shifted his gaze behind her. "Merrick! It's good to see you."

Merrick stepped around her, and her brows rose as the males embraced.

She hadn't known they knew each other.

When Merrick stepped back, there was a small smile on his face, and her brows lifted even higher.

And apparently liked each other.

But then Merrick froze beside her, and his face slowly moved from her to her father. A rush of air left him when he snagged on the hair tumbling down her shoulders—the golden shade identical to that of the male before them.

The others seemed oblivious to what had just happened. Wishing Loche and Lessia good luck tomorrow, they returned to the rest of the delegation, which hovered at the back wall.

Her father glanced at her again, his eyes narrowing slightly as his gaze trailed over her, but then he shrugged. "Merrick, may I have a word?"

When Merrick gave him a sharp nod, he smiled at her and

Loche. "If we don't speak again, I wish you a pleasant evening."

Merrick started following him as he turned to walk out of the room, and before she could stop herself, she gripped his hand. He didn't turn around, but he squeezed hers quickly before letting go and stalking after her father.

She blew out a breath.

He wouldn't tell him.

Loche downed his glass beside her, then picked up another and emptied it as well. "I know we need to work together with them, but do they need to be so damn stuck up?"

A shocked giggle escaped her, some of the tension lining her shoulders easing.

One side of Loche's mouth lifted. "I guess Alarin wasn't too bad."

She nodded, and while a sudden yearning to tell him who Alarin really was coursed through her, she kept her mouth closed.

Tonight was not the night for big revelations.

And her being the daughter of King Rioner's brother—the male next in line for the throne, should something happen to Rioner—was definitely a big revelation.

"Come on." Loche tugged at her hand. "Let's dance. There won't be any balls for a while after this."

There weren't many people dancing when Loche's arm circled her waist, but she didn't even hear the whispers she was certain came from human and Fae alike as he spun her around the makeshift dance floor.

Instead, she let his strong heartbeat drown out the sounds around them and his breathing slow her own until she could push the overwhelming thoughts flooding her mind deep down inside her.

CHAPTER
SIXTY-EIGHT

When the music picked up speed and more people joined them on the floor, Loche eyed her, and she nodded when he jerked his head toward the refreshment table.

A few groups of other Fae came over, voicing their support to Loche, and while none of them bothered her, their scathing looks burned into her back when they finally offered their good-lucks and goodbyes.

Lessia shrugged it off.

At least her father was still nowhere to be seen.

She glanced at the door he'd exited, swallowing the guilt burning like bile in her throat.

She'd never thought she'd see him again.

Especially not under these circumstances.

Even if she didn't have Ardow and everything else to deal with, the election and whatever was going on with her and Loche was already too much.

Throwing her father into the mix...

Her mind shattered.

She couldn't think about him right now.

Her feelings would have to wait until this mess was over.

Loche sat down in one of the plush chairs beside the table, and when she made to sit down in the other, he frowned and pulled her onto his lap.

She eyed him when he wrapped his arms around her and positioned her sideways on his lap.

Loche gave her a lazy smirk. "Now that I have you, I am not letting you go."

Wrapping an arm around his neck, she let her fingers play with his dark strands but remained quiet, her thoughts too muddled for her to come up with a playful response.

Or any response at all.

"I want to ask you something," Loche murmured.

She searched his eyes, noting the soberness in them and a small ember of hope.

"Will you stay with me?" Loche pulled her closer, lowering his voice. "I mean, stay and rule with me. They've opened the vote, and it seems I will win, but I'd like to share the regent position with you. I think I have much to learn from you. Besides"—he winked—"we make a good team."

The room around her started spinning.

She wanted nothing more than to tell him yes, tell him she would stay with him. Regardless of what position he offered her, she just wanted to be near him and breathe the same air as him for as long as she could.

But she needed to make sure her friends—her family—were safe.

And they would never be safe here.

Lessia clawed at her throat when it closed up.

"I need some air," she got out as she jumped off his lap, rushing out of the room.

His steps echoed behind her, and Lessia flew up the

nearest staircase, making her steps as silent as possible as she took every twist and turn she could to get rid of him.

Pausing behind a corner, she listened for steps, but hushed voices reached her ears instead. Lessia flattened herself against the wall, creeping into a dim alcove as the voices came closer.

"Both of them are in the cellar?"

Her father's voice.

She pressed herself farther into the small space, her pulse thrumming.

"Yes."

She swore to herself when Merrick's shimmering hair came into view, her father's brown mane a moment after.

"You know what you need to do," her father mumbled.

Merrick nodded, but then he stilled, his nostrils flaring.

Lessia cursed again when his head tilted her way, but Merrick only rushed his steps, dragging her father with him.

She stayed there for a few minutes until she was sure they were long gone.

Slipping out of the alcove, she slammed right into Merrick's chest.

He automatically reached out to steady her—or perhaps hold her in place, given the strong grip he kept on her arms.

"Eavesdropping, are we?" Merrick said, his voice worryingly low.

"No, I... I just needed to get away. I didn't hear anything." She glanced at the bottom of her golden dress, the hem now dirty and ripped from being dragged along the castle floor.

"You did. But it doesn't matter. It was just some orders from our king." Merrick released her arms. "Let's go back to our chambers. I expect King Rioner to come tomorrow, and I guess you'll have much to do once you're free."

Lessia nodded slowly, and when Merrick turned around, she followed him.

They walked quietly until they reached the doors to their rooms.

She half expected him to barge into hers to give her another lecture, but Merrick opened his own door instead.

He hesitated for a moment, and with a quick glance at the corridor, he turned to her. "You should know something."

She eyed him as he brushed some hair out of his face.

"Alarin's daughter isn't dead," he whispered.

"W— what?" she stammered. "How?"

Merrick shook his head. "I can't tell you, so please don't ask me. I just needed you to know that guilt you're carrying around... it's unwarranted."

A choked sound left her throat.

Her sister was alive?

Merrick reached out to squeeze her shoulder before he spun around and entered his chambers.

In a daze, she opened her door and, after closing it, slid down to the floor with her back against it.

Her eyes burned, and as she lifted her hand to her face, moisture seeped into her gloves, glistening tears dripping off her fingers when she lifted them.

She let out a strangled laugh.

Frelina was alive.

"I'm not sure if you're crying or laughing."

Lessia lifted her gaze as Loche rose from the bed.

When he stretched out a hand to help her up, she took it, wiping her cheeks with her other one.

Loche eyed her warily. "I'm sorry. I didn't mean to overwhelm you back there."

She couldn't help but smile at him.

Her sister was alive.

Nothing else mattered.

"I'm sorry for running away." Lessia stepped into his space, wrapping her arms around him. "It's just... I can't, Loche. I have too many people relying on me."

She pulled him to the bed, sighing when she kicked off the uncomfortable shoes she had squeezed her poor feet into.

Loche sat down next to her, his hand resting on her thigh. "I'll make sure they're taken care of. That's what I was about to say when you ran off. I'll even pardon Ardow if that's what it takes for you to stay."

Her eyes flew to his. "You would?"

Loche nodded. "And we'll figure out a way to make sure Zaddock and Amalise can remain in Ellow. I promise you. I don't want to live without him either."

Lessia threw her arms around his neck, laughter bubbling up her throat.

Loche hugged her back, his smile evident against her neck. "We'll figure it out, Lessia. Build a world where everyone is welcome, where everyone has a chance at a good life."

Pulling back, she slammed her lips against his, pouring every ounce of the happiness that filled her into it.

Her sister was alive.

Her friends would be safe.

She would be safe.

Perhaps even loved.

Loche's hands tangled in her hair as he kissed her, and when he pulled back, they were both out of breath, chests heaving against each other.

"Is that a yes?"

When she nodded, he shifted her down onto the bed and claimed her lips again.

She lost herself in him, kissing him until both sets of eyelids fluttered.

Their lips remained locked even as sleep took them.

CHAPTER SIXTY-NINE

When she woke, her lips were swollen, and Lessia smiled as she brought her fingers to them.

Rolling over, she found that Loche had already left.

A quick glance out the window confirmed it was still early, but she jumped out of bed, slipping out of the dress and gloves and pulling on her usual tunic and breeches.

Lessia whistled to herself while she got ready, excitement whispering over her skin at how she'd tell Kalia and Amalise how everything had changed.

After pulling her hair back with a comb, she swung open the door to Merrick's room.

His room was empty, the bed made.

When she peeked into his bathing chamber, she found it empty as well, and a frown replaced her smile.

Where had he taken off to?

If the king was coming today, he'd surely want to meet with them together.

The thought of the king had her skin tingle.

But not with fear.

No, she'd done what he asked of her, and he'd promised her her freedom.

She would be free today.

She sucked in a breath at the thought.

Walking into her own room again, she picked up the daggers from her dresser—she'd found no way to keep them on her while wearing the dress—and left the room.

Lessia smiled at the guards lining the walls outside her room, and while a few raised their brows, most grinned back at her as she made her way to the staircase.

"Lessia!"

She turned around at the top of the stairs, offering Zaddock, who rushed to her side, a smile as well.

"Did you hear?" Zaddock grinned from ear to ear.

She shook her head. "Hear what?"

"He won!" Zaddock nearly bounced from excitement. "He won again!"

She didn't think she could be happier than she was right now, but more warmth spread in her chest as Zaddock shifted his weight from foot to foot like a child eager to go play.

"I need to tell our men, but you should go to his study. It's on the floor below this one. He'll want you there when it's announced." Zaddock waved to her before he sprinted down the stairs.

Lessia didn't hesitate as she took several steps at a time down to the second floor, laughing to herself when she nearly fell in her eagerness to get there.

She asked a guard which door was his, and when he pointed it out, she forced herself not to run over. Still, her strides took her there in a few seconds, and she let her lips lift into a wide smile as she opened the door.

"Loche! I just heard!"

She started toward him where he leaned on his desk, but her muscles locked when she realized he wasn't alone, and the expression on his face wasn't happiness, but shock and betrayal.

Lessia's legs nearly buckled when she glimpsed her father, clad in the emerald uniform of the Fae guard and with an unreadable expression on his face. And beside him...

King Rioner.

Her uncle.

His features were darker than her father's, the hair that tumbled down his expensive purple robe more brown than golden, but there was no mistaking they were related.

King Rioner's eyes remained averted, fixed on a spot on the purple rug beneath him, but she knew they carried the same amber hue as her own—as her father's. While her father had kept her and Frelina hidden from his brother, he'd told them everything of the king who would stop at nothing to hurt them if he found they existed.

Her gaze shifted back to Loche.

He didn't seek her eyes, and her stomach surged when he took a step toward King Rioner, placing the wooden desk between them.

"Loche..." Lessia pleaded. "I can explain. I don't know what he's told you, but—"

"Enough!" King Rioner's voice rumbled through the room, the command surging through the oath tethering them together, and her lips snapped shut.

But when the king placed a hand on Loche's shoulder, Lessia's lips curled back in a silent snarl.

She couldn't stand this male touching him.

Loche was too good to be anywhere near him.

King Rioner let out a humorless laugh. "Behave, Lessia. I know even halflings can act civilized when you want to."

Her ears buzzed, and she went to take a step closer when an invisible rope stopped her, freezing her body with one foot in the air.

"That's better." The king smirked. "Now, where were we? Ah, yes! So, Loche, as I was saying, you have my sincerest apologies for nestling a spy into your midst. I am sure you can understand I needed to protect my people. But as soon as I realized it was one of my own who was the cause for the troubles in Vastala—like one of your own was the cause here in Ellow—I came straight here."

The pull on the oath softened, and when Lessia could set down her foot, her eyes snapped to her father.

His jaw twitched as he briefly met her eyes before shifting them back to his brother.

Loche's gaze moved her way as well, but as she desperately tried to get him to look at her, he locked down any emotion on his face and turned to the king again. "Bringing her into this was an act of war, Your Majesty. I am sure you can understand I need to protect my people as well. As for Merrick, it might have been unbeknownst to you that he conspired with the people attacking us, but he is still one of your men, and you need to be held accountable."

Lessia let out a sharp breath. "M... Merrick?"

Loche pursued his mouth, but the king didn't move a muscle, his tone bored as he responded. "My dear Death Whisperer seemed to have whispered in more ears than mine. He was found trying to break out the two traitors last night."

She shook her head as King Rioner continued. "Loche, I am sure we can come to an agreement that won't lead to bloodshed. I did ask my spy to see what you knew of the situation, but I didn't ask her to compel you to fall for her. That was all her doing. I merely needed to understand if war was brewing again."

"No! Loche, I didn't—" she started, but King Rioner closed his hand into a fist, and her voice drifted away.

Pushing against the blood oath, she tried to will Loche to look at her.

When he finally did, she held on to the small flash of pain in his eyes at seeing her gasp for air. Her eyes begged him to understand, pleaded with him to see that she had done everything she could to circumvent the king's orders.

Loche closed his eyes for a moment, and when he opened them again, determination blazed in them. "I knew there was something you weren't telling me."

Her mouth opened and closed, but the oath was too strong, and moisture lined her eyes at the little air making its way down her lungs.

"I need her to be able to speak," Loche snarled at her king.

The fingers around her throat softened, and Lessia sucked in a breath. "I'm... I'm so sorry. I—I couldn't," she stammered.

His eyes bounced between hers, the dark swirls in them blazing, before he turned to the king once more. "I will forgive this misstep if you free her and leave her in Ellow. I'll figure out a suitable punishment. Based on what my men are telling me, I don't think these attacks are over, and we need to stand united against what's to come."

"You're not living up to your ruthless reputation, regent." King Rioner laughed. "Will you allow a female—a halfling at that—to compel your love? Will she stay and rule with you? Whatever will your people say?"

"She hasn't used her magic on me, *king*," Loche snarled. "I think you should worry more about what your people will say about your right-hand man betraying you."

Ice filled her veins, and her hands started shaking by her sides as the king let out another dark chuckle. "Oh, Loche. She has. See, that's why I brought my dear brother. His special gift allows him to undo any magic performed on someone. Alarin?"

No.

Loche's eyes slammed into hers when her father stepped forward, and the air filled with the soft humming of magic.

She wanted to look away.

Didn't want to see when he remembered what she'd done to him.

But she couldn't.

She saw the exact moment her magic released its grip.

Loche's knuckles whitened as he gripped the edge of the table, and he let out a loud huff when the memories she'd compelled away replaced the fake ones she'd given him.

Bile rose in her throat when the small flicker of care in his eyes vanished, the glittering gray shifting in the blackest of loathing.

"You..." Loche clenched his jaw, tearing his eyes away.

King Rioner grinned where he stood, his chiseled face bent down, but her father winced at the devastation that must be written all over her face.

"Loche..." Lessia took a hesitant step forward. "Please, let me explain."

Her bottom lip trembled as she reached out for him, but he shoved her hand away.

"Take them away," he snarled.

"W—what?" Lessia tried to reach out for him again, but he pushed off the table and backed away from her.

"I said. Take. Them. Away. Take my feelings away. Take every memory of us. I only want to remember you as the spy who snaked her way into our election. Nothing else." Loche's hands balled into fists as he glared at her.

"No." She shook her head. "No, please, Loche. It was all real! Just let me explain."

His glare shifted to her king. "You can make her do it, can't you? Make her do it, and there will be no war between Ellow and Vastala."

"No!" Lessia fell to her knees. "Please!"

King Rioner's teeth glinted in the light from the fireplace. "As you wish."

He turned toward her, careful to keep his gaze somewhere on her leather boots. "Elessia, I order you to remove his memories of you, to remove the feelings he harbors for you."

Invisible tethers wrapped around her, trying to force her upright, but she struggled against them, pushed against the oath burning on her arm.

"Don't make me do this. D-d-don't... Please! No!"

Something warm dripped down her face, and when she wiped at it, her sleeve came back red.

Light flickered before her eyes as she fought with everything in her, but as blood continued to gush out of her nose, another tug forced her to stand.

Her feet took a step toward Loche.

Then another.

Loche's dark eyes fixed on hers, unwavering, unforgiving, as she closed the distance between them.

"Please," she whispered as she felt magic build behind her eyes. "Please, Loche. I..." She sucked in a breath and forced herself to tell him. "I think... I think I'm falling in love with you."

Loche didn't flinch.

His gaze sliced to her king again. "I thought you had her on a tighter leash."

King Rioner snorted. "It's done."

It felt like she was dying.

And she wished she was when the familiar warmth of magic filled her veins, when she opened her mouth with eyes locked on Loche's glazed ones and heard herself utter the words "Forget me. Forget every moment we had alone. Forget you ever felt anything for me. You will only remember me as the spy, the traitor that tried to ruin your election."

When the oath finally released its grip, her knees buckled, and a broken sob left her as Loche's eyes cleared and only mild disdain clouded the gray as he watched her.

Loche stepped over her broken body, his lip curling with disgust when she whimpered his name.

"I will keep my promise. There will be no war between Ellow and Vastala over the spy. But you..." He pointed at her, his eyes empty when they collided with her tear-filled ones. "You are hereby banished from Ellow. If you ever step foot here again, I will personally hunt you down and kill you."

Every word stabbed at her heart like a dagger, and she could barely see through the haze of tears as King Rioner stepped up to stand beside him. "I made a promise to you, Elessia. You are hereby free of the blood oath. But you are also banished from Vastala, and I have informed my men that if they see you entering our waters, you are to be taken out immediately."

Screaming at the fiery pain slicing through her arm, she pulled at her sleeve. The only thing that remained of the tattoo was blistered, angry skin, and a whimper left her as she wrapped a hand around it.

A freeing emptiness filled her to her core, and Lessia huffed a breath when the last traces of the oath left her veins.

"Leave," Loche ordered, his gaze pinned somewhere above her body on the floor.

"Loche..." she pleaded.

"You heard the regent," the king hissed. "Leave now, and your life will be spared."

Sobs racked her body as she clumsily got to her feet, and

she stumbled her way to the door, wondering if death wasn't preferable to the pain that burned through her, that seemed to seep into every pore.

She lingered by the door, turning her head over her shoulder, harboring a small hope that Loche would look at her again, but his back remained turned, and she caught only her father's sorrow-filled eyes before the door slammed shut.

CHAPTER SEVENTY

With her hands on her knees, she tried to mute the cry that forced its way up her throat, soft whimpers leaving her as waves and waves of pain washed through her body.

"Lessia, come with me. Quickly!"

Through blurry eyes, she made out Zaddock's worried face and didn't bother to ask where he was taking her as her heart broke, a silent scream tearing through her mind.

Zaddock dragged her into an empty room at the end of the corridor, closing the door behind them. "I heard every word. I am so sorry, Lessia."

Tears dripped down her face when she lifted it to meet his eyes. "Why? I did this to him. I deserve this."

She choked when another sharp pain jabbed at her heart.

She did deserve this.

She'd known all along what would happen when he found out.

And she'd still gone along with it—had still allowed him to fall for her deceit.

"No one deserves that." Zaddock shook his head. "I will get you out of here. You need to leave immediately. I don't know how they let you walk out alive, but you need to go before they change their minds."

"I can't!" she cried. "I—I can't leave them all. Merrick and Ardow... They'll kill them!"

"Hush!" Zaddock opened the door and peeked out, then turned back to her. "I can get you into the cellars and show you a way for all of you to leave undetected, but we need to go *now*."

She stared at him, a hiccup breaking through the sobs. "Why... why would you do that?"

Zaddock scratched his chin. "I'm being sent away anyway. And while I don't blame Loche for his reaction today, I think it was rash. He will regret it. Well, when he remembers. And when he does, this is what he would want for you."

Trying to force more than a shallow breath into her lungs, Lessia hiccuped again. "H—he won't remember. Not unless I or my... Alarin undo it."

Zaddock bore his eyes into hers. "Let's hope for his sake you will."

He opened the door again, placing a finger over his lips.

Lessia followed him as they made their way down into the cellars as quietly as possible. She expected to be stopped every time they passed a guard, but they must not have heard the news because they smiled and waved at them, some slapping Zaddock on the back for Loche's win.

When they entered, Zaddock convinced them Lessia had been granted time alone with the prisoners, and she could barely believe it when they nodded and left their posts to walk up and grab some food from the kitchen.

Ardow sat against the wall with Venko beside him when

she rushed in, and his eyes widened when he noticed her tear-streaked face. "What..."

Lessia shook her head, wiping at her face. "We don't have time. We need to leave. Where is Merrick?"

Ardow pointed to the cell opposite them, and Lessia's heart hammered against her rib cage at the blood pooling on the floor beneath the Fae.

But as Zaddock opened the door and she crouched down beside him, she realized he was conscious.

Pulling at his arm, she tried to get him to rise, but Merrick only rolled onto his side.

"Merrick, come on! They'll kill you!" she hissed.

"You need to go without me. I was ordered to stay by our dear king."

Merrick slammed his hand against the stone. "I was so stupid! I thought all the Fae had left when I came down here, but one of those sneaky bastards must have seen me and alerted King Rioner."

Lessia swore.

She'd forgotten about his blood oath.

But she'd nearly been able to resist it, and she wasn't even a full Fae...

Perhaps there was a way.

"Merrick, look at me." She pulled at his arm again. "Look at me!"

"You know I can't do that. I was ordered not to," he snarled, his hands flexing by his sides.

"Trust me," she snarled back. "You can resist it."

Zaddock paced outside the cell. "You need to hurry, Lessia. They'll figure out something is amiss soon."

"Lessia, you have to leave him," Ardow called, his voice soft.

"No! I am not leaving you behind, you stubborn male."

She grabbed his face in her hands and turned it toward her. “Look. At. Me.”

“It will kill me to break the oath,” he warned.

“It will kill you to stay here too. Wouldn’t you rather go down fighting?”

Merrick clenched his jaw, but his eyelids fluttered.

“Yes! Push back,” she urged.

A drop of blood snaked its way out of his nose, and his eyelids opened a fraction.

“Come on, Merrick. You’re the Death Whisperer, for gods’ sake! You can do this.”

With a hiss, Merrick’s eyes flew open and locked with hers.

She inhaled sharply as his eyes pierced into her amber ones.

She’d been right—they were dark.

Almost black.

But they also had swirling silver flecks in them, mirroring the pearly lock of hair that lay across his forehead.

They were like a night sky brightened by a million stars.

“Hi,” he whispered.

“Hi,” she rasped, something surging inside her as she stared into his starry eyes.

But as more blood rushed down his chin and his face blanched, she gripped his shoulders tightly.

Pulling on her magic, Lessia prayed she was right about this.

“What are you—” Merrick’s eyes glazed, his face softening, as she drew on every bit of magic inside her.

“You will break the blood oath, and you will live. You will survive it. You are strong enough,” she ordered, the purr of her voice joining the pulse buzzing in her ears.

Merrick dipped his chin, and Lessia blinked, forcing the magic from her eyes.

His dark ones focused, his face hardening, and she held on to his hand as he came to.

Please, let it work. Please, please, she begged whoever was listening.

"Fuck!" Merrick ripped his hand free to grip his arm.

As he pulled up his jacket, they both stared in wonder at the fading tattoo—how welts and burned skin were soon the only thing marring his tan arm.

Merrick released a choked breath, and as his eyes found hers again, gratitude shone brightly in the darkness. Pulling her down, he locked his arms around her neck, and Lessia let out another sob—a sob of relief that her not-so-well-thought-out plan had worked.

"You really need to leave."

She pulled back as Zaddock's urgent whisper reached her ears, and the sound of footsteps coming down a stairway joined it.

With a nod, she rose to her feet, pulling Merrick with her.

The Fae limped after her as she left the cell, and she jerked her head toward Ardow. "Him as well."

"Let me come with you." Venko pushed himself upright. "Please."

She shook her head, unable to meet his eyes.

Three was plenty when you were on the run.

They didn't also need Venko slowing them down.

"I have a ship!" He sprinted to the bars. "They can get us out of here unnoticed. I trust the crew with my life."

She glanced at Merrick, who shrugged. "Do you have a better plan?"

Lessia sighed shakily. "Fine! But let's go, they're coming."

The steps she'd heard before were close to reaching the bottom of the cellars.

Zaddock unlocked the door, and Ardow leaned on Venko as they exited the cell.

"There is a tunnel back there. Take the first right, and it will lead you down into the sewers. Once you're down there, keep to the left, and you'll find a path straight to the harbor."

Zaddock pointed into the darkness, and Lessia drew deep breaths against the unease that tightened her chest.

As Merrick and the two men started toward it, Lessia grabbed Zaddock's hand. "I don't know how to thank you."

He winked. "Put in a good word for me with Amalise when you see her next, will you?"

Her face crumpled at the thought of her friend, and Zaddock quickly pressed her hand. "I won't let anything happen to her. I promise. I'll take her with me when I leave today. Throw her over my shoulder if I must."

"W-we have some... some friends you need to help as well. Amalise will know what to do," she got out.

When Zaddock nodded, she managed to offer him a sad smile before the steps rumbled far too close for her liking.

With a final glance at him, she sprinted after the others, catching up with the males just as they found the entrance to the tunnel.

The journey to the harbor passed in a blur, and she barely noticed the vile water seeping into her clothing as they waded through it.

Fortunately, Venko kept his word.

With hoods covering their faces, they found their way to an old trade ship, and when the crew recognized Venko, they urged them into a small cabin, where they each collapsed atop a narrow cot.

But as the boat started cutting through the waves, Lessia

climbed the wooden ladder leading to the stern, ignoring Venko calling for her to stay down until they were out of sight.

Stepping up to the railing, she watched Asker grow smaller and smaller until the island she'd called home for so long was merely a dot on the horizon.

Silent tears snaked their way down her cheeks.

But she let them fall.

Let them fall for Amalise.

For Kalia and Ledger and Fiona.

For her father.

And for Loche.

For the man who'd put her heart together, only to rip it out and throw it away as if she were nothing.

Merrick joined her at some point, and when he wrapped an arm around her shoulders, she leaned into him, letting him hold together the broken pieces she was now made up of.

When even her Fae sight wouldn't let her see the island anymore, she looked up at him.

She had so many questions to ask, but right now, she couldn't bring herself to, so she settled on "What do we do now?"

Merrick eyed her for a moment. "I know somewhere safe we could go. But I have to warn you. I am not sure that we'll get the warmest of welcomes."

She forced a teary smile. "I don't think there are many places in Havlands where we'll be welcomed at all."

His mouth twitched, and a flicker of amusement sparkled in his dark eyes. "Then it's time for you to meet Raine."

ACKNOWLEDGMENTS

Wow, I have so many people to thank for bringing the start of Elessia's story to life!

I have to start with my husband, Michael. Thank you for being so patient with me as I neglected everything else to dive into the world of Havlands (and for reminding me to eat!).

To Amanda, my friend, Alpha Reader, PA and absolutely incredible support. Thank you for being there every day with encouraging words and honest feedback.

To Antonia, my friend and incredible designer. Thank you for helping me make this book beautiful.

To Elyse, my amazing editor. Thank you for bringing *A Tongue So Sweet and Deadly* to the next level. Your talent has made me a better writer.

And I can't forget Tahoe, my dog and best friend. Thank you for cuddling up in my lap in the late hours of the night and giving me the energy to finish when I was close to giving up.

Telling him wouldn't change what would happen.

So she didn't. Instead, she whispered, "You're mine," and clung to him with every nerve inside her aching and only one sentence echoing in her mind:

Please don't be the last time.

KEEP READING FOR A SNEAK PEEK AT THE NEXT STAGE OF ELESSIA'S STORY . . .

CHAPTER ONE

As she swallowed a mouthful of watery porridge, Lessia glared at the men around the timeworn table.

To her right, Merrick scrunched his nose as he lifted a spoon of the pale liquid to his lips, the disgust when it trickled down his throat as apparent as the stench of sweat and stale air permeating the small ship's cabin.

Before her, Ardow and Venko sat with blood still staining their clothing, and her gaze snagged on Venko's swollen-shut eye and the angry red line snaking its way from his forehead down to his chin.

The men's gazes remained fixed on the bowls the ship's captain had brought down for breakfast, declaring their contents was the only edible thing onboard, as their departure hadn't been planned. Not one of them looked up as they shoveled the soupy mess into their mouths.

Lessia ground her teeth as she continued to stare daggers at them.

It'd been almost a week since they escaped Ellow.

A week in which she'd given them time to rest and heal from the injuries Ellow's guards—and, in Merrick's case, King Rioner's soldiers—had inflicted.

A week in which they'd barely spoken more than two words to her, guilt building across their features every time they met her eyes.

A week in which Lessia had spent the time mainly outside, leaning over the railing and staring at the wrathful sea, trying to comprehend how everything had gone to shit.

How could she have missed two people so close to her being traitors?

She should have seen the signs with Ardow!

And Merrick...

Her gaze flicked up to the worn ceiling for a moment, following the cracks and warped beams weaving their way to the stairs leading up to the deck of the ship.

She'd assumed he was acting on orders from their king.

But whatever he'd been doing all those times he sneaked away must have been connected to the rebellion these idiots believed they were spearheading.

An ache started in her chest as she thought of Amalise—the fear she'd seen in her friend when they'd sat on that bed together on her final night in Ellow—and she clenched her teeth when Kalia's, Ledger's, and Fiona's faces flashed before her eyes.

What if Zaddock hadn't gotten to Amalise in time?

What if Amalise and Zaddock hadn't gotten the children out?

What if everyone she loved was rotting in Loche's cellars right this moment, believing Lessia had left them behind?

The wooden walls of the cabin seemed to creep closer, darkening the already dimly lit room and casting foreboding shadows on the males around her, causing a shiver to dance across her shoulders.

Lessia dropped her spoon when thoughts of Zaddock made Loche's smirk fill her mind, then the images of his cold, distant eyes as she'd taken every feeling he'd ever harbored for her away.

The spoon clattered to the floor, shattering the thick silence.

Still, when Merrick quietly bent down to pick it up, neither Venko nor Ardow reacted.

The constant pressure on her chest tightened as the men's eyes remained anywhere but on hers, and the air she forced into her lungs became heavier, filled with guilt and regret.

Her nostrils flared, and Lessia slammed her hands on the table so hard that her bowl toppled over and the gray mush spilled across the stained wood.

"Enough!"

Every pair of eyes in the room flew to hers.

Finally.

With magic pulsating under her skin, she snarled, "It's time for you to tell me what's going on! It's been a week, and I've tried to be understanding, but I'm done waiting! Absolutely. Fucking. Done."

Ardow's eyes lowered when she bore her own into his, and she slammed a fist on the rotting wood again. "Look at me!"

Lessia nearly vibrated from withheld anger, the breaths she dragged into her lungs turning choppy.

They'd put the people she loved in danger.

Could have ruined everything she'd fought for the

past five years.

And now they wouldn't even meet her eyes.

A large hand landed on her shoulder, and she turned her glare to Merrick's night-sky gaze.

She narrowed her eyes when something flashed in his dark ones, and when his mouth twitched, her magic burst to the surface, the golden glow of it reflecting in his silver flecks.

"Don't you dare laugh at me," she hissed, the shaking in her hands spreading through her body.

One of his brows quirked up, and the hand he kept on her shoulder tightened in warning.

Soft whispers responded to the magic buzzing around her, but there was no room for fear within her.

Not with the guilt and shame and worry that already festered like a disease on her every nerve and limb.

She should use her magic on every single one of them.

Force them to tell her everything.

Force them to face that guilt hunching their backs—do it as they looked right into her eyes.

But the longer she kept Merrick's gaze, the longer his whispers traced her skin, the trembles racking her body softened, the overwhelming emotions were soothed, and her eyes widened when she realized what she'd almost done.

Forcing herself to blink hard, she pushed her magic down, lowering her gaze when another wave of hot guilt washed over her.

She'd promised herself never to do that.

And now...

Now that she acted on her own will and not the Fae king's, she could actually honor that vow.